Speak Truth to Fire

By

Matthew Candelaria

Table of Contents

1. Don't Mention Demons

It didn't have to breathe. The ragged, rasping breaths were an affectation, like the body. But the breaths weren't real, and they didn't show in the lamplight, despite the evening chill. The body wasn't any more real, but it was visible, though the details were vague as it loomed over Stanley. Part bear, part gorilla, with reptilian hints in the head and in the skin, the body was a show of strength. It wanted him to know the pain he would feel when it hit him.

A huge paw made solid contact with his right shoulder, sending him sprawling across the alley. The strength was real. "Stupid," Stanley cursed to himself. He felt pain on both sides—where it hit him and where he had hit the ground and skidded across the pavement into an ice-coated puddle. "My new suit, too." He had been impatient, and suffered the consequences.

The creature roared, but did not advance. It raised its arms in a threatening display, framing an L car behind it.

He didn't know why it wasn't advancing, but then he felt the ward. The beast could advance, but not without being weakened. It didn't try because it knew its limitations from long experience. *A ward? Here?* He looked up and down the dirty, narrow alley blocked in on both sides by tall apartment buildings. He felt it now, and then he saw a sign. A tiny glyph marked the seam in the concrete.

He looked at the wall behind him. One of the apartment buildings was being protected. He looked at the rear entrance that was nearest to him, followed the fire escape up the brick wall to the third floor. He saw it and felt the unearthly thrum of its power.

He smiled. *Jackpot.* He'd come here seeking the demon's heartstone, and he was right. It must be there, warded so the demon couldn't take it. He just wished he'd known that the demon followed him. He should have taken his time, made sure it wasn't tracking him from the bar across town where he'd found it with Mr. Holland, the wandering husband he was supposed to bring home. He wanted to run right up, but he took a deep breath and realized such haste wouldn't be wise, maybe wasn't even possible.

Stanley started to get up. He winced at the pain in his side. *Deep bruising for sure*, he thought. The pain increased as he tried harder to struggle to his feet. *Maybe a cracked rib.* He got to his hands and knees.

The creature chuckled.

"That's right," Stanley spat at the beast. "Laugh while you can. You're not long for this world."

The creature stopped laughing abruptly. Then it disappeared, revealing its "true" shape—a voluptuous woman with pale, grey skin and wide, webbed wings— for just an instant.

He realized he'd tipped his hand too much. The demon was probably going to get Mr. Holland. Although the demon could travel instantly across town, it would take time for them to get back. Maybe 45 minutes or an hour. Of course, it was possible the demon had more than one man on the hook. Maybe even somebody close. Stanley had to hurry to get to that heartstone before the demon got back.

Stanley looked up at the fire escape. Normally if he wanted to get up in a hurry, that's how he'd do it, but he raised his arm and gasped at the pain. There was no way he was going to climb up now.

No time to wait for someone to let him in. He pulled out the small snuffbox that held the reagents for a spell to unlock the door. Empty. He'd been meaning to make more for a long time, but gold dust ain't cheap. He looked at the lock and sighed. "The only way you're gonna get better is if you practice," he mumbled to himself.

So he stepped up. He pulled out the picks and put one in the lock. He felt around. Five tumblers. Great.

Three tumblers he could manage easily, but five always gave him trouble— it was hard to keep the picks in the lock. They got jumbled and made it hard to move. As he was getting the fourth tumbler into place, he jostled them and they popped out. He cursed. Put his sweaty forehead against the cold solid door. Took several breaths and started again.

Another L train came by. How many did that make? He'd lost count. *How long have I been doing this?* He looked up and down the alley. The last thing he needed was a beat cop to wander by. Nothing to be done about that, though. He slipped the picks back in the lock. After a long effort, the lock spun, but before he could grab it, the door opened of itself, hitting him in the forehead. The picks came out and fell to the ground. Stanley cursed and told himself to remember to get them later. Instead, he grabbed the door.

The man coming out peered around the door. "Who the hell're you?"

"I live here."

"I ain't never seen you before. You got a key?"

"I dropped it when the door opened." Stanley made a show of fumbling around on the ground. He grabbed his tension wrench and a couple of the picks. He wondered if he had a key that would look close enough. He kept fumbling, but putting on a good show made his ribs hurt.

"Aw, hell, I ain't got all night." The guy said. He put on his hat, an old bowler of a dark color. He walked off in the direction of the L station.

Stanley kept fumbling on the ground until the man was out of sight, then he headed in.

The tile in the hallway was a dingy white. The wainscoting halfway up the wall was in good shape, but the paper above it was streaked and stained from handprints. The light was dim. About half of the gas lamps had been converted to the weakest electric lights available. The others were dark and empty. The hall was barely warmer than the outside, but even in the chill it stank. Smoke, sweat, and just the faintest hint of urine.

Stanley looked left and right. The stairs were right. There was no elevator. He started to run, felt the pain in his ribs, and slowed down to a brisk walk.

He really felt the pain when he passed the second floor. "Man," he mumbled, "definitely cracked one this time. Add a sawbones to the expenses column."

On the third floor, he put his hand to the wall. The stone thrummed with life, taking power from the demon's native plane and sending it here, pulse upon pulse, so the demon's power waxed brilliant, then waned. That's something you always had to remember in dealing with a demon. A lesson Stanley had learned painfully before the War. And unlike the gunshot and even the shrapnel in his leg from St. Mihiel, that scar still hurt. Especially now, the pain increased with each pulse. He cradled his left hand close, trying to warm the round white remnants of tooth marks. This close, he could feel the heartstone, more powerful than the rumbling of another passing L train—he was running out of time.

He found the door, felt it pulsing as if it were a living thing itself. Definitely an apprentice's place. No sorcerer of any power would let something so blatant go unmasked. Probably made all his neighbors uneasy, although they would misinterpret the cause. Thought he was a sleazy, shiftless crook. As were many apprentices in the dark arts.

The door felt solid enough, but it was old—thirty years or more. The only lock was on the knob, and it had a little turn in it, the way most old locks do. The knob was a little loose, too. Turn the knob as far as it would go, push it at an angle, apply pressure to the loose hinges, and it was probably just a little nub of the bolt holding the door closed. With a sudden jerk, he could probably pop it and save himself the time and trouble of picking this damn lock (and now with only half a set of picks).

Stanley threw himself against the door, and it popped open, but the pain of it made Stanley wonder whether it was such a great a plan after all. Stanley sucked in a breath and found that hurt, too. And it felt constricted. A second attempt at deeper breath made him cough, and that really hurt. "Just find the stone and get outta here."

Inside the room, the throbbing was dull, diffuse, dampened. Stanley stretched out his hands, closed his eyes, and felt for it. Pulse. Pulse. Pulse. It took time to narrow down the part of the room it was in, but once he was close, his hands went right to it.

It was easy to slip the little jewelry box latch with a knife, too, and once inside the pure coal stood out among the flawed gems and paste costume jewels. He had hoped it might be a real gem he could salvage. "Oh, well, that ritual is longer, anyway," he said to himself. "Just get this over and collect your fee." At least he knew the language of coal.

But as he was turning away from the jewelry box, a shrill, panicked voice called out, "Bobby, that man is robbing me!"

Stanley looked up, and in the doorway stood the succubus in her "big blonde" form, wearing the pale blue yoke frock that was obviously designed for a slender form, not her voluptuous curves. As she spoke, the trim, muscular Mr. Holland emerged from the other side of the doorway.

She was so beautiful it was obvious she was a demon. Even angry, her face had the plump roundness of a Gibson girl, and though her blue eyes flashed fire, her brow was unwrinkled.

Mr. Holland was obviously under her influence and drunk, to boot. He said, "You little bastard, stealing from a defenseless dame. I'll teach you." He put up his fists.

Stanley put up his hand. "Wait," he said, "I'm no thief. Look at this." He held out both his hands, showing the only thing in them was the piece of coal. "If I were a thief, would I be stealin a lump of coal?"

"Who knows what you're stealin. You show me a lump of coal inna hand, but what's inna pockets, huh?"

Now Stanley was glad it was only a lump of coal. All he needed was a distraction and he could get it done, quick. "Man, what's a young guy like you doing with an old battle axe like that?" Then he spoke faintly to the stone as he squeezed it.

For a moment, the demon appeared as her true self: feminine but inhuman. She still had her womanly curves, but her face was sharp, angry, and possessed of fangs. Her skin was grey but flushed all over, and it was too smooth, more like rubber than skin at all. Her hair was black and straight, oily and long.

In a moment she had restored herself, but Stanley kept his hand clamped down on the coal. It throbbed, but he kept hold of it, restricting the flow of power, even though that made the scar on his hand hurt worse.

"I can't believe you'd say that about a lady," the muscular man said, advancing a small step.

"She might be a woman, but I'm pretty sure she's no lady." And he cast the spell again.

This time it hit her harder. Not only did her appearance transform, but she staggered back as if pushed. And although she tried, she was unable to become the blonde again until the next pulse of the coal, which Stanley squeezed as hard as he could. Pretty soon she would only be able to change back every third or fourth pulse. Then it was just a question of getting this lunk to turn around. Which was going to be challenge enough, it turned out.

"I don't know who you think you are, pal, but you need to learn your place."

Mr. Holland pushed up the sleeves of his fine oxford shirt. Stanley noticed the elegant stitching, the cuffs on his trousers: the height of fashion Stanley hadn't been able to afford when buying his own suit. Stanley said, "Man, that's a nice outfit. If you can afford clothes like that, why do you live in a dump like this?"

The compliment piqued the man's ego just enough to make him pause and take note. "Idiot. This ain't my place—it's hers."

"Huh. That's funny, because this sure doesn't look like a lady's pad to me."

The man looked around. Newspapers heaped near the radio, "spicy" adventure magazines by the armchair. Soda bottles collecting in a milk crate near the door. Lithograph of a fan dancer pinned by the door. He turned and looked at the big blonde. "You little tramp. Whose place is this?"

Stanley took advantage of the moment. He put the piece of coal down on the table and quickly took out his small hammer—steel core silver plated with gold leaf on the striking surface. With a quick stroke and a word that sounded like an incoherent grunt, comprehensible only to coal, he smashed the lump.

For an instant, the blonde transformed back into her true, demonic self. She did not scream, merely gasped in surprise. Then she blew away, like a puff of smoke in a strong wind.

The man went limp with shock. He stared at the empty hallway. When Stanley walked up to him, he turned around with pleading eyes and said, "What did I see?"

Stanley tried to conceal his wincing from the hard, fast blow required by the spell. "You didn't really see anything. When you found out she was two-timing you, you realized she wasn't the woman you thought she was. Anger can do funny things to the mind."

"Yes." He paused. Blinked. Licked his dry lips. "Yes."

"C'mon. Let's catch a cab outta here." He put his arm around the man's shoulder in what seemed a comforting gesture, but really allowed Stanley to lean on him for support.

On the street, Stanley hailed a cab, glad for an expense he could pass on to the client.

Back at his office, the girl, Lane, looked agitated. Her thin face, shaped like a cross because she was wearing her glasses, looked straight at Stanley, not seeming to notice the burly man that Stanley was leaning on.

"Mr. Barton is here, Mr. Fields."

"Is he? Well, he can wait."

"No, sir, not according to him, he can't."

"What? Oh. Oof." Stanley tried his best to ease the big man down on the couch without falling over himself. "Okay. Fine. Send for Mrs. Holland. Tell her we've got her husband here and she can come pick him up. When she gets here, settle up her bill—oh, and add a cab from the Southside to the expenses list. But don't let her wake this guy up until I talk to her."

"Sure thing, Mr. Fields."

Stanley headed across the waiting room, past the partition to where Gary Barton stood. He was a tall man, slender, but not exactly gangly. His face was harsh, his eyes intense. His frame was muscular, and you'd think him an impressive figure if you really looked at him. But it took effort. Your mind wanted to wander, pay attention to anything but him. In a crowd, you'd never notice him. That was the result of a charm cast on his hat, now five years out of fashion, but looking brand new.

When Stanley reached Gary, he passed inside the charm barrier, so looking at his face became easier. And they could carry on a conversation without being overheard by anyone on the outside. It was a good charm, too, since it frustrated lip readers and even the new threat of electronic listening devices.

"Hey, Gary, what's up?"

Gary reluctantly took the proffered shake. His hand was cold and dry. "We don't know. But we want to find out. It's in Denver, and we want you on the midnight train there."

"Midnight, what? It must be after nine already."

"You can make it."

"But I got this guy in here. He saw a succubus. His wife's coming to get him and I gotta tell her the tale so she's got the right context." When he pointed he felt the pain in his ribs. "Ah, and I gotta see a doc."

"She will be here in time."

"Yeah, but then the doc."

"You shouldn't have been hurt." Barton sighed. "Very well." He placed his hand on Stanley's forehead. Stanley felt the coldness of Barton's large ring. Stanley knew its appearance from hours of study and more than a few times benefitting from its power: an ivory torch burning with ruby flames inlaid in the otherwise plain gold band. An object of great power (and expense), it could stand in as the reagents for many spells, including the spell to cure Stanley. Barton chanted. Stanley didn't understand the words—they were directed at his body in several dialects: bone and blood, sinew and nerve. Stanley felt their power enter him, reknit his bones, and draw away the pain.

After the chanting was done, Stanley took a deep, painless breath. "Thanks, but I still gotta get home and pack."

"No you don't. Travel light. Here's a grand up front for expenses and a letter of introduction."

The envelope said, "Philip S. Van Cise, DA." Stanley stashed it in his coat. "But what about reagents?"

"Take this for starters," a small box that Stanley suspected held gold dust, maybe cut with iridium. "We'll send you what you can't get locally."

"And in the meantime?"

"Be careful. You've got your chums and your John Roscoe. We don't have anybody on the ground there, and the ley readers say somebody's sucking up power. Not just for daily use. A steady drain. They're working on something big. Something we can't ignore. We want you there to find out what it is."

"If that's what you want, then I'm gone."

"Good."

Stanley walked over to Lane's desk. He peeled the outer fifty off the sheaf of bills he'd been given. "Kitty," he said, "We're gonna have to close the office for awhile. Don't know how long. Take this for a retainer." He pulled off a couple more 50s. "Why don't you grab your stuff and get out while the night's still young? I'll make sure this guy gets home."

Her eyes were still wide from the sight of the bills, which she held as if they were parchment pages from the Book of the Dead. "Yes, Mr. Fields. Thank you."

As she got ready to go, he went into his office, rolled a cigarette, and waited for Mrs. Holland so he could tell her the tale. How he'd shown her husband the woman was a tramp and was two-timing him. How that could be traumatic for a man. Might even lead to hallucinations and nightmares. He might think he saw something. But, he reminded himself, don't say what. Don't mention demons. Because if you mentioned demons, it didn't take long for people to think witch.

2. The Usual Slap and Tickle

Stefani had never thought she would be a dancer like her mother. But then, she also hadn't expected her father to die, leaving Stefani and her mother to fend for themselves. So Elizabeth Aegis went back to work—as a cleaning woman—until Stefani herself was old enough to work.

Now her mother didn't work, and Stefani was following in her footsteps. Elizabeth Stuart came to Denver because it was said that out West women could be whatever they wanted. Reporters, publishers, even business owners—the new state of Colorado had so many opportunities. Or that's what they said. When Elizabeth got here, she found that she had her choice of a much smaller set of options: dancer, cleaning woman, or whore. If she'd been religious, she could've added nun, but if she hadn't been young and attractive, she couldn't have been a dancer.

So she took advantage of her natural gifts, found a relatively clean place to dance, and got a room at the YWCA. A bad Christian and too good a dancer, she lived there on a probationary status that was jeopardized every time a man from the bar followed her home.

By the time she got tired of the leering drunks at the bar and the suspicious prudes at the YWCA, she realized her looks weren't going to last forever anyway. So she married Nikolas Aegis, a successful speculator. He invested little, but saw great returns. Unfortunately, he spent most of it on books, gewgaws, and fine wines that he had imported at great expense. But there was still enough left over to keep the family in relative comfort.

And then he died. And now Stefani, after working at Morgan's, went home not to the YWCA, but to her father's old house near Washington Park, full of all his books and trinkets and wine.

Judith Brown, assistant to the owner, said, "Don't frown so much: it creates wrinkles." So Stefani gave a big smile. But as soon as the older woman left, Stefani was scowling at her own olive-complected face in the mirror.

The dancers at Morgan's Bar didn't find many amenities in their breaks between turns on the stage and out among the patrons. They weren't allowed to smoke, since the smell was "unladylike." They weren't allowed to drink alone—they should be encouraging men to buy them drinks. They weren't allowed to eat for fear it would give them bad breath.

Pretty much the only thing they were allowed to do was take off the compulsory smile they wore in front of the customers. And Stefani took full advantage of that luxury.

It galled her that she was doing exactly as her mother had done. After all, wasn't this the age of the "New Woman"? Weren't there supposed to be more opportunities, a brighter future in which a woman could be her own person?

That may be true for some women, but when Stefani looked to get a job, she saw essentially the same options her mother had, with perhaps the dubious addition of shopgirl. She didn't want to end up like Gertrude Patterson, whose ruinous face had led to scandal and murder, so Stefani found a job dancing at Morgan's on Curtis Street, just up from the theater district. The men came out after every show, talking and excited, eager to see a woman in the flesh.

Morgan's didn't have a full band. (Bart Gallio said, "Pay girls and a band? Do they think this is *J.P.* Morgan's?") But it had a better piano player than any of the theaters, except maybe The Princess.

A wave of men from the theater had just entered when Stefani got out into the crowd. She hadn't signed up for this kind of thing, but it was getting to be the way it was all over. You weren't just a dancer, you were a companion girl. Morgan's didn't have decent booze and it wasn't cheap, so the only way to keep men coming in was to guarantee a pretty face, full bosom, and firm leg at every table. No big deal: just a smile, a laugh. Maybe let them touch your hand. Encourage them to buy you drinks. Choking down the drinks was the hardest part—it really was bad brew.

Stefani's timing was perfect. She had emerged from the back just as Judith was coming to roust her. The crowd was typical—loud and rowdy men. They were leering, laughing, and cheering at Abigail, who was on the stage doing some bawdy jokes and suggestive physical comedy. This was the most risqué act allowed, though Gallio sometimes talked about getting all the girls to pose nude on stage. You couldn't get away with that sort of thing here, nor any of those French style shows that ex-doughboys talked about since the War (and which seemed to get increasingly scandalous with each passing year). Between punchlines, she did a little dance and took something off. She never got completely naked, but the combination got the men going pretty well. They cheered loud, tipped well, and loved to talk about the act.

Stefani surveyed the crowd to see which tables needed companionship. It seemed like the crowd was mostly cared for, and she was going to start wandering toward the back when Gallio himself caught her eye. He gestured with his eyes toward a large table of men she almost recognized.

Recognition and the fact that Gallio was looking out for them personally meant they were probably associated with the bar's "protection," one of Gallio's chief concerns. She hadn't sat with them, but she'd heard they were a boorish, stingy, grabby bunch. But you had to be nice. If you got a reputation for being unfriendly, you might expect trouble from the police—they were highly connected. Now it was Stefani's turn to make them feel at home.

Every chair at the table was taken, but Stefani knew what to do. She walked around the table once, smiling at the men. Poorly shaven roughnecks, possibly beat cops on their night off, and all young. They appreciated her smile and returned it with a thorough look over. Once around the table was all it took for Stefani to identify the top banana, and when she came to his seat, she let her hand range from the chair back to his shoulder and asked, "Is this seat taken?"

Not even waiting for a reply, she slid down into his lap, giggling. "Whoops," she said, "guess my legs are a little rubbery."

Some of the girls picked the youngest or handsomest guy at the table, but Stefani knew that was trouble. The leader of any group was most likely self-doubting, insecure, and in need of constant praise. That's what drove him to be the leader. Anything that made him jealous could lead to fights once the boys got all liquored up.

Once safely in the leader's lap, Stefani was free to flirt with all the boys— a laugh, a wink, a ribald joke, anything. So long as she had her arm around him.

"Are you boys policemen?" she asked with wide eyes and slow, sensual enunciation.

"Yes, ma'am, we are."

"I hope none of you are vice, because I'm afraid you'd have to run me in," and here she held out her arms in front of her, crossed at the wrist.

They all laughed. One of them said, "No, ma'am, we're here for your protection."

"Oh, thank you! All you strong boys make a girl feel safe." She put her arm back around the leader and winked at the man who had spoken.

The leader put his hand on her shoulder. "I wouldn't feel too safe around some of these guys."

There was something in the way his hand squeezed her shoulder that put Stefani ill at ease. The words were mundane enough, but it felt like he was referring to something more than the usual slap and tickle.

They got her a drink, some of that terrible gin. Though there was just a splash of it in her gin and tonic, it was strong-tasting stuff, disgusting and bitter, and no amount of tonic and lemon could disguise the poorness of the bootlegger's product.

Still, it could get one drunk, with reasonable odds of surviving the experience, which, according to the papers, was more than one could expect from some of the gin distilled in this town. She didn't want to get drunk, so she sipped slowly and carefully while seeming to take generous drinks. She looked around the table, trying to identify what the leader had been referring to.

The leader was being respectful—they often were—though she could tell he responded to her from his blush and unconscious aversions of his eyes.

The other men were rude and it was as if they each had four hands, but it was not worse than she was used to. They were men—leering drunken men—nothing too much to be afraid of.

Then she saw that one of them was different. Most of the time, he was just like the others. He smiled, laughed, and drank. But in isolated moments, his good spirit was just gone. It reminded Stefani of when they had the electric light installed at home. She had sat in the front room and turned it on and off, marveling at how instant it was.

This man's joviality was just like that. And when it was gone, it was replaced by a strange kind of hate. When he looked at her, his face contorted in distaste, but it wasn't pure distaste. It was very like a hungry man who has been offered a disgusting dish and is trying to work out how he's going to choke it down.

Was he a fruit? She'd heard that some of them didn't just like men—some of them hated women. That didn't seem right. Although he had a special dislike for her, he didn't seem too eager for the company of his fellow officers—when they weren't looking.

So why was he with them? Was it political? Was he just keeping up appearances? She couldn't figure it out, so she tried to put him out of her mind for now, though his face seemed burned in her mind. She put her effort into appearing both charmed and charming until her next dance.

She did a little song and dance, a fast-paced number with blatant metaphors that made everyone laugh. She swished her skirts, kicked high, and paraded around the stage. Dancing was her true talent. She wasn't a bad singer, but without the dancing, she couldn't have made it work. She went out among the tables and made the most of the innuendos—smiling broadly, raising her eyebrows, almost whispering the naughty words in a man's ear with her arms around his shoulders. And of course she gave them lots of opportunities to put money in her garter. When men got to see her legs and even touch her black stockings just above the knee, it shook loose the folding money they hadn't wanted to spend. That's why Gallio put her solo number at the end of the night. He called her his cleanup hitter, and he knew that men who were otherwise tapped out would find a dollar or even two—in the moment it seemed easier to face their wives and explain they were busted than resist the temptation.

Stefani got to keep a third of the money she brought in. She had tried for half, but Gallio laughed at her. Still, it was more than the one-fifth he'd offered her first, and he guaranteed her four dollars every night, though she almost never earned less than that. Stefani liked the arrangement well enough, but she kept the details from her mother.

Tonight, Gallio tried to keep his usual stern face while counting the money she brought in, but when he got over $30 he couldn't help it, a little smile slipped out. He stifled it with a "Hmph." He had counted it into three even piles. Then he started to take out his "standard fees." Costume payment, meal allotment, dressing room rental—she forgot what they all were, but when he started taking out a dollar for the piano player, she protested, "I've never had to pay for the piano player. That's your expense."

"What? Huh? How can you dance if there's no piano player?"

"For a dollar a night, I'll figure it out." She smirked. "And you figure out how you're gonna get guys in here to see women dance to no music."

He grumbled and put the dollar back. Still, the fees were more than three dollars. But that was the cost of doing business. And tonight she was going home with over ten dollars!

After the money was totaled up, she rushed to get changed into decent clothes. As she dressed, she frowned at her reflection. The pleats on her frock were supposed to be "slenderizing," but they couldn't hide that she had her mother's Gilded Age frame. Perhaps that's why she wasn't able to enter the age of the New Woman.

She sighed and pulled on her Polaire coat. The women all got together in the lobby and walked out to the streetcar station. It was dangerous out at night, especially for women like them. Some men thought being a dancer implied that certain liberties were permitted. With this many women, they could at least act as witnesses. Even if they were women, an attack could not be ignored.

On the way, they passed the YWCA, where many of the women went inside. There were only four of them who rushed to make sure they caught the last car.

Stefani was amicable with the other three women who took the late cars, but she didn't really know them and certainly wasn't friendly. Two of them, Charlotte and Nella, lived together. Stefani wasn't sure what their relationship was, but she was suspicious. The other, Abigail, the comedic lead, lived with her mother, like Stefani, though Abigail's mother was older and more infirm. Their house was also fully paid for, so Abigail's money went further.

Abigail and Stefani rode the same line, but Abigail got off earlier, and then it was just Stefani, the dozing conductor, and the drunks who were settled in until they got kicked out at the station.

Stefani didn't recognize their faces, but she knew these men. They were the same leering drunks from Morgan's, or maybe another speak. She feared how they would act if they awoke. At Morgan's they were happy to look, but wanted to grab. When she performed, either on stage or at the table, she had her role to protect her. They were invited to look, but the boundaries were firmly defined. Even when they put money in her garter, she held her skirt and used her gaze to keep them in check.

But out here, she was just another woman in what they liked to think of as a man's world. Sure, she had the vote, but she still needed a man to corroborate her witness. So she sat on the wooden bench with her hand in her bag, clutching the tiny two-shot pearl-handled holdout pistol. She had never fired it, but her mother had, in exactly the situation Stefani feared.

Her mother hadn't killed the man, but the wound went bad, paralyzing his arm. Growing up, Stefani had seen him begging downtown. Whenever her father saw him, he spit on him and drove him off. Then he disappeared. Either he died or moved away. And shortly after, her father died, too.

Stefani got off near the end of the route. By this time, the dry air had grown quite chill. She turned up her collar and hurried home.

The house her father bought was a large two-story brick Victorian, a style no longer in fashion, but it suited his needs—lots of space for his things, which spilled out of his library and wine cellar into the rest of the house. He didn't decorate, he merely accumulated, and he made it very clear he didn't want Stefani or her mother to clean or rearrange his things.

In front of the house, a big old cottonwood tree was clinging to the last of its leaves. Stefani walked up the heavy brick and concrete porch. The door was solid wood with decorative arabesque scrollwork carved into it. She slid her iron key into the lock and turned it carefully, trying to avoid making any noise.

But the big old tumblers always made a loud click. Still trying to avoid making noise, she turned the brass doorknob carefully and entered the foyer. Without turning on the electric light, she closed the door as quietly as possible.

In the dark she reached the secretary bird statuette, then felt down its gangly legs, along the desk, until she found the rare clean spot where she kept her purse.

Stefani had to work hard to find places to put her things. And in walking through the house, she had to stick to a predefined path. Because she had been walking it since she was a little girl, her feet knew the steps by instinct, and she even knew how to avoid the squeaky floorboards.

But it didn't matter. Her mother snapped on the light in her room upstairs. "Fanny," she asked sharply, "did you have a good night?"

"It was okay."

Her mother had now come downstairs. She turned on the foyer light and crossed the room to the place where Stefani put down the money. "Just okay? That new Flynn movie is out—you ought to be making lots of money." She began to count. "Is this all?"

"Yes, that's all."

Her mother's eyes narrowed. "You should be grateful. When I was dancing, I had to come home to the YWCA, and they always looked askance. Dancing was no good trade for a Christian woman, they'd say, their eyes looking down from all the way up their noses."

Stefani thought, *But at least they only took the rent. And didn't complain about how much you made.*

"You ought to be making more. Do you want me to teach you some special moves?"

"I bet we could make a lot of money selling father's old things."

Her mother started, and her eyes got really wide. Fear? Stefani couldn't quite pin it down. "No, no," her mother said, "I think we can manage. Just try to do better tomorrow."

Her mother snapped off the foyer light and ascended the stairs by the light coming down from her bedroom. Stefani watched her climb. She still had her youthful figure despite a nearly complete lack of healthy activity. She might still have been a beautiful woman if the very things that kept her slim—worry and fear—had not taken their toll on her face.

When her mother closed the door upstairs, Stefani stood in the dark, and for a moment she wondered what made her mother so afraid. Until she felt it, the thing she had managed to put out of mind. Not her father, and not a poltergeist, but some other spirit or spirits living in and among her father's things.

Then she fled from them into her room. She comforted herself with the imagined safety of electric lights and a closed door.

3. A Deep Thirst

Otoniel Garcia sat in the bar, trying to gauge Charlie's mood. He seemed to be in a good mood, for Charlie. But how good? Otoniel wasn't sure, but probably not good enough to be hit up for another drink. Not two days in a row. Which was too bad, because even one shot of the house's gin sure helped the day go by faster.

Otherwise, sitting here, without even anyone to play dominos against, made for a very long day. Another very long day. And it was only November. The snow had set in and though the road was sufficiently clear for any determined person with a good car or horse, very few people were that determined.

There was nothing to do in Californiaville now but work the California Creek Mine, where they were also pretty resigned to waiting out the winter. At least they had work. And it wasn't any colder in the mine in the winter.

That's what Otoniel would do once he found his vein. Dig all winter, and in the spring and summer work above ground. On his house maybe. And once that was finished, he could take trips down to Denver, Pueblo, or Albuquerque for vacations, or, maybe, to get himself a wife.

Charlie, on the other hand, had it made already. He ran the best hotel and bar in town, the one where the miners went first with their paychecks for food, drink, and companionship. Charlie'd had a wife, they said, but she'd died years ago. Now he was sorta alone and sorta not. It was said that all the girls who worked through his hotel had to play nice with him or they couldn't work.

So Otoniel didn't know why the man was so grumpy all the time. Otoniel wasn't asking for much. He just wanted a drink or two every now and again. And it was only in the off season, when there were no tourists who needed guides or someone to teach them to pan for gold.

Otoniel decided today might not be the best day to ask. Charlie had been growing grumpier and grumpier since the winter wedding party left, and Otoniel had a feeling that if he asked, he might be jeopardizing his room. So he wouldn't ask today, just sit there nursing his water and try to figure out what he was going to do for eats.

The door opened, letting in a chill wave of November air. In stepped three men in long white winter coats. Two of them were tall, and the third short. The short one wore glasses and a black homburg with a red feather in the band. The tall, muscular one wore a white bowler. The barrel-shaped tall one wore a white cowboy hat. He had an immaculate goatee. He looked familiar to Otoniel. Perhaps he lived in Denver.

The barrel-chested man was clearly the local, as he gestured to the bar for the others' benefit, but the short one was definitely the leader, and he walked up to the bar first. He walked with an unsteady gait, and he trembled a little as he removed his driving gauntlets. He put them down on the bar before climbing up onto a stool.

Charlie, in good bartender fashion, didn't rush over. He finished wiping the glass in his hand, maybe the third he'd cleaned all morning, then walked over slowly to address the visitors. His face was hard, impassive, but for all that not altogether unfriendly.

The short man spoke softly, and Charlie leaned in close. Then Charlie got out three glasses and poured some clear liquid out of an unlabeled bottle. Something too expensive for Otoniel's acquaintance. Charlie and the barrel-chested man drank.

Charlie leaned in again, apparently listening to the short man's faint voice. After a moment, he said something at about the same volume and pointed at Otoniel.

The short man turned around and looked at Otoniel. He climbed down off the stool, then grabbed his glass in one hand, his gauntlets in the other, and headed over to the table where Otoniel sat. The man's steps were unsteady, uneven, and slow, so it seemed a long time before he let himself down into the chair opposite Otoniel. He slid the glass across the table to Otoniel.

He leaned forward and said, "Drink," at a volume barely above a whisper.

Otoniel threw back half the glass at a gulp and was immediately sorry. This wasn't bathtub gin, it was the real stuff, either imported or from before the ban.

The short man said, "That man tells us you can take us to Devil's Bowl."

"Sí, se puede. I, uh, I can."

"Good. Finish up. We leave soon." He took out a small stack of folded $20 bills and peeled one off. "This will serve as a starter, no?"

"Si, señor." Otoniel tried to conceal his excitement as he took the bill.

"Good."

Otoniel finished up the drink in a second gulp, reminding himself to buy more of that good stuff when he got back.

Outside, a big red Pierce-Arrow sedan was parked right up against the mudboards. Otoniel saw they wouldn't have any trouble getting started. The snow was cleared out well between the five buildings that were still in active use, down to the Masonic lodge at the end of the street and across to the outfitters and the city hall and fire department, though the abandoned cottages on the hillside lay dark, still, and buried.

In the back seat of the car, a young white woman in a white cloche was sleeping. The men walked up to the car. The tall, slender man opened the back door and indicated that Otoniel should get inside next to the woman, who was on the far side of the long bench seat.

Otoniel got in. The woman's white ermine coat was open. Underneath she wore a flimsy flapper dress. She had slouched down and pushed the dress and slip up to reveal the top of her stockings and her black garter clips. And there was a thin line of pale thigh between the top of the stocking and the pushed-up hem of her dress. Her legs were sprawled open a bit obscenely, but when Otoniel had to slide over to make room for the tall man, his leg pushed against hers, closing them a little.

The car had an electric starter, which worked right away, and the barrel-shaped man behind the wheel put the car into gear. "Okay, Otoniel," he said in an unnaturally high, squeaky voice, "tell us where to go."

"Aqui," he gestured, pointing straight ahead. "Follow this road out of town. Then keep going about five miles. There will be a road on your left."

"Any sign?"

"The post has a red ah, a blue L, and a green D on it, if it's up. Pero, sometimes it gets knocked down or the snow covers it."

"Okay."

Outside town there were just two sets of deep ruts amidst the area where cars swept off the snow.

The girl made a sound. Otoniel looked over and he was immediately sorry. Her head had lolled over to face him. Her red lips were moving, and a faint "oh-oh-oh" came out. Then they closed and her delicate throat muscles moved as she swallowed. Otoniel swallowed, too. Her skin was smooth, but goose pimpled with the cold. Otoniel was beginning to feel warm, so he looked away.

The tall man had skin almost as white as the girl's, but with a greyish cast to it. Looking at the man, it seemed like his skin was covered in dry, powdery makeup, which accounted for its dull luster. His eyes were glassy and impenetrable, and it did not seem to Otoniel like he blinked enough.

They drove on for a while, with the barrel-chested man handling the snowy road really well. Otoniel pointed out the turn, where the sign was almost completely covered in snow. Negotiating the turn and getting over the ruts in the road slowed them down, so when they hit the bank at the head of the side road, they stopped dead. The barrel-chested man gave it slow gas and the wheels caught, but there was too much snow all around the car and it didn't do more than rock a little.

The small man looked at the tall one and said simply, "Free us." The tall man got out, letting in a gust of cold air.

Otoniel moved to follow, but the small man shook his head. "No. That's what we bring him for."

The tall man removed snow with great sweeps of his long, strong arms. He wasn't wearing gloves, but he didn't seem to notice the cold. Once he'd cleared away enough snow, he hefted the car off the bank where it was high centered and onto a place where its wheels could grip. Then he gave the car a firm push. The car started moving slowly as the barrel-chested man used the engine to take up where the push left off. Then the tall man trotted alongside a short way before getting in.

Otoniel expected the man to be puffing and sweaty when he climbed back in, but he was bone dry and unwinded. In fact, if Otoniel didn't know any better, he'd swear that the man wasn't breathing at all.

Otoniel had once helped three other men lift a Model-T out of a ditch and onto the road. He remembered how much work that had been. And yet, this man had lifted a much heavier vehicle by himself. Otoniel began to be afraid.

The car drove on slowly, steadily, following the sag in the snow that marked the road. It got stuck again, but the tall man dislodged it with the same ease as before.

This time when the car got freed, the girl's head fell over onto Otoniel's shoulder. Her breath flitted up his neck and tickled the back of his ear. Her hand fell onto his thigh, the long, slender fingers stretching down between his legs. Otoniel was terrified to touch her. Then her fingers began making short, spasmodic movements. Her lips parted again, but now she was close enough that Otoniel heard her say, "No-no-no."

Otoniel said, "Is she okay? Does she need a doctor?"

The small man turned around, smiling. He said, "Oh, she's fine."

"And I'm a doctor," the barrel-chested man said.

"Oh," was all Otoniel could say.

They drove on for a while longer, following the road slowly. Otoniel picked up the girl's hand and put it in her own lap. He then leaned her head away from him so it was on the seat back.

Shortly after they left the main road, they were driving without the benefit of other tracks. Now they came to the end of the road. It seemed that no one had been up this way since the first snow, two months or more ago.

"It's up that path," Otoniel said, indicating a slight depression in the snow that led between two stands of pines.

"Yes. I can feel it," said the small man. Then he looked at the doctor. "Can you feel it?"

The doctor hesitated.

"Of course not. But you will."

They got out of the car. The tall man walked around and opened the door beside the young woman. He reached in and picked her up as effortlessly as Otoniel might lift a docile puppy. She seemed to shudder, and she reached out her left arm, placed it on his shoulder, and pushed. She said, "No, no," but the tall man didn't notice.

"Hey, hey," Otoniel said, "maybe we should leave her in the car."

The small man leaned his head back in the car and said, "Maybe you should get out." Otoniel heard this as a threat, but when he looked at the small man he was smiling, and his next words were free of all malice: "After all, you do have to finish taking us up to Devil's Bowl."

"Oh, yeah," Otoniel said, "but why does she have to go?"

"It's very important that she come along," the small man replied, still smiling.

Otoniel wanted to ask why they were going here at all. When they approached him in the bar, he'd assumed they were hunters, campers, skiers, or some other type of adventurers, but with no gear and just this girl, he had no idea what they might be up to.

But the man's smile and his gesture to lead cut off any questions. So Otoniel put his head down and began leading the way up the path to Devil's Bowl. He had a lot of experience as a guide, but following the trail in deep snow was enough of a challenge that for a while he forgot all about the men and woman he was leading.

Then about halfway up the trail, the doctor shouted in his squeaky voice, "I can feel it, by God, I can feel it!"

Otoniel looked at the doctor. His face was expanded with ecstasy, his smile huge, his eyes wide. Otoniel didn't feel anything. He thought, *¿Quien es esta hombre? ¿Que locura es esto?*

Devil's Bowl is a glacial valley with all rounded sides. They entered through a break in the north side, a narrow chink carved as a drainage channel as the glacier melted. In the center of the bowl, a large, flat stone had been deposited by the glacier. It was low, but otherwise it was the size of a cafeteria table. The composition of the stone was unusual—it must have been carried hundreds of miles by the glacier before being put down here.

It was to this table that the men went. They went quickly, leaving Otoniel behind. The small man and the doctor took off their coats to reveal long white robes, like what Otoniel had worn as an altar boy.

The tall man took the woman in one hand and with the other swept the snow off the table. Then he stripped her coat off in one powerful jerk. Otoniel heard the snapping of the buttons and he even saw one, large and black, tumbling end over end before sinking into the snow. The woman's thin frock rippled in the wind. She seemed like she felt that. She made a questioning sound, but still seemed weak and not very aware. But, when the tall man lay her down on the stone table, she cried out and began to struggle to get up.

The small man was standing beside her now. He placed his hand on her chest, above and between her breasts. He spoke a single word that seemed like gibberish to Otoniel.

The woman cried out in pain now. Although she struggled, her arms and legs flailing wildly, the man held her body still with just the light pressure of his one hand. With his other hand, he raised a long silver knife.

"Ancient Spirit, we call you, beseech you, draw you near, and promise you that soon you shall be freed again upon this world. Drink and drink and be prepared for your return."

Then the knife came down. One, two, three, four—more times than Otoniel could watch, and every stroke sent a spray of bright red blood on this man, his robe, and the ground, where it stained and melted into the snow, making it look as if the earth itself had suffered a deep, bloody wound.

The woman's cries began with an intense animal terror that drowned into the wet, choked burbling of a stream during spring runoff, and finally fading altogether so the only sound in the valley was the squish, squish, squish of the knife hand pounding a mutilated, inanimate body.

Otoniel watched in frozen shock. He wanted to act, to say something at least, but all his will was gone. He thought, *Y otra vez.* And then, for a moment, he felt it—the beating of a great heart nearby, and a deep thirst only partly slaked by the dram of human blood.

The short man pulled off his robe. Underneath he was wearing a finely tailored tweed suit. It looked incongruous—his face and hands were still covered with blood. Then he plunged his hands deep in the snow and pulled up a double handful of it, which he used to rub his face. When his face and hands were clean, he put his coat back on and looked at his companions.

The doctor's face was euphoric, like Otoniel had seen on a miner fresh from a whore after months in the mine. The tall man's face was impassive.

The short man said, "Well, shall we go?" The doctor nodded. The short man looked at Otoniel, "We'll give you a ride back to town."

Otoniel finally found his voice. He screamed and ran up out of the bottom of the bowl for the trees.

The short man laughed. "What, do you plan to stay up here and freeze to death?"

"Better than being murdered by you!"

The man smiled. "If we wanted to kill you, you'd be long dead."

A knife thunked into the tree right in front of Otoniel's face. He looked and saw the doctor straightening from the throw.

"The good doctor is a little dramatic, but he makes his point the same as me. Come now, get in the car."

Otoniel swallowed. He knew now what they were saying was true. Otoniel thought for a moment. What was nearby? Nothing. And in this snow and ice, it would be slow going. Even if he made it anywhere, would frostbite be far off? He'd seen those men. Otoniel wanted to stay whole, maybe even more than he wanted to stay alive. "Okay," he said and began walking down to the bottom of the bowl.

"Of course, you'll want to report this to the authorities. Feel free, but do not be surprised if they are unresponsive."

4. A Mausoleum on a Summer Afternoon

Mack Spar first saw Guynemer on a training mission in the south of France. During maneuvers he got separated from the rest of his group in a cloud bank. Up above the cloud he saw what he first took for the shadow of his plane, then thought it was one of his mates. When he got closer, though, he recognized the distinctly painted SPAD XII of Georges Guynemer.

He waved at the Ace of Aces, who waved back, then climbed. Mack lost him in the sun.

When he landed, he couldn't wait to tell his mates what he'd seen. He mentioned it in the mess where everyone was impressed. He described the plane in detail and talked about the Knight of the Air's deft control of his craft.

The next day they got the news. Guynemer was missing. Likely killed. And he had been at the front, hundreds of miles from the training ground at the time.

Everyone assumed Mack must have been mistaken, but he knew what he saw. The next time he took to the air, he felt nervous. He was convinced it was an omen of his own impending death. He was terrified that he would see Guynemer again. Then, when he didn't see him, he suddenly was terrified he would never see him again. He realized what an honor it was to have the ghost choose him, and he wanted to know it was real and wasn't a fluke. When the training group was on the way back to the landing field, Mack broke away and climbed into the clouds.

His wingman pursued, but in the darkening, thick clouds, it was easy to ditch him. Mack was only alone for a short time, though, as the blue and brown Spad XII appeared. It had to be Guynemer's—it had the stork and everything.

And there was Guynemer himself, in his leather helmet and fur-lined combinaison, his eyes dark and intense in his slender face.

Suddenly Guynemer dropped back and got behind Mack. Mack heard the sound of Guynemer's machine gun and saw the tracers passing between the wings of his Curtiss Jenny. Would ghostly bullets destroy his plane? He didn't want to find out, so he quickly dodged before Guynemer could engage his pom-pom.

Mack dodged a few times, then found the answer to his question as the large, ghostly shells passed through his plane and through him. When they touched his flesh, he felt a chill sensation like when he had ventured into a mausoleum on a summer afternoon. That cold, still feeling that he forever after associated with death was concentrated into the translucent bolts of the ghostly ammunition.

After he felt them, a spark of life left him. He let his plane descend below the clouds. He saw the landing field ahead of him, the rest of the group's planes landed and pulled aside. Just then his engine spluttered out. He was out of fuel.

Mack made a rough landing, but a safe one. The training commander rushed over, yelling. Mack barely heard the shouted words, but understood that he was being taken to account for his stunt flying. Mack climbed weakly out of the cockpit, but swooned when he reached the ground. The commander stopped yelling, and they called over a stretcher. Mack was taken to the clinic.

In the infirmary, Mack checked out fine. Fatigue, they said, and didn't try to explain the strange round patches of pale, dead, dry skin. At first, they'd assumed it was scars, then they dismissed it as a rash. But Mack looked at them and saw exit wounds.

He ate a meal in the infirmary, then was instructed to get some rest. In the mess, some of the men were talking about Guynemer. Mack felt he couldn't take that so he went out to the barracks tent. He heard some of the squadrons were being quartered at manors, which meant lavish guest rooms for the trainers, and the barn for the trainees. That might be smelly, but it would at least be warm. It was only September, but it was already getting quite cold at night, and tonight the chill was already deep in his bones.

As the other trainees trickled in, Mack pretended to be asleep. Then, when they were all still and breathing deep and steady, he got up quietly from bed and slipped out of the tent. He inspected his plane with a pocket torch. It, too, was pocked with tiny marks that resembled gunfire. These spots looked like old cloth, the threads brittle, fraying, moth-eaten. He reached inside one of the holes and felt the wood. White. Powdery. Dry rot. It didn't go all the way through, but deep enough that the wood couldn't be trusted not to splinter. He'd have to mention it to a mechanic tomorrow.

Then Mack heard the sound of a single airplane engine. It was a distinctive engine sound, not the OX5 used by the Jenny. It was a Hispano-Suiza. A big one. Like the 200 hp Hispano-Suiza in Guynemer's Spad.

It was circling. The sound increased again. It was throttling down as it drew closer. Now Mack saw it. The blue and tan Spad with the stork on the side. The plane touched down and passed into the one light on the airfield. The pilot's face was completely shaded by his helmet. He sat in the plane, his engine idling. Mack ran at the plane, but the engine throttled up and the plane rose back up into the air.

The plane circled, rising slowly. It went around and around until the sound vanished, swallowed by the black night and twinkling stars.

5. The Unknown Prisoner

When she was awake, Stefani was safe, but when she fell asleep, something tried to get out. It rattled its cage, pushed on the door, tested the bars, and reached for the key—the key! When its scaly foot would jingle the iron key on its ring, trying to pull it down, she would start awake, and it would skulk back into the shadows of its confinement.

It was Stefani's second worst nightmare, after the one about her father, the one that wasn't a dream.

Stefani woke hot and sweaty. She didn't sit up or move right away. She listened in case she could hear it moving around, hear its shuffling feet or the iron key ring on the nail. But there was nothing, except sometimes her mother's snoring. Tonight, there wasn't even that. Stefani threw the covers aside and took a deep breath, letting it swell up her chest, feeling the negligee clinging to her sweaty body.

After a couple of breaths, the sweat had turned cold. Suddenly, she remembered the man at the table, the one who had looked at her with such inhuman hatred. Pursued night and day, she didn't think she could stand it. She wanted to pull the warm blankets back over her, but she decided not to succumb to that temptation. Not tonight. Instead, she got up and fumbled for the light. Of course the thing wasn't in her room, but it must be in the house somewhere. She pulled on her robe, which pressed the damp and chilly negligee against her, and stepped into her cold house slippers. She lit a lamp and ventured into the hall, which had not gotten its electric light installed before her father died.

The hall was too narrow for the tables that were pushed against the wall between doorways, but her father had insisted that they be there, and then he topped them with his crazy statuettes.

The near one featured Baba Yaga, represented as a plump crone with a huge nose. Her back was hunched, her eyes deep and sinister. There was a huge wart on her nose and her fingers stroked her hairy chin. Behind her was a picture of the hut on fowl's legs, a chaotic representation of swirling dust and legs frozen midstride.

On the far table, just past the door to her father's office, fierce Kali stood on one foot. Tall, voluptuous, many-armed, she was as beautiful as Baba Yaga was ugly. Her shadow danced on the wall behind her.

Stefani had been in her father's office when he was alive, but, as far as she knew, no one had been in there since her father's death. She didn't think what was bound in this house could be found there. Wouldn't she have felt it before?

Still, the other option was the basement—what her father had called his lab, study, or conservatory, depending on the day and his mood. And she didn't feel up to checking there tonight.

So she pushed the office door open. The lamplight shone on the bookcases thick with dust, covered with cobwebs.

Stefani had never looked at the titles. Her father had discouraged it, saying the books were "inappropriate" for little girls. She did not look at them now, but kept pushing the door open. She saw his desk, with candles fused to the corners by melted wax. There was a hand-crank machine she knew produced electricity—a Van de Graff generator? There was a slit lamp, which her father had used to show her light and dark patterns on the wall.

She entered the room. The air wasn't stale as she'd expected. There was the smell of old books, and the faint char of long-extinguished candles, but the air was vibrant. It sent a tremble through her, like when the trolley got going fast on a long straightaway.

A huge tome sat open on the bookstand. Beside it, an open journal, and a pen in the inkwell where he had placed it before being called down to dinner. He had obviously hoped to return, with everything still laid out in perfect order. He had closed the door carefully behind him, but never reopened it. Nor had anyone else, until now.

Stefani was afraid to look at what he had written. She trembled with the suspicion that the words might have killed him. Her mother and the doctor had called it an advanced case of tuberculosis, citing a longstanding cough. The doctor may have been a dogmatic fool, bound to label every unknown with a familiar name, but Stefani and her mother knew that nothing so simple as tuberculosis could cause such utter bodily dissolution as had destroyed her father that night. Her mother must have hoped to keep the secret by letting no one, not even estate appraisers, enter any of father's work rooms.

Terrified by what had happened to her father, Stefani had gone along with this plan. But now she feared that whatever it was that had killed him would not stay caged. Left to its own devices, sooner or later the unknown prisoner would find its way out. It must be found and its prison secured. If possible. And if not? Stefani shuddered at the thought. She decided to read what her father had written.

So she stepped fully into the room and shone her light on the page of the journal. This page had few words, written long and slanting downward as they did when he was excited. She read, "It hungers, but what will sate its appetite I dare not imagine!" Stefani gasped and recoiled. As she did, she swept the light over the wall that had been partly shaded by the open door. A glint of silver caught her eye and she stepped closer.

Two slender silver chains hung on the wall. The outer one was held taut in a perfect circle by silver tacks. It had no clasp or break. The inner one hung loose on two wooden pegs. As she stepped closer, she noticed that there was something suspended on the inner chain, perhaps a pendant, concealed in a black velvet bag.

She drew forward and the air seemed to hum like a streetcar late at night when all the world was still except the tireless electric motor.

She reached for the necklace. She wanted to see the pendant. When her hand got close, it suddenly felt hot, like reaching into an oven, only there was no blast of heat on her arm or face.

She yanked her hand back. Could this be the prison? It didn't feel like that at all, but it was definitely strange. She put the lamp down and gave it a little more wick. The extra light was helpful for the eyes, but still far short of what the heart wanted. She reached out again, touched the wall beside the outer chain. It was cold. She walked her fingers along the wall. As soon as they crossed over the circular chain, they felt the heat. It wasn't painful—it was perhaps pleasant, like placing cold hands near the oven. Did the heat come from the necklace? She inched toward it and touched the chain carefully. It was cool. She felt along the chain to the velvet bag. It didn't feel warm—it felt electric. It was the source of the thrumming air.

She wrapped her fingers around the bag. It didn't shock or hurt. It felt like a mother's embrace in books: enfolding, strong, capable of protecting her from the world. She stayed there for a long moment, holding the velvet bag. Part of her wanted to open it—see what was inside. But then she didn't dare— whatever it was, it had power. Would it be angered to be brought out into the light? Could it be angered? What made her think it had a mind and a will?

Instead of opening the bag, she reached into the warmth with her other hand and lifted the chain off the pegs. As she pulled it closer, its power filled the room. Nothing here could hurt her, she felt. There was no need to fear. She swept her eyes over the open book, the notebook, all her father's things. None of it held any terror. And whatever spirit or power her father held captive, it would stay fast for another night. She felt comfortably sleepy.

Stefani put the chain over her head. The velvet bag came to rest at the top of the hollow between her breasts, and she felt the comforting warmth from it spread through her body.

Calmly, she picked up the lamp, closed the door to her father's study, and went back to bed. She fell asleep quickly, and remained asleep all night without a single troubling dream.

6. How to Tell the Tale

Stanley got off the train in Denver. It was late at night. Except for the red capped porters, the people coming off the train, and those waiting for them, the big cavernous marble depot was empty and quiet. The air was thin and smelled of a day's worth of anxious cigarettes and hasty meals—half-eaten and then discarded. Those with people to meet them left quickly, hard on the heels of traveling salesmen rushing to get in a nightcap or indulge some other vice before turning in.

Soon it was just Stanley and the porters. He walked up to one and asked for a recommendation of places to stay. He followed the porter's directions, but didn't like the feel of the place. It wasn't the shabby façade or the street girls out front—that was just common wear and mundane vice—there was something troubling about the place. A few too many restless spirits had missed their crossing here. It wasn't haunted, but many people had met bad ends here, and he didn't want the risk of being another one. He walked up the street to somewhere just as dirty and disreputable, but with fewer bad vibes.

The man in the lobby was wide and tall. Broad shouldered and muscular, he was past his prime, and growing a little flabby around the edges. But his mind was still sharp, and Stanley felt himself getting sized up by an experienced eye as he walked to the counter. He got a room under the name Stanley J. Fields, out of Cincinnati.

The room was small, bare, a bed and chair in the main room. In the bathroom there was a dirty tub and dirty toilet with a slightly cleaner washbasin.

Stanley put the chair by the window and looked out as he rolled a cigarette. He was on the third floor, not quite high enough to be out of earshot of the cackling come-ons of the night ladies below. Nor was he out of their view. When he lit his cigarette, one of them saw the flicker of the match and called up to him. He could come down, she said, or he could toss the key down and she'd come up. He thought, *She's just a quiff—no harm.* His loins twinged—hungry and restless. And deeper in him, less loud and less urgent, but more painful, his heart stirred, too, longing for close, quiet, whispered words with a woman in the dark. He shook his head and waved dismissively with his cigarette.

Across the street, there was a low theater advertising a "French" cabaret. Next to it, on the corner, a hotel that ran up to five stories. The rest of the street was restaurants and whatnot. When he finished his cigarette, he crushed it out and decided to head out into the night to see what shook loose.

Coming out the front door, he walked past the ladies of the night. Not that they didn't know anything, but even if they weren't succubi—and he didn't think any of them were—they were expensive sources of information. Their livelihood depended on getting good value for what they said, and they knew how to read in your eyes just how dear they could price it. Men often didn't understand the value of what they knew, and, like as not, they'd tell you all you want to know and more for the cost of a good slug of liquor and your time.

He had been sent here in search of something powerful. If it could be felt from Chicago, it probably had tendrils in Denver here that he could track. So he felt his way to a likely pool hall. Laughing and shouting showed the back room was full, but the crowd out front was pretty sparse. Two toughs in shirtsleeves playing pool, their jackets and a girl on stools nearby were the only ones beside the barkeep. Stanley went up to him and asked for a gin and tonic. He got a cold, hard, noncommittal stare, so he just ordered a tonic instead. He tasted it, then squeezed the lemon into it.

He went over to the pool table. The two men said nothing, just pushed the balls around and drank. Based on the smell and their loose movements, they obviously had something approximating gin in their glasses.

The girl talked plenty—she went on and on about what some woman named Laurena Senter was wearing, and how she just had to have some decent clothes. She seemed like she was dressed decent—black cloche hat, under which most of her brown hair was tucked, a pale sack that supposedly passed as fashionable dress these days, stockings, and pale slippers.

At one point she turned her eyes to Stanley and looked him over in a way that reminded him how he must look. New suit, but damaged and rumpled from two days' wear. Hell, he hadn't even changed his collar since the night he finished up that succubus case. That was the last time he'd had a shave, too, so he must be looking pretty scraggly. First order of business in the morning.

Watching the two men play, it was obvious one of them was a much better player as well as a better dresser, and the other one was getting tired of losing. When the game finished, the winner wanted to play another, but the loser balked.

Stanley stepped up, "I'll play you for a drink. It's the only way I'm likely to get a bracer in this joint."

The guy was suspicious. Confident in his ability, but wary of sharks. Stanley could see the wheels turning in his head, and then he decided the stakes were low enough that it seemed reasonable to take up the stranger's offer. "Sure, fella. I'll rack and you break."

As Stanley walked over to the cues on the wall, he took out a pinch of reagent—given to him by Barton. He blended it with the chalk dust as he rubbed it onto his cue, then blew it off. Unseen, gold and iridium dust sprinkled on the table.

Putting the triangle away, the guy said, "People call me Market Store Marty. That there's Panner, and the squeeze is Flo or Flew. She works over at the Alhambra. It's kind of a dump, but you can see her dance there. And if you ask nice, maybe she can find you something you can touch."

"Marty," Flo objected.

"What, doll? This guy looks like he ain't had no sugar in a while. I'm just trynna be a pal."

Stanley said, "Thanks," then leaned over the table. He drove the cue ball at the racked triangle. The balls broke with a satisfying crack. The three rolled close to the corner, but wasn't going to fall. Stanley gestured subtly with the stick, creating a little wave that traveled unseen to give the three just a little extra energy.

Stanley'd watched Marty, and he knew how well he had to play. Marty was good, but not quite good enough to run the table. So Stanley put the two and the four in, naturally, and let the seven miss on the side.

When Marty stepped up to play, he started talking. "Where you from?"

"Cincinnati."

"Yeah? You look like you had to leave in a hurry."

"Maybe."

"Why?"

Stanley shrugged, watched the eleven fall hard, then said, "Sometimes you gotta leave a place quick."

"Yeah? Somebody after you?"

Stanley didn't respond. The fourteen went down.

"So, what'd you do in Cincinnati?"

"Well, sometimes people need things done. I'm good at getting things done."

"That's a steady line. Seems like there's always some bob needs something done." The nine fell, but it was a very bad leave.

"Strue."

"You don't look like a heavy. You can handle yourself if things get physical?"

"I get things done. They don't get physical if I can help it. But if they do, yeah, I can take it."

"You interested in getting more to do?" He shot at the ten, but didn't quite make it.

As Stanley stepped up to the table, he said, "Yeah, if there's decent scratch to be made."

"And if I was to recommend you as a guy who can get things done, how'm I to know?"

"Ask Paul Snake Eyes. I done a few things for him."

"I don't know no Paul Snake Eyes."

Stanley sank the one. "He's in Cincinnati."

"And I don't know him."

Stanley sank the six. "He sometimes does work for a respectable character named John Jew Marcus, but I ain't never done anything for Marcus, and don't know anything about what Marcus does, so don't ask." The seven almost didn't want to fall again, so Stanley gave it a little wave with the stick, pushing it in.

"I guess this Marcus is a respectable character, so I've heard tell. And if this Paul Snake Eyes is in his organization, he can't be all bad neither. So maybe I will ask him what he knows about . . ."

"Stanley Fields." The five was an easy shot, but the leave was not what he had hoped for. Holding the stick over the table it was clear that the best angle for sinking the eight was blocked by the ten. Bank shot blocked by the thirteen.

Marty picked up his cue. "That was a good run."

Stanley leaned over the table and hit the shot. He'd given the cue ball a lot of spin, but nowhere near enough to make it curve around the ten, and when he tried waving the stick to maneuver it, he felt the resistance from the ball's angular momentum. He pushed through it and the ball turned just right. The eight sank, while the cue ball spun itself harmlessly out.

"That was a helluva shot."

"Amazing what a man can do when he's thirsty."

"Yeah. Speakin a which . . ." Marty looked at the bartender, who made a sour face, but poured a gin and tonic. Marty brought it over.

It smelled terrible and tasted worse. Stanley couldn't help making a face as he drank it.

"Awful, huh? They save the good stuff for the back room." Marty looked around quickly to make sure no one was around, a wasted gesture because the room still held the same five people since Stanley entered. "If you can handle jobs half as well as you handled that shot, I think I've got some work for you."

Panner suddenly spoke up, "Aw, don't take any jobs from him!"

"Shaddap! You shouldn't be talking if you don't know what you're talking about."

"I do so know what I'm talking about. And you know I do, too. You know I'm right. And Lou does, too, he just don't want to admit it."

"You're just mad 'cause you didn't get bumped up to spieler. I told you you just don't know how to tell the tale."

Stanley held up a hand. "Wait a second. Why don't you guys tell me what you're talking about?"

Panner said, "He's gonna offer you a job with Blonger, but you don't want to take it."

"Why not?"

"Because Blonger's firm ain't gonna be tops much longer."

"Does he got the fix on or not?" Marty broke in.

"But the DA's gunning for him. . . "

"Aw, go peddle that stuff somewhere else. The DA's turning out the red lights and then the bootleggers."

"I dunno, I think he's still goin for Blonger."

"As long as Blonger's got the cops, he ain't got nothing to worry about. Without cops, the DA can't do nothing. You know that. You was there when that egg come up and finger me with that copper Cokely. He fingered me, dead to rights, and did I even get taken in? Not a chance. That's what'll happen if the DA tries to move without the cops."

"I dunno, man. I think Blonger's on the way out. Somebody else is movin in."

Stanely looked at Panner. "What makes you think that? Do you know who it might be?"

Panner shrugged. "Can't tell. But the office never seems to get wise unless somebody else is making a move. I think that's what's happening here. And you mark my words, Blonger'll be out, and somebody'll move in, and all of a sudden that DA who was so strong against the old Fixer suddenly has nothing on the new guys."

Stanley nodded. That was often true, and it might have something to do with the people he was looking for. He was about to ask another question when the door to the back burst open and drunken revelers came out, including one big character, who was more than somewhat drunk.

Marty was immediately enlisted to help this guy, who was by no means light. Marty rushed to put his jacket and hat on, then they moved him out of the place and into a car. Flo followed behind eagerly, offering every possible help to "Mr. Specter." Panner followed along, too, but he neither offered help nor was asked to do anything.

When they were gone, the bartender came over to Stanley and said, "Bar's closed, bub. Scram."

So Stanley hit the street again and went back to his room. It was just a little after four. Stanley sat on the edge of the bed for a long time before he let himself lie down and go to sleep.

7. No Answer That Satisfied

Otoniel stood trembling in the cold street, unsure what to do. He had a handful of money, and he desperately needed a drink. But he didn't want to spend the money. Not that money. Not after what he had seen when he earned it. He should go to the police, tell them about the girl and her murder. But he couldn't. Not with this tremble. Not with his reputation. And not with the way Sheriff Whit treated him. He would definitely need a drink for that.

So he went into Charlie's. Charlie was still at the bar, polishing a glass, looking absently at the window. Otoniel stumbled up to the bar. He waved shakily to Charlie. Charlie ignored him. He waved harder. Charlie still ignored him. Otoniel called to him.

Charlie said, "Go away. I told you yesterday. No more free drinks."

Otoniel said, "I have money. A drink, por favor."

"You said you was busted yesterday."

"I was. Look. I will tell you where I got the money, but, please, give me the drink first."

"Sorry, Otto, but you gotta pay first. No bar tabs for the likes of you."

Otoniel balked. He needed a drink. But he didn't want to spend the money. Just one drink. Then he would tell what happened. Otoniel peeled off the smallest bill in the stack he was given—a ten.

Charlie looked at the bill, then he looked at the stack in Otoniel's hand. "Where did you get the money?"

"Por favor . . . please, give me a drink first."

"Okay, okay. Calm down." Charlie poured a drink. He gave it to Otoniel.

Otoniel took the drink, then slammed it all in one big gulp. He gasped and coughed at the roughness of the cheap imitation gin.

"Now, tell me, where did you get the money?"

"The three men, the ones who hired me--."

"What men?"

"The three men you saw. You told them to talk to me."

"I don't know what you're talking about."

"Three men. Un pequeño . . . small. Old. One tall, skinny. Blanco, no gris—grey. The other was . . . gordo . . . fat. They came to the bar asking for a guide. They hired me to take them to Devil's Bowl."

"Otto, I didn't see any men this morning. I saw you. You were hanging around here all morning and then you left for a while. I don't think anybody else came in all day."

Otoniel looked at Charlie. Clearly, he wasn't joking or lying. He was telling the truth, as he saw it. Otoniel felt a chill go through his body, and not because of his still damp feet. "Un otro," is all he said.

"Okay, Otto. I guess this off season has been hard on you." He poured another glass. He left the bottle and walked away, back to his typical spot. Now, though, instead of ignoring Otoniel, he kept looking at him askance. Otoniel looked away at first, but as he worked through the bottle, he found it became easier to ignore Charlie's looks.

Then he looked up at the painting behind the bar. A nymph disrobing to bathe in a frothy pool. Though this woman was voluptuous, her white gossamer gown reminded Otoniel of the slim young woman's white flapper dress. It was as if the painter was disrobing her for sacrifice. Otoniel finished his drink, poured another, then turned around to look away from the painting. He looked out the window at the snow, but that was no good. The snow reminded him of trudging up to Devil's Bowl through the woods.

So he looked down at his feet. This worked until he noticed something on the sleeve of his coat. A dark spot. Blood? He didn't dare find out. The coat had to go. He slugged back the last of his drink and headed down the street to the outfitter's.

Tom Blaine was a tailor by training, like his father. But also like his father—who had come to Californiaville during the Silver Rush days—he sold everything anyone might need for prospecting, mining, and, increasingly, the leisure activities that were starting to draw motorists up in the summer. He even sold gasoline for the cars. While there, Otoniel asked the tailor about the car with the three men in it who had bought gas before leaving town. He said he hadn't seen anyone. He had been inside all day—he had even lunched in his shop on cold meat and potatoes. Who could afford to eat at Charlie's during the off-season? And he said Otoniel was the first customer to come in for the day.

Otoniel bought a new heavy coat that fit him pretty well so it didn't need to be tailored, then headed back to the bar in search of another drink. This is the last time he considered going to Sherriff Whit to talk about the murder. It was questionable anyway. If he said the three white men murdered the girl and they said he did it, who was going to be believed? But now, if no one seemed to remember the men, who would be held responsible for the murder but him?

When Otoniel returned to Charlie's, it was crowded. Apparently, some miners had decided to brave the snow and make their way down from the little cluster of shacks near the mine's entrance. Now that they were in town, they were eager for distraction, and Otoniel was more than happy to oblige them. He now knew he didn't want the money, and the easiest way to get rid of it seemed to spend it.

He completely lost track of time, and his own actions. He remembered the lamps being lit, and the entire bar taking on their warm, smoky, guttering light. He remembered singing, laughing, and, eventually, someone leading him up to bed. Perhaps that someone was Charlie, and perhaps he asked questions about the source of the money, but Otoniel either gave no answer or, at least, not one that satisfied.

Otoniel woke up with a terrible hangover. He rolled over, felt the pounding in his head, the queasiness in his stomach. He felt the need for breakfast, a hot, heavy, greasy breakfast that could hold down his quivering stomach.

He took a couple of deep breaths, then rolled over again so that his feet were hanging over the edge. He sat up. As he waited for his balance to return, he reminded himself of the rules of the day. He mustn't mention the three mysterious men, and he must spend the last of the money. He had gone a fair way to getting rid of it last night, if his drink-addled memory was accurate, and his breakfast would help further. After that, he would have to make a plan to get rid of it.

He got up, staggered over to the small table by the door. He leaned heavily on it until he regained his balance. He splashed water from the basin on his face. Then he drank a little. The water was stale, but cool, and his body loved it. A couple deep breaths and he was ready to walk.

He headed out into the hall where he had to step over a few miners who never made it to their rooms.

Down in the restaurant, he was happy to collapse into his chair. He ordered a breakfast of sausage, potatoes, and flapjacks. And coffee. He would rather have had chorizo, pozole, and tortillas, but that was not an option. When it came, he alternately sipped the coffee and put it up against his throbbing head.

When his food came, he ate it hunched over. Slowly at first, then becoming more eager as it filled his belly. He started to feel less worn. In fact, he was starting to feel downright good. And that's when he saw the headline on the paper: "Search Expands for Missing Heiress," and the picture of the girl from the car.

Otoniel got up and rushed over to the table where the paper was. It was from Denver, and several days old, but the article told the story of her disappearance in late November. She had been at a cabaret, one that sounded familiar, and then she disappeared. She hadn't been seen since. For a long time, police had few clues, and those they pursued led nowhere. Then they had gotten a tip that she might have been seen in the mountains. And that's when it occurred to Otoniel why he remembered the name of the cabaret. Morgan's. That's where they had gone to pick up hooch last time he was in town. He racked his brain, which had reresumed throbbing fiercely. It was the same night she disappeared.

He fell back in his chair, suddenly sapped of all motivation, his heart pounding in terror, but seeming to give no energy to his body.

And then three men entered the hotel restaurant. They wore grey campaign coats and broad-brimmed hats. They had the bearing of lawmen—stiff, proud, interrogative. They paused at the door, looking around, assessing everything.

One of them stayed at the door. The other two walked up to Agnes, the only one working in the restaurant at the time. They showed her badges. She put down her rag and stood upright. They showed her a picture and she shook her head. Then they asked her a few other questions. Otoniel couldn't hear them, but he saw lips and eyes move. One of the questions made her point at Otoniel. The men thanked her and began walking over to his table.

Otoniel tried to pretend he hadn't been paying attention when the men stood at his table and one asked, "Otoniel Garcia?"

"Sí."

Out came the badges. One policeman spoke. The other watched and wrote on his notepad. "Denver police department. We're hoping you can help us with something."

"Uh, sure, I hope I can."

One pulled out the picture. It was her. The young flapper in the car. The heiress. "Have you seen this woman?"

Otoniel immediately thought, *La verdad es mejor.* After all, they would likely get the truth out of him anyway, and it would look better if he was open. But then he remembered how no one else had seen the three men in the car. If he talked about the woman and her murder, supposedly caused by these three nonexistent men, how could it not be pinned on him? So, even though his instincts told him to tell the truth, he said, "No."

"Look again. Are you sure?"

"Uh, yes. I am sure."

Agnes had gone over to the table of regulars and was talking to them, but it was clear she was listening, too.

The policeman asked, "Where were you the night of November 17th?"

"I was in Denver."

The talking policeman looked at the watching one and they exchanged raised eyebrows. "In Denver, really? Doing what?"

"Visiting family."

"Uh-huh. And you were with family that whole day? You have witnesses who can attest to your being with them the whole time?"

Otoniel swallowed. He didn't remember the night very well. It was Dolores' wedding, the favorite cousin. The reception had gotten pretty wild, and they'd already burned through all the booze they had, so he and his cousin Tonio had been sent out to get more. The bootlegger Tonio knew worked at Morgan's, this speak where there were cooch dancers. A little drunk, he'd gotten distracted. Tonio was pretty tight, too, and forgot that Otoniel was there. So he left him behind and took his bootlegger friend back to the party. Otoniel didn't realize he'd been left behind until he was turned out because he didn't have money to buy drinks—Tonio had it all. Otoniel didn't know where the place was, so he wandered the streets all night, trying to find his way back to abuelita's house. He made it back by the morning, but all night he could not account for his whereabouts.

"Sí, yeah. The whole day."

"Uh-huh. There're also reports you've come into a lot of money all of a sudden. Where'd you get the money?"

Now Otoniel realized the spot he was in. If he didn't say something about the three strangers now, he'd be in trouble, so he said, "I am a tour guide. I take people to see sights and locations. These three men asked for a guide. I took them. They paid me well because it was winter, they said."

"Uh-huh. And where'd they want you to take them?"

"Devil's Bo--." He stopped. He didn't want them looking around there. "Devil's Butte."

"Devil's Butte?" The man with the pad stopped writing and looked up.

"My English not so good sometimes. Maybe it is called Devil's Head. They heard the backside of it was good, and they wanted to see it, so I took them down Cripple Creek way."

"Anybody else see these men, know you were contracted?"

"Charlie."

"Yeah? We've talked to Mr. Hoyt, but he says he saw nobody. Anybody else?"

Otoniel was silent for a moment.

"Well, we think you'd better come with us until we can get this all straightened out."

"No . . . uh, okay. Can I finish breakfast?"

"No. Come with us now."

He stood up. The two men walked behind him. When they came to the door, the guard took up the front position in the line. When they reached the car, they handcuffed him, "as a precaution," then slammed him against the car before throwing him in the back. For the second time in a week, he was leaving town in a car with three men. Only this time, he knew he was to be the sacrifice.

8. Treasures in Heaven

Stanley awoke a little groggy from last night's "gin." He went to the bathroom and splashed some water on his face. In the mirror he could see the first order of business: a shave. He looked like a hoodlum, especially in his ruined suit that he had started sleeping in.

Splash of water, then his coat and hat, and he was out the door. Outside, the street had undergone the transformation typical of all cities. The gaudy nastiness of the night had changed into the dingy spent morning.

Yesterday's papers blew down the street. The ladies of the night, with their imitation dresses and imitation jewelry, were gone, replaced by a couple of skulking johns and a genuine rummy or two.

Stanley pulled down his hat a little to shield his eyes better. The sun here was very bright. The morning was cold, but it wasn't Chicago cold. It was a thinner cold, and although he felt it on his face, it didn't penetrate his coat.

There was a barber shop up the street, but when Stanley looked in, he saw an Italian man in the chair, reading the local rag. His father had brought him up with a distrust of Italians, a feeling that had been confirmed by their conduct in the War. He had to find a barber he could trust. He looked in a couple more shops and didn't like the looks of the barbers before he found one he did like: a small, fastidious Swiss man pushing a broom.

Stanley didn't trust Italian barbers, but tailors were another matter. The standard of trust was a little lower if they had a needle to your coat and not a blade to your throat, so their unmatched skill won the day.

Stanley found a tailor with an Italian name. It was closed when he got there, so he sat down on the curb. Then he noticed a church down the street. He got back up. Apparently, it was time to worship. He stood up and walked toward the church.

By now the furtive johns were gone and the street was filling up with daytime figures. Businessmen in relatively crisp new collars and freshly pressed suits looked askance at the man with no collar, shirt open, and dirty, rumpled suit. Stanley responded by looking hard at all and none of them as he walked.

When he reached the church he went in without noticing the denomination. The right place to worship was the place Destiny put you when the urge to worship arose. The spirit is everywhere, and where you are is where you are meant to be. The Initiated learn to be thankful for being in this place.

Inside, the chaplain gave him a brief look, but didn't give him any trouble when he knelt down in the pews. He was glad he'd gotten a shave at least.

When he was finished, he got up and went outside. The tailor still wasn't open. Stanley rolled a cigarette by touch. When it was finished, he lit it and walked slowly back to the shop. When he got there, he sat down on the curb and practiced blowing smoke rings. He wasn't very good, but he was getting better.

When the tailor showed up to open his shop he looked a proper dago. Old, with tanned, leathery skin, and a thin, scraggly seaman's beard. He unlocked the door and turned the sign to "open." Stanley followed him in.

Inside, the shop was sparsely populated by mannequins dressed in suits ranging from the casual and gaudy seersucker to the formal tuxedo. Around the outside of the shop were bars where hung the components of the suits themselves—three rows of pants on one side, three rows of jackets on the other. At the back of the store were racks of shirts of various colors and materials. Behind them, bolts of material were stored in cubbies. The tailor walked up to a hard wooden chair in front of the racks, turned, and started to lower himself down into it, when he saw Stanley. He let out a groan and stopped lowering himself down.

"Well, what do you need?" he asked, then quickly answered his own question: "Everything . . . but a shave." He lifted his hand to touch his own scraggly beard. He walked over to Stanley and touched his suit. The old man's steps were trembling, but his hands were firm, swift, and deft. "Nice suit. And new. Shame. Do you want another one like it?"

"I'd like one that's popular in town, something that won't stand out."

"Something cheap, then."

"Not too cheap, please."

"Well, it can't be too fine if you don't want to stand out in this cow-town."

"I'll trust your judgment. But I don't want to be back here buying another suit next week."

"If you treat all your suits like you treated this one, you could be back tomorrow."

Stanley smiled. The tailor directed him to strip to his underwear, then began taking measurements. The tailor used an extended hook to lift down a jacket and pants. He brought them over to Stanley. There was a vest inside the jacket that Stanley had not seen. The tailor encouraged him to put it on.

The suit was brown serge, not as good as the one he had bought in Chicago, but serviceable. Once Stanley had it on, he could see it was just a little large. The tailor pinched and then pinned it. Once properly pinned, it looked great.

"Okay," Stanley said. "When can it be ready?"

"Tomorrow, maybe. Most likely Friday."

Stanley looked around the still empty shop. "You can't sell me that hokum."

"I have a lot of back-orders. Loyal customers I don't want to lose."

Stanley pulled out a wad of cash. "Well, you might be able to win my loyalty, too. Look at me—I need this suit today. I'll pay a premium for your time, but if I can't get it this afternoon, I'll ankle down the road to someone who can help me."

"Okay." The tailor reached for the money.

Stanley divided his offer, giving over about a quarter of it. "I'll be back after lunch, say around noon-thirty. You can have the rest if you're finished then."

Stanley put his old suit back on, his coat and hat, and went out into the street. The air was still chilled, but for now the sun was shining into the street. Stanley felt warm enough to undo some of the buttons on his coat. He rolled another cigarette and started to look around, noting where the tailor shop was.

Denver, huh? He looked around. It didn't look as much like a cow town as he expected. The tallest building around was a clock tower attached to a dry goods, and it was pretty tall, as tall as anything he saw in Chicago.

Stanley caught a streetcar down to the other side of downtown. There was a large park with a classical colonnade on the south side. On the north side, another was under construction, though it looked like the actual work was suspended for the weather. Signs said city government was housed in a squat stone building nearby. More than anything, it reminded Stanley of the blockhouses he'd seen on the front lines during the War.

Atop the hill on the fourth side of the park was another building with columns. Its gold dome shone brightly in the sun. *Probably the state capitol,* Stanley thought. *Denver is the capital of the state, right?*

Then Stanley walked back through town. At lunch, he stopped at a place he felt was likely a speak. He showed his wad of cash and complained about the lack of beer. He got blown off, but he made an impression.

He got back to the tailor's shop to find his suit was ready. Once he'd tried it on—it was a great fit—he paid the tailor and left. He didn't speak to anyone. He blended in, became just another guy catching a streetcar. He got out at the city courthouse and went directly inside.

He went to the DA's office and gave the secretary a letter, impressing upon her that it was crucial that Mr. Van Cise get the letter right away. Then he sat down to wait, hiding his face in a magazine. Vogue wasn't exactly his style, but fortunately he didn't have long to wait.

Van Cise came out quickly, but without fuss. He addressed Stanley by name and acted like the two of them were old friends from the War. It was almost true. They'd both been assigned to the same front at the same time, but had never seen one another.

In the office, Van Cise asked Stanley what unit he was in. Stanley told him, and Van Cise lit up. "Oh, I knew a chap from there. Burt something or other."

"Conner."

"Yeah, Burt Conner. A helluva card player till you learned he never had anything. Always bluffing. No luck at cards."

"Nor life, neither. He died with rotation papers in his pocket. He was looking forward to a delousing, a good drink, and a clean bed when a Jerry sniper took him."

"Tough luck."

"Yeah."

"So many good men were lost."

"Yeah."

"Never again."

"If you say so, but I'll believe it when I see it."

"You tough guys go to class to learn to talk like that?"

"Naw. It comes natural. You gotta be more'n a little cynical to get in this racket in the first place, and it just gets worse the longer you stay."

"Speaking of your racket, you know there's no law here that protects what Barton's letter says you propose to do here."

"Good, so there's none'at restricts it, neither."

"No, the law still restricts what you can do in many ways. I want you to remember that you must still operate within the law. If you come to me for help, I'll give it, so long as I feel it serves the public interest, but if I ever feel you are acting as a menace, I will put you away, no matter my longstanding friendship with Barton. Just so we're clear."

"Very."

"Good. Private investigators can be very helpful, especially in a town like this where people don't always feel they can trust the police, but they can also be a danger. Now, if you want to get started working in town here, I suggest you talk to Shad Ruckles."

"And where would I find him?"

"Most days he hangs out at Miss Stover's."

"What's that?"

"A candy shop and soda fountain. He loves his malteds. It's up on 16th. Near Champa."

"Thanks."

Stanley headed out of the office. As he was going out, he casually blended in with the crowd of departing functionaries. He wasn't in the crowd, but he was vaguely attached to it as it left, one of many anonymous people leaving the courthouse. The tailor had steered him right, this brown serge single-breasted suit was popular among Denverites. He almost felt like a local.

After a little while, he separated himself from the rest of the men and headed down 16th street. He found the candy shop. It had a pink and red recessed façade and a similar pattern in the tiles out in front of the door. He looked inside the window and saw a small man reading a newspaper at one of the tables. His glass was tall, frosty, and half empty, with ice cream residue inside. Stanley could feel this was the man he was looking for.

He walked inside. It was warm. The man behind the counter was thin, clean-shaven, and pale. He was in his late teens or early twenties. Stanley looked over the confections behind the glass and ordered a little bar of chocolate with peanuts in it. Holding the bar by the wax paper it'd been handed to him in, he headed over to the table with the small man.

There was also a big man at the table who was studiously indifferent, staring off into space. As Stanley approached, the big man's eyes became very focused and alert. Although his body didn't move, his muscles tensed and readied to move.

"Shad Ruckles?" Stanley said.

The big guy nearly jumped. The little guy looked up from his Daily Express and said, "Do I know you?"

"No. I was sent by Mr. Van Cise."

"Phil rarely sends anyone to me. He normally sends them packing." Ruckles looked at the long, jagged, but faint scar on Stanley's right temple. "You in the service?"

"Yeah."

"Figures. Phil was always a sucker for a fellow doughboy. You got experience?"

"Yeah. 8 years."

"You from Chicago? That where you worked?"

"Yeah, I worked in Chicago."

"Okay, I can use some backup, but I can't guarantee you your own cases right away. Strictly dick for hire by the hour, likely menial."

"With all due respect, I plan to set up my own practice."

"Oh, I can't have you taking cases away from my boys."

"I won't be. The cases I take, nobody else wants."

"Huh? Why?"

"Let's just say I'm storing my treasures in heaven."

"Charity cases? You can have 'em. You must be a lot wealthier than you look."

"Benevolent backer."

Shad snorted. "Okay. So you can take the charity cases, but when I need backup I still expect you to show up."

"All right. If I can."

"If you don't, you better have a damn good excuse, like you was catching the train back to Chicago." Ruckles opened up his jacket and reached into his pocket. As he was fumbling there, Stanley noticed his piece, a .45. Slow to draw, slow to fire, but deadly. Ruckles handed him a card. "Call me when you get set up so I know where to find you."

Stanley looked at the card. It said, "Ruckles Detective Agency." He said, "Will do," and put the card in his pocket.

As Stanley was getting ready to go, Ruckles said, "Don't you like malteds?"

"Sure. Who doesn't? It's just a little cold today."

"Consider having a malted today. Not everyone lives to see warmer weather."

9. Not Altogether Unpleasant

As lunchtime approached, Stefani and Caroline had just about finished going through the catalogs kept behind the counter at the dressmakers. Caroline sighed, "These mornings are the worst. Nobody but the house girls come in the morning. The ladies don't come until the afternoon. Stef, I don't know what I would do if you didn't come here to help pass the time."

"Pick up a book, I expect," Stefani replied.

"I'm not a reader like you. They're so slow. It takes so long for a book to get good. By the time a book gets good, I could've already seen two films."

"It's not so bad as that. What you need is more practice. The more you read, the faster you get, and the better the books get."

Caroline sighed again. "I might be reduced to that, even, if the Golds allowed it. No reading behind the counter. They want me to look ready to help, not busy."

"And what about these?" Stefani gestured to the catalogs.

"Oh, that's different. I can always say I was learning about the latest fashions. Still, they're not any fun without you to talk to." Caroline looked at the clock. "It's close enough. Let's go for an early lunch."

"I could certainly eat," Stefani said. So they put up the "out to lunch" sign and headed over to a little Italian café around the corner.

It was a good thing they left a little early. It was a cheap restaurant with quality food, so the place got pretty crowded by noon. They got a table toward the back, fortunately not near the kitchen—it was by the backmost window off Arizona Avenue. They ordered a couple of lemon sodas and spaghetti plates. When the plates came and they started to eat, Stefani was disturbed by a sensation.

The necklace she was wearing felt suddenly warm. She paused, put down her fork, and looked around. She reached up to touch the velvet pouch, felt its warmth with her hands through the bib and dress.

As she looked around, she saw a man who had just entered the restaurant. He stood frozen just inside the door, his jaw fallen slack. Then he turned his head side to side, not looking, but listening, or, she thought, maybe sniffing, though what could he possibly hope to smell over the basil and garlic, she had no idea.

His wide nostrils flared and his head cocked one way, then the other. His short legs took careful strides through the crowd. He was coming right for her! She put her head down and focused on her food.

He came up and stood beside the table. Stefani ignored him, but it was only a matter of a second before Caroline noticed him. "Excuse us, sir, but do we know you?"

"She does. Or should, I think." Stefani allowed herself to look up just in time to see him gesture at her. There was something familiar about his face. "You are Stefani Aegis, right?"

Caroline looked at her. There was no denying it to an old friend of father's. Though she hadn't seen him since her father's death—he hadn't even been at the funeral--he most likely knew her. Why did she want to avoid his gaze and duck out the back? "Yes?"

"Thaddeus Marduk, a friend of your father's."

"Uncle Tad!" She looked carefully at him. He looked much older than she remembered, but she recognized his bushy eyebrows. He also looked much thinner in the face. His body was as corpulent as ever.

He put out his hand and she took it. He wasn't just shaking her hand, he was feeling it, touching the back of her hand and her knuckles. The handshake went on, and she tried slightly to pull her hand back, but he kept hold of it just a little longer. There was a slight tingling sensation from his touch. Not altogether unpleasant, but it made her uncomfortable. As did his gaze. He was staring at her chest, and she couldn't tell whether the warmth she felt was from embarrassment or the amulet. She pulled again to get her hand back.

He released it, then made a slight bow. "It was good to see you again—such a beautiful young woman you've become. And what a lovely Polaire coat, too. It was your mother's, right?"

"Yes," Stefani said. "But she doesn't come out much."

"What a shame. I would not mind seeing her again, too. But I can't take up all your day. Ladies." He bowed to Caroline as well.

When he was gone, Caroline looked at Stefani, "Uncle Tad, hm? How's he fixed for chips?"

"I believe he's pretty well off. His family were émigrés from Eastern Europe. Austria-Hungary, I think, before the war against Germany—when Hungary fought Germany, I mean. His family fell out of favor, I think, and they got out while the getting was good. Bundled up what they could, sold what they couldn't and came here."

"Huh. Not bad looking, neither, for his age. He's family to you: mind introducing me in a social way?"

"I dunno, Caroline."

"Well, if you'd rather keep him to yourself . . . If you don't think it would be weird to pursue your uncle."

"It's not that. It's just I don't know . . . I don't know him. It's been a long time since he was Uncle Tad to me. He and my dad were best friends, but I also kind of got the impression that they hated each other."

"Your dad must've been a crazy guy, may he rest in peace."

"I don't know. He always seemed more sane than just about any anybody else."

"I don't know what that says about you, Stef, but I don't think it's good." She looked at Stefani's plate. "You gonna finish off those meatballs?"

"Yeah. Lemme alone and I'll finish."

"Well, if you're gonna finish, please hurry. I gotta get back to the shop. I swear the Golds must have somebody spying on the shop, because they always know if I'm back just a few minutes late."

10.   You Is Ever Finding Stray Dogs

As the ship was tugged up to the pier, doughboys crowded the rails, pressing hard against them and straining to see over the men in front to hopefully catch sight of loved ones waiting for them. From the comfortable distance of his deck chair, it looked all too much like when they had been crowding in the trenches and he had been flying high above them in his own private war. It was just the new boys—most of the men were like Mack, trying to look and act calm because, despite their surging hearts, they knew it would be a while yet before the planks were lowered.

Mack had more reason than most to be nervous, though. Unlike the majority of the men, he hadn't been eager to come home. He wanted to stay overseas. "Home" held little promise for him, now that he had been forced to leave behind what he truly loved, probably forever.

In the brief silence between the shutoff of the ship's engines and the men's cheers, he heard the droning reminder of it. He looked up and saw the smudgy form small against the pale grey sky. Guynemer. In the time after the Armistice, Mack had used all his flight time in mock combat with the French Ace. His plane couldn't match Guynemer's spectral SPAD, but it had been fun to try, and the ghost had become something more than mere shadow, if still a long way from a welcome apparition.

Mack had wondered if the French Ace's ghost would follow him across the sea. He had seen Guynemer flying all day and night without any need to land, so he had no thought that fuel might be an impediment. Instead, he reasoned, spirits were probably linked to their native soil, either by birth or by death. The corpse, at least, must somehow bond the spirit to the mortal coil.

His speculation had proved wrong. If it were as the rumors said—that the sky had taken him—it would make sense that he would be rootless, eager to move on, and fully capable of doing so. On the voyage, Guynemer's presence had been less welcome than in France, and the sound and sight of him had kept Mack below decks as much as possible. But why was this ghost pursuing him? What could he possibly offer this ethereal airman that kept him always in the area, but never close enough to talk? Shouts went unanswered, save by a wide grin and a wave while in the air or a scornful scowl on the ground.

The men were filing eagerly down the gangplanks. Now there was a jostle between the men who were from New York and those who were from far away, the ones with the early appointment at the demobilization center. Mack knew that he wouldn't be welcomed home, but he nonetheless had a long time to wait before he would be able to collect his pay, allowances, and $60.00 demobilization bonus. Fortunately, he did have a little cash in his pocket. He hoped it would be enough to tide him over until he made it to his appointment.

As the crowd thinned, Mack grabbed his bag and headed down the gangplank. A lot of tearful, happy reunions were going on, but there were still quite a few women who were expectantly craning their necks with worried expressions on their faces. Not the ladies of opportunity, who were trying to look both eager and indifferent at the same time—no mean feat, but probably a routine talent for them. No, these were women who had really expected their men to be on the transport, and some of them had kids in tow.

As he passed these worried women, his pulse increased. It's possible that it was just simple confusion—there were a lot of transports—but it could have been something worse. He knew of at least two suicides on the voyage over. Because men didn't talk about them much, he suspected there were a lot more. The only comments Mack had heard were just after one had been discovered— hanged himself in the can. One of the guys in the room said, "Why'd he do that for? It's peace and we're going home!" Without even thinking, though, Mack had come up with at least six good explanations, and looking around at the other men, he could tell he wasn't the only one with ready reasons to make his own peace.

Mack tried to put that out of mind and pushed his way through the crowd. He was happy for the street noise that drowned out the sound of Guynemer's plane. He set his sights on the el and rushed across the crowded street to the stairs. As he climbed up, he couldn't help but catch a glimpse of the SPAD. Fortunately, the crowded train was too noisy for him to hear the engine. He transferred once, hardly thinking about it. He was almost to Harlem when he realized it wasn't home anymore.

He got off a stop early. 125th street. Even before he started down the stairs, he'd identified at least three likely flophouses—their lights stood out in the twilight. He had learned not to flinch at the No Negroes signs, and walked right into the first one. The man behind the desk was nice enough, especially once he recognized Mack's flying gear. The man was excited about planes and the War. Mack painfully answered questions until he felt he could excuse himself.

Mack went up to his room. It was stuffy and warm, despite the chill outside. He took off his flight jacket and went over to the window. He opened it to let some cool air in, expecting to enjoy the sounds of the city. But it was quieter here than it was around the port, and he could hear the SPAD. He closed the window and went over to the small table in the room. He got out his pack of cigarettes and lit one. He spent most of the rest of the night watching the smoke rise from cigarettes, taking just a few draws every now and then. Eventually, he lay down and went to sleep.

When he collected his pay, he moved down to midtown. It was noisy enough there that he was safe from the engine noise, so long as he didn't go into the Park. Still, he couldn't stop himself from thinking about the war. He thought about Bullard. Bullard had been a great pilot, and the French had let him fly, though he was clearly black. When he was turned over to US command, though, they transferred him to a service battalion. They made him a stevedore, basically. Mack wouldn't let that happen to him if he could help it.

But now he wondered whether he'd made the wrong choice. No wings and no home—it seemed like a terrible bargain, now. But if he hadn't been able to fly for those six months, it probably would have killed him.

One day while Mack was sitting by the street, letting a cigarette burn down to his fingers, a woman sat down by him. "You look like a man who could use a drink."

"Yeah, that wouldn't hurt," Mack said. "But I thought that wasn't allowed anymore."

She smiled. "It's not hard to get it, you just have to know how. Come with me."

Mack looked at her. She was very, very pale, and she wasn't young. Her straight blond hair was bobbed. She was skinny, and the shapeless bag of a dress she wore accentuated that. Still, her smile was nice, and he wasn't doing anything. "Sure," he said.

She led him a few blocks away onto a nondescript side street. She went about halfway down the block, then descended some steps to a door on the lower level. Inside, there was a tiny room. The far door had a small window in it that opened. "Private club," said a man. The woman whispered something to him. The door opened, and the smell of liquor wafted out.

As the door closed behind them, Mack marveled that liquor should be so easy to get. Inside, it was being poured as freely as at any cabaret in Paris. And it wasn't that hard to find the entrance. Surely police could get passwords to such places if they really wanted. The woman led him over to a table where several other women were drinking. One of them looked at Mack and said, "Molly, who's the sheik?"

Molly said, "Oh, he's just a poor, lost battalion. I thought we could give him a home."

The other women laughed, and one of them said, "Oh, Molly, you is ever finding stray dogs!"

"What can I say? I'm a compassionate soul. Besides, isn't he . . . ." she didn't say any more, but put her hand on his arm and gave him a squeeze through his flight jacket.

"Is he ever!" said one of the women. Another looked Mack directly in the eye. "Exotic is the word I'd choose."

"Ooh, yes. Look at his sunburnished skin!" Molly said.

The one woman kept her eyes fixed on Mack. "Yes. Or something."

She was making Mack nervous. He let himself down heavily into an offered chair.

Molly said, "He was definitely over there. That's got to be the result of all those days in the trenches."

Mack looked back at Molly, "Begging your pardon, but I was never in the trenches."

"Oh?" Molly said, trying to hide her disappointment.

"No. I was a pilot."

This made the women hoot, and they called the waiter over to get another round, including a drink for Mack. Then they began plying him for stories of his days in France. It took him a little while to figure out what kinds of stories they liked. They weren't very interested in dogfights and engine troubles—they liked stories of the bunkhouse. The mess hall, the showers, and the occasional fight over a pretty French maid or whore. He quickly became an accepted part of their group.

This was their favorite speakeasy, but there were other joints they went to, including a couple of dance halls. Mack wasn't really a good dancer, but he could jig it up just enough to keep the women happy. That and the occasional trip home with one of them was all it cost him. It was a good time for a while, but it started to drag after a few weeks. And that's when one of the women recommended they head up to Harlem.

Emma, who still took advantage of every opportunity to praise his "exotic" good looks, laughed and fixed Mack with her stare to see his reaction. But he didn't have time for much of one. The rest of the women thought it was a wonderful idea, and he was pulled along with the tide as they piled out of the club to hail a cab. He did down the rest of his drink quickly before leaving the table, and another that had been abandoned.

In fact, it took two cabs to transport all six of them to Harlem. They'd told the driver to take them to Barbary Coast, a popular club in Harlem, the one that drew all the white people north. When he got out of the cab, Mack looked at it in horror.

The place was a sham, a mockery of blackness, a show made up for all the whites to enjoy. If he hated himself now, he knew he couldn't live with himself if he were to participate in that, play the part of the white patron, buying little bits of blackness that had been cut up and graded to ensure they were acceptable.

He was rooted where he stepped out of the cab. The ladies went a few steps before they noticed he wasn't following them. Molly said, "Are you okay?"

"I can't go in there," Mack said.

"Oh?" Emma said. "And why not?"

Mack said, "Lemme show you the real Harlem."

The women "Ooh"ed and told him to lead on.

His first worry was that he wouldn't remember the way, but it turned out he had staggered drunkenly down these streets so many times that he could have found his way blind, and probably had more than twice. His next worry was that the place would be closed, but it wasn't. The Club Niger was a lot less flashy than the Barbary Coast. The lights weren't nearly so bright, and the music was quieter. It drew him in.

But as soon as he stepped inside, he realized his mistake. There were blacks of all shades: high brown, nut-brown, olive, maroon, and even a few high yellows, but there was not a single white face to be seen. He should have turned around and walked out, but his pride didn't let him. This was his home. He belonged here, and he deserved to have at least one drink. Then he would go. He pulled out a chair at a large table and the women followed. They were silent now, and a couple of them were obviously terrified. Mack gave them a look that said, "It'll be fine."

And when Mack saw the bartender, he knew it would be, too. Jake, an old friend, who even now greeted Mack with a smile. They would get their drink and then they could be on their way.

But then a voice came from behind him, "You've got a lot of nerve to come here, after France."

Mack turned around. It was George Turner, another friend. Or former friend. Mack tried a smile.

"I was a fool to sign up for the white man's war, but you didn't just sign up for the war. You signed up for the race. And wasn't that grand? Too grand to acknowledge a brother Negro on the street."

Mack put his hands up, "France was different. Let me buy you a drink and start to make it up to you." The music had stopped, and Mack could feel more than a few pairs of angry eyes on his back.

"And when they jumped us, you sided with the whites."

Now people were murmuring. A few chairs moved. Mack said, "I didn't side with anyone. I didn't get involved."

"You watched us get beat and didn't do nothing. Get beat over white whores. And then you bring them here."

Emma said, "I beg your pardon!" She was forceful, but an angry look from George shut her up.

Mack stood up. "The lady's right. You've got no business dragging them in this. Your beef is with me. I made the mistake of bringing them in here. Let me fix that by getting them out, and then you and I can settle up." Mack turned toward the women and made a gesture that they should go.

They got up and started heading for the door. And that's when Mack got hit. A jab to the head that dazed him. The women screamed and began running. As Mack staggered, he watched the women run, saw that they made it safely to the door at least before he turned to face George.

Though he was dazed, Mack had more fight in him than George expected, and a quick charge landed a couple of punches. That's when the rest of the club joined in, and Mack lost a few minutes in the pummeling.

When he became aware of himself again, he was staggering back out toward Lenox Avenue. He collapsed on the sidewalk there. In his field of vision, he saw the women climbing into a cab. As she was about to step in, Molly turned and rushed over to him. She crouched down and looked him directly in the eye.

"Dirty nigger," she hissed, "I hope you die here, where you belong!" Then she ran back to the cab.

Mack closed his eyes. He knew it was true. Here, in Harlem. This is where he belonged. And he had given it up, for what? For nothing.

But then the drone of the engine pierced his mind. He opened his eyes. He couldn't see the SPAD. The lights were so bright, he couldn't even see stars. The sky was just a featureless black void. Infinite and unreachable, it had grabbed him by an emptiness in his own heart, and it pulled. He ached from the pull of it, the pull that tugged on every blood vessel in his body, but wouldn't tear that heart loose.

Suddenly, the drone of the engine stopped. Mack panicked. Was he dead? Was Guynemer gone? But then he looked around and saw the plane was taxiing to a stop in the center of Lenox Avenue. Guynemer climbed down, took his helmet off and walked over until he stood directly over Mack.

"I would offer to help you up," he said, and gestured with his hand, "but I think we both know how that would end up."

It was clear that Guynemer was comfortable with no one noticing him. They didn't see him—they sometimes walked right through him. But it took Mack a moment to respond. "It doesn't matter. I'm going to stay here. This is where I belong."

Guynemer shook his head. He pointed up. "That's where you belong. With me."

"Goddamn you. Why are you here to taunt me? Is it for my sins?"

"Which sins are those?"

"I gave it all up. Gave it all up for nothing."

Guynemer shrugged. "I don't pretend to know what you're feeling." He gestured at the street and the Club Niger. "Frankly, all this seems pretty alien to me. But it wasn't for nothing that you gave it up. Would I be here if it were for nothing?"

"What is it for, then?"

"I don't see any more than you. I don't know any more than you. I just feel the pull and I follow. I know you feel it, too. And I think that someday soon that pull is going to drag you back into the sky."

"But you don't know that. You're just saying that. You're here to tempt me with hope, keep me from slipping the noose before you can tighten it."

Guynemer shrugged. "It's possible. But if so, why are they leading me on, too? I'm already dead. We'll see."

Mack watched him go for a moment. Guynemer put his helmet on and began climbing into his SPAD. Then Mack got up on his own and began staggering back toward midtown. When he made it to his hotel, he rested in the lobby before heading up to his room.

11. Pulling a Carcass out of a Burrow

It took Stanley a few weeks to get set up. He found a space downtown, California Street, over a dry goods, sharing a hallway with a dentist and a real estate agent. It seemed about perfect. He had hired his receptionist young and pretty but not his type. No sense in inviting that kind of trouble. Lettering was being put on the door: Fields Detective Agency.

He willfully forgot the address where he slept. He kept it written down, but he had long ago learned not to keep such information floating around in his head where anyone could see it if they put in the effort. Once a person's going through your pockets, the game's half over, and you've got worse problems than having them find out where you live.

He was standing inside the office watching the guy stencil the last letters on the glass when he felt it. Fear, worry, and trepidation trembling in the air, the first hints of business coming his way. At first it was just tickling the inside of his ear, but then when she—he didn't know who she was, but she was definitely a woman—opened the door from the stair well, it flooded down the hallway and made the hair on his arms stand on end. He went to his desk and sat down to wait.

The woman came in through the open door, squeezing past the man stenciling on the door. Then she walked hesitantly up to the receptionist's desk. Her steps were slow and shuffling. There was a brief exchange between her and Gail Downs, the receptionist. Then Gail buzzed the intercom. "There's a woman to see you . . . about a case." Her voice was a little too high and excited. That would pass.

"Tell her to come in, Gail."

"Okay, Mr. Fields."

The woman came in through the partition door. She closed it carefully behind her. She was small and slender, despite the oversized hand-me-down coat she wore. Her hair was black and fell loose over her shoulders. Her complexion was a light reddish-brown, and she had the high cheek bones and narrow face of a Mexican with more Indian than Spanish blood. Her steps were timid as she made her way to the middle of the office, where she stood, trembling.

Stanley felt her fear, throbbing off her in nervous waves. He was pretty sure any demons in the area would feel it too and flock to her. At the very least he could not let her leave in this state. He said, "Please, miss, have a seat and tell me how I can help."

She moved carefully around the chair and sat down. "Mr. Fields, Shad Ruckles sent me to you. He said you might be able to help."

"Maybe I can. Tell me what's wrong."

"It's my brother. He—they say he killed someone. A girl, I think. They won't tell me—." She broke off in confusion.

"Who says? The police?"

She nodded. Tears were beginning to rise, such powerful tears filled with pain that Stanley hated to see them wasted. He was not the sort of conjurer to induce tears for the purpose, but when the opportunity arose, he liked to collect them. He handed her his silk handkerchief. If he was lucky, it would retain some of the energy, and maybe he could transfer it.

"Denver police? Or somewhere else?"

"Denver." In her sadness, her Mexican accent became more pronounced.

"Good, then I think I can help." Stanley took out his notebook, wrote down what she had told him. "Start by telling me your name and your brother's name."

"I'm Maria Garcia. My brother's name is Otoniel."

"Now tell me everything . . ."

About an hour later, he put down his pencil. "I think that's all I need for now. I'll see what I can do." Between the verbal commitment and the act of writing notes, he had assured her immensely. He could let her out of here and she wouldn't be a beacon for every hungry spirit in this dangerous little town.

"Thank you," she said.

"Maria, I'm going to start looking into this. Is there any way I can get a hold of you?"

"I work at the Oxford Hotel. It's near here."

"Good, I'll get in touch with you there."

"I . . . I can't afford much of a retainer."

"I know. Shad wouldn't have sent you to me if you could pay. I'm new in town—I can afford to take on a few cases for free to help build up my reputation. You just have to promise me that if I help you out, find the truth about your brother, whether it's what you want or not, you'll tell everyone that I do good work. Deal?" He offered his hand. She shook it timidly and nodded.

"Okay, now why don't you head on home? Gail, why don't you help Miss Garcia find her way to the streetcar?"

"Sure thing, boss." She came in and helped Miss Garcia to her feet. "Let's get you home. Mr. Fields has things under control now. He'll make sure it works out."

Maria nodded as she was being led out. Stanley gestured at the handkerchief with his eyes. She saw and handed it back over with thanks. He held it carefully, so as not to disturb the energy.

The handkerchief tingled in his hand. Definitely some powerful feelings there. And in the flavor of them, very faint but distinct, was the touch of something powerful and evil, possibly his first true taste of what he had been sent to find. He might be able to tease the knowledge out of the tears, use a spell to trace this problem back to its source, and learn what he was up against. Like pulling a carcass out of a burrow to see what had its teeth stuck in the other end, this wasn't always smart, and it could be very dangerous. But sometimes it had to be done.

12.   A Face Like President Wilson

The holding cell was cold. It was drafty and even icy in places. The colored quarter of the jail was secure against escape, but not against winds. The arresting officers had confiscated his coat and personal items, including the rest of the blood money.

Like a lot of the prisoners in the holding cell, Otoniel kept to himself, standing close to the other prisoners in the warmer part of the cell, but saying nothing. When he felt warm, but tired of standing, he would take a turn sitting down for a little while on one of the chill benches that were mostly unoccupied along the outer wall of the cell.

One time he sat down beside a Negro who stayed on the bench and was in relatively high spirits. The man said, "Why you so glum? You lucky to be in here."

"Yes?" replied Otoniel. "Howzzat?"

"Iffen you wasn't in here, you'd be out there with the Klan."

"The Klan?"

"The Ku Klux Klan. You are one dumb spic if you don't know about the Klan. If the Klan even suspect you of a crime against a white woman, they might pick you up. They have a court of they own, with just one verdict: guilty. And they may not kill you, but you may not be grateful for that. You may wish you was dead. Ain't you heard about them? Ain't you seen their bonfires?"

"Yes. I have heard of them."

"Not enough."

Another Negro who had come over to sit down said, "You ain't, neither. They's in the police, too. Bein in here ain't no safe place. One day you're a prisoner of the city, and the next you get disappeared. Next anybody hears of you is your scream as you're burning alive."

"Shit, don't listen to that guy," said the first guy. "He's crazy. What'd you get arrested for?"

Otoniel was silent.

"Don't wanna say? Well, I kin understand that. But unless it was jaywalking or parking tickets, you ain't got much to worry about from the Klan. Your average Klansman is dumb as a post and couldn't pass an exam to become anything but a beat cop.

"If you was arrested by somebody in vice, or, shoot, homicide, he weren't no Klansman. Even if you just got picked up off the street, once you make it here somebody with stripes is in charge of you."

"They ain't all dumb," protested the second Negro. "They say the king of the Klan is some kinda doctor."

"King of the Klan? Don't listen to this jiggaboo. The Klan don't have a king. He's called the Grand Dragon. And yeah, the high ups in the Klan are society types and shit like that who are just joining a lodge. You don't got to worry about them. They pays they dues and don't show up to the meetings. They especially don't interfere here. Cops in the Klan are different. They believe. But they dumb. And they stuck handing out parking tickets."

"Shit, any colored man anywhere in Denver who ain't afraid of the Klan deserves what they get. "

A guard came up to the bars and said, "Otoniel Garcia." When Otoniel stood up, the guard gestured for him to come over. Then he was told to turn around. He was handcuffed, and the door was opened. He was quickly led out. The door was closed behind him.

Otoniel was led down the halls to a small room, an interrogation room.

In the interrogation room, the questions were blunt and angry. "What did you do with the body?" "Did you rape her or just rob her before you killed her?"

"Is this your first murder, or have there been others?" And then, among the badgering, accusative questions were a few about specific details related to the night of the girl's disappearance.

He tried to keep his answers straight, but between his drunkenness on the night of the disappearance and the browbeating questions, he was sure they got enough out of him to show that he couldn't possibly remember the night in question. The policemen worked in shifts, and Otoniel grew more and more tired.

Then, during the third shift, there was a knock on the door. The police opened the door from the inside, talked briefly with the man outside. Before they could finish, another man pushed his way past. "Let me see him. Let me see him right away."

The man pushed the door open and came in. He was tall, thin, and pale. He wore a dark blue three-piece suit and small metal-rimmed glasses. His face looked not unlike President Wilson's. He quickly looked Otoniel over before putting an indignant expression on.

"How long has he been here?" the man asked shrilly. None of the police seemed ready to answer that. He didn't need their answer, apparently, "He was arrested last Thursday. Today is Monday. That's two Saturdays that have passed without an arraignment. And no bond hearing, either.

"Get him a drink of water and then this interrogation is over. If he's still here tomorrow, you can ask some more questions, but I tell you, gentlemen, I plan to go before the judge and get him out today."

The policemen looked at each other nervously. Then one of them said, "Now see here, you can't just . . ."

"What do you mean, I can't? You, sir, are engaged in an illegal interrogation. I can have anything you've gotten here thrown out. How do you think this case'll go forward then?

"Well . . ."

"Just as I thought, you don't think. Now, let's get my friend his glass of water and then we can take him back to his cell, shall we?" The man came over to

Otoniel, put one hand on his shoulder, then gestured for the guards to hurry. When the water was brought, Otoniel drank thirstily. Then the tall man gestured for the guards to lead them out. He used his body as a shield between Otoniel and the guards. The guards led the way back to the cell block, but when they opened the door, the tall man held up his hand.

"Excuse me, officer---uh, uh, what's your name?"

"Carmichael."

"Officer Carmichael, if he's being charged, he should not still be in the holding cell, should he?"

"But he's a . . ." Officer Carmichael started then stopped under the glare of the sergeant.

"Oh, he's a what? Tell me, please. Is that why he hasn't had a bail hearing? Is that why he wasn't given a chance to talk to a lawyer? Why don't you tell me all about it?"

"Carmy," the sergeant said, "put him in another cell."

They led Otoniel down the dimly lit corridor of cells. One was opened. The tall man remarked, "Look at that. A bed and everything. Not that it matters, because I plan to have you out of here tonight. As soon as I can arrange a bond hearing."

"Gracias," Otoniel said, "pero, I don't know who you are."

"I am Derrick Biltmore, and I'm your lawyer."

"Pero I don't have a lawyer."

"You do now."

13. The First Time over the Top

Stanley had a hard time getting ahold of Maria before the hearing. The lawyer Van Cise recommended sure worked fast. He had his secretary try her at work—she'd just left—and she didn't have a phone at home, so he went to her house. She wasn't there. Her mother didn't speak much English and his Spanish was minimal, but he managed to figure out the direction she walked from and met her at the streetcar.

She stepped off the streetcar wearing a man's coat. Army surplus. The hem of her grey skirt protruding from the bottom.

"Señor Fields . . . What?"

"I got a lawyer for your brother. We think we're gonna get him out today."

"You have already proved his innocence?"

"No, but we're hoping we might get the charges dropped or at least get him out on bail."

"Ay, por la virgen!"

"Well, let's hope. And let's get there. This car go downtown?" Stanley asked, pointing at one approaching from the other direction.

"Sí."

So they caught the streetcar back downtown and made their way to the courthouse. Inside, they were directed to courtroom two, and they made it just before the doors closed.

Otoniel was led in by a guard and took his place next to his attorney at the table. This was the first time Stanley had seen the attorney Van Cise recommended, Derrick Biltmore. Even seated, he looked impressively tall and slender. His suit was very high quality, dark blue, and of a heavy weight, though not wool.

The prosecuting attorney was shorter, round, although not so round that you'd notice and comment on it if he weren't sitting next to someone so tall and slender. His suit was of a similar quality, but darker, close to the color of his hair, although his hair was flecked with silver.

Otoniel looked many years older than his sister. Very thin and slightly hunched, his skin was weather-beaten, the color of old shoe leather, the texture of onion skin. His clothes were threadbare and shiny. Overall, he looked very much the vagrant, albeit of the harmless variety.

Then the judge was announced and everyone stood. Stanley saw people in their true proportions. Biltmore was even taller than Stanley'd thought. Beside him, Otoniel seemed like a dwarf, hunched over from a life of hard labor or despair. The judge entered in a swirl of robes. He sat down at the stand and disturbed some of the emotional residuum of the courtroom. A dull rainbow of accumulated anger, fear, sorrow, and joy fluttered up. The judge said, "You may be seated."

The bailiff read the case name and number. The judge looked at the prosecutor, who stood and said, "Your Honor, the issue at hand is of a very serious crime, and the accused is a major flight risk. I ask that bail be denied."

"Mr. Jaegens, be reasonable," the judge said, his voice tired.

"Very well, your honor. I ask that bail be set at $5,000."

"$5,000?" Biltmore shot up from his chair. "Ridiculous! Setting bail at that amount is like a denial. Look at my client. He is in no condition to go on the run. I think $500 should be sufficient, considering the financial state of my client."

"He cannot be in that dire a condition, if he can pay your fees," Jaegens said.

"Your honor, I ask that Mr. Jaegens' remark be stricken from the record as misleading—I have a reputation for performing much of my work pro bono."

"Withdrawn," Jaegens said. "The accused is a flight risk. A spic with no family, we need security to keep him here."

"Your honor," Biltmore responded, "My client is a family man. I believe his sister is here today, and he also has his mother and many relatives in town. He is a US citizen who moved to Denver when he was a child, and since then has strayed no farther than the Rocky Mountains where he gives visitors guided tours of the sights."

"Mother and sister are not the same kind of anchor as wife and children, especially for a spic."

"Enough, Mr. Jaegans," the judge said. "Bail is set at $1,000." He pounded his gavel and rose, retiring to his chamber.

Bitlmore smiled and shook Otoniel's hand. "We should be able to get you out of here now."

Otoniel was led back out by the bailiff and Biltmore came over to Stanley and Maria.

Stanley said, "That was quick work, Mr. Biltmore. I'm Fields, by the way."

"Derrick, please. The Colonel told me to expect you. And this must be Miss Garcia."

"Yes, this is she."

"Mr. Biltmore," Maria said, "I know I should thank you for your assistance, but how are we to get my brother released? We do not have $1,000."

"Miss Garcia, you only need to put up a fraction of the money, maybe $100. Surely you can get that? Especially since you only need it temporarily—it will be refunded when your brother returns for trial."

"Mr. Biltmore, I'm not sure if we can even put together $100!"

Stanley broke in here, "I can cover that."

"But, Mr. Fields, I'm sure I could not accept such a gift."

"Tain't a gift. If I'm gonna find out what your brother's mixed up in I need him out of jail. And I'll make damn sure he makes it back for trial."

"Oh."

"Now, let's go see a bondsman. Derrick, I believe you have my number if new information arises?"

It was after dark by the time they got Otoniel released. Stanley watched him hug his sister, and he thought he saw a faint residuum of magic rising off him like a black dust. When Maria introduced him and they shook hands, Stanley could feel it shuddering through the palm of the man's hand: Otoniel had been around one or more powerful sorcerers, possibly even been near the casting of a powerful spell. And Stanley could see in his eyes that it hadn't been a pleasant one. He had the look men had after the first time they went over the top. If, that is, they lived to look again.

Stanley resolved to get Otoniel alone for some questions as soon as possible.

14.   Pure, Clean Water

Bart Gallio liked to open Morgan's by himself. When he first bought the place from Duncan Morgan, there was an old bartender who opened the place, which was about all the guy was good for, since he wore out by about 2pm. Then the old guy had an apoplexy and couldn't do anything for himself, let alone the club. Bart started coming in to open the place while he was looking to hire help, then realized he didn't need it in the morning. So he opened up the place in the mid-morning.

He set the tables, swept up anything they'd missed the night before, and took the day's deliveries. Bread, every day. Cheese and meats most every day. And once a week he got a visit from his bootlegger. A couple kegs of local beer, a barrel of local hooch, and a few bottles of import.

Another benefit of opening the place himself was getting the chance to interact with some of his most important customers. This morning, three men burst in and the lead one said, "Bart, get the liquor flowing and don't stop until close."

Bart knew who they were, sort of. They were part of the Blonger gang, a couple of steerers and a spieler. The steerers were new to the game, but the spieler had been coming back for half a dozen seasons or so. His nickname was Cajun Chris because he could do a really good Louisiana accent, and he hooked many marks from that state.

Bart thought it was remarkable that the type of con they ran worked so well and so reliably that it could fund the entire Big Store's protection racket. But it did. The steerer sidled up to a mark in the crowd they recognized as a tourist in Denver (often because they bought an out-of-state paper or maybe by their accent). They pretended to be from the same place as the mark, and struck up a casual friendship, saying they should hang out and talk about home. The steerer then took the mark to a spot where the spieler was waiting. The steerer then "recognized" the spieler as someone who had made a great killing in the stock market.

Reluctant at first, the spieler would be made to spill his secret: he had a system that guaranteed profits. He was banned from the large exchanges, but sometimes he could make a little bit here and there at a small exchange where he wouldn't be recognized. He said he would share his secret if the steerer and the mark asked him to, which they would. The steerer and the mark were then led to a fake exchange run by a bookkeeper, another member of the gang. The spieler then made some great profits on a few fake exchanges, then the steerer and the mark were invited to do the same, and they could do it on credit.

Pretty soon, the mark made so much "profit" that he wanted to cash out. At which point he was told that he needed to show that he could have made good on their credit by producing real cash, say about $5000 to cash out the $250,000 the mark thought he saw. Since he didn't have that kind of cash ready, he was told to wire it or bring it in cash to a certain location. Which he did , confident of the $250,000 payday. That never comes.

It was not Chris that'd shouted, but it was to him that Bart spoke, "Big score, Chris?"

"Yessir."

Looking at their faces, Bart could tell that only Chris and the man who shouted had shared in the score. "Another Creole, Chris?"

"Nossir. Fritz here roped in a boy from Minnesota."

"Well, Fritz, the first drink is on you, then, huh?"

"Not Fritz," the steerer said in a thick German accent, "Cal. Cal Schla--."

Chris cut him off, "Might as well be Fritz. You may be talented, but you're still raw. Telling people your real name makes you easier to track."

"But we is all friendly, no?"

"Maybe for now, but what if our Brooklyn Buddy gets pinched while collecting a mark in a hot town down south? The less he knows, the less they can make him say."

"Well, you is right. Let me buy the drinks then. Beer?"

Bart leaned forward over the counter. "You could have a beer, but lookit what I just got today." He went in the back room and came back with a tall, narrow, unopened bottle. As he put it on the bar, Fritz's eyes opened wide.

"Kümmel! Very good."

"Might as well have the good stuff while you can still taste it, hmm?" He poured three glasses.

Fritz said, "And not you?"

"Well, why not?" He poured himself a glass and they all drank together. It was sweet, but tasty. Good stuff—genuine old world product. Bart let it linger on his tongue. He rarely had stuff this good. He rarely drank at all—the liquor was too valuable to drink himself—and if a patron spotted him a drink, it tended to be just a beer, almost nothing this good. Buddy choked and coughed a little. Chris made a frown, but Fritz was delighted.

"That is the good stuff. Reminds me of my father. Very, very good."

Bart thanked him for the drink, and Chris said the next round was on him. Beers this time. So Bart took the bottle into the back. He felt a twinge in his heart as he put a little water in the kummel: guilt. Not because he was cheating his customers, but because it was such good liquor it was really a crime to dilute it. Then he poured three beers and came out.

Now Bart thought it was the right time to address the issue with Chris. He pulled him aside from the steerers and said, "It's a little early for fishing, ain't it?"

Chris didn't look up. He looked at his beer, clearly wishing he could just drink and avoid this conversation.

"And you know how the Fixer feels about off-season fishing, right?"

"Well, sometimes the fish is just biting. Why shouldn't we reel 'em in?"

"I'm not here to tell you your business. I'm just saying this is how things have been in the past. You've been here a few seasons, and you're making a name, but you have to make sure you don't act like too much of a big shot. You wouldn't be the first grafter to get banned from the Big Store—or the biggest."

"So why is you telling me this? This is my business, and you mind yours."

"I am minding mine. I'm part of the Firm, too. I didn't think I could let this go without saying something. But like I said, I'm not here to tell you your business. Enjoy the beer and lemme know if you need another."

Bart went back to getting the club ready to open, pulling down chairs and cleaning the tables. After a while, Chris called out, "Hey, Bart, when do the girls get here?"

"Just afore lunch."

"Well, when they do, send one over here. And tell her not to spend all her time looking at Frenchie."

If he did send one over, Bart would tell her no such thing. French was Blonger's right-hand man, and Blonger was his protection. A speak needed nothing so much as protection. Even before you had booze, you needed protection, and Blonger offered the best protection you could get in Denver, maybe the country. The Blonger Firm could fix almost anybody's problems. He had the Denver Police in his pocket and could pull strings in at least a dozen cities around the country.

When much of his gang went to get graft in Arkansas and Florida over the winter, Blonger often went with them, and that left French in charge. Which meant that wherever French was drinking would never get raided. So that meant you had to try to keep him happy for as long as possible.

French liked the ladies. And they loved him. His moll was a hot dish, but that didn't stop him from enjoying the attention of dozens of others. In fact, getting that attention was what kept him drinking at Morgan's.

Bart had just about finished getting things ready when his bartender showed up, and he turned the work over to the burly middle-aged man with well-manicured mustachios. Bart went to stand behind the bar.

The door opened and stood open long enough for a gust of cold wind to blow in. Bart looked over and saw a tiny, tottering old man followed by a man so tall and square that he seemed to fill up the entire doorway. The old man staggered and stumbled forward. The big man walked with long, slow strides, always keeping deferentially behind the old man.

They came up to the bar. The old man pulled himself laboriously up to the bar stool. At this point, the Blonger gangsters stopped laughing and joking and took notice. They just sat, looking vaguely uneasy, their celebration momentarily quashed. Bart felt it, too, an uncertainty so strong it bordered on nausea.

The old man looked parched. His skin was dry, his lips cracked, even his eyes looked dry.

"Uh, drink?" Bart asked.

"Yes," the old man rasped, "water."

Bart brought the man a tall glass of water. The man drank it up in one large gulp. Then he gestured for Bart to get him another.

While Bart was pouring him another glass, the man said, "I am looking for Stefani Aegis. I believe she works here."

Bart froze. The last time anyone had coming looking for a girl by name, it had been *her*. Bart didn't want to risk anything like that again, so he said, "I think you're mistaken. She don't work here."

The man finished the new glass in a second long drink. He put the glass down and motioned for another. Bart didn't move immediately. He was staring at the man's dry, scaly hands and wondering where the man had been to get that kind of exposure. They had the look of frostbite, darkened and a little shrunken at the tips. But they worked just fine to hold the glass and didn't seem to cause the man any pain. He tapped the glass, which woke Bart up. He took it and poured it full again. The man said, "Are you sure?" His voice was much less raspy than when he had entered.

Bart quavered inside. The man knew he was lying. For the first time, Bart looked up at the bigger man. The big man had rough-hewn features—big clumsy nose, blocky chin, prominent cheeks—and a dull complexion: pale, almost grey. It looked like he wore a lot of makeup, and his hat was pulled down low over his nearly hairless brows.

Bart got the small man his glass of water, all the while steeling himself to say, "No, I am sure she doesn't work here."

The small man drank down the water. He put the glass down. "Very well," he said, his voice sounding almost normal. Then he put three crisp one dollar bills on the bar. Bart's eyes popped at the sight of them. Then he trembled slightly inside. The money can't be for the bill. It had to be for information. Could he keep up his lie in the face of that much money? But the man said, "Thank you. I may check back in a little while, see if anything's changed."

Then he got down laboriously from the stool. Surprisingly, the big man didn't help him, didn't even look at the small man's struggle. He kept his cold eyes fixed stonily on Bart. But once the old man went past him, the big man turned.

Bart grabbed up the money, then watched the two men leave, the little man tottering and the big man taking his intermittent long strides. After they were gone, he stood there watching the doorway, thinking. The money wasn't enough for a bribe, really, but it was enough for a promise—or a threat.

Suddenly Bart realized the bar was filling up. He turned the work over to the bartender and the first girl who had just showed up. When Stefani arrived, he called her over. "Two men came looking for you today."

"Oh," she said, pulling herself up. "Was one of them about this tall, round, thinning hair?"

"No. One was short, one tall. The short guy was very old and acted like he already knew you were here." This seemed to affect Stefani. Her face showed fear and she grasped the pendant at her neck.

She said, "If you see them again, send them away."

"What? If you got problems with men in your life, you take care of it out there. I'm not going to send away paying customers for you, and I don't want any melodramatic scenes in here, neither. Now, get back there and get your costume on."

As Stefani left, Bart held the three dollars close to his chest. They felt warm, somehow, and he wished the men would come back and he could keep pouring water at a dollar a glass. At that rate he could give up the booze and the dancers both and just pour pure, clean water.

15.   I Think I Must Be Damned

Stanley went home with Otoniel and Maria. Maria insisted—she wanted him to be there when their mother saw Otoniel. She thanked him many times for getting her brother out, and said their mother would like to thank him, too. Otoniel was quiet. He seemed thankful, but there was a cloud over him still. And then he realized that Maria, too, was perhaps not as excited as he would've expected her to be

In the front room of the Garcia home, they were met by Mama Garcia, who jumped all over her son, smothering him with kisses and a torrent of happy Spanish. Stanley caught "Gracias" several times and the names of several saints. Then she took a break and turned to Stanley. She took his hand and thanked him directly.

"Don't thank me yet. This is a long way from over."

Maria translated for her mother, who tried to look solemn for a moment, but quickly burst back into a smile and hugged and kissed her son again.

After a while, Stanley was offered a seat, and he took one—an old wooden chair topped by a cushion with inadequate stuffing, its fabric worn, faded, and frayed. He waited patiently as Mama continued to shower her son with affection. Otoniel began to look more comfortable and relaxed. *Good*, thought Stanley. After a while, Mama seemed to remember herself and asked him if he wanted a drink, café con leche or chocolate.

"Dutch chocolate?" Stanley asked.

Maria said, "Chocolate Mejicana. Mamacita would never give a guest Dutch chocolate."

"I'll have some chocolate, then," Stanley said, trying to mimic the lilting Spanish pronunciation.

When the drinks were brought, Stanley said, "Can I have some time alone with Otoniel? I have to ask him some questions so maybe we can make sure he doesn't have to go back."

Maria nodded, then explained to her mother ,who looked worried and sad but didn't fight. They left Stanley and Otoniel alone in the small entry parlor.

"Now, Otoniel, tell me what happened."

Otoniel took a long time to respond. Stanley felt his nervousness. Otoniel's heart was racing. His breath was ragged. His stomach churning. But below the rhythm of his body in stress was something else, just an echo, but it told of contact with a great power. "Three men came," he began at last. They needed a guide. They hired me—I was the only one there."

"A guide? To where?"

Otoniel licked his lips. He took a deep breath. He didn't seem inclined to answer.

Stanley took a sip of the chocolate. It was rich, creamy, and spicy. Cinnamon, for sure, but perhaps something else as well. Then he put the cup down and looked sternly at Otoniel. "You're going to have to tell me if you want my help. Trust me, I'm not with the police, and whatever you tell me won't get to them if it will hurt your case. We have to make the jury believe you are innocent—how can we do that without more information?"

"I am not worried about the jury. Pienso que—I think that I might be . . . damned."

Stanley looked at Otoniel. His eyes were damp, but he was trying very hard to keep from crying.

"Why? What did you do?"

"I took them to it."

"Where did you take them—who were they?"

"I took them to Devil's Bowl."

"Who did you take there?"

"The men in the car."

"Who were they? Tell me about them."

"One of them was old. Very old. Small, too. Another was about my height, but big, portly. He had a . . . perilla." He made a motion on his chin to indicate a goatee. "The other was tall. Very tall. His skin was pale. But not really white . . . gris. He was . . . fuerte." He made a muscle on his arm and felt it with his other hand.

"Strong?"

"Sí, strong."

"How strong?"

"He lifted el coche . . . the car."

"What?"

Otoniel nodded.

"Okay. I'll watch out for that. Was there anyone else?"

"Sí. There was a girl."

"What girl—the one you're accused of murdering?"

"Sí. They took her to the bowl."

"And . . . ?"

"And they killed her."

"How?"

Otoniel didn't respond. He was looking out the window.

"Otoniel, you have to tell me. It's important."

"With a . . . knife. They . . . apuñalaban muchas veces." He made a stabbing motion.

"And what did you feel?"

"Scared. Sad. And scared."

"But did you feel anything else—something not you?"

Otoniel didn't balk at the question. He knew exactly what Stanley was talking about, and he seemed relieved. *Good*, Stanley thought, *this will be easier if he's at least a little sensitive.* Otoniel said, "I felt un hambre. A hunger. O una sed. No . . . una lujuria sanguinaria."

Stanley nodded. That was good and bad. It was good to have confirmation that what Otoniel had felt was the same phenomenon he had been trying to track down, but what he felt was dire. Those men—whoever they were— were trying to revive something evil and powerful. "When this happened, did you sense anything else, any smells or tastes? Did you see or hear anything that didn't seem to really be there?" He gestured at his nose, mouth, eyes, and ears.

Otoniel's face changed. Suddenly his expression brightened in a way it had not all during his mother's ecstatic greeting. "¿Me crees? You . . . believe me? Gracias a dios. I have been afraid to tell anyone. I thought no one would believe. But you do?"

"Yes, I do. From the moment I saw you, I knew you had seen something, experienced something most people could not understand. Now, tell me about what you felt."

"Sí. I smelled something. It smelled como un perro mojado. A wet dog."

Stanley wrote it down. "That's all?"

"Sí."

"Good. Maybe it will be enough." Stanley stood up and put his notebook away. He patted Otoniel on the shoulder. "Señor, get some rest, and let me know if you think of anything else. Also, tell me if you have any nightmares, uh, pesadillas."

"Sí. I will."

As Stanley was getting ready to leave, he noticed that Maria had been eavesdropping. She clearly wanted to talk to him, but he merely waved and headed out the door.

As he headed toward the streetcar stop, Stanley heard Maria rushing out of the house after him. He walked on, despite her cries of "Espera, wait."

When Stanley got to the stop, he began rolling himself a cigarette. He was licking it when Maria caught up with him. He put it in his mouth as she panted.

She said, "Do you believe what he said?"

"What I believe or don't believe doesn't really matter, does it? Clearly, what he needed to hear was that I believed."

She was not convinced, "Es loco, what he said. Crazy."

"Well, maybe that's how we'll save him."

"Mi hermano not is crazy. Pero, what he said—that's crazy."

"And if he killed the girl, that'd be crazy, too. Take your pick."

"He didn't kill her. He's not a killer."

"Says who? You?" He lit his cigarette. "Right now the only evidence suggesting your brother isn't a killer is the presence of these three men, men who only your brother saw. So anything he can tell me about that day can help. What he saw, or thinks he saw or smelled or heard, may be what they told him to see, and it may help me figure out who they were or what they were doing. That'll help me track 'em down and bring 'em in." He paused for a drag on his cigarette, then used his cigarette hand to point at Maria as he spoke. "Any time you think I'm not handling this case right, you just tell me and I'll refund your money and drop the case."

"But we aren't paying you anything."

"My point exactly. Try to find someone else ready to help you with this case."

She looked at Stanley with a hard expression for a moment, then said, "Bueno, you keep working. But if you get my brother sent to the . . . manicomio . . . . madhouse . . ." She wanted to say more, but it seemed her vocabulary failed her.

"Fine. Goodnight."

Maria spun around, silent in her anger. Stanley watched her go, finishing his cigarette. As she left the glow of the streetlamp, he flicked his cigarette off in a different direction. As he waited, he fought hard to resist the temptation to look at his address.

16.   A Simple Thing

After her conversation with Bart, Stefani headed through the kitchen to the dressing room. She took off her cloche hat and blue coat with Mandel fur. She hung them up and was about to sit down at one of the dressing tables when she was disturbed by a rattling sound. It cut through all the bumping, shuffling, and general fussing of the ladies in the dressing room. It cut through her skin and flesh, rattling her bones.

She asked Gloria, one of the nicer girls, new here, but an experienced dancer. "Do you hear that?"

"Hear what?"

"A rattling. It's really loud. Don't you hear it?"

"No. Maybe it's coming from the kitchen?"

"Maybe," Stefani said as she strode out of the dressing room. Opening the door into the kitchen, she said, "Hey, cut it out!"

But the kitchen was empty.

Stefani walked into the kitchen thinking the rattle might be a knife or a dish precariously balanced and rattled by traffic in the street or the stamping of feet in the bar. She walked through the kitchen, getting closer to the sound as she approached the sink and saw the source, a glass sitting in the dry sink. As she approached, she realized she wasn't really hearing the rattle. Instead, she was feeling it, deep inside her bones. No, not in her bones. It wasn't in her body at all. It was in her mind, or her spirit. It touched her in the same place as the beast rattling in its cage at night.

With that thought, fear gripped her, and the brightly lit kitchen became suddenly like the unknown darkness of her father's closed rooms. Shadows in the corners loomed larger. The doorway to the back corridor that opened in the alley, always gloomy, grew deep in darkness, and a figure lurked there. It wasn't large, just something vaguely like an old, feeble man.

And still the glass rattled, the way they did in Caroline's apartment when a freight train thundered by. Only this one went on and on, rattling.

Now she was standing in front of it, looking directly at it. It was a plain clear glass sitting on a dirty lunch plate. It did not visibly move, nor did the crumbs on the plate move. But the glass rattled.

She almost picked it up, then stopped herself. Instead, she grabbed a dish rag and used that to pick up the glass. It vibrated in her fingers, sending tingling sensations through her nerves, sensations that turned into chills in her shoulders and down her back.

She suddenly thought of Bart, and she burst out of the kitchen carrying the glass and looking for him. She saw him absently wiping a table near the stage. He was looking at the table's surface, already damp and shiny, but who knows what he saw. When she came up to him, he looked up at her, startled.

Inexplicably, she shoved the glass in his face and said, "What's wrong with this glass?"

His face went momentarily pale and his mouth fell open. Then he recovered himself and spluttered, "What're you talking about? If it's cracked, toss it out, but otherwise what could possibly be wrong with it?" Then he went back to wiping the table, but his hands were shaking, and it was obviously an effort to ignore her standing there.

Stefani watched him for a moment, not knowing what to make of the whole situation. Then she went back to the dressing room. She didn't want to put the glass down—she was afraid of just having it lying around.

Instead, she took it into the dressing room and put it down on the long vanity in front of the mirror. She sat down in a chair in front of the glass. She wanted to silence it the way she had quieted the thing in the cage. That had been silenced when she put on the pendant. Maybe this could be, too.

She touched the pendant with one hand, then closed her eyes and tried to make it sit still. Her heart was already beating quickly with fear, but as she thought about the glass, her heart sped up even more, until it was beating in rhythm with the rattle of the glass. She didn't know when the glass stopped rattling, but as she became more relaxed and her heartbeat slowed down, she realized it wasn't rattling anymore.

She opened her eyes. The glass was still sitting there. She reached out hesitantly, then touched it. Nothing. Whatever she had done, she had stopped it. She felt extremely happy and proud, and she was smiling broadly until she noticed Gloria in the mirror, looking perplexed at her.

Stefani turned to Gloria. Gloria said, "What happened? You came in with that glass, looking like the devil was chasing you. Then you sat down and closed your eyes, and now you're all smiles."

"Maybe it was the devil. I just said a little prayer and now I feel much better."

"And the glass?"

"Oh," Stefani said, trying to think. "I like to have a drink of water after my prayer. I meant to fill it up, but it looks like I forgot."

"Well, go get yourself a glass. And, damn, you look happy. Maybe I'll have to try a prayer before my shift tomorrow."

"You should. Can't hurt, right?"

Stefani scooped up the glass and went back out into the kitchen. She filled the glass with water and got a long drink, though she found it a little hard to keep from spilling, she was smiling so hard. She didn't know why she felt so happy. No, it wasn't happy she felt. It was powerful. She felt very powerful. It was a simple thing, something no one else had even noticed. But she had noticed it, and not only that—she had made it stop.

And if she could do that, she wondered what else she could do. She was very excited to find out.

17.   A Framed American Flag

Otoniel was happy after talking to the detective. He sighed a deep sigh of relief. He had told someone his deepest secret—and been believed! It occurred to him briefly that this might mean even worse things are to come. If the thing he had felt were real, who knew what that could mean? What did that mean those men were? And what were they trying to accomplish? Otoniel shook his head and found it surprisingly easy to focus back on the positive feelings in the present moment.

Mamacita came back in and smothered him with kisses, then sat down next to him. She held his hand and looked at him with that motherly look that said, "I love you, no matter what," but had a significant doubt of "what" might be.

After a while, Maria came back in. Otoniel had been surprised at the way she charged out after the detective, but she hadn't given him any chance to respond, just a quick glance. And now it was the same, just an angry look at him very quickly, then she went into the kitchen. There was some rattling in there. It was also angry and purposeless.

Then Mamacita apologized, and said she would get dinner ready. After a moment's rattling in the kitchen, she asked Maria what was wrong in a whisper she evidently hoped Otoniel would not hear. Maria responded with a loud, acrid, "Nada, mamacita. Nada." Mama responded, "Que Dios nos salva." In his head, Otoniel could almost see his mother crossing herself.

Mamacita apologized for the dinner, but to Otoniel it was delicious. It was simple—the end of this week's pot of beans, some hastily-made tortillas, and chili sauce—but compared to prison food and before that the comida gringo he had eaten in Californiaville, it was heavenly. At first he lost himself in the food and his mother's smiles, but then he became aware of Maria glaring at him from across the table. He tried to ignore her, but it was clear that something was irritating her.

After dinner, Mamacita showed him up to his room. It was the same room he had shared with his three brothers growing up, but now the second bed had been removed and much of the décor changed. There were many pictures and mementos of Otoniel's older brother, Manuel, who had died in France.

Otoniel looked at the framed folded American flag, the picture of him in his uniform, and his last letter home. Manuel complained of everything, but in an excited, almost happy tone. The family had moved to Denver before he was born, so he'd been no farther from home than Greeley before he enlisted, and now his body rested halfway around the world. In the letter he said he was looking forward to finally making it to the front line.

It was only a couple days after that letter was sent that he was killed. His first engagement. They didn't know anything more than that, but looking at pictures of what it was like over there, Otoniel imagined it. He imagined his brother had climbed up out of the trench and started to run. He got no more than two or three steps before he fell. Machine-gun fire.

Otoniel tried not to think about it. He was getting ready for bed when Maria burst in. She stood there for a moment looking at him angrily. In that moment, Otoniel was struck with the memory of a similar confrontation when she was just eight and had caught him necking with his first serious girlfriend. She was older now, but perhaps no more mature. He knew better than to prompt her. She was working herself up to tell him.

"He doesn't believe you," she said suddenly in English, so Mamacita wouldn't understand.

"Huh? Who?" he said, then realized what she was talking about.

"The detective. He thinks you're lying."

Otoniel rebelled at that thought. The detective had to believe. "If he didn't believe me, why did he say he did?"

"Because he wants to use an insanity plea to keep you out of jail. To look insane, you have to believe your story."

"¿Que? Eso es loca."

"¡Ingles! Your story is crazy. Maybe you are crazy." She took two steps into the room and began waving her finger at him. "Why do you have to say those things? Men who weren't there? Strange feelings? Weird smells? You'd have to be crazy to say that!"

"Is that what you think? He is not the one who doesn't believe me—it's you!"

She was silent.

"What do you think?"

"You want to know what I think? I think . . . I think . . ." Her words were choked off by sobs. She turned, fumbled with the doorknob, then rushed out of his room, slamming the door behind her.

Otoniel almost ran after her, but when he reached for the doorknob, the magnitude of what she was feeling struck him.

If Otoniel were lying, or, worse, insane, then the only conclusion was that he had killed the girl. He stepped back from the door until he ran into the bed. He sat down on it, looking at his hands. Suddenly, he doubted his own story. He collapsed back on the bed, clenching his hands. They felt moist and sticky

18.   Fastest Thing on Wheels

Mack spent the next few weeks mostly in bed, recovering from his rough night in Harlem. First he was healing, and he got up only for food and drink. Then he was healed and he got up even less. Every week, the landlord would come by, knocking for the rent, and Mack would pull the money out of his pocket until one week there wasn't enough money and the landlord threw him out.

Mack sat down on a park bench. He didn't know where to go. Worst of all, he didn't hear the SPAD. He let his head sink to his chest. He looked at his hands, and, past them, his uniform pants, which were beginning to show their age, and his boots, which were still sturdy.

A man yelled, "Hey, flyboy!" but it was the sound of the engine that made him look up. It wasn't a plane engine, but it sounded good. It sounded real good. The engine was in a red roadster, real low and real long. A four door. And behind the wheel was a doughboy, a young man, who said, "Oh, yes, you'll do nicely." Mack suspected he lied about his age to enlist. The doughboy leapt over the door and ran up to Mack, sliding onto the bench next to him. Mack looked at him briefly, then looked back at the car. With nine out of ten cars on the street black, that red just looked so gorgeous.

"Lemme tell youse a story," the doughboy said. Mack looked back at him. He was young. Very young, though from his eyes Mack could definitely tell the boy had seen combat.

Mack looked back at the car.

"Oh, yeah, she's a beaut! Haynes 45. Light six. Fastest thing on wheels. And she's in my story, if you'll just listen."

"Sorry," Mack said, and turned his attention back to the doughboy.

"There's these six Brooklyn boys, see, and they all sign up to go Over There. It'll be great fun, they thinks, and bein just kids they don't take it none too serious. And they don't have much family, anyhow, so they thinks it will be a lark to make each other beneficiaries for their death benefit and whatnot. Only when they get to the Argonne, they find it ain't such a lark as they thought, and they get kinda chewed up and only one of these kids survives. So he's got all kindsa money, so he goes out and buys a swell automobile. I mean, ain't she swell?" He gestured at the 45.

"Yeah," Mack said, and took the excuse to look at it again, idling there, eager to go.

"So, anyway, this boy sees a doll he wants to take a ride in his swell machine, and she want to go, only she's got a girlfriend and won't go without her, so the boy needs to find another guy, a vet, she says, and he don't know nobody on account of losing all his friends in the Argonne. You see what I'm sayin?"

"Yeah, I understand," Mack said. He stood up and grabbed his hat.

"You do? Oh, youse a real swell guy, thanks." He offered his hand. Mack shook it. "I was prepared for youse to be a hard case and I was gonna tell you about how my buddies died. Thanks for not bein a hard case."

The doughboy jumped over the door into the driver's seat. Mack went around to the other side and jumped over the door, too. The doughboy took off the brake and put the car in gear. It leapt off the curb and cut easily into traffic. The kid wasn't a great driver, but the car handled well and had loads of power and speed.

As he was driving, the doughboy looked over and said, "Hey, flyboy, what's your name?"

"Mack."

"That's easy to remember. Mine's Sam. The doll, her name's Millie. I dunno her friend's name."

It turned out to be Sarah. "After Sarah Bernhardt," she explained as they climbed into the back. Sam drove the car out of town and they found a nice stretch of grass off the road a ways. Sam and Millie fooled around a bit, and Mack did his best to pretend to listen to Sal. She appreciated the effort and kept talking. Mack thought, *This isn't so bad*, but he was eager to get back in the car.

When they did, he suggested that they go out for a drive and really see what the car could do. The women thought that was a great idea. As they drove out, the women were excited by Sam's driving, but Mack was a little frustrated. The car could go much faster than Sam was letting it.

"Boy, this is just like flying, ain't it? And, hey, you oughta know, right, Mack?"

Mack had to admit that it was a fair imitation, with the wind whipping over the open body of the car. Then he said, "But I bet we can go faster."

"You sure? Why, we're doin over fifty already."

"Listen to that dog growl. You hafta let her off the leash."

"Yer gonna have to show me how," Sam said. "Millie, hop in the back and let me take your seat. The pilot's taking the wheel."

As they performed the complex maneuver, Mack noticed the SPAD. It was flying pretty low and circling, waiting for him. Mack smiled. He gave the 45 some juice and they were gone. He quickly got the car up to nearly 60, and they went over a little hill. Sam said, "Whoo-boy, I think we really were flying there for a moment."

Guynemer was pulling ahead, so Mack gave the 45 a little more pedal. They went over another hill, and the women screamed. Sam said, "Okay, that's enough. You're scarin the dolls," but he couldn't conceal the tremble in his own voice.

Mack knew he'd never be able to keep up with a SPAD, but that wouldn't keep him from trying. He worked hard to get every ounce of speed out of that six-cylinder engine, and soon he was going over 75. They went over another hill and the wheels came high off the ground. Mid-air, he realized it wasn't a SPAD he'd been racing. It was a Jenny, a trainer. No wonder he'd been able to keep pace.

And that's when the pavement gave out. When the 45 came down on the gravel surface, it veered, and it was all Mack could do to keep it on the road. And slow down. But then the tire hit a rut that cut the next curve too tight, and the car bounced up, slid, and went off the road.

He'd slowed down enough that the car's body was able to absorb most of the impact, and it was only Mack who went through the windshield.

Mack was stunned when he rolled over, aware at first only that his face was bleeding. But when his eyes focused, he saw a pilot's face appear over him.

"And a pilot, too!" the stranger said. "Hot damn, if you can fly half as crazy as you drive, I've gotta have you in my circus!"

Mack smiled, but couldn't reply. Past the man's head, he could see the silhouette of the SPAD against the sky, but his ears were ringing too loud to hear the engine.

19.   Not a Complete Parasite

The morning after talking to Otoniel, Stanley went to the home of the murdered heiress, Irene Pitcher. The family was "old money" in Denver, which meant they had made their fortune last generation rather than this. Silver money. Colorado's silver deposits were not just valuable, they were powerful. The metal was prized by many conjurers for the earth energy it contained. Unfortunately, the supply had, for a while, been controlled by an evil cult. The Slaves of the Silver Serpent did more than just organize parade events. Even in Chicago they had made an impression.

The house was a three-story stout red stone mansion near Cheesman Park. It had a tower on the south side of the house. As was the fashion for these old mansions, it was close to the street, an intimidating looming castle.

He walked up to the door and rang the bell. A servant came to the door, took his card, and invited him into the foyer. Stanley told the man, who was doing his best imitation of what he supposed the perfect British butler must be, that he had come in regards to the late Miss Pitcher. He was shown into an interior parlor where he waited briefly before Mr. Pitcher entered.

Old Pitcher had once been a laborer, and his workingman's frame filled his tailored clothes almost to bursting. Gunmetal grey hair, eyebrows, and Van Dyke beard stood out sharply from his pale, almost translucent face.

"Well, sir, pray tell me what business you have with the death of my daughter?"

"I am an investigator trying to help find your daughter's murderer."

"Hmph. At least you're not a complete parasite. You think you work for a living."

"Have there been a lot of them, parasites, come calling since your daughter's tragedy?"

Pitcher grew cautious. "There always are, in these cases, aren't there? Scandal seekers and rag writers who want you to think they've uncovered something about your lost one. Hmph. You can always tell them by the way they hold out their hands. If there were something really scandalous and provable against her, it would be worth more to the papers than I could pay. Hmph. Think about how much they must have made off that Gibson Girl affair."

It took Stanley only a moment to recall what Pitcher was talking about. "Yes, that was quite the scandal. I'm from Chicago, and they made a lot of ink with that one, for sure."

"You're from Chicago, hmph? Indianapolis man, myself. Chicagoans are so full of themselves. What did you say you were here for?"

"I'm an investigator, helping to locate your daughter's murderer."

"They found him, didn't they, that spic?"

"Yes, well, they arrested him, but I'm not sure they have the right man."

"Hmph. He did it all right. Lead that spic up to the gallows now and pull the lever, says I, not wait for his lawyers to find a clever trick defense."

"Yes, well, you will admit that the police are not wholly honest."

"Crooked as a crankshaft, you mean, hmph."

"And that they might not be above framing an innocent man to protect someone who paid them?"

"Maybe in some cases. I've heard about this guy they call The Fixer, but this beaneater ain't none of that gang. He did it, I can tell you, hmph. I feel it."

And he did, too. There was a subtle enchantment on him. The faint trace of it lingered there, almost imperceptible until you knew the man well enough to sort out what was him and what was not.

"Now, hmph, please to leave and continue your investigations elsewhere."

"I have just one question, something no one has been able to tell me so far: she was kidnapped from a night spot. But surely she didn't go there alone?

Who went with her? Why not a chaperone or family member? Was she seeing someone there?"

"Hmph. I told you to be gone. Your curiosity may have to go unsatisfied. Garth will show you out."

Garth, the imitation butler, did show him out to the foyer, but before he was shown out the door, a voice said, "Wait, I want to talk to him."

"Very well, Master Hugh."

The owner of the voice was a young man wearing a suit much like Mr. Pitcher's, save that it fit his more delicate form much better. There was a definite resemblance, but Hugh obviously had neither the build nor the inclination for hard physical labor.

"You're looking for Irene's killer?"

"Yes."

"I think the Mexican probably did it, but it can't hurt to have someone looking into it."

"Can you help me?"

"A little. Maybe. She was seeing someone at Morgan's. They met there often. I think he was married. An older man. Greg or Craig or something like that. If you go down there, I'm sure you'll see him—or find someone who knows him. I was there when they met. We went out on a lark. A cabaret seemed so fun, so wicked, but so harmless. It seemed harmless."

"Can you tell me more about him?"

"I don't know much else. She didn't talk about him—shut up if I asked her."

"Well, can you at least tell me what he looked like?"

"I think he was about my size. Thin moustache. Dark hair. He looked Latin, but I think he was white, but tanned."

"Anything else?"

"No, I don't think so."

The butler had not left. He remained an intimidating figure standing just outside Stanley's peripheral vision when he looked at Hugh. This made Stanley glance constantly to the side, which was starting to make him nervous. He said, "Okay, thanks. I'll check it out."

Then Garth finished showing him out the door.

Outside, Stanley saw the streetcar pulling away from the stop. He started to run to catch it, but it was too far. Stanley took a few more steps, trying to decide if he wanted to just walk all the way into town when he saw a church a couple blocks down. He headed there. He walked up the front steps, but the door was locked. "Worship where you are," Stanley mumbled. Then he knelt down on the stone landing. He bowed his head and put his hand flat on the wooden door.

He felt the power of the wood. It had been treated properly—lovingly hewn and tenderly sanded and oiled. The hinges had been properly made: heated, hammered, quenched, and tempered. Just enough silver along the braces to make them hold. The structure had a strong blessing as well. If he needed a place to make a stand, this would be a good one.

But that was nothing to do with what he needed now. Stanley sighed, then turned around to wait. He sat on the top step and began rolling a cigarette when a middle-aged man in a dark suit came around the Pitcher home. He followed the sidewalk until it met the walk up to the Pitchers' door. There he hesitated. He put his hand on the gate. Then he resumed his rapid walk.

Stanley put the cigarette in his mouth and smiled, "Always where you need to be, when you're needed." He lit the cigarette and headed down the steps to follow this would-be visitor of the Pitchers.

He followed the street for another block, then turned and headed toward the park. Stanley let himself get closer. When he was a few steps back, he called out, "Greg!"

The man stopped and turned. He looked at Stanley, and his face showed his surprise. "Yes?" he asked.

"My name is Stanley Fields, and I'm an investigator." He handed a card to Greg. "I wanted to talk to you about Miss Pitcher."

"That young lady who was murdered? I am glad they found her killer. Why would you want to talk to me?"

"Because I know you're the reason she was in that drum, Morgan's."

The man's jaw dropped momentarily, but it didn't take him long to get his gums flapping again. "What an absurd suggestion. I think I've heard about enough of this."

"Maybe you'd rather talk to somebody from one of these local rags? Which do you read? The *Express* or the *Post?* Or, more to the point, which one does your wife read?"

Greg stopped and turned around slowly. "What do you want from me?"

"I just want information. I know you've got it. Tell me what I need to know, and I'll do my best to keep it secret. You won't get the same promise from the newspapers."

"Okay, okay. But can we go somewhere to talk about it?"

Stanley gestured at a nearby bench.

"No, I mean somewhere private."

"On a cold day like this, that park bench is about as private as the grave. Have a seat."

Both men sat down on the bench. "So, you were meeting the dame at Morgan's?"

"Well, yes, but it wasn't anything serious. We were both just looking for fun. Cut some fancy steps, have a little juice, and gab a bit."

"How often did you meet?"

"Once a week. It was easy to schedule that way."

"Sure. You don't have to pass notes or get on the horn, which can lead to trouble. And your everloving wife just thinks you have a lodge meeting or something."

Greg blushed a little. "Yeah, that's it."

"And it also means that anyone who's looking will know where to find you—or her."

"Uh, yeah. I guess so."

"So, what happened the night she disappeared?"

Greg hesitated.

"C'mon, tell me. You know you want to tell. That's why you keep coming by the Pitchers'. You wanna confess what you know."

"Okay, okay! Yes. I want them to know I had nothing to do with her murder, but maybe I know something about her disappearance."

"Yeah? So tell me that."

"Well, see, we were kind of fighting that night. I guess. I guess I was just looking for some fun, but she started getting goofy. She kept wanting to go somewhere and neck, and that's fun, but down that road lies trouble, I say. You start out driving a fumble-buggy and end up pushing a pram."

"I think I get the picture. So what did she do when you were fighting?"

"Well, she started hanging around the necks of other guys, just to get my goat."

"I see. Mexicans?"

"No. There were spics there, but she didn't hang around them. She mostly hung around this big guy. Had a neat Van Dyke. He spoke with a squeaky voice. I think somebody called him "Doctor." I shoulda stopped her. He kept leading her on, but when she wasn't looking his eyes were cold."

"So, what did you do?"

"I was sore. So I left. I walked around outside for a while. It was cold that night, and it didn't take long to cool my head. But when I got back, she was gone."

"That's it, huh?"

"Yeah, that's it."

"Okay. Take my card. What's your last name?"

Greg looked disgusted at himself. "What did I tell you all this for—you didn't even know my name?"

"I knew enough to go to the papers. I still can. Name?"

"Harrison."

"And where's a private place I can look you up?"

"Well, I still have lodge meetings, but I don't go to Morgan's. Saturday night you can find me on Curtis Street. Ask a few people and you'll find me."

"Okay. Hopefully that won't be necessary."

"I hope so, too."

Stanley got up from the bench and walked at a natural pace toward the streetcar stop. He waited just a minute before it swung around the corner to pick him up.

20.   Steps Quick and Light

The evening's performances kicked off with an "Over There" number. There weren't many WWI vets in the crowd, but everyone knew the music and it was a nice little number. It was a big chorus line of women in trench coats and helmet-like hats. They came out singing, strutting, and kicking. The coat was just held closed by the belt, so when the ladies kicked, the coat opened and showed some leg above the knee, a tantalizing hint of what was to come.

Between the first and second verses, there was an extended musical bridge. The chorus line stepped back to the rear of the stage. As one, the women shrugged off the coats. The noise of all those heavy coats hitting the ground at once made a big impact on the crowd, who responded by hooting at what they saw, because now the women were wearing very short pants and army blouses, sleeves rolled up, and unbuttoned dangerously low. So when the women came forward again, waving their hats, marching, and kicking, the men were much louder. It was a fun number and got the audience excited for the evening's performance.

No matter what anyone said to her about it, Stefani loved this part of her job. The dancing and the singing felt so good. Being under the lights, all the men watching her, bending to her voice and responding to her figure. It didn't matter that she knew she was not the best singer or dancer. She was good enough for them, good enough that whenever she was between numbers, they called her over, bought her drinks, plied her with questions, trying to get close to, maybe even touch, the bright star of the stage. She answered them with a carefully written script, introduced them to her persona, a gypsy fleeing communists in the Old Country.

But tonight felt different. Instead of simply feeling their eyes on her, she felt the audience's appetite, its lust. And in opposition she felt the energy of the chorus line, pouring out what the audience needed. The two pulsed together, like the beating of one great heart, one pushing and the other drawing this invisible but palpable fluid. When her arms were around the girls on either side of her, she could feel the energy flowing from one to the other, through the skin of her arms. And when they all raised their hands in salute and marched forward separately, she could feel it, diminished but binding them still with rhythm and with spirit. It was powerful, but diffuse, and though the audience drew some of it in, much of it dispersed into the air.

As one of the larger women on the chorus line, Stefani had always found this number to be exhausting, starting off wearing a heavy coat and marching and kicking through the entire song, but today she felt her heart pounding harder than usual. Then she realized that it was not her heart at all, but the amulet she wore, which pulsed rapidly along with her heart, but stronger and deeper. For a moment, it felt like her ribs would be crushed by these two hearts striving to draw together.

The pain made her miss a step, but then she drew in a deep breath and her heart took a half-skip so it beat in echo of the amulet, and the two became like the performers and the audience, one pouring out and the other drawing in. Her heart now felt a million times stronger. The dance was easy, her steps quick and light.

Then the dance was over and she joined hands with the women on either side of her for the bow. When they ran backstage, the women whose hands she'd held complained of her grip.

While the other women went into the dressing room to catch their breath, Stefani felt curiously untired. She changed out of her stage costume, then went into the bar. As she walked around, she felt the men's interest reaching out to her. It was more than just their eyes on her, it was something of their thought, their intent. She knew a man was going to call her over for a drink a moment before he did it. She enjoyed the sensation and the power it gave her.

Then three men came in who felt different from the other men in the bar. The first rattled and creaked with power, like a strong gust through dry leaves in autumn. He was small, old, and his steps were unsteady. Behind him, a tall man with broad shoulders and a square face. He felt like a hammer blow. The third man was average height, medium build, maybe a little wiry. She didn't feel any thoughts or emotions from him. His hat was pulled down over his eyes and his overcoat was drawn tight, and it was as if he had done that with his spirit as well.

The first two men went to a table, but the third one went straight to the bar. Bart looked horrified, even worse than when she'd presented him with that glass. Suddenly Stefani realized that what she felt from the glass was like an echo from one of these three men.

Then, all three men had their eyes on her. Her heart dropped to her belly. The man at the bar glanced over at the two men at the table, then got up and began heading toward her.

She swallowed hard, involuntarily. She croaked out an "excuse me" and bumbled over herself and the man she had been entertaining to get to her feet. She headed directly backstage, toward the dressing room. As she reached the door, she saw the man was still following. He had walked past the bouncer as if invisible. So instead of going into the dressing room, she ducked out the rear exit.

His hat no longer covering them, she felt the power from his eyes, reaching out to her, trying to grab and hold her. She shut the door on him, then began running down the alley in her indecently short costume. Looking back over her shoulder, she saw him come out of the bar. His eyes shone like fire, burning through the chill dark of the alley. Then she felt a pair of strong hands grab her shoulders. She screamed, but as she turned, she saw Uncle Tad.

"Oh, uncle, I'm so glad to see you. There's a man following me."

"Really? Well, let's go take care of him."

"No, no, please. I'm scared. Let's get out of here."

"What? Okay. My motor is just over here."

He helped her into the open cab of his Ford. Then he put his coat over her nearly-bare shoulders. As they drove off, she placed her hand on his shoulder, panting away the last of her fright.

21.   Background Noises and Interference

After leaving the Pitcher home, Stanley rode the streetcar with his eyes closed. Otoniel's story had troubled him. Of course, rites were performed all the time by people who were ignorant or foolish. Rebellious youths, rich playboys trying to break out of the dull monotony of their indulgent lifestyles, so-called free-spirits who thought of the rituals as a poke in the eye of religious orthodoxy. Stanley had been told it was especially bad in the '60s, after the spirit of '48 had died out and the labor movement stalled without a global revolution. So it was possible that Irene had just been mixed up with a man who didn't know what he was doing, and they were drunk or in a state induced by opium or cocaine or peyote or something else exotic.

But Stanley was convinced that wasn't what was going on here. The specificity of place, of action, of people—and the way they concealed themselves from the eyes of the law and the public—made him feel that whoever had performed it not only knew what they were doing, but also had expectations of results.

So Stanley rode with his eyes closed, reaching out, trying to feel the hungry thing, whatever it was. Past the hum of the electric lights and motors, the chattering of the telephone lines, he reached up among the slumbering pines, the latent life of wildflower seeds waiting for the water and warmth of spring.

He touched it, just briefly, before it withdrew completely into wherever it was hiding. He couldn't tell much about it, couldn't experience it directly, but he got clues about its existence. He knew it was there almost the way you know someone has picked up the phone even if they aren't speaking: a hum of the closed circuit, the faint trace of background noises and interference on the line. He knew it wasn't very powerful, because it was still able to hide, and at a certain point power just can't be hidden.

He also knew it had potential. The silver mines opened by the cult touched the veins where it skulked, and it left footprints there, footprints wide but shallow, like a puppy yet to grow into its paws. And now it knew he was looking for it. It knew him like he knew it. It had a sense of his power and potential, maybe even an approximate location, though it was hard to tell anything too precisely with this kind of sense.

Stanley opened his eyes and saw the car was almost to his stop. It had become crowded with people coming downtown to enjoy the nightlife. He found himself pressed between the workmen who had splashed water on themselves and changed shirts and the clerks who had taken off their ties.

Stanley got off the car amid a crowd. He looked around quickly to convince himself that he wasn't being tailed, then pulled out the piece of paper with his address on it.

When he reached his building he was surprised by the crowd gathered outside. There was an ambulance-like vehicle marked Denver Manager of Health. Many of those standing around had their undershirts pulled up over their mouth and nose, others covered up with a cloth. He felt the disease emanating from the body as it was loaded into the ambulance. Then he heard its name: smallpox. Smallpox in a modern city. The creature from the hills, whatever it was, had been here. Now that he had touched it, he could detect the faint traces it left as it fed.

There were many kinds of sacrifice that could feed a creature such as this, and it would need all of them to become fully manifest. Direct blood sacrifice, of course, but also wherever there was disease in the presence of a cure, it could feed. Wherever there was famine in the presence of plenty, it could feed. Wherever there was random murder, pointless war, or any of the thousands of other ways that man showed his cruelty and indifference to man, it could feed. Apparently here, it had chosen some fertile ground. Listening to people talk, there had been hundreds of smallpox deaths lately. Hundreds when simple immunizations could prevent it, when it had been eradicated from most of the civilized world.

Stanley remembered being in the trenches with the sick, the wounded, and the hungry. The men could not see the things that preyed on their sickly spirits. Most of the creatures were smaller, opportunistic scavengers, no more unpleasant or dangerous than the rats that grew fat feeding on the corpses. But behind them was something more, something insatiable and powerful, something they had tried to bury in that field in France, staked with all those white crosses, but something that refused to stay buried. This thing was kin to that, and, if loosed, would seek to exhume its fellow beast.

Stanley shivered. He needed a smoke. And a drink. He headed into the hotel lobby and asked for his key. He took it up to his room, checked that the door was still secure, had not been forced or jimmied, then let himself in. He locked the door behind him and threw the bolt.

He let himself fall down onto the bed. Eyes closed, with his elbows resting on the bed, he rolled a cigarette and put it in his mouth. Before it was even lit, the air felt oppressive, thick, hot, and still. He got up and went over to the window. The radiator didn't seem to be putting out too much heat or humidity, but the room felt muggy. He threw the window open and felt the cold air come in. He leaned out. His window opened on a narrow alley between buildings. He could reach out and touch the painted brick of the next building. He lit the cigarette, watching the shadows the match cast on the bricks opposite.

He looked down at the icy ground, puffing lazily on his cigarette. He held his watch in his hand and tried to focus on watching the seconds pass, but in a little while his mind drifted back to the war. When he found himself thinking about men's spirits being slowly gnawed away even as their bodies rotted, he tried to focus again on the watch, but noticed only the whiteness in his fingertips as he began clenching the timepiece.

He sighed—it was impossible to forget now. He knew men who came out of the war claiming that what they had seen proved there was no God and certainly no Satan, because what man was capable of doing to his fellow man was far beyond any supernatural evil that had been imagined. What they did not realize was that men and their actions were just the tip of the iceberg that sank deep in the spiritual ocean. No man was merely a puppet to the hidden, malevolent forces, but neither was he free.

"Who is he that sayeth . . ." and of all the invisible forces that worked behind the scenes, God's were the subtlest. They either worked unobserved, or sat back and watched as men strove and typically failed in their battles against the principalities of darkness. Or maybe they didn't. Maybe the priests knew or saw something to justify their faith, but from where Stanley stood, it was just mortal men arrayed against mortal men and the immortal forces of corruption and decay. And that's why the world was going down the crapper. Entropy, they called it, a scientific principle inviolate and essential, written into the universe at its creation. It was easy to see how men might be drawn to that principle and its obvious power. It was much harder to justify his own faith in a force that required one to sift the sands of an entire beach to find a single uncut diamond, then believe it had been left there for you.

Stanley sighed again and looked at his watch. It was close enough, and, besides, he needed that drink. In France he had developed a taste for cognac, but right now even bathtub gin sounded good.

He bumped out his cigarette and dropped the butt into the alley. He closed the window, grabbed the key, and set out. He focused on the sidewalk, its cracks, bumps, and imperfections, to avoid noticing too much about his building or its neighbors. Paying just enough attention to avoid being hit and killed by a motorcar, Stanley went several blocks before he looked up and oriented himself. He was just a few blocks from Morgan's, so he headed that way, thinking he could check up on the clues he'd gotten out of the boyfriend

As he was getting close, he felt a tremble in the air, like a loud cry, muffled. Stanley looked around and saw the source, an old man, tiny and withered. There was power there, cloaked, so Stanley couldn't tell just how much, or what kind. The old man's companion was big: tall and broad—taller because of his hat and broader because of his double-breasted overcoat. This man looked huge and strong, but from him Stanley felt nothing. His strength was merely physical, his senses wholly mundane. He was the corporeal guard for the tiny man who looked as frail as this giant was sturdy. The frail man was probably as powerful in a psychic sense as this man was physically, if not more so. This made following them his number one priority. Morgan's and the bearded doctor could wait until tomorrow.

Since they were going his way, it was easy for Stanley to begin tailing them without being too conspicuous. Then he saw that they, too, were going to Morgan's. Could they be connected to the heiress's murder? Just as the doorman was letting them in, the little man looked over his shoulder at Stanley. Their eyes met, and as much as he tried to prevent it, the old man pierced him and there was a recognition. They knew one another as sorcerers. Stanley broke the contact quickly, but it was impossible to say how much had been seen. Stanley cursed himself. It was a stupid move on his part, or a brilliant one on the part of the elder sorcerer, to feign indifference, then suddenly catch his eye when he wasn't ready.

He pulled his hat down over his eyes and fully cloaked himself to prevent further discovery by the elder sorcerer, then headed up to the bar. The bartender was watching the old man with a look of horror. His gaze didn't deviate, nor did he respond when Stanley asked about the heiress and her associations with Greg. Stanley was just about to try harder to get the barman's attention when he felt the unmuffled throb of another source of power. He looked at it, noting from the corner of his eye that the old man looked too.

It was a young woman, in her 20s or thereabouts. She was dressed in her entertaining costume, her voluptuous body almost as exposed as the powerful charm she wore around her neck.

One look in her eyes and Stanley knew she had no idea of the charm's power—or her own, for she had been able to tap into it and seemed capable of wielding its force. Stanley looked at the elder sorcerer, who was now grinning broadly, his crooked, discolored, crocodilian teeth dry and dull in the dim light. Stanley looked back at the girl.

She seemed to suddenly realize her peril and turned running from the room. Stanley bolted after her, but she knew her way through the back corridors and quickly outpaced him in the narrow kitchen. At the back of the kitchen, a well-meaning dishwasher stepped in to stop the man who was chasing the dancer. Stanley knocked him over, barely slowed, and continued pursuit. At the end of the hall, he saw the exit door closing and ran toward it. When he exited the club, he looked around. He saw the woman being helped into a car by a man.

Hoping for a crank starter, Stanley sprinted, but it was an electric starter and the car was away before he was even close enough to see the license plate in the dim of the street lights.

Stanley turned around and walked back to the club. When he reached the back exit, he ran into the old man and his huge companion. The big man was holding the well-meaning dishwasher off the ground by the throat. The dishwasher was gagging and turning red.

"It seems we have a shared interest. Perhaps we can talk, pool our resources."

Stanley gestured with his chin at the struggling dishwasher, whose movements were weakening. "That doesn't seem an omen for friendly conversation."

The old man made a gesture. The big lug waited until the dishwasher had just stopped struggling, then let him collapse in a heap.

Stanley bent down and felt the man's faint pulse, listened to his ragged, desperate breaths.

"Happy?" the old man asked, his "h" sibilant, his "p" faint,

"Not happy, no."

"But you will consent to a meeting?"

"Yeah, okay. What about two o'clock tomorrow?"

"Very good. I am at the Brown Palace. My associate here will be waiting in the lobby and will lead you up."

With that, the old man left, followed by his bodyguard. Stanley bent down and helped the dishwasher up. The man had almost fully regained consciousness, and Stanley led him around to the front, more eager than ever to get a drink.

22.   Mystic Medicine of the East

Stefani's heart was still pounding from the chase, and as Thaddeus' Ford ran rattling down the road at what must have been nearly thirty miles an hour and skidded around corners, she didn't feel relief at being whisked away from her pursuers, she felt panic.

She noticed right away that they weren't going the same way that the streetcar went to her home, but at first she thought he was just going a different way. Thaddeus didn't talk, and he didn't look at her. Nor was he really focused on the road. His eyes were looking into the middle distance—he was lost in thought . . . or something.

As they tore around a few more corners, Stefani knew they weren't going to her house, and her heart began to beat even harder. Then they pulled up at Thaddeus' old house on a dead-end street far from the streetcar lines.

Thaddeus opened his door and began to get out. As he was stepping down, Stefani said, "Excuse me. Where are we?"

"What? Oh. Oh! I'm sorry. I forgot you were there. My apologies. I just drove home without thinking."

"Can you please take me to my house?"

Thaddeus walked around the car and opened her door. "First, let me offer you a cup of tea."

"Oh, no. I'd rather just go home."

He took off his hat and bowed slightly. "Please, I must insist. I owe it to your father's memory to make sure his only child is recovered from her ordeal before taking her home to a big, empty house." He stretched his hand out gallantly.

"Well, okay." She took his hand. It was cold and soft. He helped her down. He took her arm and guided her up the walk to the porch. The air was cool and dry. The porch was an old, low, wooden one. Its boards were worn free of paint and warped.

Thaddeus opened the heavy wood door and switched on the electric light. For a moment, Stefani thought she felt something like her night terror, something that didn't like the light and scuttled away into the dark. Was it caged or was it free? Then she pushed that thought away—it was just another big empty house full of old knickknacks like her father's.

After he closed the door, he gestured, and said, "Do you still need that, or are you warm enough?"

She realized he was gesturing to his jacket, which she wore draped about her shoulders. When she had rushed, panicked, from work, he had immediately and unquestioningly put it around her shoulders as he led her to his car and then to safety. She looked at him, saw on his face the same friendly smile she recognized from his visits as a child. She suddenly felt a little ashamed. She was being rude to one of her father's oldest friends. And why? A scare at work (that he saved her from), a fast car ride (to which she was unaccustomed), and a nightmare she was reminded of because he collected the same oriental knickknacks as her father. "Yes, thank you, I'm still a little chilly." And, she didn't mention, a little embarrassed by her skimpy cabaret outfit.

"That's fine. Go ahead and have a seat over there. It'll take me just a moment to get the kettle going."

"Thanks. A cup of tea sounds wonderful."

"The cure for what ails ye—mystic medicine of the East."

Stefani went in to the parlor and sat down. A lot of dust puffed off the chair. It was old—heavy wood scratched and chipped here and there, the upholstery's deep pile worn thin on the seat and back.

She heard Thaddeus moving around in the kitchen. The water ran. A match struck. She might have heard the little puff of gas lighting or she might have imagined it. She looked around the room. The electric light was in the center of the ceiling, but its one filament was inadequate for the gloom. Darkness lurked in every corner and loomed on the shelves and knickknacks. Thaddeus' taste in collecting really was very much like her father's.

Father had served in the army in the Philippines, but his passion for collecting didn't run to the Catholic faith of that island, but to the Hindoo or some other pagan sect of the region. Instead of virgins with downcast eyes or saints looking plaintively skyward, those statues looked directly at you. Their eyes deepened and darkened with the gloom. They challenged you with their unholy emotions: anger, greed, lust. The carving and casting were so detailed and so lifelike, it was almost as if they were life in repose, as if they had been moving a moment ago and would instantly resume, but had just now stopped.

And there was one in particular that bothered her. A large statue in the corner opposite the door. It was behind and to her left if she just sat straight in her chair. Almost three feet tall, it had four arms that held various tools--or maybe knives of different shapes—a short squat body and the head of an animal. What animal, exactly, she couldn't say. A wolf, perhaps, or a rat. Probably something in between the two so that it resembled nothing to her so much as a feral cur. Whatever it was, its eyes seemed to focus on her.

She looked back at it to decide if it was her imagination and became convinced it was not. It was looking at her, hungrily. As her eyes met its, she felt its hunger, its desire to gnash flesh and bone and offal. Her heart began to pound, and her amulet to throb.

"I assure you, it will win," Thaddeus said.

"What?"

"If you are trying to out-stare that statute, it won't blink first. Believe me, I've tried." He offered her a steaming cup atop a saucer.

Stefani smiled as she took the cup and saucer. "I guess so." Instead of using the delicate handle, she first grabbed the cup, letting the warmth grow to dispel a chill that seemed more than just physical. She held the cup until the heat turned into pain, but the chill remained.

She took a sip of the tea. It was rich and fragrant, exotic and sweet.

"It's jasmine tea," Thaddeus said. "I acquired a taste for it when we were in Manila. Not much of a city, but after the jungle it didn't take much to seem luxurious. Did your father ever talk to you much about the war?"

Stefani shook her head, then sipped the tea again. The warmth went through her and helped her feel a little more soothed.

"Well, most of it was pretty terrible, not suitable for repeating to young ears like yours, but some of it . . . I suppose you've heard how little food and supplies we had?"

"Yes, I think father mentioned that. Was it very bad?"

"Criminal. There was no way to stretch what we had into what we needed, but to make sure our company at least got its share, your father proposed that the division divide up all we had and let every company manage its own resources. This was a good idea, but it meant that we had to haul it around in a cart. Our cart was pulled by this old jenny, Esperanza. The cussedest, stubbornest beast you ever saw. Since dividing the supplies was Old Nik's idea—that's what we called your father—managing the mule fell to him. It was clear Old Nik had never had an animal before."

"No, he was from New York. He never even had a dog."

"He treated it like a child, talked to it, cajoled it, bargained with it, anything he could think of to get it to go. It was pretty comic. The first day the column had to leave us behind—I don't think he got that jenny to move more than a mile. But eventually the two of them got to be a team. When we reached Manila, and we got some more food shipped in, he kept her, at his own expense. And when we shipped out, he tried hard, but couldn't hide that he was crying. He ever tell you that?"

"No."

"Well, I bet he was pretty embarrassed. The rest of the men made pretty good sport of it to pass the long journey home." There was a pause. "Finished your tea, I see. Well, I'll take you home, then."

Thaddeus took her cup and set it aside. "I'll handle that when I get back." As they were walking to the car, Thaddeus said, "I can't help but worry you might not be safe leaving work alone so late at night. Listen, my club is right around the corner from there. An old bachelor like me needs something to fill up his time, so I'm there most nights swapping stories with a bunch of other old vets. I can take you home. Although I took a wrong turn tonight, it's really on my way, and no trouble at all."

She looked into the smiling face of her father's old friend. She felt safe, comfortable, and warm, despite the chill. Her head was a little groggy, too. But then her amulet throbbed, and her head became clear. The chill she had felt all evening returned, and she was no longer certain how safe she was. "Oh, no. I'm fine. I walk to the streetcar with some of the other girls. I wouldn't want to leave them to do it without me."

"As long as you're sure. And if you ever feel you need me, just come looking for me. It's the Decameron Club."

"Thank you. Thanks a lot."

"You are utterly welcome," he replied. His smile seemed a little forced, but he gave her hand a little squeeze as he took it to help her into the Ford sedan.

23.   Near Misses

Otoniel's mother kept him busy all day. It was as if she'd been expecting him and she had a list of chores prepared for him. Although she was working in the kitchen all day—making chili, beans, and tortillas—she still needed him to move the furniture so she could clean under or behind it. He strained and pushed the heavy old wood pieces much too large for the space out of the way, then she rushed in with brooms, brushes, and rags in a whirlwind of cleaning and he had to move everything back. By late afternoon, he was exhausted and craving a drink, but he knew there was no alcohol of any kind allowed in mamacita's house, unless some of his brother's old stash was still hidden around.

It was late and they were just about done when the investigator, Mr. Fields, arrived. He looked like he'd just woken up and was probably still hung over. Nonetheless, he didn't complain when Otoniel asked him to help move the last couple of pieces back into place.

Otoniel said, "Thank you, Señor Fields."

"Sure. But that ain't why I came. Can we step outside to talk?"

Otoniel looked quickly over his shoulder to where mamacita had gone back to busying herself in the kitchen. "Si," he said, and gestured to the porch.

The porch was a heavy brick and mortar structure. Although the walls were low and the ceiling high, it gave a sense of confinement and isolation from the neighbors, even though they were less than ten feet away. Otoniel watched as Mr. Fields got out his tobacco and began rolling a cigarette. As he was lifting the cigarette to this tongue, he said, "I met your sacrificers last night. Or some of them, anyway."

"You did? ¡Que bueno! Will they be arrested?"

Mr. Fields lit his cigarette. "I dunno. I dunno if we're going to get them arrested."

"But how will you keep me out of jail if you do not bring in the killers?"

"Well, there are ways. But, anyway, I can't go to the police until I have more evidence, which I hope to start getting together here soon. After I meet with them tomorrow."

"No—you must not! They are butchers. They will kill you if they think you know."

"They might try. It's part of my job to make sure I don't get killed." Mr. Fields took a long draw on his cigarette. "So I suppose you don't want to go with me?"

"No, I don't"

"Why not? You got something else going? A hot date?"

"I don't want to see those men again."

"Maybe they're not even the same people. I need you to tell me."

"You would know these people."

"Perhaps you're right. I am pretty sure these are the right people. But you said there were three of them. I only saw two. So I want you to come along to make sure."

"No."

Mamacita called from the kitchen, "Dile a tu amigo que cene aquí."

"He's not my friend."

"He brought my son back to me. He's my friend. Invite him to stay for dinner."

"Sí."

Mr. Fields had been waiting patiently while the exchange went on. When it was over, he said, "well?"

"Mama says you should stay for dinner."

"I'd love that. I'm not making any money for this job--I might as well get some food out of it."

Otoniel and Mr. Fields washed their hands in a basin in the entry hall. By the time they got to the table, it was all laid out. Otoniel breathed deeply, inhaling the scents. Nothing said home to him more than this—these were the scents of his childhood, the smells he had missed while living and working in Californiaville, and, especially, while in jail.

They sat down and mamacita said the Lord's Prayer in Spanish, tacking on additional thanks for having her son back. As they were serving the food and getting ready to eat, Maria entered the small dining kitchen. She stopped dead at the doorway, her eyes locked on Mr. Fields, her face unable to conceal her anger. It lasted only a moment, then she composed herself and sat down at the table.

As she was getting some beans, she asked, "So, Mr. Fields, what brings you by today?"

"Your brother may be out temporarily, but if we want to keep him out, we have to be working on his case. I came to ask him to help me identify some suspects."

"Oh?"

"I may have found the men truly responsible for the murder. I'm going to meet with them tomorrow, and I thought Otoniel might come along to provide a positive ID."

"Oh, no," Maria burst out."

"¿Que?" Mamacita asked.

"Nothing," Maria replied in Spanish, "They are just such terrible men, and Mr. Fields wants to take Otoniel to them."

After dinner, as mamacita and Maria were clearing off the table, Mr. Fields nudged Otoniel. "You wanna drink?"

Maria said, "Thank you, but I'm sure we don't want to hold you up from other important business."

"No," said Otoniel, "I would like a drink. But Mama doesn't like liquor. Let's drink upstairs." As they were going up the narrow stairs from the back hallway, Otoniel had mixed feelings. He sure wanted a drink, but he was not sure he wanted to have it with Mr. Fields. He did not want to be reminded about what he had seen. The door to the upstairs room was flat in the ceiling and opened upward. The light button was just inside the door on the floor. Otoniel pressed it and the room lit up. It was a small, uninsulated attic, half-converted to livable space. The light was on the wall. When Otoniel climbed in, he had a momentary flash that the room looked just like it had when his brother was still living.

But the illusion passed and along with it the room's mystery. It was like a cathedral without the bishop. The holy relics of the family's life on their New Mexico ranch still hung on the wall, but without his brother to tell their grandmother's stories, they were just rusty tools and cracking leather.

"My brother used to keep his stuff up here. Even before it went dry, Denver was not friendly to drinkers, especially Chicano drinkers. And Mamacita was almost as bad. Pero, there may still be something stashed here."

"No, I invited you. Let's drink from my supply. Wait . . . you said there might be some left, as in from before Prohibition?"

"Si, if mama didn't find and get rid of it all."

The roof of the attic room was a comfortable height in the middle, but quickly sloped down. Otoniel went first to a saddle on the wall and checked one of the bags. Empty. Then he reached in a spittoon and came up with nothing. Then he went to one of the kickwalls and felt the boards. One came away in his hand to reveal a half-full bottle stashed inside.

"Is tequila okay, señor?"

"Tequila? Oh my, yes. I haven't had tequila since I was in Mexico with Pershing."

Otoniel decided not to say anything about that. He felt around inside the cavity for glasses, and found only one. He suspected his family had a very different idea about that campaign—it was something mamacita brought up when his brother said he was enlisting for the war. "They hate Mexicans," she said. "They will kill you." Otoniel poured about two fingers worth of tequila for Mr. Fields.

Mr. Fields raised his glass, "To absent friends."

Otoniel seconded the toast. He took a belt off the bottle, and enjoyed not just the burn of that first sip of liquor, but the rich flavor of the tequila. His brother had always kept the good stuff hidden away. It was the first time he had drunk anything but bathtub gin and watery beer since he moved to Californiaville. Unless you counted . . . but he didn't like to think of the drinks the old man had given him.

Mr. Fields rolled himself another cigarette. Otoniel noticed the scar on his hand. It looked like a bite. Several clear tooth marks and some more jagged and torn. They curved from his knuckles across the back of his hand. When Mr. Fields finished rolling the cigarette, Otoniel noticed the scar was on his palm, too. The scar gave off a faint resonance that reminded Otoniel of the thing in Devil's Bowl. As Mr. Fields took the first long drag, Otoniel rolled the spittoon over near him for the ashes.

A couple of sips in and Otoniel felt the fire in him. "When you were in Mexico, you might have shot my uncle. He joined up with Poncho Villa"

Mr. Fields seemed unphased by Otoniel's angry tone. He drew a long puff on his cigarette, then said as he ashed, "Not I. My unit never even got sight of any of that tricky bastard's troops."

Otoniel looked at Mr. Fields, whose wry, honest smile went all the way into his eyes. His anger diffused and he laughed, "We don't even know if my uncle ever made it down there, anyway. That's where he said he was going, but the last time anyone saw him he was falling-down drunk in Albuquerque, and the last letter we got from him was from Texas, y sin palabra de Poncho Villa." He raised the bottle, "To near misses."

"And far ones."

When Mr. Fields had finished his glass, Otoniel offered him a refill, which was quickly accepted. Before he took a drink, though, he said, "So, any chance you might reconsider coming with me tomorrow?"

Otoniel looked at the saddle on the wall, focused on the shiny spot where his hand had wiped the dust away. "No."

"I know what you saw, and I understand why you're afraid."

"You think you do? No lo creo."

"You saw a young woman murdered in the most brutal, cold-blooded, and cruelest fashion. They stabbed her, probably dozens of times, probably long after the life had left her body, the brutality of the blows as unimpassioned as if they were cutting vegetables. I've seen that."

"Pero los brujos."

"I've seen sorcerers. I've seen them perform their rites, and I know what kind of beasts they summon. You felt the hunger of one—I've looked them in the face, and believe me they are as hideous and perverse in person as you might never be able to imagine." Mr. Fields gulped down the rest of the tequila. His eyes had no trace of smile in them now, they were almost like obsidian in their sockets. He held his glass near his face, displaying the scar on the back of his hand. "Maybe you'll grant me now that I know a little of what you saw. And I know they didn't pick you as a guide by accident. They want you linked to this crime, and whatever their evil purpose is, you can't fight it by not facing them."

"Lo siento."

"'Sokay. I understand." Mr. Fields put his glass down. "Sorry about your uncle. What he did was very brave, whether he actually joined Villa or not. Sometimes it takes a lot of courage just to get out the door. If you find your courage, we're meeting at the Brown Palace, about 2 in the afternoon."

24.   A Friendly Clasp

Stanley tried to keep himself steady as he came down the narrow stairs. The tequila was good old stuff and stronger than most of what passed for liquor these days. He huddled close to one wall as he came down. When he reached the bottom of the stairs, he nodded to Maria and her mother, then got his coat and hat down off the rack. He headed out the door, and Maria got up to go after him.

"Mr. Fields, stop," she called out. He was on the bottom step of the porch, but he said, "Yes?" and came back up the stairs holding his hat in his hand.

"What are you doing?" she asked him.

He smiled and put his hat on. He hadn't meant for it to be so cockeyed that the brim covered one of his eyes. "I'm trying to keep your brother out of prison."

"Are you? Are you? By taking him tomorrow to confront some imaginary murderers? And what happens when he lashes out at them?"

"He isn't going."

"Good. At least he's that smart."

"No. He's afraid."

"Oh."

He rolled a cigarette and said, "Lemme ask you something. If these people are your brother's imagination, why is he so afraid of them?"

Maria's voice was annoyed as she answered, "Imaginary fears are always the worst."

"For children, maybe, but a man like your brother . . ."

"Brujos. That's crazy. He's crazy like a child."

"So who killed the girl?"

Maria started to answer, then faltered. She clearly had a thought, but didn't want to say it.

Stanley smiled a little wider. "So you'd rather believe your brother is a murderer than accept that there may be things in this world you don't understand?" He chuckled, then blended his laugh into crackling words unintelligible to human ears. There was a rush of air that disturbed Maria's wavy hair. Her startled expression was clearly illuminated in the blue flame that surrounded his hand. He touched a fingertip to his cigarette, puffing. The cigarette lit. He extended his hand to her, palm up. "What do you think now?"

She tried to slap his hand away, saying, "A trick!" Stanley saw the pain on her face in the instant before he took her hand in a friendly clasp. Then the flame spread over both their hands like a blue viscous gel.

Maria looked at Stanley for explanation. He closed his eyes and began concentrating, listening to the flickering laughter of the bright blue flame. He muttered to it slowly, coaxing it gently. The fire grew until it had spread over her entire body, and the pleasure of the warm sensation showed on her face for a moment. Then her expression grew hard. "Let me go," she pleaded and pulled at her hand.

"No," he replied. "If I do, you will be burned. Let me take away the flames first." He dispelled the flames. Then he let go of her hand and looked into her eyes. There were conflicting emotions there.

He smiled wider. He could tell she wasn't as convinced as he had hoped, but he tried to sell it to the hilt. "Still think your brother's a murderer?" He tipped his hat and turned away. He headed down the stairs and sidewalk before turning toward the streetcar stop. He took a long pull on his cigarette, enjoying the smoke in his lungs and the orange ember at its tip.

25. Fetid Life and Rancid Death

When Stefani got home, her mother was already asleep. Stefani almost started upstairs to go to bed herself, then paused. She already felt unsettled from the men chasing her this evening. She did not see how she could possibly sleep, with that stress added to her normal disquiet. But what was she afraid of? Nothing. No, not quite nothing. She was afraid of the unknown, at once less than nothing—and more. To overcome it, she must face it.

She pulled Thaddeus' jacket tighter over her shoulders, felt its comforting warmth, and, thus girded for battle, she went to the door of the basement. The door was locked, but the key was nearby, on the ring that the doctor had brought among the few personal effects that were found on his "body"—little more than a heap of soggy clothes when it was removed, Stefani remembered with a shudder. Her mother almost couldn't stand to touch the ring. She had dropped it in an offering bowl under a Hindoo goddess, and there it sat, gathering dust over the intervening years.

She looked into the bowl and could immediately identify which key it was—the old, heavy iron one. Although her father had curiously ornamented the door with elaborate silver trim, the lock remained the only one in the house original to its initial construction.

She reached into the bowl and picked up the key quickly, suddenly fearing she might lose her nerve. The key was cold and heavy in her hand. The other keys on the ring made a dull sound when she lifted it.

She put the key in the lock, turned it. There was a click, nothing more. She turned the knob slowly. Still nothing. When she pushed the door open, though, there was a faint whoosh, and out rushed the accumulated animal smell of many years. But was it alive or dead? She couldn't tell—it stank of both fetid life and rancid death.

She reached into the room, grabbed a candle and matches sitting on a shelf there. There was an electric light, but it was at the bottom of the stairs. She lit the candle and carried it down the stairs.

As she began heading down, something scurried in the darkness. A mouse? Too big for a mouse. A rat? Here? But that's what it made her think of, only it was almost as if she only thought of that because someone was whispering it in her ear. When she focused on the voice she could really hear it: sibilant, wet syllables.

She reached the bottom of the stairs. The air was still and thick with dust. The light of the candle was steady, but limited. It illuminated a work table that was spread with glass beakers, flasks, and vials. She switched on the electric light. It was a single bulb over the center of the large room. Although it lit the room, it also cast deep shadows. There, in the exposed space between the joists overhead. There, under the worktable. Behind the heathen idols, among the books. Shadows were everywhere, so she didn't dare put out the candle, but began to use it to explore.

She looked at the big book on the nearest table. She could not read the words in it, but she recognized that the glass apparatus diagrammed in it had been set up by her father, apparently for some experiment in progress at the time of his death. There was only one piece missing, the flask that she guessed was supposed to receive the final formulation. Next to the tome was a small notebook, and in it, her father's shorthand scrawl—she had learned to read it many years before.

There were only two sentences on this page: "The beast is held, but for how long? How much time do I have?"

When she read those words, her eyes began to tear up. Her father knew he was doomed, and he had chosen to spend his last hours with her and her mother. She thought of him at dinner. He had been so pleasant, so normal, right up to the moment when everything went horribly wrong. And then he looked at his suddenly liquefying hand, not with surprise or horror, or anguish, but merely with sadness. First his hands, then his face: skin, muscle, and bones melting like ice cream on a warm summer's day, softening, deforming, collapsing on itself. And then the screaming that must have been her, because her mother was also so calm.

The doctor was called, told that her father had been tubercular, but kept it hidden. And that stain on the tablecloth, it was soup. He must have spilled his soup.

As she was thinking of her mother's words, Stefani heard the creature scratching again at the lock, emboldened and strengthened.

This was it—this was the thing that had killed her father and forced her mother into denial, repression, and paralyzing terror, all while confined here in the basement. What could it do if it were free?

Stefani's heart was pounding, and she felt the amulet in the bag throbbing in response. She stared into a shadow, and though the beast wasn't really there, she perceived its outline. She tried to look at the creature, saw a scaled foot, like a bird's, another scaled foot like a lizard, but smelled something musky like a great shaggy beast. As she looked at the thing, hatred and horror mingling in her heart, the power of the amulet was shaped and focused on it. It made a pained sound and scurried back into the darkness.

Then Stefani blinked, and what had seemed so real, so corporeal, vanished like a momentary haze over her vision. She was in the basement alone.

Clutching the candle in her hand, she began carefully looking for the great iron cage that held the beast. As she remembered it, it was so large that there was no place to conceal it in the room.

Still she looked under tables and in corners. She did not find it, but at the far end of the room she found the crawl space. Raised about halfway up to the ceiling, the space was a narrow dirt tunnel that receded into darkness beyond the light of the feeble bulb and flickering candle. From the crawl space emanated that musty, skunky odor. Could the cage be in there, hidden in the dark? It would still be much smaller than she remembered it.

She dared not go in to look, but she did stretch her arm out to get the candle into the crawl space—the air felt cool and clammy, as if she were reaching into cold, greasy water. She quickly pulled her hand back out.

She looked at her arm and shook it, but it was dry. She put the candle down in the dust at the edge of the crawl space. She grabbed the amulet, closed her eyes, and tried to push with her mind into the darkness. She could tell it was working. The creature was driven back deeper into the darkness. Then she was startled when her buttocks bumped up against the edge of the table. She had moved back, too. But she felt comforted and headed up the stairs to bed. She closed the door to the basement and put the candle out now that she was safely in the glow of electric light.

That night, she dreamt of the thing in the cage, but it seemed far away. And though it still reached for the lock, its clawed fingers were no longer so close to reaching and unlocking it.

26.　　All the Faces

Otoniel left the house in the late morning. The day was fully underway, but the sky was still grey and the air had a November chill to it, though it was late spring. He looked both ways, then turned left and headed quickly up the street. He glanced over his shoulder once or twice, but saw no one following him or watching from the neighbors' windows.

He had been released from jail, but he wasn't free. This was the first time he had left the house, and he'd only done it at his mother's insistence. She needed some tripe and she wasn't going to walk all the way down to el carniceria when she had such a strong young man in the house again.

Outside it was worse than ever. It had gone beyond a vague sense of discomfort or unease to a very specific sense of being watched, and every time he looked, there was no one, but always something. A dark cloud against the sky that seemed strangely close, a shadow under the window ledge that seemed too dark for the light of day, a black branch on a grey tree that didn't belong at all—a mad, hopeless graft put there to die.

As he came to el carniceria, it was even worse. He expected to know the people there—he had only moved away a couple years ago—but all the faces were strangers. Yet they all seemed to know him. Their conversations stopped when they saw him, and resumed when the people thought he had moved out of earshot.

But although he had moved beyond the ability to understand their words, he still heard their tone when they began speaking again. Vicious whispers, strangely sibilant, almost inhuman. The words were never clear, but he always knew they were about him, words punctuated by the intermittent "thunk, thunk" of the butcher's assistant cutting steaks behind the counter. And then there was that one man moving through the crowd of mostly women. Short, with a limping gait. His face was pale, but ruddy, his eyes completely black, eyes that stayed focused on Otoniel.

Otoniel tried to ignore them, but those eyes seemed to pierce his back, sink deep in his flesh, and strike his heart. He was losing faith, courage, and when it was time for him to go up to the counter, Otoniel almost lost it completely. But, instead, he shuffled up to the counter. Before he could speak, though, he was frozen by what he saw in the case.

There was a big pile of human arms and legs heaped up in the middle. Over to one side was a bowl labeled "Hands and feet 5¢/lb." On top of the counter was a jar half-filled with pickled eyes. The bowl of ground beef had a human ear sticking out of it. And in the middle of the case was the heiress's head.

The thunk of the cleaver startled him and he looked up, helpless and trembling, at the butcher. The butcher said, "Whatcha want, José?"

Otoniel could barely manage an incoherent sound as the cleaver came down again, cutting a steak off a woman's shoulder. The cleaver came down again and the arm was detached at the shoulder. The arm was fat, dark-skinned, and wrinkled. Then Otoniel recognized a ring on one of the fingers, it was mama's. The finger squirmed, its fingers seeking purchase on the wooden block.

"Well, whaddaya want? Or don'tcha speak English, spic?"

Otoniel blinked several times. He pressed the heels of his palms into his eyes, hard, until he felt pain and saw bright bursts of color. Then he opened his eyes again, and he saw what he expected to see. A case full of animal parts arranged around a cow's head, a jar of pickled eggs on the counter. A cold, close voice laughed. He turned around and looked to see who it might be, but no one was laughing. A few people were looking at him impatiently. Only the man with the pale ruddy face was smiling, but his black, impenetrable eyes had the same intense, emotionless stare.

Otoniel stepped away from the counter, suddenly feeling dizzy. The laughing seemed like it was inside his ears, making him feel off balance. He staggered as he tried to walk out of el carniceria. Several people reached out to try to stop him from falling, including the small, ruddy-faced man, who extended sharp, talon-like fingers. Otoniel dodged them and staggered out into the street, the laughter still pounding in his ears. The street seemed to pitch and roll under his feet. The ruddy-faced man was following him. The man's steps were quick, birdlike, with a very high stride. Otoniel tried to run while looking over his shoulder, but the dizziness made it impossible, and he barely managed to stagger from lamppost to lamppost. The man followed, running in short bursts, also from lamppost to lamppost, never falling behind, but never gaining ground, either.

When Otoniel reached his house, he had to scramble up the front stairs on all fours, as the increasingly loud laughter had him almost incapacitated. He stumbled across the porch and lunged at the door. He fumbled for his keys, but dropped them. Just bending over to look for them made him nauseous with blurred vision, so he pounded on the door and called for his mother. The small man was perched on the concrete wall of the porch, his smile curling halfway up his face around his long, beaklike nose.

Otoniel stopped pounding on the door with his hand and began to use his head, trying to silence the deafening laugh. He pounded several times, each harder than the last, until he felt some warm wetness, and then the door opened and he fell in, yelling, "He's following me!"

His mother looked out. "¿Quien?"

He half-pointed, but then crawled in, shouting, "Close the door!"

When his mother closed the door, the laughter died away, except for the echo and the ringing in his ears. He breathed several times deeply, panting. He blinked and saw the blood beading on his eyelashes. Then he saw drops falling to the wood floor. Behind him, his mother was crying, and she bent down to put her head on his back.

27.   Mutual Interests

The next day Stanley made his way to the Brown Palace, a large, surprisingly elegant hotel for a city of this size. It took him only a quick glance around the lobby to spot the bodyguard, who was standing in the middle of the triangular space, right next to a chair. He did not move or even look around. Stanley walked up to him. Once he got the big man's attention, he was led upstairs.

Once inside the door of the suite, the big thug began to search Stanley. The old man waved him away. "Please, please, Mr. Fields is our guest. Let us treat him courteously."

The room was full of a strong perfumed chemical odor. The old man sat at the couch, rubbing lotion onto his hands. Stanley said, "Perhaps the best courtesy would be telling me your names so I know who I'm talking to."

"But of course. I am Phil Saluzar."

"And his name?" Stanley gestured at the big man.

"What does it matter? You're not here to talk to him. His name might as well be mud. Come, sit, sit. A drink?"

"Sure. Whiskey?"

"I would ask 'bourbon or scotch,' but these days they are sadly all the same. And even applying the label 'whiskey' is being generous by far."

Stanley looked at what his host was drinking. A clear liquid too viscous to be water or even gin. His own whiskey was a pale brown. A little anemic, but a passable shade. The taste, however, was not really passable. It was barely drinkable.

"Okay," Stanley said after he took his sip, "you called this meeting. Tell me about our mutual interests." Stanley tried to peer into his host, learn more about him and his powers, but he was unreadable. Stanley hoped he was just as opaque.

"Ah, but I had hoped you might tell me about our mutual interests in that lovely creature we both seemed to discover yesterday."

"You didn't know of her before then? How long had you been going to the speak?" Stanley looked around the suite. It was all gold and white. Marble floor and hearth. Gold trim on everything. The sofa he sat on was white velvet, the cushions plush and thick.

"It was perhaps my second visit, but my first time during a show. It seemed well worth the return visit."

"Are you from Denver?"

"Me? Do you think a town as wild and uncouth as Denver could produce a creature of my refinement?" He smiled. Though his face glistened with lotion, his skin was dry, wrinkled, and cracked.

"Where are you from?" Stanley could not place the accent. Perhaps somewhere back East, but with a lot of time elsewhere, maybe Europe or the Orient.

"I will pay you the respect of not telling you. I think that if you truly care, you will be able to find out. After all, you seem a man of discernment and capable curiosity."

"So, tell me about our mutual interests."

"Excellent. Discernment and capable curiosity. You waste no time on fruitless questions, but return precisely to the main point."

"Well, what do you want from her?"

"Your tone is perhaps a bit too defensive. I have a legitimate reason for desiring to speak with her. You see, I am an antiquities dealer, and her late father was in possession of a great many very valuable pieces, which I believe are largely hers now."

"So why talk to her at the club? Why not visit her at home?"

"The girl lives alone with her mother, who owns the house. The mother has refused to see me, forcing me to contact the girl elsewhere, such as her place of employment. Now, sir, if you will repay my kindness by being as open with me about your interest in this girl."

"None whatsoever. Just pure coincidence I happened to be there."

"Pardon my skepticism, but why then did you run after her?"

Stanley finished his whiskey. "A girl runs, seems frightened. I follow to make sure she isn't in danger. I have a tendency to butt into everybody's business. Occupational hazard, I guess."

"And what is your business, Mr. Fields?"

"Private detective." He handed a card over that had his business address.

Saluzar looked at the card. "I see. And your reason for being at the club, was it professional or personal?"

"Professional. I've been hired in relation to the Irene Pitcher murder, and I suppose I wouldn't mind talking to the girl for background."

"So you should mention my business when you see her. I think perhaps you will see her first."

"You think so?"

"Indubitably." His voice was thin and cracked. He took a drink from his glass.

"What makes you so sure?"

"You have important questions to ask her. My business is purely monetary. You no doubt will seek her out first."

Stanley thought it likely. He wasn't sure what questions he had for her, but it seemed to him that there was likely some connection, something that linked her somehow with the beast he was tracking. And what of this sorcerer? What was his connection with the beast?

"Okay, so if I'm gonna mention this, you should tell me what their names are so she knows I'm not making this up."

"My friend's name was Nikolos Aegis. I believe his daughter's name was Stefani."

"Okay, I'll remember that for the next time I see her. You got any other helpful information?"

"I don't think so."

"What about Irene Pitcher?"

"Sad, what happened to her. I heard they captured her murderer."

"Maybe. We don't know. I'm trying to help figure that out. You come into Morgan's often before this?"

"As I told you, maybe once or twice."

"Did you ever see Irene?"

"If I did, it was brief and I did not know her at the time. I cannot remember."

"Okay. Did you ever run into a guy named Greg that hung out with Ms. Pitcher? What about a doctor, a big man with a Van Dyke beard?"

"I don't think so, but perhaps my memory is faulty. I will keep your card and let you know if anything else comes up."

"Thank you."

Stanley was led out.

28.   Never Get Wise

It was late morning, and Bart was just beginning to set up the joint. He was pulling chairs down off the tables when his first customers came in. It was Audley Potts, Bill Sturns ("the Painter Kid"), and Fritz, the young steerer who'd scored in the off season. Word is he'd been chastened, but most of the blame had fallen on Cajun Chris, the spieler, who should have known better.

Now the two experienced spielers were being very free of their wisdom with the young man. It started out as some general bits of advice, but after they each put away a belt of whiskey, Sturns started in on a story of a big score he'd made in Little Rock, where he spent the off seasons. It was an old story, and even Bart had heard it more than once, but it was a fun one, and it had grown more embellished since the last time, so it was almost as if it were a whole new story. Potts even had a supporting role, one he had clearly played more than once, though not the last time Bart had heard it.

Just as a matter of caution, Bart cleared away the empty whiskey glasses, but left the soda glasses. You could never be too careful. Even with protection there was always the chance that a rogue element like the DA, Van Cise, would bust in, like he had at Quincy's. He'd threatened to keep raiding until he shut down all the gin joints in town, and that didn't sit well with Bart.

And it was not five minutes later that the door burst open suddenly, forced off its hinges by a huge bruiser of a cop. And who should follow him in but that goddamn little weasel of a DA, Colonel Van Cise himself, brandishing a piece of paper high and saying, "This is a raid, nobody move!"

"Aw . . . shit!" began the young steerer Fritz, but he was silenced by a touch from Potts. Bart came back toward the entrance from where he had been working. He raised his hands slightly and said, "Wha's going on, officer? Why are we being raided?"

"We have reports that liquor is being served in here."

"Liquor? Never!"

The DA had walked up to the bar. He sniffed the air. "Then what do I smell?"

"Probably the cleaner. It's pretty strong."

"I bet it is. You three, up against the wall, there." He indicated a short stretch of wall to the left of the door, then said to the other cop. "You search their coats." Their coats were hanging on the other side of the door.

The cop patted the pockets a couple of times and quickly pulled out a flask. "Well, what have we here?" He unscrewed the lid and sniffed it. "Hooch, all right."

As Van Cise was patting the three con men down, he said, "You all do know liquor is illegal, don't you?"

"Yes, sir," said Bart. "That's why they're not allowed to drink it in here."

"Oh, no? You mean that if we look around this . . ."

"Cabaret, sir. It's French style, very high class."

"Yes, I'm sure. You mean to tell me that if I search this . . . cabaret I won't find more hooch?"

Bart worked very hard to keep his eyes off the wall panel where most of this week's delivery was hidden. "No, sir, you won't."

"Good. Laughton, tear this place apart."

"Will do, Colonel."

The burly cop began searching behind the bar. He sniffed every bottle of soda and extract. Then he began searching around the room, ripping up plants, looking in every cranny, feeling along the wall. He seemed to pause at the secret panel in the wall, his hands hesitating ever so slightly at the subtle crack, but he kept on.

Then the Colonel found Potts and Sturns' paperwork and was reading it aloud—"Audley H. Potts has been bonded with the company to the sum of

$100,000 for a period of one year. Metropolitan Bonding and Security Company of Newark, New Jersey. And one for you, too, Sturns. Hey, Ed, looks like these two are pretty big-time outta town businessmen. Maybe we oughta let 'em go with a warning."

"Yeah, maybe that'd be nice. But they gotta know this is a one-time deal."

"Yeah. Okay, misters, you can go, but just so's you know, here in Denver we enforce the law, and the law says liquor's illegal. I don't wanna catch you guys with hooch again, or it'll be straight to jail."

Bart looked at the Colonel. The DA was a good actor, but Bart was suspicious. As soon as the two bunco artists skedaddled out of the room, the Colonel and Laughton changed. They cuffed him, roughed him up a bit, and took him to the police station.

It took longer for Bart to get out than usual. Ike Goldman typically got him pulled aside at the sergeant's desk for special handling, but he had to wait in his cell until he was pulled up before the judge, who immediately recognized his connections and let him go. Of course, Blonger was the Big Fix, so everything really moved at his pace. That was not reassuring, either.

When Bart finally got back to Morgan's, The Painter Kid was waiting there. "I heard you was getting out today."

"Yeah? What of it?"

"Not much, 'cept I keep thinking bout when you was arrested. That seem funny to you?"

"As a $3 bill."

"Me too. And I keep saying so, but nobody wants to listen."

"Tell it to the Big Fix."

"I been telling it, and he wants to hear it lessan anyone. I was thinkin if you might come along, maybe he'd listen to you, you being there and being such an upstanding citizen and all."

"I don't know if he'll listen to me. I haven't worked with him very much, I'm mostly Goldman's man, but I'll come along."

The two men went to the American National Bank Building. They went up to Blonger's office on the third floor, and waited for a while until they were let in.

"What do you want, Painter?"

"I was just thinking you might want to reconsider what you was saying earlier about the DA iffen you gets convinced by what he has to say."

Bart gave his account of the arrest, including his suspicions about what the DA was thinking.

Blonger was unconvinced. "That fool don't know anything. The damn fool had you and Potts, and read all your kit, and doesn't know a con-man's layout when he sees it. He's just a big bag of wind and will never get wise to anything.

"Asides, even if he did want to move on us, he's too busy dealing wit the hen houses. He doesn't have the manpower to do both."

"But if things ain't changing—why was I in the hoosegow so long?" Bart asked.

"Exactly what I said. You're Goldman's man, right?"

Bart nodded.

"Well, Goldman's main business is the hen houses. He's probably busy worrying about them and it took him some time to find out you's in there, too.

"And don't forget, if the DA does decide he wants to arrange an accident for us, well, we still have the police on our side, so he won't be able to make a move, especially not without us knowing."

After a few more arguments like this one, the Kid was still not convinced, so Blonger threw them both out in frustration.

Back on the street, the Kid said, "He ain't never gonna get it."

"You may be right."

"Well, I ain't stickin around to get pinched. I'm hitting the road. See ya."

Bart waved to the Painter Kid. As he walked back to Morgan's, he wished he could just pick up and go, too. But he couldn't. There was too much sunk into the place. Suddenly, the speak began to seem like a noose hanging loosely around his neck, ready to tighten if he made the wrong step.

He couldn't let that happen. If Blonger was going to get taken down, then he would need protection from someone else. But who? Who? He thought of the old man and trembled. But you might expect that anyone who could give you protection might also be terrifying.

29.   Vestiges of Discipline

Since his meeting with Saluzar, Stanley had spent a lot of time tracking down unproductive leads, including trying to figure out who Saluzar was. He'd confirmed that Aegis had served with the Colorado Regiment in the Philippines, but not Saluzar. He felt he'd exhausted his local resources, so he went to the telegram office and sent off requests for information related to Saluzar, Aegis, and his daughter. When he returned to the office, he was surprised to find a note from the district attorney. It seemed like a social invitation, coffee and cigars for that night. Normally, Stanley would also expect some scotch from a well-connected high society type, but he remembered the district attorney was a teetotaler, so he made a note to get a drink before going over.

Stanley, who didn't have any friends in town, appreciated the invitation, but he had the feeling it was more than just a social call. He didn't know what the business was, but there was something. Since he depended on the district attorney's support, he sent his acceptance of the invitation right away.

The girl he had seen the other night—Mr. Saluzar called her Stefani—was definitely wrapped up in this case, and he would have to try to speak to her tonight, hopefully without running into Mr. Saluzar and his thug. But if she was working anything like the same shift as last time, it would be many hours before she was back to work, so he sent word to his secretary, Gail, that he was taking a nap, put his feet up on the desk, and let himself fall asleep.

Gail woke him up in the early evening. "I'm getting ready to go. I finished putting together the clippings you wanted." She put the folder on the corner of his desk.

"What? Oh, thanks. Have a good night."

"You, too. You okay?"

"Me? Yeah, yeah," he said. In truth, he was still troubled by the touch of that thing in the mountains. There was no doubt that the blood sacrifice had brought it very close. To give it adequate power to wreak its destruction would mean feeding it with living force—emotion—as well as blood.

He needed a drink, and he needed it quick before heading over to the DA's house. So he took his hat and coat, locked up the office and headed toward Morgan's. When he got there, the doorman let him in easily.

He started to head for the bar, but paused to look at the stage. A woman was doing a hoochie-coochie. Not the best he'd ever seen, but not bad, either. She was graceful, beautiful in her movements. A bare arm, slender and soft. A bare leg, tapered and long. A face bejeweled and made up to suggest the mysteries of the Orient. She had gossamer material over much of her body.

Not willing or able to take his eyes off her, he felt and shuffle-stepped his way to the bar. He put his hand on the wood, but couldn't quite find his way to a seat, so he kept standing.

When the music finished, and she bowed with the same grace as she danced, Stanley did not clap as enthusiastically as he might have because he was still a little numb. A thin, worn curtain came down and Stanley turned to the bartender. "I'll take whatever you got that passes for bourbon."

The bartender was the same as last night. He didn't move, but looked stonily back. "You ain't gonna cause trouble again? I kin have you thrown out right now."

"You think that was me? She took one look at those other guys and took off: the old guy and his big silent bodyguard."

When he mentioned Saluzar and his thug, the bartender's expression changed. "Yeah, alright. What'll you have?"

"Whatever you got that passes for bourbon. And tell me, whaddaya know about those guys?

"I don't know nothing." He said and shuffled off to serve Stanley's drink.

When he came back, Stanley said, "I know that wasn't the first time you'd seen them, so . . . what do you know?"

"I toldja I don't know nothing. Four bits."

Stanley fumbled for the change. Prohibition was probably the best thing that ever happened for business at places like this. They charged more for inferior products and a place like this—hell, it practically operated just as openly and freely as before. Probably had a lot more expenses in graft, though. Except for the price, he was glad they were still open.

He took a sip of the whiskey. It was terrible. If it weren't for the bitter aftertaste, it wouldn't have any taste at all. But it worked. He felt the warmth of it spread out from his throat and gradually diffuse through his body. How could anyone live without this simple comfort, and, worse, make others live without it?

Relaxed, he turned around on his stool, putting his back to the bar and scanning the place.

He felt her before he saw her. There was power there, and no ability to shield it. It radiated out and throbbed over the bar. Even fairly insensitive people could probably sense it, though they likely didn't know what they were feeling, confusing it for mere attraction or some other baser emotion.

Stanley watched her. She was at a table with several men, wearing what was presumably a work costume, a dress that showed she was not of the slender flapper type. She was a voluptuous woman, and that would make it easy to mistake her power for attraction, even for someone as experienced and discerning as Stanley.

She came up to a table and began working the marks. The men were eager, and cheered even before she sat down. A drink was ordered for her. She became the center of attention, and men at other tables, even those with dancers at them, kept glancing over at her. The men would tell her jokes, stories, anything they could think to get and hold her attention. But even when her mouth was smiling, her eyes were distant, sad. When the men were not watching her, her smile collapsed in on itself, and she showed her genuine emotion. Loneliness, oppression, almost despair. This was not the life for her.

Of course, with the power she had, she need not live it. That meant she was truly ignorant not only of how to shield her power, but even of how to use it. That could make her very dangerous, not only to herself, but to everyone. Someone like Saluzar could manipulate her as a very powerful tool.

However, Stanley could not approach her tonight, not after last time, but he must try to get to her sometime soon. Help her understand her power, both its promise and its danger.

Stanley pulled out his watch, saw the time, realized he would have to hurry. He slugged back the rest of the whiskey, and left to catch the streetcar. He got off in a residential neighborhood. He could see the large houses in the light of the dim electric streetlamps.

Van Cise's house was a large brick manor. It was not new, but it was in good shape. He rang the bell and the door opened. He was led into a parlor, where, to his surprise, there were a dozen other men, but Mr. Van Cise was not to be seen.

A colored servant came by, offered him some tea or coffee. He took coffee, added a generous portion of cream and sugar. The cheap whiskey had left him feeling groggy, not clear, and had left a bitter taste in his mouth that still lingered.

As he drank the coffee, he looked around at the other men. They were mostly older, and, save for him, they were pretty upper crust. Some of them seemed to know each other, and two small groups kept up a steady level of banter, but what really unified this group was service in France. All of them retained, to some degree, the vestiges of discipline, the resting awareness, the careful lethargy designed to conserve energy while maximizing readiness.

When Mr. Van Cise entered, his military bearing was accentuated. He walked crisply, refused an offered seat, and stood rigidly beside the coal stove. "Men," he said, "I've invited you here to ask your help. We are about to undertake a major enforcement operation, and we need reliable, trustworthy men to drive cars. I have invited you here because your characters, as known to me or in the judgement of those I trust, are beyond reproach. However, if you are inexpert drivers or if you do not want to participate, now is the time to back out."

One gentleman raised a hand and asked, "Enforcement operation? You mean like police work?"

"Yes."

"Does that mean we've got to arrest criminals?"

"No. We have many officers capable of performing that task. You will primarily be drivers. You will take officers where they need to go, then take officers and criminals back to the designated lock-up. That doesn't mean, of course, that things won't get hairy. You all know how unpredictable desperate men can be, and I'm sure none of you would be averse to putting in a little muscle to keep the scum in line."

"In fact, Colonel," one of the men shouted, "some of us would relish the opportunity!" There was a little chuckle in the room.

"That's the spirit. We've got to show these underworld types that we decent human beings won't stand for their kind here." There was a general cheer. "Good, good. So—any of you feel you want to back out—do it now, and then you can leave while the rest of us talk operational details."

Another man said, "I don't feel comfortable risking my personal car in a police operation. We have just the one, and I can't think what my wife will do to me if it's damaged."

Another man peeped, "Darla, no—worry about what Chuck will do. Remember when you drove to the Springs? Harriet had to drive him to the social—you never saw a boy so glum!"

"No worry. For people who are concerned or don't have a car, we have a few cars available. Any more questions?" Van Cise paused. "No? Okay. Last chance to back out."

Two of the men who were not part of the group excused themselves. Then Van Cise told the rest of them when and where to meet. A couple of people pressed him for details, but he refused, saying they knew everything they needed. The utmost secrecy was required he said, and if they could not work under those conditions, they must leave as well. They did not. Van Cise thanked everyone and invited them to stay for cigars and coffee.

Stanley took a cigar, and stayed to smoke it, but he didn't join in with the groups conversing in the parlor. He was thinking about what the men in the pool hall had said on his first day. He wondered whether the criminals running Denver were indeed about to be taken down, and who was waiting to take their place.

30.   May the Sky Take Us

Mack loved it when the flying circus got to a new town. It was the best thing. The goal was to attract as much attention and raise as much interest as possible, so they started by buzzing the main commercial drag. They flew single file as low as they could go. Then they would break up to spread around town and the surrounding farms. The trailing plane usually had a wing walker—currently Pete Buell—and it carried fliers, so that on the second pass, when everyone was seeing the man out on the wings and marveling, he would drop the papers announcing where they were going to be. They knew the spot either from a previous visit, intelligence from another flying circus, or from Joe Grand's scouting visit.

This was a new town. As near as they knew, nobody has been here before—and with good reason. It was a tiny town, but with the number of circuses flying the Midwest circuit these days, it was getting hard to find virgin territory. Once they had tried getting into one of the big towns to try to cut in between the bigger air shows, but they had learned that was not a good idea. An expensive lesson: it cost Joe Grand a broken arm, bruises and bloody noses for everyone else, and a couple of trashed planes. So they were sticking to the smaller towns—they'd made it most of the way across Kansas and may have to head across the border for the next target.

Mack hated it when he had wing walker duty. Any half-decent pilot could fly low and slow and steady so the rubes could see the wing walker. He'd complained about it to Joe, who insisted that they all take turns, but Mack had to do it less often after that.

Today he was totally free, so after they buzzed the main street—Maple, he thought it said—he banked left, low, and tight to buzz the secondary commercial district. After he pulled up, he looked back to see that he'd spooked a couple horses, which wouldn't be good for business, but there was also a crowd of people looking up excitedly and gesturing. The kids were jumping up and down. He'd probably see all of them tomorrow.

After buzzing up and down the streets, Mack joined up with Guynemer and started doing the mock dogfights that he loved. He knew it looked really impressive, a series of deep dives, tight turns, even a stall or two that must seem somewhat random to someone who didn't know they were being inspired by the maneuvers of an invisible enemy. Mack had thought it might be more impressive to have the company do an actual duel between him and another pilot, but it had turned out that none of the other pilots were really up for it. So it was just Guynemer and him.

After everyone had finished stirring up the townsfolk, they headed over to the farm where Grand had arranged for them to stay. They landed in a fallow field. They would camp out here, and tomorrow they would start the show. So tonight it was early (and sober) to bed.

The next day, it turned out they had done a good job of building interest. There were plenty of people crowding in to watch the show. Sure, there were plenty of pikers who chose to watch from neighboring fields, and the farmer who owned the field let all his friends in free, but it was still a pretty good crowd.

Besides, it was the rides that made the real money, and everybody was crowding the planes after the first exhibition. Pilots got to "keep" 50% of their proceeds from the rides, too, but they had to pay for their plane. They could either buy their plane and pay for maintenance, or rent it and leave maintenance to Grand. The take would've been better if they could manage to get more people in per trip. He knew that circuses with better planes managed four or five passengers up per flight, but with the Jennies, they typically only took two. Maybe three if they were small—or only one if it was a really big guy.

On the third night after dinner, Grand gave them "the talk," that they'd all gotten accustomed to. Mack watched his face carefully for tells, but in the flickering firelight it was hard to see whether his upbeat tone was genuine or feigned. At the end of the speech, Grand said, "Well, that's about the size of it. I think we should move on tomorrow. Or the next day. Mr. Windermere's already hit me up for a second payment. I put him off once, but I don't think I can do it again. And there were fewer people today. Probably less of a crowd tomorrow."

Bill Geiger asked, "We know where we're going to next?"

"I've got three possibilities: Hill City, Lamar, and Pampas."

Chuck Stewart said, "We can't go to Pampas. Bully and his crew were there already this summer. It's picked pretty clean."

"So Hill City and Lamar, then."

Geiger said, "Hill City and Lamar are pretty small. Better do another day here before moving on."

Stewart said, "They ain't any smaller than here."

Mack looked around at the other aviators and their two mechanics. There were a few nods of assent and some grunts, but no real shows of enthusiasm. Thin gruel filled out with pilfered carrots didn't give them much energy for enthusiasm, nor their situation much cause. And the terrible moonshine they passed around didn't help, either.

Mack didn't say anything. It didn't matter to him whether they moved or stayed here, so long as they kept flying.

Being grounded might not have been so bad if it weren't for Guynemer. The liquor helped to drown out the sound of the engine, but when he was outside, he saw the distinctive outline of Guynemer's SPAD, circling high above the birds. And then he just had to get up. So when Grand offered him the opportunity, after he cracked up that poor doughboy's speedster, he leaped at the chance to join this half-baked flying circus. Since he'd been back up in the air, he and Guynemer had been dueling, and it was probably only a matter of time before he cracked up his plane, too, but until then he loved this life.

Once they'd made a decision (they were heading to Lamar day after tomorrow), everyone dispersed from the fire circle to sleep. The night was warm and clear, so the bedrolls had been pulled out of the pup tents and everyone slept under the stars. There was a little bit of moonshine left, so they passed it around, people propping themselves up on their elbows to take a slug. After one more round, it was empty, so people lay back and got quiet.

Mack stayed up, looking at the stars and listening to Guynemer's engine in the night. Of course, he knew that if Guynemer were in an earthly plane, there's no way he would fly on this dark Kansas night. No lights, no landmarks, only the stars to fly by and an unlit field to land in. Guynemer's spectral plane had no concerns about navigation in the dark, nor did he worry about fuel. His Spad never seemed to need fuel, and he only landed just before Mack took off, so they could fly together.

After a little while, Geiger spoke. "Hey, Mack, you sleepin?"

"No."

"I figgered not. You almost never sleep. You just stay awake listening, but to what I don't know."

"The ghost plane."

Geiger laughed. Mack had told the story about Guynemer one night when people were sitting around the fire exchanging ghost stories. Everybody loved it, but you could tell the guys who had really been in the War and lost friends in the air. They were really cracked up by it. So people asked him to tell the story again sometimes, and Geiger knew it well.

After a pause, Geiger said, "Hey, you going to go on to Lamar?""

"Yeah. Why not?"

"I'm thinking about it. This can't keep up. Practically begging for money, stealing fence wire to replace baling on the wings. I think I'm gonna bail before we crack up."

"Really?"

"Yeah. It can't be long. You saw Grand's face tonight. He's out of his depth—he's not a great promoter like Gates. And when we're thinking about going to places like Hill City, there can't be much left."

"Maybe, but I'm not going to bail. I love flying too much."

"You've been at this as long as I have. You must own your plane by now. You don't have to stay with this winged dog-and-pony show just cause you want to fly."

"What's the alternative?"

"Air mail. Look, they've got the main route set up, right, but they ain't got the feeder routes yet. One's supposed to head out of Denver to meet up with the main route in Cheyenne. They can't have that many great pilots in Denver, can they?"

"No, I don't think so."

"So, here's what I figger. We fly along to Lamar and check out the action there. If it's good, we can stay, but if it's as bad as I think, we can fly on to Denver, see if we can get in on a mail route."

"Mail flying seems kind of boring."

"That's the best part. You wanna keep flying the same stunts for the yokels in these dumb Jennies? How's about night flying, huh? And maybe a newer plane. These things were washed up in '18—they've got some hot birds out there today."

"I bet."

"You remember what it was like when we went from these granny wagons to the Nieuports?"

"It was like flying for the first time all over again."

"No doubt. The way they could climb!"

"The best birds of the war. Guynemer told me how much he admired them."

"You knew Guynemer? You wasn't in the Lafayette Escadrille."

"I wasn't. Did I say Guynemer? I meant Foncke. I always do that. I really wanted to meet Guynemer. I started flying because of him."

"Me, too. He was the best. Three Boches in five minutes. Nobody's matched that!'

"Nobody." Mack paused, listening to the drone of the spectral plane for a moment. He thought about the exhilaration of night flying.

After a pause, Geiger said, "I never believed that he died. They never produced a body, just that Hun doc who said he saw the body and had to run because of artillery. He belonged to the sky and the sky took him."

"We should be so lucky."

Geiger felt around him. He lifted the moonshine bottle up. It was barely visible in the starlight. "It's empty, but a toast nonetheless. May the sky take us!"

Mack raised his hand in a fake toast. "May the sky take us!" Then he put his hand back down on the ground. He looked up at the stars and listened to Guynemer's engine droning into the night.

31.   Unique Pieces

It was chilly in the morning at about 6am when Stanley showed up to drive for "Colonel" Van Cise's raid. They warned him he might be waiting a long time. They wanted to make sure they had arrested the Big Fix, Blonger, and his manager, Adolph Duff, before the general raid began. Fifteen cars and their drivers were scattered around waiting for the order, but the Colorado Rangers and special deputies Van Cise was using instead of police were gathered at headquarters, a church.

Where Stanley was, he couldn't even see the headquarters, so he just leaned back and tried to get as comfortable as he could in the cramped seat of the Tin Lizzie.

Not his first choice for making a quick getaway or pursuit, but you could still outrun a crook on foot. At least it was one with an electric starter. Having to crank the motor any time you stopped or the car stalled would definitely give your quarry a chance to escape. He only hoped it wasn't too noisy, since even in an unmarked car the ranger in the seat would probably tip off anyone who looked to see the source of the noise.

Then the ranger came out to the car. He introduced himself as Chaz Hayworth, said they weren't in the first wave. "We're gonna be one of several cars rushing 'The Lookout' when the time comes. After the first cars goes, we pull up in front of the church, then wait for Samson, the Fed, to come out."

Chaz waited a few minutes, then said, "Okay. They oughts to be gone by now." Sure enough, there were some open spaces right by the church. Stanley was going to pull into one when Chaz looked behind them and said, "That's the Fed's car. Let them pull in first." So Stanley had to drive around the block and park behind the shiny Buick 8.

They waited in the car at least another half hour as the summer sun began to dispel the chill and make them feel pretty warm. It wouldn't be long before they'd be putting the windows down to cool the car. But then Samson, the Federal Investigator, ran out of the church, gesturing wildly.

Stanley fought the starter and managed to get the protesting Lizzie going shortly after Samson closed the door on the Buick. Stanley kept mere seconds behind the Buick as they streaked toward their target, "The Lookout," which served not only as an observation post, but also a sort of headquarters for the bunco artists. No one knew just how many crooks may be meeting there at this time of day, though surveillance suggested it could be anywhere from just a couple to over a dozen. And it might be more or less once word got out that people were being arrested.

The Colonel was taking no chances with the Lookout. He was sending three cars, five rangers, the Federal Investigator, and drivers who could all act as "toughs" if called upon. The three cars pulled up close to one another and the investigator and rangers jumped out, positioning themselves to stop any crooks who tried to make a break for it. Apparently there was some concern about a tip-off. Duff, Blonger's second in command, had a copy of the Colonel's list of suspects when he was arrested. No one knew how much the bunco artists knew or how they planned to respond. After a brief exchange, Chaz leaned back in the car and asked Stanley to come out.

A man was coming out the door as Samson reached it. Samson drew his gun, showed a badge, and sent the man back inside.

Inside the large room were five more men, a few cheap desks, tables, a telephone, and a typewriter. The men were arrested, handcuffed, and led back out to the cars. There was no real resistance. They hadn't been tipped off and none of them seemed suspicious that this arrest was different from any they'd had before.

Stanley and Chaz drove two crooks back to the church. They took a different route to reduce the chance that people would see the stream of cars and get tipped off that it was a police raid. It was hoped they would still be picking up members of the gang throughout the day.

As they drove back, Stanley felt something, a tinge of some power, brief but intense, like a match struck in a dark room, then snuffed. Neither of his passengers seemed to notice it, and Chaz didn't show any awareness, so both sides in the Colonel's gambit were deaf to the greater world. It was a mundane game of cops and robbers, but it operated against the backdrop of greater power, probably manipulated by it to some degree, to help bring the terrible beast across.

At the church they dropped off their passengers and Stanley drove back to the Lookout. Things were cleaned up pretty well there so the Fed went back to the church to talk strategy. They left behind a few rangers and a driver. Stanley volunteered for that duty.

Over the course of the next few hours, a couple more bunco men showed up. Stanley and Carl, a tall strong ranger with a boyish tanned face and short greased blond hair, had to take them back to the church. This time he decided to go a little further out of the way, toward the source of power. The ranger objected, "Hey, where you going?"

"Sorry, I missed the turn." Stanley went up a couple blocks, then took a likely left. There, he could feel it, the dull throb of a protective charm, probably around a sanctuary. The building was made of red stone, with a sign proclaiming it was the Denver Athletic Club. Stanley noted it, and also noticed that the ranger seemed to sense something, too. Stanley found his way back to the church. While they were taking the crook inside, Stanley heard the bunco artist say, "It's been twenty years since I was in church last. I'll be damned if it won't be another forty before I ever go again."

Stanley smiled, looked up at the Sunday school motto on the wall: "The way of the transgressor is hard." They took the men down to the cellar.

At the end of the day, the Lookout was locked up, though it was kept under observation. Most of the people involved in the roundup assembled at the church. Other than a couple of drivers to transport prisoners to Golden and Brighton, the rest were dismissed. Stanley couldn't find a good opportunity to talk to the Colonel, and he was so busy there wasn't likely to be one in the future. Besides, the other thing he wanted was a drink, and that definitely meant leaving the company of the teetotaler lawman.

Stanley was turning to leave the church when suddenly Samson ran out of the door. "You," he said, "please stop. We need you. We've just got a tip where French is at."

French, the top bookmaker for the bunco ring, was the last of the ring's elite who was still on the loose. Stanley stopped.

"Come back in here."

Stanley walked back up the steps to the church door. Inside, the place was pretty cleaned out. The bunco men who had already been arrested were on their way to Golden or to Brighton, and with them the DA and most of his men. The tip had come with only the Fed and a couple of others still in the church.

"I need to head out now and try to get him. Can you help?"

"Where's he at?" Stanley asked.

"A speak called Morgan's."

Morgan's. Where he had first met Mr. Saluzar and Stefani. If something was drawing him back, he had to go along. "Yes."

"Good. Let's go."

They jumped in the car and pulled up suddenly behind the club. Stanley got out of the car. He went around to the front, got let in by the doorman. After a few seconds, there was a moment when no one was watching, and Stanley slipped into the back where he had chased Stefani. He opened the door for the agents and they rushed in. "Stop," Armstrong said, "Federal agents. You are all under arrest unless you cooperate."

There was a smattering of talk, and a few protests, but it calmed quickly.

"We are looking for Jackie French."

A few people said, "He's not here," or "He was here, but he left."

Armstrong ordered a search of the place. Stanley remained in the back hall, sort of guarding it, when Stefani came out of the dressing room. When she saw Stanley, her eyes went wide. He put his finger to his lips and directed her back into the dressing room. Once inside, he closed and locked the door behind him. "I don't want you running off like last time."

Stefani didn't say anything. She backed toward the corner of the dressing room.

"Why did you run last time?"

"You were with those men."

"I wasn't. I didn't even know them. I looked at you because they were looking at you." Stanley felt that was an easier explanation than his real reason. He could feel it now, again, the pendant in the velvet bag hanging between her breasts. Hanging in the deep cleft between her large breasts, he noted now. After a moment, Stanley realized what he was doing and looked away, blushing. "What do you know about those men?"

"Nothing," she replied.

"Those men say they knew your father, say they want to try to buy some unique pieces from his collection. Does that sound plausible?"

"Maybe. My father had a large collection."

"Was that amulet part of it?"

"Yes."

"It's a valuable piece. It may even be the one they're looking for."

"How do you know? You haven't seen it—it's in this bag."

"I bet you haven't seen it, either, but you know it's valuable. That's why you wear it."

Stefani reached up and touched it.

"If you didn't know those men, why did you run?"

"I, uh, felt something."

"And it told you to run?"

She nodded.

"Well, that's a good instinct. Keep it up." Stanley pulled out a business card and handed it to her. "If running isn't enough and you need help, here's how you can get in touch with me." Then Stanley unlocked the door and stepped back into the hall.

Out in the main room, Armstrong was furious. "French was here, and you let him get away? That's like aiding the escape of a felon." There was a slight pause, then he said, "Look at this booze! That's it—you're under arrest and this place is closed until further notice. Everyone else better get outta here before the paddy wagon gets here!"

Stanley rejoined the rangers in the main room. He looked at the only man being arrested, the bartender. The man seemed about to pass out as he stood, held firm by the wrist.

32.   Things Get Dangerous

Bart paced his cell. He'd been to college plenty. True, he wasn't as educated as some of Blonger's men, but you couldn't run any sort of legitimate business without getting pinched once in a while. And this was the first time in a long time that he'd made it to a cell. His arrangement with Constable Goldman meant he got separated out for special handling at the sergeant's desk.

He hadn't been in the cell very long, but already he didn't like it. His cellmate was entirely too comfortable. That meant he'd been here a while. He looked somewhat familiar, but Bart couldn't quite place him. Maybe he'd seen him on the street. Maybe he was a purse snatcher. He was definitely some kind of petty thug.

He reminded Bart that cells were for little people, people without connections. People without protection. Bart didn't like the thought that he was now one of those people.

He paced the first day. By the second day he spent most of his time sitting on the edge of the bunk. By the third day he was lying down and that made him worried. He could feel his motivation and his strength slowly ebbing. It was late that day when he finally got word from one of the cops he knew. Sam or "Sham" Gilroy came up to the bars and said, "Bart, if you're waiting for Goldman to get you out of here—don't."

"What?" Bart got up and went to the bars. "He's always taken care of it before."

"Yeah, but this Blonger bust's got all the guys spooked. Nobody knows how far the DA wants to take it. He's a crusader and he ran this whole thing outside the department. And rumor has it he's not done yet.

"Nobody wants to connect themselves to the Big Store. You got pinched at the same time. They think you might be tainted and won't do nothing, just in case."

"Thanks, Sam. Next time you want a drop, you come by my place and it's on the house."

"Thanks. But you know I'm a teetotaler, and I never go to speaks."

It was Sam's lie that drove the point home most to Bart. Things must really be bad if he didn't feel comfortable talking about drinking here in the jail. Was Vice going to start busting the protected bootleggers?

Bart got in touch with his actual guard. He said he no longer wanted to wait for a hearing to be arranged—he would take the first judge available. He also sent word to his lawyer.

His hearing was scheduled first thing the next morning. He was granted bail, but it was high enough to be a sharp reminder that the Big Store was closed, maybe for good.

He paid his bail and met Sven, his sometime bodyguard and driver, outside the courthouse. They walked across the work site where the Civic Center Park amphitheater was being installed. It was nearing midday and the workers were half-loafing around looking forward to their lunch break.

They got in the car and Sven drove them the short distance to Morgan's, Sven's huge Swedish frame bent comically over the tiny steering wheel of the Model T. But Bart was in no mood for laughing. Instead, it made him think how fouled up the whole situation was now.

Without the Big Store, who would give protection? It didn't seem like anyone was in a position to take over, he thought, which meant there would be a struggle. And that's when things got dangerous. That was how his dad got ventilated. And it was the same stupid set-up: a crusader judge was letting police put the squeeze on wine rooms for corrupting young women. The top guys got taken out and there was chaos.

The gangs don't let you wait to see who comes out on top. They need support early, so they make you choose, especially if you have a business that makes money, which they're desperate for more than anything. Except it isn't really much of a choice. You get the gang that controls your area. And if it turns out they can't protect you . . .

Back at Morgan's, Bart saw Sven had started cleaning up from the last raid, but like everything the big man did without direction, his efforts were unfocused and superficial. The burst beer barrels had been removed, and the main area had been mopped, but under the stools and tables the beer had dried around bits of broken glass and splinters of wood. "Sven," he said.

"Ya?" the big Swede looked at Bart. His eyes were big and empty.

He was hopeless. Bart sighed. "Just take your place at the door." Sven did as he was told.

Bart set to cleaning up the floor. He dislodged the sticky glass shards and swept them into his dust pan.

Then Sven returned. "Boss, there's two guys at the door that wants to see you."

"What're their names?"

"Uh . . . I knows I's sposed to ask, but they been here before, so I thought you might be expectin them. There's this really big guy, and a skinny small old guy with a scratchy voice."

Bart's blood chilled. He knew exactly who these people were, but he had not been expecting them, and definitely did not want to see them. "Can't they see we're closed? Send 'em away," he said, hoping his words sounded more angry than scared.

Sven left. A moment later, Bart heard his choking cry. Bart grabbed his heater from behind the bar and turned to the entryway.

Bart saw Sven's feet lifted off the ground. He was being held aloft by the big man. With his hand on Sven's throat, Bart could see that he was nearly as pale as the Swede, but with an ashy grey cast to his skin.

Bart turned his gun on the short man, who smiled threateningly. "I am not one to be kept out, not when I have a business proposition to offer. Please put the gun down."

It was not a request, and though every instinct in him screamed "Shoot!" he lowered the gun.

"Excellent," said the little man. He touched the leg of the big man, who lowered Sven to the ground. "Now, can we retire to the bar? I am parched."

Bart led them into the bar. Sven stumbled along at the back, still a little dazed. "As you can see, I got busted so I don't have a lot to offer. Whaddaya want?"

"Water will be best, anyway." He took the glass and drank it down in one long gulp, then passed it back. He began speaking when Bart refilled the glass. "My proposition relates to your unfortunate entanglement with the law. I think a number of people in town have suffered the same fate, and with the—what do you call it?—Big Store being shut down, people are nervous about the supply. And rightfully so. The natural response to these recent events would be increased enforcement on the part of an embarrassed police department. They have to show they are not bought."

The man took a long drink, then resumed, "I am in a position to bring liquor to this town, but I need someone local, someone with connections, to distribute it."

"And why would I stick my neck out for that?"

"The District Attorney thinks that by taking out the Blonger Gang he will ensure the police force is independent and will serve the people. But you and I know that someone else must soon take over. More water, please."

Bart looked at the big, grey-faced man, then back at the small old man. He turned his back to refill the glass and said, "You think that's gonna be you, huh?"

"Not me, but someone over whom I have a certain amount of influence."

"And why should I trust you? Or believe you?"

"It's not a question of whether you can trust me, but of whether you can risk working against me. As far as belief, I can give you a sign and I can give you proof. For a sign . . ."

The old man half stepped, half fell from the bar stool. He hobbled into the kitchen and pulled aside the curtain that hung by a blackened window. He scraped off a small square of the window. "For a sign, look here at midnight. I will be happy if you will take the sign, and you will be happier, too. But if you need proof. . ." He hobbled back out to the bar. He grabbed a piece of paper and wrote in a shaky hand. He folded it and handed it to Bart. "This is the next mayor. When you get your proof, you must come to me or you will suffer."

He picked up his hat and hobbled out, followed by the big grey-faced man.

When they were gone, Bart opened the paper. It said, "Ben Stapleton."

33.   Like Calling to Like

Stefani first saw Thaddeus—she immediately thought of him as "Uncle Tad"—through bars and then through tears. *Thank god,* she thought when he went up to the officer's desk. They talked. He paid some money. The officer called over another policeman, who led Thaddeus back to the door of the cell. He unlocked the door and called out, "Stefani?"

She rushed to Thaddeus, grabbing his hand tight. "Thank you, thank you," she said.

He put his arm around her. "My child, you must be freezing. Didn't they even let you take a coat?"

Stefani couldn't say anything. She bit her lip hard. Thaddeus looked around the cell. He pointed at the other woman in the cell, who was conspicuously looking away as she held a coat tightly around her.

"Isn't that your Polaire coat?" he asked. Stefani nodded, but when she tried to say "Yes," all that came out was a tremendous sob, followed by other broken bits of sobs. Stefani buried her face in Thaddeus' shoulder, trying to block back the tears and sobs.

"All right, Nancy," the officer who had opened the door said, "give it up."

The woman in the coat responded in an angry shriek, "My name's Gladys!"

"Tell it to the judge. Just give the coat back."

Stefani felt the coat being placed over her shoulders. Thaddeus put his arm around her shoulder and led her out of the station.

Securely in the car and on the road, Stefani said, "It was awful. They broke all the glass. They broke *everything*. And they yelled at us. They threatened us. They threw me in there with those women. Those women." She watched the street lights go by, then hissed, "Whores!"

"Now, now," Thaddeus said. He put his hand on her shoulder. His strong grip calmed her and she let herself sink into the seat.

She was still seething, though. At him. Mr. Fields. He had come to her, peppered her with questions, and pretended to care, and then it turned out he was just with the cops. Why didn't he do something? Help her escape, or at least say something? But he stood there with his head hung and guarded them while the others took the place apart.

Thaddeus interrupted her thoughts, "There are some who think you are little better than those demimondes. A burlesque dancer. The costume may even be worse."

Stefani said, "Morgan's is a cabaret, not a burlesque," and gave Thaddeus a cold angry glare. She could see him noting it out of the corner of his eye, but otherwise he ignored it.

"I know your father wouldn't be happy."

"Damn you," she said as she hit him. He didn't wince or respond other than with the same sideways glance. "You don't know him. He married mom when she was a dancer."

"But did she stay a dancer? Did she go back to it after he died? Is she happy with you? Don't you think his words might be why?"

"Daddy didn't think like that. He was above that kind of thing. He knew things. Saw things. Other people . . ."

"I think you give your father too much credit."

"You stop. Right now."

"Your father was a good man—a great thinker and a reliable friend. But he was a man. And perhaps more bound by social convention than you think." He turned away from the road for a moment. He met her eyes, glanced down at her scanty costume visible through her gapped coat, then back into her eyes.

Stefani understood. They were silent for a while. The road passed by.

After a while, Thaddeus spoke, "Maybe this isn't such a bad thing after all. You can find another job. Maybe come work for me. I need a research assistant. Someone to fetch books, catalogue materials, file notes, and make sure everything stays in order."

The pendant between her breasts throbbed. It wasn't exactly a warning, though there was caution in it. It was more akin to crickets in the field at night—like calling to like. And far away in the darkness, something responded.

Stefani gasped and clutched the pendant.

Thaddeus looked over. He smiled, his yellow teeth looking white in the dim light. "You don't have to respond now. Here, we're at your house. Think it over."

Stefani didn't wait for him to open the door. She did it herself and ran to the house without looking back. As she fumbled for her keys, she heard the car idling there, its four-cylinder motor tumbling unevenly like crazy laughter.

34.   Chop Suey

SALUZAR NOT IN RECORDS AS POSITIVE ID OR AKA. GET FINGERPRINTS. Stanley put the telegram down. He took a long drag on his cigarette, then reached for his glass. It was empty. He picked up the hooch bottle and shook it. It was getting low. He sighed. He'd have to find a new supplier soon. City this size, it shouldn't be a problem, but since the Blonger gang had all been rounded up, a lot of hooch dealers were rightfully a little jumpy and reluctant to take a chance on a guy they didn't already know.

He looked at the clock, saw it was early evening, well after business hours of course. Now he remembered that Gail had left what must have been hours ago. Still, it was possible that the Colonel was in his office. They'd been working late to put together the case against the bunco artists.

So Stanley got up from his desk, put his hat on, locked up and headed down to the street. As he stepped off the curb, he heard a loud "honk" and an automobile sped right past him, barely swerving to avoid him. Stanley cursed a little. He didn't think he was ever going to get used to those things. People drove them like crazy, parked them every goddamnn where and never cared about the inconvenience they were causing. Whoever thought these automobiles were such a great idea had made a big mistake.

Stanley caught a streetcar, rode it down to the courthouse building. The door nearest the Colonel's office was unlocked. Stanley went in.

Inside the heavy stone building, the corridors were dark—most of the electric lights were off. Stanley followed the light and sound to the DA's office. When he poked his head around the corner, Chaz and a couple of armed guards popped up, but quickly settled down again as the Colonel's smile and friendly greeting told them what they needed to know.

"Stanley," Van Cise said, gesturing to a chair, "haven't seen you since the raid. Me and the boys here just ordered in—you like chop suey?"

"What? Yeah, sure, but I can't stay to eat. I just gotta ask you a couple questions, then I'm outta here."

"Sure, sure." He turned to the others, "Go ahead and dig in without me, boys, I won't be long." Then he said to Stanley, "C'mon through."

Inside, the Colonel's office looked like the site of a battle between two mighty armies—one of order, the other of chaos. On one side, the Colonel had meticulously and neatly laid out all the documents in preparation for the raid. On the other side were laid out the documents seized during the raid, boxes and boxes of papers that had been dumped out of Blonger's desk, the Lookout's files, and more. The zone of conflict, where the two were being integrated, was a mixture of folders, crude piles, and scattered papers that spread across the room and spilled out into the reception room where the Colonel had been working when Stanley arrived.

The ashtray in the office was piled high with ashes and cigarette and cigar butts. The couch on the right wall looked as though it had been slept in, and this was obviously not the first time they'd ordered in chop suey, since the remnants of an earlier meal were near the trash can, itself overflowing with crumpled paper.

By the couch was a copy of *Tarzan the Terrible*. It caught his eye because it tingled slightly. It had been handled by someone not with power, but with potential, which was stirred by reading descriptions of fantastic deeds.

"So, Mr. Fields, what'd you want to ask me?"

"Well, I was hoping you might be able to help me out with an investigation. I'm looking for a person's fingerprints, and it'd be helpful if you happened to have them on file."

"Mr. Fields, I don't think I could turn those over to you."

"If it'd help, I can get an official request from the Chicago Police Department . . ."

"I think that'd be necessary."

"But I don't want to go through the trouble if you don't have them on file."

"Understandable." Van Cise got out a pen. "What's the name?"

"Phil Saluzar."

"Phil Sal-uh-zar?"

"No. Sal-oo-zar. With a 'u,' I'm pretty sure."

"Odd. I'll check it out. Anything else?"

"What can you tell me about the Denver Athletic Club?"

"That's right, you're not from here. Well, the DAC is just what it says, an athletic club. Only, it's probably the most elite club downtown. Nothing much else to say. Why do you want to know?"

"We have reason to believe it might be a meeting place for some suspects in our investigation."

"We who? Who are you working for again?"

"A friend of a friend. One with common goals. Public safety. Good government. Justice."

"Yeah?" Van Cise regarded Stanley with a long look. "I guess Gary wouldn't have sent you to me if you represented something I wouldn't support. Best damn lieutenant I ever had. Always seemed to sort of know when something was going to happen. But it seems like he doesn't know what's going on this time, so I'll give you some help.

"If you're interested in good government and public safety, you should be looking into something that I would be investigating if my plate weren't full with closing the Big Store. The Ku Klux Klan. They have been growing in power and interfering with some of my other investigations. Drove a likely innocent suspect out of town. Have been intimidating witnesses. We had to prosecute one of their members for contempt because he refused to testify. And look at this." Van Cise reached into his desk and pulled out a typed letter, addressed to him.

Stanley read the letter:

Mr. Van Cise,

You know as well as we that the Denver Police and even your office are not sufficient to guard public safety. The case of Ward Gash shows this. The Ku Klux Klan begins where the law leaves off. If you will work with us, Denver and its white women will be safe from harm. If not, you will suffer the consequences.

Sincerely,

The Dickey Brothers

"Anything about that strike you as odd, other than the general oddness of trying to tell a public official he's not good at his job?"

"Why the mention of white women?"

"Well, it could be a reference to the Gash case. A Negro janitor who may have had intimate relations with white women. If they actually happened, they were probably consensual, but the Klan drove him out of town with threats, and he hasn't come back, so we'll likely never know for sure. Or it could be . . ."

"A reference to Irene Pitcher."

"Exactly, although I can't officially comment on an investigation that's in progress. Well, not really in progress until we can get some more concrete information. But maybe you can start poking around for me. If you're going to start looking, there's a quack downtown who's pretty deep in it, we think, though we don't know how deep because the Klansmen swear their oath is too sacred for them to testify about the meetings. He's got an office next door to the Denver Athletic Club. Name's Locke, John Locke. So, that satisfy you or do you need to know something else?"

"That's certainly a lot. Thanks. But one more thing: whose Tarzan is that?"

"Heaven's mercy, don't tell me you're into that stuff, too."

"A little."

"That's Carlton's. Can't get enough of the stuff. A grown man. Otherwise, he's all right, though."

"I worked with him a little during the raid. He seems better than all right. Thanks."

"Any time. Sure you don't want any chop suey?"

"I'm sure."

"I'm starving. Lemme know if there's anything more I can do for you."

"Will do."

Stanley emerged from the city and county building into the full darkness. There was a slight chill in the air. Disproportionate to the season.

35.   Yanked around by Strangers

Stefani was riding the streetcar headed downtown to pick up some supplies. She had two lists. One for her mother, which included some thread and fabrics, and one for herself, which included some new shifts and a corset.

At one of the stops, she felt the trolley was taking too long, its normal rhythm interrupted by something. She brought her gaze back from the distance, looked around to see what the problem was. An old man was being helped onto the train by a tall, strong man. Suddenly, her blood froze. She recognized them from Morgan's. She tried to look out the window before they could see her, but it was too late—the old man's eyes caught hers and they locked long enough that she knew they recognized her.

Still, she turned back to the window and hoped he would leave her alone. For the first time, she was thankful for the annoying jasper who had sat down beside her two stops ago and periodically tried to strike up a conversation with her. But then the tall man led the old man to her seat. The old man gestured at the seat. The jasper gave a disdainful look. He clearly valued the seat, but the stony gaze of the tall man and a hand's firm pressure on the shoulder of his seersucker suit convinced him he should look for another seat.

The old man sat down heavily in the vacated seat, the rattan creaking just barely perceptible over the hum of the electric motor and the groan of the rail. Stefani couldn't help glancing over at him. He didn't start talking right away. First, he opened his mouth and spritzed it a few times from an eau de cologne bottle. The stuff didn't smell sweet. It smelled oily.

Then he began to speak. "Allow me to introduce myself: Phil Saluzar, and I am sorry for the abruptness of our first meeting."

"I . . . I didn't know what to do. I didn't know who you were."

"Of course not. I'm Phil Saluzar, an old friend of your father's and Thaddeus Marduk. I knew them before they went to the Philippines."

"You say you're a friend of father's, but I don't know you. I know Thaddeus, but I don't know you."

"True. We had fallen out of touch. I travel a lot and I haven't been back in Colorado since you were a baby."

"So, how did you know who I was?"

"Your pendant, my dear. It was your father's. He got it in the Philippines."

Stefani touched the pendant.

"Yes. Your father came back changed. So did Thaddeus. They had always had a jealous friendship, and when they came back it was even worse. They were hard to be around after that. But, then, your dad did win the girl, and Thaddeus couldn't stand that."

"Thaddeus made love to my mother? She hates him."

"She didn't then. She was having a hard time deciding between them. But that was a long time ago, when she looked much like you. I would've thought Thaddeus was out of your life." He looked at her reaction. "He's not? Is he courting your mother again? I should not be surprised. He is not one to give up on what he wants."

"No . . . He . . . offered me some work."

"While the club was closed? Of course he would make that offer. You do look an awful lot like your mother." He paused, swallowing hard. Then he began again, his voice growing ever more thin and dry. "We are approaching my stop. I must tell you—I know what killed your father."

Stefani's heart jumped. She felt the color drain out of her face. She quickly recovered. "Yes. Tuberculosis."

The old man got up and walked to the door, aided by the tall, muscular man. "No, friendship. And something else. Something that may still be in the house."

Stefani practically popped up out of her seat. The trolley pulled away. Stefani turned and watched the old man's back recede in the distance.

Then she let herself sink back into her seat. What did he know? What did he know?

Then she tried to calm herself. Saluzar must have known that would set her off. He had been at the club. Perhaps he had talked to one of the girls who knew how much her father's death haunted her. He knew about Thaddeus from the night when he had pursued her and Uncle Tad drove her away. What did he want? What interest did he have in setting her against Thaddeus?

She knew better than to let herself be manipulated so easily. She had to put this to rest. She needed to check her mother's story so she could trust her mother and not be yanked around by strangers on the trolley.

She got off the train downtown and got on another one, headed to the hospital. She wanted to see tubercular patients, know what they looked like—see how they died. Then she would know.

When Stefani finished telling her story, the head nurse straightened herself stiffly. She looked down at her desk, arranged some papers. A long, chloroform-scented pause.

"Well," she said at last, "some of what you describe sounds like tuberculosis. But some of it does not. Perhaps the best way for you to know would be to see for yourself."

"Yes. That's what I want."

"It won't be easy to look at."

"It can't be harder than not to know. Please!"

The head nurse sighed. The wrinkles in her face deepened, and her entire appearance hardened like a mask of Medea Stefani had seen in a book as a child. "Very well. Come with me." She took her large ring of keys in hand. She led the way out of the office into the great marble hallway. The nurse's stout clogs sounded confident, strong. Stefani's heels click-clacked uncertainly.

The head nurse ascended a short flight of stairs, stopped at a door marked "observation room." Inside, the room was long and narrow. One wall was a bank of windows with a rail before it. The floor was raised high above the room beyond.

Stefani walked forward and leaned over the rail. She looked into the tubercular ward.

The nurse spoke coldly, firmly. "These patients are advanced cases. They will all die soon. You may even see one. There." The nurse pointed.

Stefani's eyes followed the nurse's bony finger. The man in the bed had deep sunken eyes. He was very pale, save for his lips and chin, which were stained with blood. He broke into a coughing fit, which ejected blood from his mouth and nose. Some of it spilled onto his face and some landed on his gown, which was splattered with numerous red-brown stains. A nurse wearing a cloth mask came over and wiped his chin, but residue remained. As she turned away to attend another patient, Stefani saw her eyes. They were tired and detached.

Stefani looked back at the bedridden man. His eyes stared up at the ceiling, but they were glassy and exhausted, sleepless. He looked like he was already dead.

"Do they always get worn down like that at the end?"

The head nurse's face took on its mask-like appearance again. "Tuberculosis is a wasting disease. It takes a terrible toll before the end. His appearance is typical."

"Are they ever energetic and vivid and then just one day: blood and death?"

"They sometimes get lucid before the end. They may suddenly be surprisingly energetic and talkative. They may even get up and walk around, then die. But not before they've been like this."

"And the blood normally comes out of their mouth and nose?"

"Yes. Well, sometimes there is a little in their tears."

"But what about their skin? Does it ever come through their pores?"

"No, I don't think so."

"What about their skin? Does it ever come off?" Stefani couldn't help herself. Her voice was growing louder and more shrill.

The nurse's marble mask had cracked. Her eyes were growing moist. "I—I don't think I've ever heard of that."

"And what about their bones? Does tuberculosis ever melt their skull and their eyes and their brain and their spine?"

"No, child, no. What horror are you talking about now?"

Stefani was shouting and crying now. "I'm talking about my father. And I'm talking about a lie. That's the goddamm horror I'm talking about."

The head nurse's face was still horrified, but now it was also sad. "No, child, no. Don't take the name of the Lord in vain. Only He can save you." She reached out and put a comforting hand on Stefani's shoulder. "Let us pray."

Stefani straightened up, choked back her sobs. "Thank you, but no. Only I can save me." She turned and rushed to catch the trolley. The nurse stood still, her clogs silent as Stefani's heels clicked confidently down the hall.

Stefani returned home, trembling with anger and trying to slow her rapid breathing and racing heart. Her mother sat at the dining room table, as usual, staring out the window with a half cup of cold coffee in her hand. She was still wearing her kimono, tied sloppily over her nightgown, even though the sun would soon be low enough to shine directly on her face through the west window.

Stefani put down her pocketbook and empty shopping bag. She tried to take a deep breath, with modest success, then walked over to the table.

"Mother," she said. Elizabeth Aegis gave no response. "Mother!" she said again, louder, and hit the table with her fist. She had not meant to hit so hard or shout quite so loud.

Her mother turned around with a startled noise. She looked up at Stefani, who noticed how faded and worn she looked, how frightened her eyes looked. Narrow, chocolate brown irises, expanded pupils, and so much white, as if awakened from a nightmare.

Stefani hesitated, then said, "I know you were lying to me. Father didn't die of tuberculosis."

"What? What are you talking about? Of course he died of tuberculosis."

"No. I've seen tuberculosis victims. I know what it looks like. And I know what happened when father died. They aren't the same. Tell me how he died."

Her mother's eyes narrowed. The whites practically disappeared. The pupils narrowed. Her eyes looked like they belonged to a racehorse in the stall, with fury barely contained. "I told you how he died. I told you it was tuberculosis."

"That's not all you've been lying about. I know about you, father, and Uncle Tad. Why didn't you tell me he loved you? Did you love him? Or did you just lead him on to set him against father?"

"No. It wasn't like that at all. They fought, but I wasn't involved. I wanted them to stay friends."

"Then why did they fight?"

"I don't know! I don't know!" Her mother glanced to the side, and the whites of her eyes became visible again, along with a little bit of the fear.

Stefani looked where her mother had glanced—the basement door. Her father's laboratory. "You know more than you're telling. Why did they fight and why do you hate Thaddeus now?"

They looked at each other for a long moment. Then her mother said, "Because he killed your father!"

Stefani felt unsteady. She pulled a chair out from under the table and fell into it. "But . . . but . . . how? I was there. He wasn't there. How could he have killed Papa?"

Her mother looked out the window again. "I don't know. I don't know. I don't know what they did or why they fought. It was hidden. Partly, I daren't look. And what they showed me—I couldn't look. I couldn't understand. I can't remember. I don't know. If anyone can tell you, Thad can." Then her mother paused. She looked away from the window and back at Stefani. She reached out her hand and grabbed her daughter's elbow. "But don't! Don't! Don't! Leave it alone and don't talk to him. Don't see him. If he thinks you know! I don't want to lose you, too."

Stefani felt the chill of her mother's hand, saw the fear in her mother's eyes. This was not a lie. This was real. But Stefani felt she already knew more than her mother dared. Too much to stop. She had to find the truth. She had to ask Thaddeus about her father's death.

36.   Deaths Will Have Their Echo

Stanley found a good place from which to watch the Klan headquarters. It was a little soda fountain with a speak inside, but outside was occupied by a steady stream of apparently shiftless individuals. Some were obviously lookouts, and these changed regularly. Others were hangers-on who flattered the lookouts in hopes of getting a drink. Others were truly down-and-out individuals who looked to accomplish nothing more than nurse every possible second out of a nickel cup of coffee to keep them out of the chill, then buy another.

Stanley knew what that was like. He blended in easily.

There was a lot of activity at the Klan headquarters today. There were people coming and going, and as the time wore on, more of the people were carrying robes, or even wearing them. Stanley did his best to learn the faces of all those coming and going, but it seemed likely that this stakeout was going to be a bust, like so many before it. He didn't see anyone who had power. He did, however, sense the traces of brushes with power from many of the people, but none that were capable of wielding it directly.

Then the rain began, a cold autumn rain that was thin and needly. Not many people had umbrellas, it was an unexpected rain, and from the café he could see the pain on people's faces as the rain was driven into their reddening skin.

And then the man he was looking for appeared. There was a group of Klansmen, all wearing their hoods as they came out of the white stone building. They turned and headed down the street and Stanley followed them with his eyes while draining his cup. Then he pressed his hat down on his head until the brim was low on his forehead.

The rain was as cold and painful as it looked. It gave him a good excuse for keeping his head down and just following the Klansmen with his peripheral vision. He followed the Klansmen around the corner, where, to his dismay, they climbed into a long, low red car with a cloth roof. The engine growled to life, but the car didn't immediately drive away. As he passed, Stanley noticed the gold lettering on the side: "Pierce Arrow."

Stanley walked on a few steps, until the car began to move, then flagged down a cab. A likely cab stopped. A model T, but in decent shape. The inside was drafty and the springs were obviously in bad shape, but the engine sounded healthy and the driver handled his machine capably. Stanley noted the number in case he might need a pursuit cab later. Today, though, he was content to just follow the traces of power through the rain.

"It's nice to be out of the rain. Can we just drive around?" he said.

"Sure, buddy, if you've got the cash."

Stanley handed the driver a sawbuck.

"Alright. Any preferences?"

"Yeah. Head up here then turn west."

The taxi turned and Stanley could see the red car with the white top. They headed west on the major street, for a while until it became obvious where they were going. The pull of the cemetery, already visible atop the hill, was strong. Stanley was not exactly eager to go there, but he had to follow.

Although the red car was continuing around the outside of the cemetery, Stanley told his driver to stop on the near side.

"Getting back in the rain? In the cemetery, no less."

"Just got some stuff to think about."

"Well, I dunno how much thinking you're gonna wanna do out there. You want I should hang around? The fare's only a dollar."

"That's okay. Gimme back five and keep the rest for yourself." Stanley looked around, saw the streetcar lines on an adjacent street. "If I need to get back, I can take the streetcar."

The driver took the money happily and said, "Well, if you change your mind, you can always get me. Just call the company and ask for Taxi Max. Nobody knows this town like I do."

Stanley nodded. Taxi drivers always said stuff like that, but he might just ask for Max if he thought he needed a good driver.

He pulled up his collar and pulled down his hat against the rain. He didn't like being in the cemetery. All the bodies crowded together reminded him of France. Although many of these were peacefully dead--unlike the Somme--the air was still charged with regret, anger, and jealousy. There was a lot of power here, but hard to control because of its unfocused emotions and general despair. That's why necromancy was more easily turned to dark purposes. Their pain and anger could be better turned to death and destruction. Much harder to build anything with that grey, formless stuff.

As he walked among the graves, Stanley's mind kept going back to France, all those dead, unsettled souls. Those deaths would have their echo. Stanley shook his head and tried to focus himself again on this cemetery.

Looking over the graves, Stanley saw his likely goal: a long procession of people. As he got closer, Stanley could see through the rain that they were policemen, a hundred of them, at least. The family waited by the grave as the pallbearers took the coffin and laid it down on the catafalque. The pallbearers moved aside, but before everyone had reached their places at the graveside, they all stopped suddenly. Everyone looked over and an even deeper silence fell.

Six figures in white robes approached the graveside. The lead figure bore a large white floral cross hefted over his shoulder. The base said "Knights of the Ku Klux Klan." The lead knight put the cross in front of the other flowers. The family made a brief noise—they were obviously unhappy—but no one else moved or spoke. One of the figures handed out papers. Then the robed figures departed.

Political theater, clearly, but underlying it was sorcery. While the figure was handing out papers, two other figures were casting. The motions were subtle, hard to notice, and probably no one nearby could even hear the words, but Stanley could sense the spells being made. Stanley could feel it, trying to control his mind, plant the notion that these men represented the good, the right, the true Americans. The family resisted, but most of the people in the crowd, many of them police and politicians, were affected. They seemed to accept the message. Stanley saw that the Colonel was among the crowd, one of the others that was resisting. Stanley decided he would hang around and try to talk to him before leaving.

The other spell was even more sinister. They were placing an enchantment on the body that would allow them to use it as an anchor to help focus the power of the graveyard for use. Necromancy at work, then, which would fit in with the sacrifices. Just the sort of casting that would be necessary to free the spirit in the silver.

Stanley found a place to hang out in the shelter of a mausoleum. It was dry enough that he could roll and light a cigarette. Then he took a swig from his flask to keep warm. The cigarette, he hoped, would disguise the smell of liquor on his breath when he was talking to the Colonel.

When Van Cise passed by the mausoleum, Stanley called to him. The Colonel jumped, still affected by the ceremony.

"Oh you," he said. "What're you doing here?"

"Just taking in the sights. What was that all about?"

"A funeral. One of the few good ones on the Denver force was killed. Ambushed and shot dead by a group of assassins because he was trying to enforce the law."

"Yeah? And what about the Ku Klux Klan? What were they doing here?"

"Oh, you can read their ridiculous drivel if you want." He handed Stanley a crumpled up piece of paper, damp on the outside. "But what they really want is power. Just another gimmick to get power so they can become corrupt and rich." The Colonel took a deep sigh. Apparently, though he had closed the Big Store, and it looked like maybe for good, he was despairing of the impact of it all. The Colonel shrugged and said, "I'm tired and wet. I want to get home and get a cup of hot tea. You want a ride?"

"No, thanks. I've got something to do, still."

The Colonel turned and left. Stanley watched the Colonel go, thinking that he was at least partly right. They were looking for power, looking to harness the living and the dead for their dread purpose, but what that purpose was, who could say? It was unlikely something as mundane as getting rich.

37.   Much Harder to Squash

The old man pushed the door open slowly. Then his big body guard pushed it, causing it to swing open quickly and bang against the wall before swinging back slowly. Patrons in the bar barely looked over.

Bart watched nervously as the old man stumbled up to the bar. He pulled himself up onto the stool. He was obviously worn by the effort.

"Can I get you something?" Bart asked.

"Water, please," the old man spoke. His voice was as raspy and dry as ever.

Bart poured out the glass of water. The old man took it and drank for a very long time, evenly, slowly. When he finished, he didn't gasp, but began speaking immediately, "Now it is time for us to go meet your new associates."

Bart looked away. "I-I dunno. I'm not sure about this. I think somebody else might be better for helping you. I'm just a saloon operator. That's what I do. I'm not a fixer, and I don't want to be."

The old man took a deep breath, then said, "You mean you are afraid to be a fixer."

"I'm not afraid."

"Yes, you are. You are like this cockroach." The old man pulled up the mat on the bar and a cockroach scuttled away. "You see, you want to hide in the tiny cracks, where you think you are safe." The cockroach found a crack in the bar, where it sat, its antennae twitching. "This may seem safe, but once you are flipped into the light," the old man sent the cockroach out of the crack with a flip of his nail. "You are easily squashed." With his other thumb, he crunched the cockroach on the bar.

"Now a man," he continued, wiping his thumb on Bart's shirt, "he is much harder to squash." The old man pushed hard and Bart staggered back a step. "With Blonger gone, everyone's in the light. You have two choices. You can scurry for cover and hope that you get there before someone puts their thumb on you." The old man raised his thumb to Bart's face. "Or you can get ready to go."

Suddenly, Bart realized what was being offered—the opportunity to be his own protection. "Who am I going to leave in charge here?"

The old man looked around. "Him."

"Caruso?"

The old man nodded. "You can trust his loyalty."

"Uh, okay. Caruso, you're in charge until I get back."

The big man with the grey complexion helped the old man down from the stool. The old man hobbled to the door, which the big man held open for him, but not for Bart. They led the way to a car waiting at the curb. The big man opened the door for the old man, and helped him into the seat. Then the big man went around to the driver's seat.

Bart paused for a moment, trying to figure out where he should sit. He took a deep breath, then decided on the back seat behind the driver.

As the car took off, Bart tried to wipe the cockroach remains off his shirt. Most of it came off, but a greasy stain remained. "I wish you hadn't done that. Now I hafta meet these people with this stain on my shirt."

"You're a fool if you think that is your worst stain. Just cover it up with your hand. No one will notice."

The car headed west out of downtown. As it drove past Sloan's Lake, Bart looked out to see the remains of the Manhattan Beach amusement park. He remembered enjoying the carnival there as a child, but little enough of it remained now. The car stopped at a small house in the area called Edgewater.

"Now," said the old man, "go in there and meet with your new partners."

"What? I can't do that. Not on my own."

"You can, and you must." The old man pointed at the grease spot. "Just remember, be a man, or you will get squashed. Go. Now. They're waiting."

Bart covered up the spot on his shirt, then walked up to the house. He thought about ringing the bell, but the crank was broken off. Instead, he just entered.

There was a large common room just inside the entrance. All the curtains were drawn. Three men sat at the table. A fourth was standing in the far corner. They all looked at Bart angrily.

"Who are you?" the standing man asked. He was tall, thin, and wearing a blue suit. His hat was pulled down over his eyes, which were like flame when Bart caught brief glances of them.

Bart remembered the stain and his hand went quickly to cover it tightly. He felt a wave of confidence wash over him. "I'm Bart Gallio, and I'm here to help you guys keep this business running."

The standing man laughed. "That's the dumbest thing I ever heard. What makes you think you can help us?"

"I don't think, I know. Here's how: Blonger was the fixer cause he had people on the inside with the fuzz. If you don't have that, it's only a matter of time before you have an accident."

"And you do? That may work for your beat, and we've all got our mulligans, but that don't make you anything special."

"You don't understand. I know who's going to be the next mayor. And he will make my man chief of police."

That won their attention. They invited him to the table. He listened to the plans of Tommy Lowe, the standing man, Diego Herrera, a spic, "Pal" Moygnihan, and "Fast" Frank Wilson. When they had worked out their plans, Bart shook their hands and rose. He walked out, and found it was dark, but the car was still there. He walked up to it, opened the door, and stepped in.

The old man asked, "How did it go?"

"Great!"

"I'm not surprised. You can stop covering that stain now."

"Oh, ha!" Bart took his hand off the stain and suddenly felt strangely deflated.

38.   What Kind of Sap

Stanley went into a soda shop with a juice joint in the back where he was known. He had a couple drinks, then found the oppressiveness of the small, dark room to be too much. There was too much smoke, too much talk, too many breaths in the air he was breathing. So he went out to the front room, ordered a cherry fizz. Terrible sweet stuff, but it gave him something to drink, and it helped the joint show legit business.

A few other people were in the soda shop part. All of them had obviously gotten a little tight, too. They were sitting around nursing sodas and coffee and like drinks. Stanley was just about finished with his drink when there was a tapping at the door. The door opened and a small, frail man with a white cane came in. He held out his cup as he went around the room.

Stanley saw that his face was intensely scarred. Obviously a smallpox victim. Not fully healed. Not fully accustomed to his blindness yet, either.

From behind the bar a man shouted, "Get outta here, scabby! I told you, you can't peddle in here no more."

"Please," the blind man said, "show some Christian mercy. I have nowhere else to go right now. No place warm."

The man behind the bar came out using the bar gate near Stanley. He grabbed the blind man by the lapels. He picked him up, then threw him down, "I told you to get lost. Now do it, before you get hurt."

Stanley rushed to the side of the blind man, who had begun to sob a little. Stanley said, "Don't worry, sir. I'll take care of you. Here, please take my hand. These men won't hurt you anymore."

"What business is it of yours?" the barman said.

"I hope it's everybody's business when a helpless invalid gets worked over by a coward."

The barman folded his arms. "I ain't no coward. He was told to leave and he didn't. He needed to be knocked over or he would just come back."

As Stanley helped the man toward the door, he said, "If that's the only way you can think to keep him out, you've got problems. If he doesn't respect you, he's gonna keep coming back, even if you do knock him down sometimes. He knows you're more afraid of him than he is of you."

"That's a lie! A damned lie, that's what. I ought to pop you, piker."

"Go ahead and try it, sap, and see what it gets you!" At the door, Stanley put a few coins in the man's cup, then sent him on his way.

The barman said, "And you give him money, too? Whatchoo wanna give money to a goof like that for?"

"I dunno. I give money to you, don't I?" He climbed back up onto his stool. "Gimme another of them cherry fizzes."

The barman went back behind the bar. He sprayed the soda and added the syrup. As he stirred, he said, "It's sad, anyhow. He used to be a good customer. Damn pox."

"It's those fucking doctors and their fucking vaccines that caused this."

Stanley, who had been fighting hard to keep control of the anger that the bathtub gin was loosing in him, couldn't let this pass. "Where'd you get that hooey? Lay off if you don't know what you're talking about."

"I know what I'm talking about." The man, who had thin stringy hair plastered by sweat to his head where his hat had crushed it, turned to look at Stanley. His eyes had the tremble that showed he'd been drinking, too, and probably more than Stanley. "You're the one that don't know. You just a sheep and you go where you hear the bell, or if they have to set the dog to nip at ya!"

"Oh, yeah? And what puts you in the know?"

"I read the ad the Medical Liberty League puts in the paper. They tells it straight. They tells us to never let no doc put sickness in your body." As he was talking, he got louder and his gestures became animated. He almost knocked over his neighbor's Coca-Cola. "That's crazy! Put sickness in your body to make you well? That don't make no sense. They think we're stupid? The doctors they all get together and come up with this scheme so they can sell us their vaccines. What's a healthy person need a doctor for? Nothing. So they give us that fucking shit to make us sick so's we need 'em."

"The Medical Liberty League? Boy, are you the biggest sap--."

"Me? No, you's the sap. They inject you with that stuff to make you sick and it make you a fruitcake, too. Ever wonder why there's so many damned fruits around? They didn't used to be no fruits before the vaccines."

"Oh, there didn't did there?"

"No. So I ain't letting 'em put that shit in my body."

"Nobody's gonna force you."

"But that's what they trying to do. They start up this whole "epidemic," and try to scare us into taking their shit. Everybody. And when everybody gets that medicine, what's that? That's socialism. That's un-American, is what that is."

Stanley was forcing his fingernails into the palm of his left hand, while he tried not to clench the glass too tightly in his right hand. He had to try to keep himself under control. "You quite finished?"

"Yeah, I guess so. I guess I can hear to your sheep bleats now."

"A'ight." Stanley looked around the front room. Everybody was watching. He had to play it cool. Straight. He remembered there was a paper around. He saw it, so he got up and grabbed it, then came back to the bar. "You beat your gums so much, I don't wanna waste everybody's time with most of that hokum. But there's one thing everybody's gotta know, and that is that vaccines don't make people sick. They keep people from getting sick." He flipped through the newspaper for a couple of pages until he found what he was looking for. He pointed at the column showing the smallpox dead of the week, and he said, "So, let's look. This week there were 22 new cases of the pox. Of these, 15 hadn't been vaccinated, and seven had been. So it looks to me like two people without vaccine get the pox for every one that gets it with the vaccine. That doesn't seem like the vaccine causes the pox, now does it?"

"But--!"

"Still my turn, so pipe down. Now, let's look at the dead here. Five died this week. Four without vaccine. One with. So it seems like four die without the vaccine for every one that dies with it. That sounds to me like the vaccine is saving lives."

"And what kind of sap believes what he reads in the paper? A sheep, that's what kind!"

"Oh, yeah?" Stanley flipped a couple pages over to the Medical Liberty League ad. He showed it around, "And what kind of sap does that make you?"

The man's face was red with rage. He was close to going over the edge, and Stanley should've left well enough alone, but he couldn't help himself. He smiled and said, "Baaa!"

The other men in the joint who had all been listening quietly suddenly busted up. Stanley started laughing, too, but the red-faced man was coming at him along the bar, kicking glasses as the barman yelled, "Hey, hey!" The man tried to jump on Stanley, but Stanley grabbed his arm and threw him to the ground.

Before the man could get up, Stanley hit him a couple of times in the face, hoping to subdue him, but he wouldn't stay down. He grabbed Stanley's left arm and tried to throw him down, but Stanley rolled away. As the man was running by, Stanley gave him a sucker punch in the kidney. The man groaned and wobbled a little, leaning against the wall.

"Look," Stanley said, "I don't want to hit you any more than I hafta. And we both want another drink. What say we go back into the mill here and get us some hooch? On me."

The man had turned around and now he was leaning his back against the wall. He was panting. He shook his head for a moment, obviously trying to clear it, not to say "no." Then he said, "Okay. Sure." He reached out to Stanley, who helped him to his feet, and the two of them leaned on one another as they went back into the speakeasy.

39.   Bible and Guns against Liquor

Bart went over the shipment. "Beer, two dozen cases. Gin, two hundred pints." He opened one and sniffed it. "Domestic, obviously. Is this brown liquid . . . ?"

"Whiskey," said Tommy Lowe, bowing his head in a nod that brought the brim of his hat down over his eyes.

"Whiskey, yes. Also domestic, I assume."

Lowe gave a similar nod.

"So, where is the imported whiskey?"

Fast Frank said, "The border's getting a little hard to run."

"The Canadian border? The Mounties giving you trouble?"

"No. At Wyoming. A bunch of the farmers have started patrolling the road. They set up road blocks and they stop all the cars. A couple of my guys are in jail up there now. And it ain't just the main roads, neither. Practically any place we can come across, they're watching. I think they got dep'tized. They got new guns and cars."

"So, have you tried persuading them to work with us, instead of against us?"

"They been approached afore. Old temperance types. The womenfolks is all Bible and the mens is all guns and they is all against liquor."

"So what are you going to do about it?"

Pal Moygnihan said, "We're working on increasing our production."

"Making more of this?" Bart sniffed one of the pints of "whiskey."

"Okay, that may well work for some of our customers. They're just wanting to get drunk or get a warmer. But even if we can get our production up to supply all the need, we want to have some imported stuff."

"Why?"

"For two reasons. First, those who know the difference will pay the difference. They will pay a lot. Second, the people who want the good stuff are the people we want on our side. High society. Money. Connections. If we don't supply them with quality liquor they can serve to their high-toned friends, they'll find someone who can. Especially with Christmas and New Year's coming up.

"We need to have some, but if we don't have a lot, that's okay. We can always charge more. It's even more premium, and the gifts will get us more favors. But we do need some. If we can't get it through the north, what are our other options?"

Herrera said, "Not much chance of bringing it in from the south without having to pay. La policia in the Springs are in control and the ways around them are controlled by the local gangs. We can do it, but it'll be expensive, and I wouldn't count on it being genuine."

Tommy Lowe said, "I gotta connection in Scottsbluff. He might be able to supply us."

Fast Frank said, "No good. That route is patrolled, too. Not many roads. Not many options. And they is all being watched."

"Well, we can give it a try," Tommy Lowe said.

"Can't we just remove the obstacles?" Bart asked.

"'Spossible," Fast Frank said, "but we dunno how many of them there is. And they is pretty well armed. We's had shootouts with these Temperance types afore. We don't always win, and it's always expensive. I'll look into what it will cost and whether we can even do it."

"All right. You do that. I'll come up with something in the meantime. I can't believe you guys. What did you do before I came along? Now get outta here and lemme think." His hand was clenched tightly on the charm in his pocket. It felt hot in his palm and thrummed. Or was that the beating of his own heart?

Pounding, deep beats—he couldn't believe he was talking to these mobsters like this.

Nonetheless, they accepted his words, took his abuse, and obeyed his commands. With almost no grumbling they climbed out of their chairs and left the room. Bart sighed. He let go of the charm. He took a couple deep breaths. He needed to relax, but he didn't think he could relax here.

"Caruso," he called out. Caruso was cleaning the bar absentmindedly, but he immediately jumped to attention. "Get the car. I wanna go for a ride."

Caruso looked surprised, but he didn't hesitate. He took the keys from under the bar, then ran to get the car.

Bart was waiting. The car was an old Model T in the open style. Some day, maybe soon, he should get a sedan. The car used to be just for picking up booze and running other errands, but now that he was using it to run to meetings and the like, the jostly open air vehicicle was not ideally suited. Maybe he should get a Buick or an Overland. Maybe a brougham and then he could get a driver. When Caruso asked, "Where you going, boss?" Bart just said "East." He didn't want the mountains looming over his thoughts.

After a little while, he came to a big field, bustling with activity. He stopped the car and got out. He walked up to some other spectators, and he said, "What's going on? The circus?"

"No, sir. An air show." A kid said.

When Bart didn't say anything, a man added, "Air show. With airplanes." He pointed.

A biplane swept down low over them. It banked slightly, revealing an empty seat in front of the pilot. As it straightened up and began climbing, Bart felt his heart soar. He smiled. That was the answer. They could fly over all those farms and their gun-toting teetotalers.

40.   Like a Real Flyboy

When Mack and Geiger landed in Denver, they immediately began to inquire about the air mail route. They figured out that it was being run by a small company out of Jefferson County Airfield. When they got there, it seemed that that was pretty much the only thing being run out of there. There were maybe two other planes hangared there on anything like a permanent basis.

The two men visited the air mail office and found that it was also the office for a local airplane factory as well. The man in charge ran both sides of the business and he was firm in his denial. "Look, even if I could use more pilots, which I don't need, then I still wouldn't need your planes. This is partly a promotional venture for our planes. We want to fly our planes so we can show how good they are.

"If you want to check back in a few months, maybe I can use you guys as pilots, but I still couldn't use your planes."

There was a second air mail route running in town, but they used De Havilands with Liberty engines, which were faster and had a longer range and higher ceiling than the Jennies Mack and Geiger were flying. The ceiling was a real issue here, too. With the high plateau Denver sat on, their Jennies couldn't clear the ground by much more than a thousand feet, and even that took some work. The man in charge at the second outfit also had a disdain for acrobatic pilots, and he made no secret of it.

So Geiger decided to move on and try to meet back up with Joe's flying circus. But Guynemer seemed to like it here. He landed his ghostly Spad more often and lounged around beside it like a real flyboy. He even wandered off the airfield sometimes to sit beneath a tree or look at a little patch of wildflowers. He didn't always fly away when Mack approached. Sometimes they would sit together under the tree, smoking. It felt good. Guynemer had become a friend, and he liked this strange new, wordless friendship. So Mack decided to stay.

Turns out it wasn't too hard to make a living. At least, not to the standards Mack was used to. He got a commission as "deputy security officer" at a couple of the local airfields. The pay was miniscule, but it allowed him to set up his bedroll in the hangar, which saved him a bundle. There were plenty of people looking for joy rides, and he could charge them $3 apiece for a simple ride or $5 if they wanted a flying lesson. A lot of his students were well-heeled businessmen and playboys, so they kept coming back, and sometimes they took him out for lunch after a lesson. The amount of food they served at a restaurant for a meal was about what Mack had been used to eating all day, and he became content to just have a cigarette for dinner and breakfast afterwards.

One of Mack's students even bought his own plane. He was a young heir to some kind of packing fortune, but of course he wasn't interested in his father's business. He wanted to fly, so he was down pretty regularly for lessons. Not just him, either, but his flapper wanted to learn to fly, too. Mack had no problem with that—he had seen Quimby fly before he earned his license. (And, truth be told, the doll was a better pilot than her squeeze.)

The plane he bought was an old Jenny, too, and because he knew Mack maintained his own plane, he hired Mack to be his mechanic. Between all these miscellaneous odds and ends, Mack was able to put away enough money that he would be able to rent a bed in a flophouse (or, heck, maybe even his own room!) when the weather turned cold.

And then there was Caruso. Jay Caruso was an enthusiastic student, if you judged by the frequency with which he came for lessons. He was there every day. Of course, if you judged by his actual level of enthusiasm, he was anything but eager. He was like a man who was learning to fly at gunpoint. And he wasn't too talented, either.

Caruso didn't have a feel for the controls. He could understand what they did, but unless he was being constantly told what to do, he gradually drifted one way or another. He tilted slightly left or right, and then when Mack told him to correct, he overcorrected, and Mack had to take over to keep them from rolling. Or he would begin a gradual dive, then when he noticed he was diving, he tried to pull up so hard he almost stalled the plane.

It was a hopeless situation, but Mack was happy to take the money. Then one day, Caruso left his lesson and went over to the car that was always waiting to pick him up. Only this time, instead of him just climbing in, there was someone waiting outside the car. He was a short Italian man who spoke angrily with his hands.

From over his shoulder, Mack heard a voice say, "What do you suppose they're talking about?"

Mack looked over and saw Guynemer's ghost standing right there, holding a fag between his fingers. Mack almost jumped. "What are you doing?"

"I'm asking you what you suppose they're talking about."

"Well, uh, I dunno. I think the short man by the car wants to know why Caruso isn't a pilot yet."

"I think you might be right. And why isn't he?"

"He's got no feel for the controls. He'll never be a pilot."

"I think you're right again. So what are you going to say when they come over here and ask you?"

"I'll say the truth. And I'll tell 'em that if they really needs a pilot, well, I needs work."

Guynemer almost patted Mack on the shoulder, then thought better of it.

After a moment of talking and gesturing, the short Italian came over and looked up at Mack. "See here, what's the problem you got with my guy here?"

"I ain't got no problem with him."

"So, whyse you won't make him a pilot?" He pointed angry. He glared angry. He spat the words angry.

Mack might've stumbled or had a hard time saying what he had to say if he hadn't already talked to Guynemer about it. "Cause he ain't a pilot. And what's more, like as not he won't never be a pilot. He's got no feel for the controls. If you don't like it, if you don't trust me to make that call, then why don't you take him to an official school? Someplace where they'll charge you twice as much and want you to fill out a bunch of paperwork."

The Italian man was still pointing and glaring, but he didn't say anything.

"But I'm thinking you're not gonna do that. I'm thinking you and your buddy sit down here every day and watch him fly, and you see he's not getting any better. And I'm thinking you come to the same conclusion I do, only you want to blame me for it. Well, I ain't to blame for it, and I think if you think about it a little bit, you'll see that's so."

"Well, shit, that's about the goods, ain't it?" The Italian looked at Caruso and the other man with them, a big, pale, Scandinavian-looking guy. They smiled at him, mimicked his laugh. "So, tell me, smart guy, what am I supposed to do if I need a pilot?"

"Well, that's easy. Why train one when you can hire one? I mean, you already been paying me."

"And how do we know we can trust you?"

"Who can you ever trust? But, if you want, I can fly Caruso around to places you want, and then you can see I'm on the level. So, whaddaya think?"

"I think we can try this. For a little bit. Then we see."

"Sounds great. Just great."

41.   That's Why I Don't Believe You

Although his brother was gone, Otoniel still felt safer in his sanctuary. The attic was infused with his energy. It was almost like when he would put his arms around Otoniel and hold him close. It wasn't for long, just a brief squeeze, but it was enough. It was strength and love that took all the pain and fear out of him.

Otoniel remembered one time in particular. He was just eight, and he had lost a fight. Bad. He had gone in feeling so confident and strong. But it only took a couple of blows and everything turned upside-down and sideways. He was just overpowered, and soon he was confused and hurt and exhausted. The bigger boy had even rubbed his bloody face in the dust before he left. Otoniel got up as soon as he could, but when he did, he felt himself trembling and he could feel the sobs coming up and his eyes getting moist and heavy. He knew he was going to cry, and that was the last thing he needed—for the other boys to see him crying after he had been beaten up so badly.

He began to run toward home, but he only made it a few steps before a strong arm grabbed him and almost pulled him off the ground. With the tears and the blood and the dust, he couldn't even see who it was, but he recognized the voice. His brother said, "It's okay, Oto. Everyone who fights loses sometimes." And then a second arm wrapped around him and pulled tight. Then it let him go.

Otoniel stood there for a moment, and the urge to cry left him. He still had a little bit of adrenaline shakiness. By the time he felt well enough to look, his brother had joined some of the other older boys playing ball.

Today, Otoniel came up here to flee the things he saw on the street. He could see them from the window of his room or the parlor, but up here the tiny window let in little light and didn't offer a view of the street. And, even better, he didn't feel compelled to look.

He wanted to maintain the magic and sanctity of this place. He went to the cabinet in the rear corner of the attic and opened it up. Inside, there was a bottle of oil and some old rags. He took them out and walked back to the center of the room. He took the saddle down off the wall and inspected it to see whether it needed cleaning. But it didn't. It was in great shape. Mamacita was thorough in her housework. It was just a little dry. He poured some oil on the saddle and began rubbing it in with a rag.

He had never oiled the saddle before, but he had watched his brother do it. His brother had been proud of how he could get the oil into all the filigree decorations, and he had told Otoniel all about it. Otoniel tried himself. He poured the oil at one end of the decoration, then tipped the saddle to help it run all the way through. Unlike his brother, he didn't know exactly how much to pour in, so he had to pour a second and third time to get the entire filigree, and then there was a little extra.

That was okay, though. He just began rubbing there. He rubbed in small circles the way his brother had told him. The motion warmed the oil and leather, and the smell of it rose up into his nostrils. He remembered his brother smelled like this sometimes. It got up in his nostrils and his eyes began to feel wet. It must be irritating his eyes.

He put down the saddle and laid the rag on top of it. Then he went to the kickwall and pulled out the bottle of tequila. There was a little left. He opened it up, took a drink, then carried it back over to where the saddle was.

The tequila soaked in him like the oil in the leather. He felt warm and loose. He resumed rubbing and the motion felt good. The oil didn't seem to bother his eyes anymore. When he had finished oiling the saddle, he hung it back up on the wall, then headed down the stairs. He left the empty bottle in the middle of the floor.

At the foot of the stairs, he turned and headed down the short hallway toward his room. In the narrow space, he almost ran into Maria. Initially startled, her expression quickly changed to one of anger as she crushed herself against the wall and hurried past Otoniel.

Otoniel's reactions were dulled, so she was almost out of reach by the time he decided to grab her wrist. He pulled her back to him. "Why don't you believe me? I didn't kill that woman!"

Maria struggled for a moment, then said, "Let me go!"

"Tell me!" From their place at the entrance to the hallway, Otoniel could see the parlor window. Things that had been loitering on the sidewalk and in the street, now began to hop with excited glee toward the house.

"No!" Maria said, and tried to get free again. She lifted herself up and pushed with one foot against his knee.

Some of the creatures were now pressing their faces against the glass. Their claws scraped sharply and excitedly, making screeching sounds that sent irritating chills through Otoniel's muscles. They were speaking to one another in agitated whispers. Otoniel could hear them, but either their words were too quiet to be intelligible or they were in some strange tongue. He gripped Maria more tightly. "Tell me!"

"Ungh!" Maria was pushing with all her strength—he could feel her low heel digging into the flesh just over his knee--and now she was trying with her other hand to free herself. "Let me go! You're hurting me!"

"Not until you tell me why you don't believe me. I can see it in your eyes. You think I killed that woman."

Maria pushed hard again, but her shoe slipped off Otoniel's knee, and she partly fell until she was supported only by Otoniel's hand on her wrist. "Augh!" she yelled. Then she looked him fiercely in the eye and asked, "Did you rape Victoria?"

For a moment, Otoniel was stunned. His grip loosened slightly, and Maria almost got away. Then he recovered himself and said, "No—I told you that."

Maria was now standing and trying to pull her arm free, but she wasn't fighting vigorously. She looked Otoniel angrily in the eye. "Did you rape Victoria Guerrero?"

The voices at the window had stopped. Now they were snickering. Their amusement grew, and soon they were laughing deep, hateful, masculine guffaws. "No!"

"Did you rape Victoria Guerrero?"

"No! Shut up!" With his free hand, he struck Maria. She went limp. Shocked in the sudden silence, Otoniel couldn't help but release her.

She caught herself with her hands. She looked up at Otoniel. "That's why I don't believe you." She rubbed the red spot on her cheek.

Suddenly, a key turned in the front door lock. Mama was returning from the market. Maria got up quickly and headed for the back door. She slipped out quickly.

Otoniel turned and retreated to his room. He closed the door behind him and leaned against it. He put his hands on his shoulders, turned his head to the side and tried to hug himself, but his arms were not as strong as Manuel's.

42.   Something I Can Trust

Bart was bustling around Morgan's to try to clean up when the men began to show up. Fast Frank was first, followed by Diego Herrera, then Pal Moygnihan. Tommy Lowe came last. He didn't look too happy about the meeting. Bart ignored his heavy insouciance and kept busying himself working around the place.

Fast Frank looked to Lowe, who made an impatient gesture back. Frank said, "We been looking at our supplies, and we think we can bring together maybe a little more'n half of what the town needs."

"Aw, Hell, Frank, that ain't what we's supposed to talk about first." Frank lowered his head until he was looking at his belly. Lowe said, "We's supposed to talk about how we ain't heard nothing more about this mysterious mayor Bart here is bringing in."

"No, you haven't heard anything. You don't need to hear anything. It's all going forward according to plan."

"Yeah? But how's we supposed to know that?"

"Well, if you thought about it for a while, you'd realize that the elections aren't for a couple months yet. Many of the candidates, including our candidate, haven't even announced for the position."

"So, until then, we've just got your word on this?"

"Yeah."

"So, how's we supposed to believe what you're saying here?"

"You have the same choice of evidence I had: you have a sign, and a proof." Bart pointed to the window at the back of the club where a little bit of the blacking had been scraped away. Fast Frank got up and headed toward the window. "You can look through there and see the sign of things to come. Or you can read the proof." Bart pulled out a beat-up but still sealed envelope.

"Proof?" Tommy got up from his seat. "What's that, and how's it proof?"

"In this envelope is written the name of the next mayor. When he is elected, he will put our people in place. He will do as we ask, and he will ensure the safety of our operation."

"Oh, yeah? Lemme see it!"

Tommy reached for the envelope, but Bart pulled it away. "Patience. First the sign." He pointed to the window, but never took his eyes from Tommy's.

"Jess," Fast Frank said, "It's lighting up!" Diego and Pal rushed to the window. Tommy stayed in front of Bart, their eyes locked.

"Hijo de puta," Diego said, "It's a cross. A flaming cross. The Klan."

"Exactly, my friends. The Ku Klux Klan is taking over and we can ride their robes to power."

Pal said, "But ain't they said they're against liquor?"

"Who doesn't say that in public? Trust me, my liaison within the Klan assures me that once their people are in place within the police department, we will be able to run as much liquor as we can handle. Others will get pinched. Others will get raided. Others will go to college. But we, my friends, will be free to do as we please."

"Hmph," Tommy said. "Signs is all well and good for religion, but they ain't so good for business. I wanna see the proof." He reached again.

Bart again pulled the envelope just out of reach. "You think you want proof, but do you really? A man who demands proof is a man without trust. A man who cannot trust is a man who is also not trustworthy. A man who is not trustworthy is a man who must be watched. Do you really want to know?"

"Yeah, I wants to know."

"Very well." He handed the envelope to Tommy.

Tommy took the envelope and tore it open. He looked at it for a moment, and then he read aloud, "Stapleton."

"Stapleton," Pal repeated.

Fast Frank said, "Yeah, yeah, sure. Wasn't he a judge? Got brought up on charges because he was corrupt?"

"So he's our man?" Tommy asked.

"Yes. He's a Klansman. He might sound distant or even publicly deny it. He may even condemn the Klan in public. But he is one of ours, and he will do as we need him to do."

Frank said, "But he ain't even a candidate yet."

"No, he's not. But there are still months before the deadline to register. He will be registered and he will win."

"And how do we know he'll win?" Tommy asked.

"Because the Klan will make it happen. You think it's a coincidence that the Big Store got shut down when the Klan came to town?"

Frank said, "But that was Van Cise, and he hates the Klan."

Bart looked at Frank. "All tools have their uses. Now that his is finished, he will be discarded."

Frank scratched his stubbly chin. "I dunno. Some folks talkin like he's gonna run for mayor. Takin down Blonger made him pretty popular."

"He won't run. He's finished. You'll see."

Tommy said, "And in the meantime, we just trust your word?"

"No." Bart walked up to the bar. "In the meantime you trust the money." He reached behind and pulled out four bundles of bills. "And if you don't, go ahead and try to work against us and see what happens."

"Hey," Tommy said, "now you're talkin." He picked up the bundle, riffled it, then hit it against his other hand. "That is something I can trust."

Pal Moygnihan and Fast Frank also walked up to the bar and grabbed their money. Herrera stood by the window, still looking at the flaming cross. Finally shook his head and said, "No sé. No sé." He looked at Bart. "I don't know if I can work with the Klan. I don't think—it's not safe. For me. Y mi familia."

Bart walked over to Herrera. "It will be safer to work with them than to work against them."

"Maybe. Pero . . ."

"Look at Fast Frank," he pointed at Frank, who was lounging in his chair, sloshing the little bit of whiskey in his glass. "He's a Negro, but he's not worried."

"Actually, Gallio, I didn't think about it so much. Maybe he's right." He reached into the pocket of his jacket and pulled the money out. He looked at it.

Bart walked over to the bar and picked up the last bundle of money. "The Klan may say a lot of things out there, but in the end, they's just a business. What they say, that's just advertising. It's like when Coca-Cola puts white folks in their ads. That don't mean they don't want Negros and spics to drink it. They just use white folks cause they look better. They put a Negro in the ad, and some people don't like that. But if they put white folks on there, especially a pretty white girl, who objects to that?"

Bart looked around at everyone. No one said anything.

He continued, "They gots their side of the business, and I got mine. They don't interfere with me and what I'm doing. They don't care who I work with, so long as the liquor keeps going out and the money keeps coming in. And as long as you keep working with us, you's protected. And that's what you want, right? For you and your family." He walked over to Herrera and held out the money. "You want to be protected."

"Protected and paid," Frank said. As he and everyone laughed, he hit the money on the edge of the table, then put it back in his coat.

Herrera laughed too. He took the money and put it in his pocket. But his eyes were unconvinced.

Bart realized that Herrera was the one he would have to watch closely.

43.   Six Fragments from Hermes Tresmegistus

Stefani didn't know what to expect when she reported for work at Thaddeus' library. The library was in an outbuilding behind the house, a converted stable and coach house, it seemed. She had been directed to go around the house, so she came across the front lawn, which was immaculately cared for, and went to a gate beside the house. Unlike the front lawn, the back lawn was blighted. Close to the gate and the house, there were some scrubby weeds, stunted and twisted. As she got closer to the building, there was nothing but bare earth, desolate and hard-packed.

When Thaddeus opened the door, he barely looked at her face. Instead, his eyes went fixedly to her breasts. As a dancer, she was used to men looking at her body, but this was different. He looked at her as if they were not part of her body, as if they were somehow separable. She half-expected him to reach out and snatch them. After a moment, though, he stopped looking and instead led her into the building.

Inside the library, the main level was crowded with bookshelves. There were so many that there was barely any room to move between them, and at the end of every passage, more books were heaped on the floor wherever they could fit.

Thaddeus picked his way through the bookshelves to an open staircase. It led up to the loft, which had been converted into a series of cagelike enclosures. The first one was open, and Thaddeus went in and sat down.

It was clearly a study area. It had a single bookshelf half-full of large volumes. Several more books were sitting on the desk, along with a few notebooks. One was open, both pages filled with tiny, cramped writing.

Stefani looked down the row to the other caged areas. She couldn't be sure because the light was dim, but the next one looked like a chemistry lab and beyond that perhaps an operatory.

Thaddeus lit a lantern. He adjusted the wick, then searched briefly through the papers on the desk before coming up with the piece he was looking for. "Fetch me these volumes. You'll find a taper at the bottom of the stairs."

Stefani looked at the list. The first title was "Six fragments from Hermes Tresmegistus." Nothing else. All other texts were listed similarly.

As Stefani looked down the list, Thaddeus suddenly said, irritably, "Well? Get moving!"

Stefani rushed away, out of the cell and down the stairs. At the bottom of the stairs, sure enough, there was a table with a couple of candles on chamber style holders. There was also a box of matches. Stefani struck a match and lit one of the candles.

She picked it up and headed into the library. In the dim light of the candle, the bookshelves were labyrinthine. There was no central aisle or any easily discernible order for the way in which the shelves were placed. One aisle was on the left side, another on the right. Sometimes the shelves were arranged to create dead-end corridors where books were heaped up against the wall.

The books, too, seemed to be placed in no discernible order. It only took a brief scan to eliminate alphabetical schemes by title or author, and there seemed to be no categories or themes to unify the texts, except maybe a dedication to incomprehensible concepts.

She wandered through the shelves, her nostrils full of the scent of the books: dust, old paper, vellum, glue, the residue of smoke, and under it all an earthy, spicy smell, like cloves and rare mushrooms.

The smell was intoxicating, and the seemingly endless corridors hypnotizing. She soon lost her way and began to lose hope of ever finding her way out, let alone finding the book. And what would Thaddeus think when she came back to him and confessed her failure? Through his disdain, she could feel her father's.

Did she want to dishonor his memory? If he were watching her now, what would he think? She had been given a chance to show she was good for more than just showing off her body, a chance to use the mind that he had always praised so eagerly. He had loved to see her read, to watch her draw, or to listen to her elaborate thoughts. And now here she was, failing to find even a single book in a library. She sank to the ground, feeling exhausted and hopeless.

Through a film of tears, Stefani watched the candle flame. Suddenly, the flame guttered. She felt a chill underground breeze, and smelled it, too, an earthy scent that was much stronger and damper than the general atmosphere. A wax dam broke on the side of the candle, and a runnel went down the side. The flame suddenly brightened. Her amulet throbbed once.

She gasped and found the strength to rise. The breeze was gone but in the candlelight she could see a trace of it in the air, like luminous pollen drifting off a tree. She followed the trace and it led her to a staircase that descended into darkness. The stairs were rough-hewn stones, piled and mortared. They were worn smooth from the tread of many feet.

The chamber below was round. A double row of curving shelves circled the outside of the room. A gap in the shelves led to the middle of the room. She stepped forward slowly, letting the light lead her. The back of the inner shelf was not more shelf space, but a smooth wall covered with inscriptions. She recognized petroglyph-like patterns, Greek letters, and Latin words, but others she could not—pictograms, strange curving letters of sensuous shapes, and other characters she could only presume were letters of some sort. They had been inscribed successively, sometimes one overlapping another. The floor was made of earth, a dusty brown in most places, but in the center it was red like southern clay.

In the middle of this red earth was a small, circular hole. Darkness seemed to splash up out of it in the flickering candlelight, and inside something stirred, like a large fish in too little water, writhing, straining, gasping open mouthed, staring with lifeless eyes, staring suddenly at her. She opened her mouth, but the airless sound came from the creature.

A voice broke in on her reverie. "Do you feel it?"

Stefani spun around and saw Thaddeus standing at the edge of the circle. His eyes were rapacious. She quickly regained her composure. "Feel what?" she asked in what she hoped was a calm voice.

His eyes narrowed. He tilted his head and looked at her carefully. "The air. It's cool and humid down here. It's good for the books."

"But won't they get moldy? Don't the pages stick together?"

"You are thinking of regular books. These are different—they thrive down here."

"Thrive? They're just books." But even as she said it, she could feel the hunger in them, the way they swarmed at the energy coming from the pit like small fry grabbing at scraps from a big fish's meal.

He looked at her again for a long moment, then said, "Vellum. Animal hide. It's best to treat them as though they were alive. You will see. Have you found the first title?"

Stefani shook her head.

"Why not? If you can't find my books, perhaps this might not be the right job for you. And your father always said you were so clever."

"I'll figure it out. It's not like you use the Dewey Decimal System."

He glared at her, then turned and left.

She backed out of the central area. She decided to look for the book again, but this time she would try something else. She stretched out her hand and held it just over the spines of the books. She closed her eyes and felt her way along, not touching the books but close enough that something leapt to her hand like sparks arcing on the streetcar wires. Edging along. She took about a dozen steps, then crouched down. She put her hand on a book. She opened her eyes. It was the title she was looking for.

It was about a foot tall, ten inches wide and four inches thick. The cover was made of leather, but an unusual leather, paler and thinner than she was used to. The pages, too, weren't paper. Perhaps they were the vellum Thaddeus had mentioned. She could see how it required moisture. Now it was pliable, but she could imagine that if it dried, it would become brittle and crack. The writing had been scratched deep into the page, but the rusty red ink was growing faint.

Not that she could read it. The symbols were not a language she knew, but they were not completely foreign. She had seen them before—perhaps in her father's library. As she ran her fingers over the words, the amulet on her breast throbbed, responding as if it knew the words by her touch.

Then she realized that maybe the key to understanding the amulet, finding the identity of the thing in her basement, and perhaps learning what happened to her father, was here in this library.

Suddenly, Thaddeus called, waking her. She had to be careful. He already knew more than her, and he suspected her of being sensitive to the mysteries of the library. If he knew she was learning to read and understand these texts, who knew what he'd do. She could handle that, though. After all, it wasn't like he was the first man she'd played dumb for. She picked up the book and headed up the stairs, making sure to put a little extra wiggle in her hips.

44.   He Doesn't Think They Are Demons

Otoniel didn't sleep much, but he spent a lot of time in bed. At night he stared up into the darkness toward the unreachable ceiling. During the day he couldn't look at it too long or his imagination began to spatter it with blood. So he rolled over onto his side and looked at the empty bed on the other side of the room.

He ignored his mother's calls for breakfast and lunch, but when dinner came around, he got up, hoping to get a chance to talk to Maria. But she shunned him. At the table, she talked around him, making a convincing fiction of not ignoring him, but still not talking to him. Mama was clearly concerned, but she let peace reign.

One day, though, his mother didn't let him ignore her. She pounded on the door for a long time. It was earlier than she usually came to the door, but it was already light outside, so he was lying on his side. After a while of the banging, he yelled, "Go away."

Mama replied, "Tony, it is time to get up. You have to go to church."

So, it was Sunday. Otoniel had lost all sense of what day it was. "No, I don't," he replied.

At this, Mama opened the door and came in. "Yes, you do," she said to Otoniel and went to his closet. She pulled out a nice suit of clothes that Otoniel had left behind when he went to Californiaville. "If you want to spend another day in this house, you will visit the house of the Lord." Then she left, closing the door loudly behind her.

Otoniel knew he didn't have much of a choice. He got up and went over to the closet. He put on the shirt and slacks. Both were just a touch short, but for the most part they fit well. He put on a tie, something he hadn't done since the Thanksgiving wedding. As he was tying the tie, his hands began to tremble. He realized that he really was going to go out of the house, something he hadn't done for several weeks. He took deep breaths and tried to steady his hands.

When they met in the front hall, Maria noticed his trembling hands with disapproval, but she said nothing. Mama didn't seem to notice anything except that her children were ready. She herself wore a black dress with a very high collar. It was attractive and stately, if a little old-fashioned. They went outside the house and saw a lot of people trying to get into relatively few cars. They were mostly Model-Ts, but someone had one of the newer Oldsmobiles.

Otoniel managed to get Mama up into one of the cars, but when he didn't climb in, she began to climb out, so he stood on the running board. Fortunately, it was a short trip up the street to St. Leo's.

The red brick church had two towers, some stained glass, and a grey stone foundation. It was also an Irish church. The Irish were allowing the Hispanic congregation to meet and hold a Spanish-speaking mass in the basement. Otoniel didn't know all that much about American society, but he knew that if you were living with the scraps the Irish threw away, you must be very low.

Nor was it a scrap that was willingly given. As Otoniel helped his mother in through the foyer, past the holy water basin, he looked over at the Irishmen who were standing guard across the doorway into the sanctuary. They were cold, resentful, and on their shoulders there were small, demonic creatures that whispered loudly into the assembly's ears. These men were making it clear that the Spanish mass wasn't being offered for the benefit of the 'Spics,' it was being enforced to keep them from mingling with the others in the congregation.

At first, Otoniel was shocked to see demons in the church. Then he realized that of course they would be here. How else could one account for the fact that so many basic, clear instructions from the Bible were simply ignored? When he reached the basement and saw no demons down there, he didn't think, "There are no demons here." He thought, "Of course a man can't see his own demons. He doesn't think they are demons. He thinks they are justice, piety, and common sense."

But Otoniel was also becoming aware of them. Now that he knew they were there, he couldn't help but see hints of them. There was a young woman two rows ahead, and when she bowed her head her bobbed black hair lifted up to reveal the pale brown skin of her neck. Every time it happened, Otoniel felt something shift. Leaning one way or another, its claws pressing into his shoulders, he felt its surprisingly heavy weight pushing into his back. He heard it, too. No words, just a raspy breath hot and moist on his ear.

When the mass was ending, and the priest raised the goblet of wine, Otoniel was struck anew by the bloodiness of the ritual. Suddenly it seemed as if the goblet were overflowing with real blood, red and viscous. It poured down the priest's sleeves in a heavy stream, splashing against his cheeks. Then he lowered the goblet, but the stains of blood were still on his cheeks. He went to get the communion wafers, and in his shuffling step, Otoniel heard the squelch, squelch, squelch of the knife, and the white vestments of the altar boys became like blood-spattered snow. Then the priest turned around, but instead of a communion wafer, he held a piece of bloody meat.

When the priest called for people to come up and receive communion, Otoniel pushed his way past his mother. He rushed up the stairs and past the ushers in the alcove into the street. His staggering step turned into a run as the demons came out of their hiding places to curse at him. They hissed and chased, nipping at his heels but never getting too close. Other people's demons. The demons of Americans who feared for their jobs and thought Mexicans would take them away. Or moralists who worried what a brown-skinned man might do to a white-skinned woman. Or the women themselves who held court through slits in curtains and passed judgment over tea.

Otoniel ran up the stairs to the porch and into the house, closing the door hard behind him. Then he fell to his hands and knees in the middle of the room, panting and sweaty.

He didn't know how long he had been in that position, but he became aware that time had passed when the door opened and closed behind him. His arms suddenly ached. He let himself fall to the ground, then rolled over onto his back. He wasn't panting now, and his sweat was cold as ice on his back.

Mama and Maria were looking at him. Mama was concerned. Her eyes were moist. Maria was angry.

Mama dropped to her knees beside him. She grabbed his nearest hand and bent down as she raised it to her lips. "Oto, Oto. Jito." She kissed his hand again, then pressed it to her cheek. Her warm tears ran over his knuckles. Then she sat up straight, still holding his hand in both of hers. She looked at him, her eyes still pitying, but her face growing stern. "Oto, you must talk to the father. When was your last confession? Whatever is hanging over you, give it to Jesus to forgive. The Virgin Mary will make soft his heart. There is no crime so terrible that it cannot be forgiven."

Otoniel looked from his mother to Maria, who was still staring at him, unmoved. He pulled his hand away. He crawled backward away from the two sets of eyes on him. "You don't understand. Sins confessed with the lips do not touch where the real problem is." He almost began telling her about the demons, then suddenly realized that she wouldn't understand. Instead, he raised his left hand outstretched to her. "If it were my hand, I would cut it off. If it were my eye, I would pluck it out. "He motioned as if to tear his eye out, then beat his chest, "But even if I cut my heart out, the sin would be still deeper than that. There is no way to confess and be forgiven for sin that seeps out of every part of me. Sins that are me." Otoniel got up and rushed down the corridor to his room where he slammed the door and threw himself on the bed.

It was not long before Maria came into the room after him. She spat at him, "You're guilty, you dirty bastard!"

Otoniel rolled over and looked at Maria, his arms wide and suppliant. "Please, please, please! Leave me alone. Out there I am pursued and hounded mercilessly. In here, I am supposed to be safe. Please believe me that I didn't kill that woman."

"I don't know about that. But you raped Victoria."

Otoniel shook his head. "No, no, no!" He rolled over and fell out of bed. He got onto his knees and crawled toward Maria. "I am innocent!"

"Why should I believe you?"

"Please don't make me tell. Believe me because I am your brother."

"I can't trust you."

Otoniel sobbed for a few times, then he took a deep breath. "Victoria was drunk . . . passed out. Juan C had brought her. There were a few of us. Someone said she wanted it. Someone said we should take turns." He hit his head on the ground twice, then took a deep breath. "When it was my turn, I couldn't make it happen. I didn't do it—I couldn't do it."

Maria stepped back away from him, heavily. Otoniel looked up, and her eyes were angrier than ever. Her face was red. "You think that makes you innocent? You think that excuses you? You were there, and you would have done it. You didn't try to stop it, and you never told the truth. Impotence is not innocence!"

"No, you don't understand—I couldn't do it, because I knew it was wrong."

"You knew it was wrong, but you let it happen anyway? When you see a woman being raped, and you do nothing, you aren't an innocent bystander—you are a rapist." Maria ran from the room and slammed the door behind her.

Otoniel lay on the floor. Although he could feel its solidity below him, he still had a sensation of falling. He realized that he hadn't really believed what he told Mama about confession. He had thought confession would bring relief, but now he realized how terribly right he had been.

45.   Break the Machine

Bart stood at the front of the room with a small notebook in one hand, held open with his thumb. "Frank, it says here you've got a guaranteed 700. Tell me what they're doing tomorrow."

"They's votin, then they's drinkin. My people are putting Carlson first, then Stapleton."

"You have six meeting places. Did you get your supplies?"

"Yes. It's all ready for the morning.

"Good. Herrera—1000 voters?"

"Sí. We meet at eight places, then we go to the polls. My people vote for Briggs first, then Stapleton."

"Excellent. Lowe—1000 voters?"

"Yeah, yeah. That's right. We're all set. We meet at 10 places, and I think we got all the booze we needs."

"Right. And your vote?"

"My people put Stapleton first and Briggs second."

"Moygnihan?"

"I think I's got 1500."

"Don't overestimate. We need a real count."

"Okay, okay, I'm thinking maybe 1200. My people put Stapleton first and Carlson second."

"Yes, I think that's right. And I think that'll do it. The numbers look right, but only if we deliver 'em. It's supposed to keep snowing tomorrow. Very cold. You'll need to employ cars or trucks to get people to the polls. And keep count. If you don't hit your numbers, you'll need to go to the doors of people in your neighborhood. Let them know the benefits of voting and what happens to people that don't vote. And make it worth their while. Booze and a meal for everyone who voted. We may need to be able to count on them in the future."

"But," said Lowe, "If the Klan is such a big deal, why they need us to help mobilize the vote?"

"Mayor Bailey has thousands of city employees here, including many he just hired. They are all going to vote for him. If we are to break his machine, we need something impressive. And that means you guys, along with the Klan, and along with the unions. That means getting out a bunch of rubes that don't pay enough attention to care. That means giving them something they do care about: some hooch and some food and maybe a couple bucks here and there if they bring some friends along. It means getting out one of the biggest turnouts in Denver's history. If we do that, we can break Bailey's machine."

"Yeah?" said Lowe. "And then what?"

"Then we've got the city in our hands. And if you thought the Big Store was good for business, you ain't seen nothing yet. We won't just have the cops, we'll have the entire city in our pocket, from the beat cop to the mayor's office himself. And then just watch the dough roll in. Just you wait."

There was a moment of silence as Bart looked out at the men sitting at the tables. Then he said, "But that only happens if we get the vote out tomorrow, and win. So go do it!"

People got up out of their chairs sluggishly, but it was clear that they had been affected. They would do what needed to be done to secure their own "Big Store."

When everyone was gone, Bart sighed. He didn't like working on the elections. It reminded him too much of what his father had said about Robert Speer's Big Mitt. "We came across from the Old Country because of a delusion. They say it is a land of freedom, but it's really a land of money. And the government, it is by the rich for the rich.

"Let me tell you, the man who owns a factory, he tells all his employees they are lucky to have a job, and he tells them that if they don't vote the right way, they won't have a job tomorrow. So the people in the factory go out and do what they are told. And if the man their boss wants doesn't win, they get fired anyway. That is not freedom."

No, that was not freedom. And it was not democracy, especially with the kind of scheme that he was running here. But it was the country that his family had come to, and the one where he had to make his living. And it was easy enough to do, because everyone seemed to agree on the rules: making money was the goal and everything else was just the means to do it.

The door pushed open and the bell disturbed Bart's thoughts. The place was technically closed because of the storm, but he had forgotten to get up and lock the door after the others had gone. The man holding the door open was the big grey-complected bodyguard. And under his careful protection, the old dry man walked through. Or tottered rather. He moved slowly across the floor and then even more slowly climbed up into the seat.

Bart had his glass of water waiting for him. The man drank thirstily, then put the glass down. Bart refilled the glass. The man said, "I trust everything is ready for tomorrow."

"Yeah. It's all a go. We're gonna get the vote out. All old-fashioned-like."

The man had drunk another half glass "Good," he said.

Bart looked at the man, and he suddenly had a feeling that here was a man who didn't seem to agree on the same rules. "So what's your line?"

"Hmm?"

"Your work. What do you do to make dough?"

"Ah, yes. I suppose you could say I am a teacher."

"A teacher, huh? And how does this make money for teachers?"

"That is what makes you people so easy to predict: you all only want one thing. But there is much more to our world than just money."

Bart felt annoyed at the old man's raspy superiority. "Oh, yeah? And what's that? What do you want?"

The old man was in the middle of drinking water. He put it down, then said, "I am a teacher. I live to spread knowledge." He pointed a trembling finger at Bart. "I have already taught you a thing or two, but perhaps I can teach you one more right now. Gallio is an Italian name, isn't it?"

"Yeah," Bart said, and involuntarily stopped wiping the glass in his his hands. "My grandfather came over."

"Yes, well. Perhaps Gallio is not the smartest name to have when allying with the Klan. Perhaps I might recommend Galey or Galler. I would start rehearsing it. They will ask."

The old man got down from the chair and began tottering out of the club. Bart watched him go. Bart realized he was still holding the same glass. He tried to put it on the counter, but he only made it halfway, and the glass slipped off, crashing on the ground and shattering into pieces.

46.   The Mule

Mack landed in the designated field. He knew it by the French flag on the side of the barn. An unusual sight this far west in the Provinces, but nothing to arouse suspicion.

For Mack, it did his heart good to see the familiar Tricolor that he had grown to love and admire during his fighting days. He zoomed over the field once, saw the men waiting there with the crates of hooch. Then he banked, cut his engine and glided in for a landing. There was plenty of room in the field, which seemed like it was kept close by grazing.

Guynemer didn't land, just circled up above. He landed less and less these days, which was okay. He was a distraction on the ground.

The farmers brought the crates out across the field. The crates weren't labeled, but they opened them to show the contents. Canadian whiskey, Irish whiskey, Scotch whiskey, French brandy, Russian Vodka, and more. All good labels, too. He recognized many of them from his time in France, and he appreciated the potential value of the cargo. A cargo of just regular whiskey in his plane was worth more than enough to justify his fee, but this cargo of rare, imported liquor would be worth a fortune.

Mack loaded it into the plane himself. He wanted to make sure it got in there secure, so none of it was damaged in the loading process, and none of it would shift during flight. The passenger space of the Jenny wasn't ideal for transporting cargo, but with some ropes and a blanket, he was able to get them securely in.

One man didn't come across the field. He just stood by the barn, smoking. It was clear he was no farmer, in his stylish suit, chesterfield, and fedora pulled low over his eyes. The representative from the gang in Denver, here to oversee the delivery and pay the bill.

Once the hooch was loaded, the farmers brought out a couple of cans of gasoline. Mack filled the plane's tank, then walked around the Jenny. In the air circus he had learned to be his own mechanician, which was easy with the Jenny. Slow as the mule it was named after, it was also as reliable, except for the OX-5. But since the engine was anything but as strong as an ox, the Jenny was designed to fly with little power, so it was an excellent glider, and engine failure was rarely a disaster. Mack pulled on the guy wires, checked his oil, looked over the OX. Then he climbed back into the plane. He yelled "contact," then listened appreciatively as the engine sputtered to life.

He taxied to the end of the field, gave the motor a few revs to make sure it was ready for flight, then put the throttle all way down. He could feel the weight of the hooch in the plane's sluggish response, but about a dozen feet before the end of the field it began to rise and easily cleared the low sheep fence at the field's edge.

The engine wasn't happy, so Mack throttled it down. The day was good for flying, not too hot and not too cold, which was good because the water-cooled OX had a tendency to overheat or freeze. Up ahead, Guynemer was climbing up into the clouds, so Mack pulled back on the stick and began to climb as fast as the OX would let him. He had to get up higher anyway to find the road that would guide him south. There it was. The junction at the river must be Big Beaver, and that road was the one he wanted. He could follow it over the border and then he would have to dodge over to take another one.

The day was sunny and the clouds were high, so navigating by the ground was easy. Guynemer wanted to do more than just fly, and he swooped and taunted. "Easy enough for you," Mack said, "You don't have to worry about your cargo—or fuel!"

But after a little while he decided to engage Guynemer, just to relieve the boredom. After a couple of test maneuvers to make sure his cargo really was secure, the two were swooping and diving in a mock dogfight in which the French Ace's spectral Spad proved again and again its maneuvering superiority to the Jenny.

Another couple hours later, Mack was regretting his choice. The Jenny was making intermittent sputtering noises. The gauge said half full, but it often stuck. The motor never lied about its need for fuel.

Mack kept scanning the ground for that little town with the red clock tower. There, he spotted it. Now, banking from south toward the setting sun he should see the clearing he was looking for. There it was. And none too soon, as the Jenny's motor gave up and died. In the whistling quiet that followed, he was very thankful for the Jenny's optimal glide ability.

Still, with the extra weight and the low altitude he had been flying to navigate, it was going to be a close thing.

The Jenny was falling too quickly, and soon he could hear the disturbance in the tree branches by his wheels. The spreader bar then clipped the top of a tall one with a jolt, and the entire plane tilted downward as it broke away the top cluster. But toward the clearing the trees were shorter, and he just coasted in.

The grass in the clearing was tall, but sparse. It wasn't an old homestead, and there were a few patches of volunteer winter wheat, but the place was likely used as a hunting lodge, if it were regularly used for anything at all.

Mack jumped down and ran to the root cellar where the gas cans were hidden. He ate a quick lunch of cheese, hard bread, and pickles. Really hard bread—he had to dip it in the brine to make it edible. It was hard to get the motor started, but once the fuel pump had been primed, the motor caught and he was on his way.

As it was getting darker, navigating got tougher. There weren't good maps this far north, and the lack of electric lights made it hard to spot all but the largest towns. It might have been easier to be able to use the main roads, but of course he didn't want to attract attention and get too near any of the major populated areas.

It was almost full dark by the time he reached the last town he was supposed to follow. It was hard to recognize—he only knew it as the town with three steeples. In the dim glow from the town's sparse lights, he had to circle it twice to see the third one and confirm it was the right town. As he veered off to the southeast, he hoped the guy at the next field remembered to light the signal fire.

There was a heavy breeze out of the south and it buffeted the wooden frame of the Jenny. The motor sputtered when he tried to put the throttle down. So he just let it pull along, a little over stall speed, and looked for the signal fire.

He was just about to give up when he spotted it. He had been heading too far south, so he banked to the east. When he got close, he cut the motor and glided down.

The tough tending the field didn't smile and didn't talk. He barely looked at Mack, but went directly to check on the cargo. Once he had counted the crates and checked their contents, he afforded a grunt. Mack responded with a grunt and a gesture to ask for help pushing the plane into the barn. As they were pushing the plane, Mack noticed that Guynemer had landed, too. He leapt adroitly out of the cockpit and walked casually across the field as he took off his flight helmet. What could he want?

After they stowed the plane, the tough went out to his car to sleep. Mack laid down on a cot set up in the barn. He smiled—it reminded him of when he was at the Somme. Those were heady days. He would have been happy to drift off to sleep with his reminiscences, but Guynemer was there and clearly had something to say.

He tried to ignore him, but in the silent dark he could feel the French Ace's eyes on him.

Finally, he said, "What?"

"Nothing. I just hope you're happy with yourself. You've been given the gift of flight, and this his how you squander it. The stunt show I could understand. It was gauche, almost degrading, but it was flight.

"This, though? Your plane, the mule. Appropriate, no?"

Mack propped up on one elbow and looked at Guynemer. He was smoking and spectral smoke drifted around his head. The tip of his cigarette never glowed, though.

"There won't always be wars. There may be many less. I'm not so naïve to think there won't be more, but there may be fewer now that Europe's sorted out. Now the airplane needs to be used for other things. Like airmail. Important letters can be delivered faster now. Maybe that will help stop the wars, too."

"Perhaps, but this work is not for you. There will be another call. You need to make sure that you and your plane are ready when it comes."

"What does that mean?"

"You will see. When the opportunity arises, take it."

The rest of the return journey took two more legs and most of the next day. At the airfield, his plane was wheeled into one of the temporary hangars, where the liquor was unloaded.

He was paid $150. Not bad wages, much better than what he was making at the flying circus. He was thinking he could afford a little extra fuel for recreational flight, so he went over to the fuel hut. He was stopped in his tracks by what he saw inside. There was a gleaming engine, barely used, set up on blocks behind the counter.

He leaned forward to speak closely to the man behind the counter. "Is that a Hispano-Suiza?"

"Yep," said the man, "it's practically the only thing left of a jenny that crashed here last week. Guy didn't want to fix the plane, so he sold the engine."

"How much?"

The man looked hard at Mack and said, "Two hundred."

Mack countered, "One hundred."

"One seventy-five."

"One fifty."

"I don't think I could go lower than one seventy-five."

"What about one fifty and an OX-5 in trade?"

"That piece of junk." The man was quiet, but his lips were moving. He seemed to be doing math in his head. "Okay, but you gotta help me break down the engine for parts."

"If I get to use your tools to install the Hispano-Suiza."

"That's a deal. If you know what you're doing, maybe you can even earn a little money around here monkeying with the planes."

"Since I just spent my last dollar, I think I could use that money. After all, a guy's gotta eat."

47.   Peaceable Assembly

The president was in town, and it was a great nuisance. Stanley wanted to speak to the Colonel, but he and most of the rest of the city was in an uproar. It was Monday, but Stanley still carried the Sunday paper under his arm. He probably couldn't have gotten to see a church man like Van Cise on Sunday, but most Mondays the man would be hard at work, not traipsing around like a minor sideshow freak in this ridiculous moving circus.

The parade finally came to its end near the Auditorium, where the president's guards in dark suits and dark hats got out, followed by the president himself. Rotund, jovial, waving. Dressed in white pants, white shoes, and a straw boater, the man was clearly enjoying his rolling party. "Harding," Stanley almost spat the name under his breath. After Wilson's desperate, futile attempt to sell the last shred of the peace he envisioned, Harding's "Voyage of Understanding" was a ridiculous farce. Harding was a man who turned out to be so much less than he had seemed. Just a few years before he had seemed such a good candidate. Stanley himself had almost voted for him. But now, after the man had surrounded himself with cronies and some of them had shown themselves very, very corrupt—he was such a diminished figure.

Wilson, on the other hand, was the opposite. The slight scholar had seemed such a no-account person with his absurd occupation of Vera Cruz and sending his expedition after Pancho Villa. But when he came to France, it was clear he knew what was at stake. Unlike most of the politicians there, he was not so insensitive that he couldn't feel what had been buried in those fields of France. And that's why it had struck at him, taken him down.

And now this joke of a president was keeping Stanley from doing what he needed to do to stop another such beast from rising up here, in the middle of America.

Toward the end of the retinue, Van Cise came out of a car, trotting along like the little dog at the back of the pack. "Colonel," Stanley shouted, stepping forward out of the crowd. Two Denver police put their hands on him. Stanley could feel that one of them was a Klansman. But Van Cise turned around. Stanley looked at him sternly to convey the importance of what he had to say.

Van Cise waved the policemen off. "It's okay, officers. I know this man. He's obviously got something important to say. I'll talk to him over here."

Van Cise led Stanley over to an area that the police were keeping clear, but was out of the main flow of dignitaries. "Okay, Stanley, what's so important that it can't wait until the president leaves town?"

"That clown is a distraction," Stanley said, angrily.

"Harding is our president. He deserves our respect."

"Wilson was our president," Stanley said, gesturing between the two of them. "That man just took his place."

"Nonetheless, Harding is the president and deserves respect."

"He's still a distraction."

"From what?"

"From this." Stanley pulled out Sunday's paper and pointed at the large ad that read, "At Last—You Can Know—All about the Ku Klux Klan!" Van Cise took the paper. As he read, Stanley said, "Two days from now. In that very hall," he gestured at the Auditorium, "they are going to be gathering to recruit new members."

Van Cise hesitated. "They have a right to peaceable assembly."

"You know it won't be that. Have you forgotten Memorial Day at that cemetery? When those men booed you, that didn't feel like a normal audience, did it? Do you really want that kind of audience here, thousands of them in that enclosed space?"

"That's the mayor's business. He probably won't let it go forward. As you said, this is a distraction. Once it's over, he can deal with that."

"I don't think you can count on Stapleton for that."

"Well, we'll see, won't we? Now, if you'll excuse me, I've got to go." He handed Stanley back his paper, then scurried to get into the Auditorium before Harding started talking.

Stanley rolled a cigarette. "Yeah, we'll see," he said as he began puffing and walking away. He pushed his way through the crowd, then walked further down the street. Although many local high-muck-a-mucks were gathering at the Auditorium for Harding's speech, Dr. Locke wasn't.

Stanley made his way up to the café where could spy on Locke's office. He sat down with his back to the office and closed his eyes. With his mind, he felt his way across the street and up the stairs. He tried to feel his way in under the door, but he encountered a ward. Like most wards, it didn't feel like a wall. More like a strong current, and it made it very hard for him to push his way inside. The effort strained him. With practiced ease he brought his coffee cup up to his lips without opening his eyes and took a sip of the strong, sweet drink, then chased it with a long drag on his cigarette. Thus fortified, he managed to push his way in.

Locke was there. As were Saluzar and his body guard. And another man. Stanley didn't know him, and just got a vague impression that the man's temporal power was greater than his spiritual. Then Stanley felt himself sucked out the door, and he opened his eyes. Panting and sweating, he got up from his chair. He went over to the counter and put his empty cup and saucer down. "I'll have another, and this time make it stronger."

The man behind the counter, Chet, who had long since learned to trust Stanley, nodded faintly. After pouring the coffee, he took a metal cream carafe off the shelf and poured a thin brown liquid into the cup.

Stanley finished the cup in two long drinks. Mixed with the poor-quality coffee, Stanley found the moonshine almost palatable. He had a second "strong" cup, then settled in to nurse a cup of regular coffee.

The wave of people leaving the Auditorium washed over the café and receded. Stanley had another cup. It started to grow dark. Locke and the unknown man turned in. Saluzar and his bodyguard left. Stanley didn't dare get out and tail them. It was all he could do to keep himself concealed here in the café. Out on the street he would be conspicuous. He did reach out tentatively, though, just enough to confirm that Saluzar was heading to his hotel.

Stanley decided to do the same. There would be plenty of time for them to face off tomorrow. But then he remembered that little room where the only one waiting for him was a bottle. Ever since he saw Harding, he had been thinking of France. Not of the fighting, but of afterward. Digging in the blood-soaked earth. Filling it up with bodies. And parts of bodies. And the maggots in them. He thought of the ritual, trying to lock that beast in there. Though there were a hundred sorcerers working together, it was the hardest work he'd ever done.

So if he went back to his hotel, he was pretty sure he would hit that bottle and finish it. In his current mood, there was no avoiding it. His only hope was having a couple more here then heading back. He might be too exhausted and just pass right out when he got there.

After a couple more drinks, Stanley managed to get himself up and out of the café. He got himself into the general area, then stopped to pull out the piece of paper with his address on it. He frowned. It was just what he thought. Despite himself, he was beginning to remember where he was staying. He would have to move soon.

The next day, Stanley let himself sleep in. He wanted to give events some time to show their shape before he talked to Van Cise. That and he felt terrible. Goddamn moonshine. He couldn't wait for real liquor to be legal again.

Stanley rolled himself a cigarette and sat on the edge of the bed smoking until he was ready. Then he headed downstairs. In the lobby of the hotel there was a late morning edition. It was just as he expected: the NAACP and the Knights of Columbus had demanded that the mayor not let the Klan speak. People were reminded of the mayor's condemnation of secret government, and of President

Harding's own condemnation of the masked order: "It is un-American and inherently vicious."

When he read that, Stanley snorted under his breath, "Even a stopped clock is right twice a day."

Stanley put the paper down and headed out to the café, where he ordered a cup of coffee. While he waited for his cup, Stanley started his breathing exercises so he would be ready to peer inside Dr. Locke's office. When the coffee came, Stanley took a couple of sips. When he felt himself renewed, he reached out to the office.

Dr. Locke and his unknown guest were awake and eating. Stanley couldn't tell much more without risking being seen. He wasn't quite ready to eat yet himself, so he finished up his cup of coffee and headed toward City Hall.

Stanley made his way down to Van Cise's office. The door was open. Stanley walked in. Van Cise sniffed the air, then looked at Stanley suspiciously. Stanley said, "Well, whaddaya hear?"

"If you read the paper," Van Cise said, "I hear the same as you. The mayor's been visited by groups objecting to the Klan rally, and he's thinking about it."

"You wanna put some money down about which way his thinking is going to go?" Stanley began rolling a cigarette.

"I don't believe in gambling."

"Yeah, it figgers. You don't believe in gambling if there's even a chance you might lose. It doesn't matter that your office almost demands that you take the risk on this one."

Van Cise stood up, wagging his finger angrily at Stanley. "Are you saying I don't live up to the commitment I made when I took this office?"

"I didn't say that, but it might say something if that's what you came up with outta what I said."

Van Cise hit the desk with his outstretched finger. "When I took this job, the police in this town were run by a fixer and his mob." He pointed in the direction of the jail. "That fixer and most of his mob are in jail now because of me. Don't tell me I don't have the courage for a fight."

"Yeah, and what happened next? You have the police run by a mayor whose strings are being pulled from somewhere else. And all of a sudden you no longer have the courage for a fight."

Van Cise sighed. He sank down in his chair. "It's not that I don't have the courage. It's just that I get the sense that this isn't really my fight. It's somebody else's. Maybe yours."

Stanley gently hit the edge of Van Cise's desk. "That's too bad, because we could really use your help in this fight." Then he turned and left Van Cise's office.

Stanley went back to the little café. He got a cup of strong coffee and reached out across the street. Dr. Locke, the mystery speaker, and a couple dozen other Klansmen were gathered in the cellar office. Again, he didn't dare listen to what they were saying for fear of giving himself away, but he sat meditating and monitoring their movements.

At one point, Saluzar and his bodyguard arrived. They were delivering something. They handed it off, then sat at the back of the room, letting Dr. Locke and his out-of-town guest continue running the meeting. Stanley couldn't tell what they'd brought.

Stanley was surprised when the attendant came out from behind the counter and asked him if he was going to order another. "You can stay if you've got more money to spend, but you sure as hell can't sleep here."

Stanley blinked, surprised at the man's angry tone, off balance from the dim light and his achingly full bladder. "Yeah, gimme a reg'lar coffee. And a sandwich. I don't care what kind." He looked at the falling light outside, then back at the attendant. "You got the evening editions?"

"Yeah," the attendant responded, much friendlier now. His thin face, saggy around a mouth half-empty of teeth, was practically beaming.

"Then gimme as many as fit on this." He put a quarter down. "If any of 'em got the Klan story on the front, pick 'em first. Otherwise, I don't care which ones."

Then Stanley headed to the toilet. When he came back, there was a steaming cup of coffee, a ham sandwich with a pickle, and two newspapers, both with the Klan story on the front.

Stanley ate eagerly. He had no idea how hungry he'd gotten. He read, too. It seemed that the mayor hadn't made any decision about the upcoming talk. He'd met with more delegations, too, including major supporters of his campaign. And there was rumor that the governor had sent him a telegraph to say the meeting should be stopped. But it was all still up in the air.

Stanley was about halfway through his coffee when there was a disturbance behind him. Stanley turned around just enough to tell what was happening through the corner of his eye. Men were dispersing from Dr. Locke's office under cover of dark. Stanley finished his cup of coffee as the last of the men set out. Then he got up, went through the door into the speakeasy, past the guard who knew his face, and into the back alley that allowed him to catch up with the Klansmen. Even if they picked up they were being tailed—which they wouldn't— they'd have no idea where he came from.

Stanley got close enough to the group of three men to see what they were carrying—what Saluzar had delivered—a sheaf of posters. He tailed them as they traveled past the state capitol to a large cathedral, the Immaculate Conception. They plastered the doors with posters, then headed on.

When they were gone, Stanley went up to the doors. As expected, the posters advertised the talk the next day. And they radiated power. Stanley could feel a faint hint of fear tingling in his hands as he held them over the posters. *Confident bastards*, Stanley thought, then turned to head back to his hotel. He rolled a cigarette and drew deeply on it as he passed in the shadows between streetlights, as if he relied on its glow to lead him home.

The next morning, Stanley wasn't eager to get out. He couldn't tail all the Klansmen, and he knew where to find them when it mattered. He just went down a couple times to get the paper. In the morning, he read that the rally was off. Not the mayor, but some administrative civil servant had made the call. In the afternoon, he read that the mayor had reversed the decision. The rally would go on as planned.

About seven, Stanley put on his jacket and headed out. When he reached the Auditorium, the place was already crowded. Half an hour before the doors were to open, and the crowds were lined up around the block. It was almost as big a hullabaloo as the president's speech had been. Stanley used a few tricks he knew to get up close to the front of the line.

When the doors opened, Stanley went in and wasn't very surprised to see that the hall was prepacked with supporters. He found a place toward the back and watched as people filed in. Between the crowd and the stage there were many officers in uniform. It didn't take much concentration to tell that they were Klansmen. The residue of it was on them from a recent meeting. After a while, the organ recital started with "Onward Christian Soldiers."

As the organ died out, a Klansman who introduced himself as the Manager of Safety said he wouldn't tolerate any rowdiness. If rowdiness did break out, the rally would be broken up. Then the speaker came out. Applause roared. He unfolded an American flag and draped it across a table on the otherwise bare stage. Then he led a rendition of "The Star-Spangled Banner." After the caterwauling stopped, he introduced himself as George C. Minor. He said he was here as a law-abiding American who only wanted to talk to people who were open to his ideas. If anyone had any objections, he would cancel the meeting.

And the objections started right away. One man stood up, then another, a man in uniform, who announced that he was a priest at the Cathedral of the Immaculate Conception. Further remarks were lost in the hooting and hollering of hecklers. This went on for a while, as all the energy that had been built up in the meetings and singing began to be released.

Then the Manager of Safety came out and declared the meeting over. Stanley got up out of his seat and stood against the back wall, watching as the hall quickly emptied. As the last people were filing out, Stanley saw the Colonel. He made his way over to the DA, catching up shortly after they left the hall.

The DA was ashen, but he seemed relieved to see Stanley. "You said there would be violence," Van Cise said.

"Yeah," Stanley said as he began to roll a cigarette, "but I was wrong. It was much worse than that."

"Yes," Van Cise said.

"They've demonstrated they can fill that hall and empty it as they please. That's what everybody who was here saw and everybody who hears about it will know for sure. The Klan has shown its power."

Van Cise looked at the hall for a short while, then said, "When I took office, I dedicated myself to the eradication of organized crime. If the Klan isn't organized crime, then I don't know what is. This is my fight, too. Let me know if there's anything I can do to help."

Stanley scratched his chin. He was overdue for a shave. He said, "I dunno. I might need some muscle for my fight. There was a Ranger I worked with when we were doing the raids. Carl something-or-other. I trusted him and he might be useful. Think you can put me in touch with him?"

"Sure," Van Cise said. After a short pause he said, "That's not very much. I'll have to do more on my side."

"Of course. Every little bit helps." But when Stanley exhaled, he watched the smoke get swept away instantly in the warm night air.

48.   Puta Americana

Despite Otoniel's protests, the family was coming over. They wanted to celebrate his release. Otoniel said it was too late for that. Or too early. Probably both. Although he had been released months ago, he had not been cleared. A lack of evidence kept the case from moving forward, but it hung over his head. It seemed there were too many police walking down his street too frequently. Mama had said it was in his imagination. She thought a party would cheer him up and wouldn't be put off any longer.

"It's the perfect time for everyone to come over. The plants in the ground are tall, but it's not time to harvest yet. We have more beans than we need at this time of year and plenty of salt pork. Besides, you sit around here and mope so much, you might as well be in prison. If you won't go out to see people, I will bring them to you."

And so it was. It became the biggest gathering since Dolores' wedding. Dolores herself did a lot of the cooking, bringing over a pot of beans, a pot of chile, tortillas, and conchas. She was just visibly pregnant with her second child. The first was unsteadily walking around and was constantly underfoot, mostly clinging to Dolores' legs. Dolores didn't seem to notice and moved around the kitchen freely and quickly.

Her husband, Paolo Muñoz, was dour and untalkative until Padre Tomas showed up and took all the men into the back yard to open the first couple bottles of wine. After that, Paolo became very friendly and spoke glowingly about his wife, her mother, and, as the evening wore on, pretty much every woman in attendance.

Though cousin Berto made a little beer, and some others had hooch hookups, it was when Padre Tomas broke out the sacramental wine that the party got really good.

Otoniel didn't go out back to enjoy the wine. Although the party spilled out into the front and back yards from the small house, Otoniel was afraid to go out. So, with the women in the kitchen and most of the men outside, he found himself alone in the parlor with old Marcos. Although Marcos' body couldn't support him anymore and his spindly frame had to be carried from chair to chair, his eyes were as intense and mean as ever. And the collapse of his nearly toothless mouth gave him an even more sinister appearance. Otoniel remembered his childhood, when Marcos had walked around ordering everyone about, and cuffing those who didn't move fast enough when commanded.

Otoniel sat down in a chair on the far side of the parlor and stared at the opposite wall to avoid seeing Marcos' hard stare. It was several minutes before Marcos said, "Why aren't you in the kitchen?"

Otoniel looked at him. "What?"

"With the other women. You're scared. I can see that from here. A man doesn't get scared, and you're too old to be a boy. You must be a woman. So, woman, get in the kitchen and fetch me a concha y café." Though he was sober, his Spanish was slurred because of his lack of teeth and a slight tremor in his jaw.

Otoniel was stunned for a moment. He wasn't sure he understood what Marcos was saying and didn't know what to say.

"Get!" Marcos said after a moment.

"Call one of the women from the kitchen."

"They're working. They're being valuable. You're sitting there on your culos as if you expect them to make money for you. But that's not going to work anymore. Now you've learned what happens if you become a puta Americana: they will use you up and throw you away."

Otoniel looked into Marcos' lean black eyes. He said, "I've never been a whore for Americans or anyone else."

"You take their money and you lay down. That sounds like a puta to me. My father didn't fight, either. He thought God would watch over him whether his land was in Mexico or Los Estados. He had land. We all had land."

Otoniel remembered the stories about how the family land was lost. "But your land was taken—you didn't fight, either. When they came, your land was turned over the same as everyone else's."

Marcos smiled broadly. He had two dark brown teeth visible, both on the top, decayed and worn. "When they came for everyone's land, Papa didn't fight. And neither did anyone else. There were too many of them. Too many guns. But before that . . . our land was dangerous. One or two men walking out there with nothing but a piece of paper and a badge to protect them could get into real trouble if they didn't know their way around. C'mere."

Marcos' eyes fixed Otoniel like Nosferatu's. Otoniel stood up and walked over. Otoniel expected him to whisper, but instead he reached out and grabbed Otoniel's hand. The grip was painfully strong, and Otoniel found he couldn't break free.

"These are hands that can squeeze the life out of someone. This is what happens when you kill someone, puta. It makes you strong. But you wouldn't know that, all you know is—."

"Marcos!" Mama yelled from the edge of the kitchen.

Marcos released Otoniel's hand. He smiled, showing off his two narrow teeth. "No need to worry, Fe. I was just telling your boy that I think he's innocent."

Mama frowned. "I think it's time you got some sun. I'll call Berto and Manny in to carry you outside."

"Gah!" Marcos' smile became a childish disgust. "If they've been at the Padre's wine, they might drop me."

"Serve you right. Remind you that you're a cripple, and that you depend on other men to support you. Remind you that you depend on Jesus for your daily bread."

Mama, true to her word, rustled up the cousins to carry Marcos outside. Marcos cursed them as violently as he could, but underneath the anger and the hard words was the fear and petulance of a helpless baby.

Still, Otoniel had been pierced by what Marcos had said. Should he have fought when the men came to take him away for a crime he didn't commit? Or should he have fought the men when he realized that they were likely going to kill the heiress?

After they had taken Marcos away, Mama said to Otoniel, "Sometime you should talk to the Padre about how Marcos really feels about the men he killed. He has cried many hours about it."

Otoniel was not sure that helped. Marcos had acted and now he cried. He had earned that right. But Otoniel cried as well. And he had nothing to show for it. Otoniel stood up and wandered around as he thought. At the end of the narrow hallway that led to the bedrooms was a window into the back yard. He looked outside, and he immediately froze. There was Juan Castillo, laughing and smiling.

Otoniel wanted to rush outside and confront him right away, but then he saw demons perched atop the trees at the edge of the yard. Some of them jumped around the branches like monkeys. Others stock still, watching, their leathery wings ready to carry them down to the ground, talons sharp and gleaming. For a moment, Otoniel almost expected the demons to swoop down on Juan. Then he realized that although the demons were watching Juan, they weren't there for him. They were waiting for Otoniel.

Here was the man who actually had raped Victoria. He felt no guilt, and there were no demons for him. He was talking to Marcos, and the old man's eyes made it clear that he considered Juan C to be a real man.

Through dinner, Otoniel tried to keep up his rage, but it was hard to keep the keen edge on his anger with the good food and fun conversation. There were stories about the old days, good natured teasing, and gossip. Otoniel didn't feel like talking, but since most of the men were pretty quiet, with the exception of Padre Tomas and a couple others, it wasn't really noticed. And he did feel better listening to everyone talk. After dinner, the women and men split up again, with the men in the front hall and spilling out onto the front porch, and the women in the kitchen and spilling out the back. Now it would have been a toss-up as to which was the louder as the men engaged in passionate disputes about cars, tractors, livestock, jobs, politics, even streetcar routes.

It was late when everyone dispersed into the night. When the door was closed for the last time, the dishes were washed, everything was in order, and but for the smell one might never have guessed there had just been a party here. Mama and Maria were exhausted and went straight to bed.

He kept turning this betrayal over and over in his head. How could God let Juan C walk around so carefree, when he was so tormented? He realized that Juan's punishment must be left in the hands of God, but Otoniel would have to be responsible for his own atonement.

49.   Kool Kozy Kafe

Stanley could feel that the situation was getting out of his control. The number of Klansmen had swelled dramatically since the Auditorium incident. They were now involved in so many activities that it was hard for Stanley to keep track—and many of them ran out of City Hall.

There were a lot more Klansmen in the police now, especially in the vice squad. Supposedly, the Klan was a moral crusade, and its rhetoric often targeted prostitution and liquor, but in truth, being on vice mostly put them in a position to take graft and to knock over speaks and brothels that didn't pay up.

With the huge Klan gatherings, the Klansmen were mingling a lot, allowing spiritual energies to be transferred from one to the other. This created a lot of noise. It was very hard for Stanley to tell who had been involved in rituals and who had just been a regular attendee at rallies.

Part of his problem was that he didn't know what their plan was. He was just following, observing, and trying to react. If he could figure out what they were trying to accomplish, Stanley might be able to get ahead of them, anticipate some of their strategies. There were many ways to bring a spirit across. For spirits without a lot of power and those that were unbound, a simple conjuration with a circle of power could be used.

But what they wanted to loose was a powerful spirit that had been banished and bound. That required a lot of power and a strong way to focus the power. They were building up the power they needed with this whole Klan ruse. Recruiting the living and the dead for their needs would make the conjuration possible. But just how powerful was this spirit? He did the estimates based on ten thousand Klansmen, and he didn't like the figures he was coming up with. Especially since he thought there might be twice that many Klansmen by the time they were ready to conjure it. It could be a beast as powerful as the one they had put down in Europe. But Stanley had never been very good with these kinds of calculations, so he could be wrong. He hoped he was.

Drawing the energy from the followers took a number of steps, but they could be taken in many orders. Even if the sacrifice Otoniel witnessed were the beginning of the conjuration, there were still dozens of patterns—that they knew of. The Serapeans were constantly innovating, and they may have many other ways to accomplish their ceremony.

It would help if he could figure out how they planned to focus their energy. That could be done in many ways, too. A ley line nexus could be used as a lens to aim the energy. But doing that meant you had to get all your followers out to the nexus, which was probably impractical in this case where so many participants were ignorant rubes. You could also wait for a conjunction. But that was problematic because you had to wait for one, and when Stanley looked in the almanac, it didn't seem any were coming up in the near future.

So they were probably going to rely on a guiding spirit. If they could find a spirit already on this side that would be willing to act as a guide, it could carry and focus the energy to help the other spirit get across. But where were they going to find the right kind of spirit? Stanley wondered about the woman from the club, Stefani. She seemed to have had a brush with something. And the man who picked her up the night Stanley first saw her—he was definitely no stranger to otherworldly powers. But neither of them seemed connected to Saluzar or the Klan. And although Morgan's had opened up again shortly after the raid that shut down the Big Store, Stefani hadn't been back since.

There was another possibility that terrified Stanley, though it was only theoretical: radio. Nobody knew yet whether radio could be used to transmit spells, though early tests seemed to indicate no. But a Klan hangout that had gotten very popular in recent months was The Radio Café. The place had a receiver hooked up, and it played a station inside the restaurant. How the radio was mixed up in all of this, Stanley couldn't figure out, but he was afraid there might be a way to use a tower to focus spiritual energy. Then they wouldn't need a guide or a nexus or a conjunction or anything. They could just do it as soon as they had enough rubes. That thought made Stanley shiver.

So he spent a lot of time outside the Radio Café, which advertised itself as a "Kool Kozy Kafe." Stanley found another place he could watch it from, just across the street and two doors down.

Summer gave way to autumn, and Stanley was putting things together, but, he felt, not fast enough. The pattern wasn't emerging. Then the break came late on a Saturday night. The theater crowds had gone. The Radio Café was getting ready to close. There were just a few men in there still. Then, suddenly, five of the men got up together and headed out. Stanley realized something was up. He got up, too, and headed out to follow.

But just then a large crowd of toughs and molls came into the café where Stanley was. They clogged up the door with their bodies and raucous movements. Stanley tried to push his way through, but the men were just not going to let him by. It took him nearly two minutes to get out the door. Next time, he would remember to bring a charm for pushing through crowds.

The delay was enough. Stanley caught sight of the men just in time to see them take a man at gunpoint into an alley where a car was waiting. As the car pulled away, Stanley angrily punched the corner of a brick building he was passing. He cursed himself even worse, then, because it hurt.

It took several minutes of searching around to find a cab. "Taxi Max!" Stanley called out when he saw the man, almost dozing behind the wheel of his waiting cab.

Max perked up. "If it isn't old Sawbuck himself. Where can I take you tonight?"

Stanley climbed in. "Just drive around. I'll tell you where to go."

"Again? Without even the rain as an excuse today?"

"Drive. Fast! Please."

"Okay, okay!" Max put the car in gear and they headed off.

Stanley closed his eyes and concentrated. The men had been resonant enough that he should be able to track them, if he concentrated. He could feel them, but just faintly. And not knowing how the roads went, Stanley led them down several wrong turns. But then he found the trail steady and he led them far north of the city center. When Stanley could feel they were close, he asked Max to stop the engine. He did, and they rolled to a stop in sight of a tiny little shack in the middle of nowhere. With a car parked outside and a light on inside. And the sound of a number of men actively working as they yelled out.

Stanley wanted to rush right in, but with the five men, caution dictated that he at least survey the situation. That took only a moment. Five guys beating the sixth with the butt of their pistols. Stanley felt that the light in the place came from an oil lamp that was on the shelf just the other side of the thin wall. An oil lamp. Good. Stanley knew its language. He spoke, causing it to flare up brightly, burning its fuel up and going dark in an instant.

The men were startled and scared when Stanley burst in. He cuffed all the five men standing, and they fled out of the room. As they left, Stanley crouched beside the injured man. He had been beaten unconscious, but he would be fine. After Stanley heard their engine igniting, Stanley called on the heat left in the lamp to light it again.

Stanley gave the man a brief inspection. Nothing to worry about immediately. Stanley went back to the taxi, saying, "Take me to a phone."

"You're the boss," Max said.

As they drove, Stanley thought. He had figured out the pattern. He knew what they were up to. Unfortunately, it was not something he could handle himself. He needed help.

Stanley hated writing telegrams. He felt he was either being too cryptic to be understood or he was wasting too much money on extra characters. He was finally okay with this one. POWER ID. REPORT IN MAIL. NEED HELP. 1 TOUGH. 1 SLICK. After the telegram was sent, he went to the post office and mailed the report.

Stanley hoped they wouldn't wait on the report before sending help. He didn't know how much time they had.

50.   Poppies and Burning Crosses

Stanley had received a cable telling him which train his backup was coming in on, so he waited at Union Station. When the train came in, he watched for them, and he picked them out easily. Or one of them anyway. He assumed the man with him was the other one, but he couldn't be sure, until he saw their faces.

The man who gave off an easy-to-pick-up power signature was Mike Tarkus. He was a brute. Very powerful muscle. Both physically and magically. He was a little short and wide, like a bulldog, and you could say he looked like a bulldog—if you were out of earshot.

The other man was Burt Fallow. Slender and subtle, he was one of the best tails you could ask for. Great natural talent for following and staying hidden in plain sight coupled with some of the best stealth magic of anyone in the Chicago Coven. Getting these two made Stanley wonder what Barton had figured out since he told him to come to Denver. Something was making the Coven nervous.

Stanley met up with them, shook hands, then wordlessly turned to lead them out. They got on the streetcar. Got off. Went up to Stanley's room. When the door was closed, they sat down in Stanley's two chairs. Stanley checked around the room, then said, "Did Barton fill you in on what is going on here?"

Tarkus shook his head. "Not much," he said, "but as much as he knew."

"Yeah," Fallow said, "He said he had a lot of unanswered questions. He said your reports were less than helpful."

"There are some things I just don't like to share over distance. I think there's a major conjuring going on here. They're trying to loose an imprisoned spirit."

Tarkus and Fallow leaned forward. "I didn't know there was one shackled here."

"I don't think any of us did."

"You mean . . . ?" Fallow almost jumped out of his chair.

Stanley nodded. "It's an unrecorded spirit. Imprisoned either by a native shaman or possibly prehistoric."

"How powerful?" Tarkus asked.

"I couldn't gauge it according to the standard scale, it's still too hidden. But it's big. Very powerful. It reminds me of some of the entities we encountered in Europe. Something with a huge appetite for blood and the power to feed itself. Once it makes it over."

"How far along is the conjuration?" Fallow asked.

"I don't know for sure. There has been sickness—a smallpox outbreak."

"That damn disease. It gives them so much death to work with."

Stanley nodded. "And they've set up to draw strength from the dead."

"So two out of six, at least. A preliminary sacrifice?"

Stanley nodded. "I think so."

"And the rest?"

"I don't know."

"What about the guiding spirit?"

"I think I've got a lead on one, but I don't know. I don't think they have it. But for the rest of it, we need to do more research before we know for sure." Stanley looked at Tarkus. "That's where you come in, for now. While Fallow and I are tailing people, I need you to research recent local papers and let me know if you find anything that might be a fear event, or rage, in case I missed it. Those are best harnessed closer to the conjuration, so it doesn't seem likely, but we still want to know."

The three of them caught the streetcar down to the library, a tall, stone building with pale grey columns. Tarkus went in.

Stanley and Fallow walked down the street to the Brown Palace. When they first walked in, a bellhop kind of did a double take and almost started to walk toward them. Then he blinked, shook his head and went back to keeping a watch on the lobby. It took Stanley a moment to figure out why, but then he remembered: Fallow was a Negro. Though his concealment charms allowed him to "pass" and walk unhindered into many places where Negroes were not welcome, sometimes people might see through the charms . . . at least temporarily.

They set up in a smoking lodge next to the lobby to wait. Fallow spilled a little water with essential oils in it onto the table. He traced a figure on the surface and muttered some words to help conceal them. Stanley said, "This is the primary sorcerer. He's behind it all. I need you to follow him because he knows me. I think he's pretty sensitive, but hopefully you can keep out of sight." Stanley peeled off a few twenties from his roll and gave them to Fallow. "For expenses." Fallow nodded.

It was a couple of hours before the old man showed up in the lobby with his escort. The two of them cut across the floor and headed up the elevator. Fallow said, "Think they're in for the night?"

Stanley shook his head. "I don't know. I haven't had the chance to follow their movements at night. That's what you're here for. Good luck." He patted Fallow on the shoulder and used the lounge's street exit. Then he walked over to the coffee shop where he kept watch on Dr. Locke's office.

The doctor literally lived in his offices—it was his home as well as a small hospital, so Stanley waited for a long time, nursing several coffees to the extreme edge of his ability before the doctor emerged and headed down the dusk-dimmed street to the garage where he kept his car. As soon as he was out of sight around the corner, Stanley got up and hailed a taxi. He had the driver go slowly around the corner and, sure enough, by the time they had rounded it, there was the doctor in his red Pierce-Arrow.

They followed the doctor at a distance until he pulled off the road and stopped. Stanley had the taxi drive on a bit further, then he got out and paid his fare, telling the driver to go. Stanley doubled back on foot for a little ways, then snuck around a darkened shop. Looking around the corner, he could see three men clustered in front of a truck, the Pierce-Arrow a little ways back.

Dr. Locke had met up with two men, but one of them was obviously his compatriot. The other was a merchant. They were haggling over the price of the cargo of the truck. Stanley took the opportunity to sneak through the darkness to the back of the truck. It was a flatbed with the cargo on it covered over with tarps. The men were still haggling, so Stanley took a wide route around the truck. Then, keeping it between him and them, he snuck up to the truck.

Their deal concluded and one man was heading back to the truck. Stanley realized he was in direct view of the sideview mirror, but he had to check what was under the tarp, so he rushed forward quickly and lifted it up. Wood. Lots of posts. Stanley could feel power emanating from them, but he couldn't immediately identify the wood, so he got out his knife and cut off a small sliver. Then he looked at the truck's mirror and saw a face in it, looking directly at him.

"Wait," the man said, "I see somebody by the truck. He's messing with the load." As the man began scooting across the truck cabin, Stanley blew through his hand, causing black obsidian powder to spray out the other side, which he changed into a thick shadow that covered him as he rushed into the full darkness.

The three men converged on the spot where Stanley had been. They all looked around to try to see him. The merchant said, "It was probably a hobo looking for something to liberate from the truck. How disappointed he must have been."

"Yes," Dr. Locke said, looking more or less in Stanley's direction. "How disappointed." Then Locke and his compatriot got back in their vehicles. The merchant waved as the truck and the Pierce-Arrow drove off, but the drivers didn't wave back.

Stanley watched as the merchant went into the darkened shop, waited a few minutes, then headed back up toward the street. It was quite late by the time he made it back to his room. Tarkus was already sleeping. Stanley shook him to wake him up. Tarkus woke up mid-snore and raised his hands to Stanley. Then he realized who he was looking at and relaxed. He rubbed his eyes and sat up. "'Sthere ye are," he mumbled. "What time is it?"

"Late. Has Fallow been checking in?"

"Yeah, I think so. Pretty regular, anyway."

"Good. Next time he calls in, tell him to get back here. We've got to figure out what to do next."

"Yeah, and what are you going to do?"

"I'm going to get some sleep. I don't know how much we'll be getting from here on out."

"Right." Tarkus stood up and slapped himself on his cheeks to wake up. He started pacing to try to keep himself awake.

Stanley woke up slightly when the phone rang. Tarkus answered it. Stanley heard him mumble, then dozed off again. When he was awakened, Tarkus was standing over him and Fallow was sitting by the door. Fallow said, "You got anything to eat in this joint?"

Stanley shook his head. At the mention of food, his own stomach growled. "That's part of what the expense money was for."

"I was on surveillance. And everything's closed now."

Stanley nodded. "Work will keep us from thinking about food. Something's definitely afoot."

"What'd you find out?" Tarkus asked.

Stanley told them about his encounter with Dr. Locke at the truck. He described the wood pieces, then said, "Any idea what they're for?"

"Burning crosses," Fallow said. Tarkus nodded. "It's something the Klan does."

"Right. A perfect intimidation tactic that would be designed to incite fear across the city."

"And easy to incorporate into an appropriate casting. With twelve burning sites across the city, you could cast a pallor over the entire population."

"Yeah, so now we just need to figure out when they're planning on doing it. Are there any auspicious occasions coming up?"

Tarkus said, "They just missed All Hallow's Eve. That would've been a perfect time."

"And so close," Stanley said. "It's hard to believe they would've missed that if they were aiming for it."

"And the full moon, too," Fallow said, "just the week before that. And the new moon was yesterday. It can't be a lunar cycle."

"So what kind of cycle are they using?"

Fallow said, "I think it's going to be political, the date they use. I mean, you said that they were leveraging some kind of political group to keep people from getting vaccinated and extend the smallpox outbreak, and they used that policeman's funeral as an excuse to harness the dead."

"Armistice Day."

Fallow and Tarkus nodded.

"An all-American organization that is celebrating the veterans and striking fear into the hearts of citizens at the same time. It's perfect."

Fallow said, "They'll do it the night before so everyone will be thinking about it during the day. As they're celebrating Armistice Day events, it will be poppies and burning crosses."

Tarkus said, "And that means they're probably out delivering the wood tonight. And if we want to find out where these crosses are going to go up, that means we have to be out tonight, too."

Fallow yawned. "All right. Let's get going. Where's your car?"

"I don't have one."

"Old man, I can't believe you don't have a car. Didn't they give you expense money?"

"Yeah, but why would I blow it on a car? They're too conspicuous for pursuit, and once your target marks your vehicle, it's completely worthless."

"Old man, take a look at the streets next time. It isn't like it was a few years ago. Even in this cow town there are thousands of cars out there. You can drive a car without catching any attention. And most of the cars are Fords—your target will pick you out before they can pick your black Model T out of all the other black Model T's out there."

Stanley was taken aback. He thought for a moment and he realized that Fallow was right. He had always worked in Chicago using train, bus, and taxi. And he'd gotten along just fine here, too. But sooner or later he would need a car. "Okay, sure. But for tonight, let's use a taxi."

Stanley led the way from the hotel to the taxi stand where they could be found at all hours. There were just two cabs there. Both drivers seemed to be asleep. Stanley knocked on the window of the first cab, and a familiar face looked up.

"Taxi Max," Stanley said.

The sleepy driver smiled. "The very same. Good to see you again. And with friends. Get in."

Stanley opened the back door and everybody piled in.

Taxi Max yawned, then said, "So, where to tonight?"

Stanley said, "We're looking for a truck out making deliveries."

"Shouldn't be too hard to find. Probably not too many of those out at this hour. Everybody is either at home asleep or they've found a cabaret. Whereabouts are we looking?"

"Could be anywhere. So start in downtown and spiral out on some of the better roads a truck might use."

"Will do." He yawned again, but put the car in gear and started off.

Fallow yawned, too.

Stanley said, "Burt, you should catch some sleep. Mike and I have already dozed off for a few."

"Thanks," said Fallow, who leaned his head against the window and let himself doze off.

They drove around for quite a while, then Tarkus said, "There! Look!"

And there was the truck. It looked like it was almost empty. Stanley said, "Follow at a distance, unless you think it's stopping. Then go by."

They followed the truck for a few minutes, when it pulled off the main street into a residential neighborhood. It slowed down and a door opened on a house. A man emerged and walked toward the truck. As they drove by on the main street, Stanley confirmed that the truck was stopping and seemed to be making a delivery. Then he said to Taxi Max, "Okay, now drive around the area for a little bit."

"Anything in particular you're looking for?"

"No. Just drive."

After a while, Stanley said, "Stop the car."

Max stopped the car. Tarkus and Stanley got out. They looked around. They were standing on the top of a hill. The steep slope dropped away suddenly and spread out before them they could see the entirety of the city. "This is where it will be placed," Stanley said.

Tarkus nodded. "And this is where we'll stop the spell."

"Yeah. If we can. C'mon, let's head back to the hotel and catch a little more shuteye."

Although they had been out late, they were back in their places by early morning, except Tarkus. Tarkus had been up on guard through the night, so he was allowed to sleep in while the others got up for surveillance. Stanley was glad of his place at the coffee bar, and he happily splashed out on a second cup of coffee relatively quickly. A lot of people came and went from the doctor's place, but Locke himself stayed in. Stanley tried to remember as many faces as possible, hoping to look for them in the DA's Klan rogue's gallery later. Couriers brought notes from Fallow and Tarkus. Fallow said that Saluzar hadn't been down all day. Tarkus was just noting that he had gotten up and made it out to the site, which he said was called Ruby Hill. It was a little bit of a chilly day for hanging around outside, and Stanley felt sorry for him as having the worst post today.

At lunch time, Stanley moved himself to a café that also had a good view of the doctor's place, though not as commanding. He stayed there until midafternoon, when he was expecting another courier from Fallow and Tarkus. Then he moved back to the counter where he had spent the morning. Couriers came in with notes saying there was nothing to report.

As dark was approaching, Stanley got up and left. Although knowing about Locke's movements was important, he might just as well be taking part in conjurations in his sanctuary, as might Saluzar. The place they could best hope to interfere with the conjuring was at the site of the cross. Stanley and Fallow met at the pre-appointed streetcar stop. They got on the 3 line and rode it out close to the end of the line. Then they got off and headed west. At the streetcar stop, they picked up some food at a chop suey place.

It was a long, uphill hike from the streetcar line to the hill. Tarkus was camped out at the bottom of it, and he hailed the two of them when they reached the park, though it took some time for them to see him in the growing gloom. They got together and ate. Stanley rolled a cigarette and smoked. By the time they had finished, it was full dark and growing quite cold. There were few streetlights out here at the edge of town, and the three of them appreciated the cover it gave them. Stanley took out a flask of hooch and passed it around. The three of them drank slowly in silence, watching the top of the hill.

It was a couple of hours before the car drove up. The three men had long since finished the hooch and now were keeping warm by chanting a heat charm. It was a little more effective than pacing and kicking, and a little less energy intensive, but not much. By the time the car appeared, they were ready for a fight and eager to get home out of the cold.

At the top of the hill, the Klansmen were working in the light of their headlamps. They were struggling to set up the cross, which seemed to be wood wrapped in burlap. There were four of them. Three struggled with the cross, while the fourth sat waiting with a gas can.

Tarkus rushed forward a couple of steps, planted his feet, and let loose with a quick spell. A single word and the cross blew apart. Two of the men who had been helping to set it up fell to the ground. The third turned to face the men coming up the hill. He clearly knew what was happening and was prepared. The man with the gas can put it down and ran frantically for the car.

The third man wound his hand up like a softball pitcher, spoke a word, and sent a flare of violet energy—something between a flame and a spark—at Tarkus. Stanley was in front of Tarkus before it hit, his own shield absorbing the energy, which sparked and burned across the invisible hemisphere. He felt the energy tingling in his outspread fingertips. Not very powerful. As they expected, this shouldn't be too difficult a group to handle. All Stanley had to do was part the shield for Tarkus to make his next attack. Stanley brought the two middle fingers on his right hand together, then split them apart suddenly, creating a gap in the shield.

Tarkus launched his attack through the gap, something like a spectral punch that knocked the man down and out cold. At this point, the other two who had been helping out with the cross realized what was going on and started to run.

That left just the man by the car, who seemed to have found what he was looking for. It was a long, smoky quartz crystal. He pointed it at Tarkus, and a blast of visible energy came out, this time looking like a bright and sharp spearpoint. It hit the shield and at first did not disperse. It pierced several inches in, and Stanley could feel it pressing the shield, faintly touching his hands. The pain of the attack was momentary, but intense.

But now Tarkus was ready with another blast, which sent the man up against the car. Stanley, Fallow, and Tarkus then rushed up to loot the scene. They took the bag of what was clearly the reagents for the casting, and the smoky crystal.

As they were headed back down the hill, Stanley said, "This time it was easy. They didn't even know we were coming. Next time, expect people who really know how to use the power against us. Next time we'll have a real challenge."

Fallow said, "I don't care about next time. Let's get home and rest tonight."

51. A Lot of Promises

As he was wiping down the bar, Bart noticed that his hand was trembling. Coming in in the morning used to be calming, but these days it didn't help. He worried about the door opening and someone coming in demanding something he couldn't deliver. Being in charge was supposed to make him feel safer, but it wasn't. All it did was make him very aware that he was absolutely without protection. Of course, he wasn't supposed to need protection. That was the point.

But Bart didn't feel safe. He wasn't protected, and he didn't have the power to ensure his safety. Or the safety of those he had promised it to. He needed many things he just didn't have. Especially money. He needed money.

The door opened and in came Tommy Lowe. "Hey," he said, angrily, "what's goin on? I thought youse said we was gonna get a commissioner that would keep the police offen us."

Bart stood up straight. He grasped the rag tight in his hand to keep from trembling. In the corner, Caruso folded up his newspaper, took his feet off the table, and let his chair fall so that all four legs were on the ground. The sound distracted Lowe, and startled the two toughs he'd brought with him, who lifted their hands to their jackets.

The sound gave Bart an extra moment to think without Lowe's eyes on him. He said, "That's what I said, and that's what will happen."

"Oh, yeah? When? It's been almost a year since we elected that piker into office, and we ain't seen nothing yet."

"Patience. Rome wasn't built in a day."

"Thas exactly what I expect a lazy dago to say. You says patience, but Ise got people who's gettin pinched. Well, I ain't payin for stock lost because your store ain't open yet, and I ain't goin to college over this, neither."

Bart walked up to Lowe. Lowe was a taller man, but Bart looked him right in the eye and said, "Tommy, I thought you were a big six, but here you are throwing kittens like a weepy flapper. What stock did you lose? Did you get a stash hit or was it just a shipment that got nixed. That's gonna happen, even after the store is fully open. And who said anything about college? Ain't none of us going to college over this."

Bart turned his back and resumed wiping the table. His hand was still trembling, but his voice was steady. "You gotta know how this works. A new mayor, he's gotta look like he's on the up-and-up. If there's no arrests, it looks suspicious. And if he appoints a new police commissioner too soon, people is payin close attention and they might be suspicious. Go back to your joint. Wait a week. You'll see."

Lowe was quiet for a moment. "Okay, but next time one uh my guys gets pinched, you can count me out."

"We'll make sure you know what to expect next time. Oh, and Tommy," Bart turned around, leaving the rag on the table. He fixed Lowe with his eyes. "Next time you bring muscle with you into my club, you'll be leaving here on your back, not on your dogs. Capiche?"

Lowe didn't say anything, but it was clear that he felt the power of Bart's eyes. He gestured to his two men and the three of them all but scuttled out the door.

When Lowe left, Bart felt as if something left him, too. He felt suddenly weak and his legs were wobbly. He pulled out a chair and let himself fall into it.

He was startled by a raspy chuckle. He turned around and saw the old man shuffling out of the darkened hallway that led to the back door. "I was beginning to be afraid you were going to let that simpleton push you around, but then you rose to the occasion." Behind him, the tall grey man walked with his slow, stately gait. Behind him there was another man, big, too. He wasn't as tall as the grey man, but he was much fatter. He had a Vandyke beard and a big bushy moustache. He wore a bowtie and an expensive suit that might have been just a touch small for his body.

"I—I, uh, it just seemed to come to me."

"Yes, yes. Funny how that happens. His timing was appropriate, though. Turns out it is time for us to pay a visit to our recalcitrant mayor. He needs to be told again what he's supposed to do." He gestured to the fat man with him, "Since you are so keen on names, this is Dr. Locke. He is the head of the Klan, and he's going to do the talking when we see the mayor. Come, let's go."

Bart stood up and walked toward the old man. Caruso also rose and started to follow. The old man gestured for him to stop. "We'll take care of your boss. There's no need for you to come."

Caruso looked to Bart. Bart nodded, "I'll be fine." His voice suddenly squeaked, and that's when he realized that he was terrified. He distrusted his voice now, so he said nothing more, but instead fell in between the grey man and Dr. Locke.

They went out the back door. A long, red car waited for them. Locke got in the front passenger seat. The old man and Bart got in the back seat. The grey man drove.

They parked in front of City Hall. It was a tall, stone building with narrow windows. It crowded the sidewalk and shut out the light like something medieval. A blocky tower on the front had a clock near the top below its sloping cap. The doorway was a small, dark alcove with a short flight of steps and an arch overhead carved with the words "City Hall" on it. There was some awkward scrollwork on the sides of the arch.

They went inside and up to Stapleton's office. There was no secretary outside, so they went straight in, with Dr. Locke in the lead. Stapleton's secretary was standing beside his desk. She was young and dressed in a shift dress with a big bow at the neckline and wore a cloche hat over her bobbed hair. The mayor had dark hair and a sun-browned complexion. He wore a simple suit of grey serge. His eyes were looking down at the desk.

When he heard the big man's footsteps, he suddenly looked up, and said, in a startled voice, "D--Dr. Locke! What are you doing here?"

Locke said, "We are here to talk to you about the appointment of your police chief. We think you owe it to your public to fill this vital position."

"Yes, yes, of course." He looked at his secretary and handed her a paper, "I think you get the idea. Just fill the rest in along those lines. Thank you." She took the paper and left the room, closing the door behind her. Before she took it, Bart could see the paper was trembling.

"Now, I've been meaning to talk to you about that. I think we should look at some other candidates. I don't think he's right for the position."

"Candlish is perfect for the position. And he's who we've chosen. We want to see his appointment announced before the end of the week." Although Locke spoke with a high, squeaky voice, it had a surprising force.

"I don't know. The man's an incompetent buffoon--."

"Yes, it's amazing how often such people find their way into office." Locke walked over to the window. He leaned against the sill with one hand, placing the other on his hip. This pushed back his suit jacket to reveal a holstered gun and knife. "But he does have one virtue. He's loyal. He knows who his friends are and won't cross them." Locke turned back to Stapleton. "We know you've been seeing some new friends since you got in office. We want to make sure you remember your old friends."

"I promised during the campaign that I wouldn't let my administration be run by secret interests."

"You made a lot of promises during the campaign. This one, at least, is one no one will have to know you're breaking. If we don't have to keep coming here to talk to you about it."

"Yes, but--."

"Now is the time to uphold this promise. Even as we speak, the body of Irene Pitcher has been discovered. The city is about to boil over with anger. They need somewhere to direct their rage. Having a police department that is being stewarded by a man who resigned a year ago, which is directionless and unmotivated, which you promised to clean up and change, will start to look very bad. It's time to act."

Locke didn't wait for the mayor to respond. Instead, he turned and headed out of the office. Bart followed, with the old man and the grey man behind him. Bart took a look back at Stapleton, whose face no longer looked dark—it was pale as a sheet.

52.   St. Leonard

"Otoniel? Otoniel!" Mama pounded on his door. "You must come out!"

"No!" Otoniel tried to keep his voice from betraying his tears.

"You must eat something, jito."

"No."

Mama pushed the door open finally. Looking in her eyes, he could tell his feelings were fully visible on his face. He tried to rise from the floor, where he had been kneeling in the hope that he could say a prayer, but only sobs had come. She rushed to him. "Otoniel, ¡mijito!" She put her arms around him, pulled him to her. He did not resist—he had no energy for resistance. She cradled him, made comforting noises. He cried some more.

After a while, she asked, "Otoniel, what is wrong?"

He didn't answer.

"Otoniel, did you kill that girl?"

"No!"

"Then what is wrong? Why are you crying?"

"Because they're after me. They chase me everywhere. They're going to take me!"

"Who? The police?"

"No. The demons."

"Demons? Saints protect us, the devil is trying to take away my son! You don't need to stay in here, God will protect you. Come with me, and we will pray." She helped him to his feet. "Ah, you must get dressed. A man's clothes are his armor." She helped him select some pants and a shirt, and he put them on. Then he leaned on her as they made their way into the main room of the house.

She let him sink down into the couch, then rushed over to a sideboard. She opened a drawer and felt around inside. Otoniel could hear the sound of metal rubbing against wood. Finally she stopped and returned. She placed a medallion in his hands and said a couple prayers over him.

Otoniel felt the medallion. It was worn smooth—not much relief and no sharp edges.

When a knock at the door caused Mama to get up, Otoniel looked at the medallion. It was oblong, and the figure in the middle stood tall, holding chains in one hand, while the other was raised. Around the edge, the medallion read, "St. Leonard." The patron saint of criminals and fugitives. A sign that it was never too late.

The medallion must have been his father's. He had never asked too many questions about his father's history. He knew there were problems with the law, and that his father had spent time in jail. Why, he didn't know. And there was one story that his father had not died of consumption—he'd been shot, something Mama wouldn't confirm or deny. She just said it had been his lung that caused his death.

Mama answered the door. From where he was sitting, Otoniel couldn't see them, but he could hear them. "We have a warrant for the arrest of Otoniel Garcia. We believe he is here."

Otoniel turned around and peeked out the curtain behind the couch. The man at the door wore a brown suit. Behind him, two officers in uniform. Behind them, a host of demons, dancing eagerly.

Mama said, "Sí, esta aquí. Esperen, por favor." She left the door open. She walked over to Otoniel.

"I can't go with them," Otoniel said.

"You have to. They are the police."

"Not the police. The demons. Don't you see them?"

Mama pushed the curtain aside and looked out. "No. But they're not my demons. They're yours. You have to go. St. Leonard will protect you."

"Get Mr. Fields."

"I will. Jesus has many servants. He may be of some help as well."

53.   The Library Was Not Deceived

Stefani learned to feel her way around the library pretty well. Not only could she find the books Thaddeus wrote down for her, but she also found the ones she was looking for, the ones she hoped would help her banish or dispel or just lock up the thing in the basement. It wasn't as loud in its rattling these days, but neither was it content to stay where it was. It still wanted out.

Stefani would take the list from Thaddeus and quickly find all but one or two titles on it. Then she would look for something that would help her. She would feel her way along the shelves, skimming the emanations from the books to get a sense of their contents, and when she came to one that seemed promising, she would stop and pull it down.

As she read the tomes, she was beginning to get a sense of how it might work. She needed some way to be able to concentrate her strength and push without letting the thing push back. Apparently, that meant she would need some type of protective circle. She was, however, having a hard time finding out what exactly that meant.

After a couple hours, Thaddeus would typically yell for her. Stefani would put back the book she was reading and rush to his study cage with Thaddeus' books. She would apologize for not having found all the books.

"By George, girl," he would say, "why is it taking you so long? I thought you'd be better at this by now."

"But I am better, Uncle Tad," she would say as she tilted her head and fluttered her eyelids in her best Lillian Gish impersonation. "Your library is so big, and the organization is so complicated—I don't think I'll ever get a hold of it. But

I am getting better. Please don't give up on me." And she would reach out and touch his hand sometimes, or other times just look in his eyes.

"Oh, go on," he said. "Get those other books and be quick about it."

She would rush off to get the last books, then either go back to the book she had been working with or find a new one. She had a small notebook that she kept on a cord around her wrist where she would jot down the most important information. She sometimes conspicuously made false notes about the organization of the library.

She felt she had Thaddeus pretty well fooled, but the library was not deceived. It watched her closely—she could feel its eyes on her. And she could feel the amused contempt with which it regarded her. She was not entirely sure that it was the library itself that was watching her, or the spirit from the pit. She also wasn't sure whether the entity would or could tell Thaddeus about what was going on. It had never spoken to her, not even when she'd tried to engage it in conversation, but that didn't mean it couldn't speak. And it seemed to gravitate around Thaddeus. Was it loyal to him, or did it regard him with a similar sort of contempt?

The watchful eyes, though, were the reason why she never messed with the books at the center of the library, near the pit. The books that felt almost alive, with their strange pages and rust-colored ink. She knew they held knowledge that might be vital, but she dare not approach them. As she read more books, though, she assured herself that her knowledge was adequate and that she had no need of the material in those closely guarded books.

One day Stefani came home from the library and found her mother in her accustomed spot at the table. Instead of looking out the window or sleeping with her head on the table as she did most days, Elizabeth was looking at Stefani, as if she were waiting for her to come home.

"Stefani," she said, "please come over here for a moment. I think we need to talk."

"Sure, Mother," Stefani said. She took her notebook off her wrist and put it in her handbag. She came over to the table and sat down adjacent to her mother, neither the spot she had been sitting when her father died nor the spot where he had sat. No one had sat there, she thought, since father died.

"Stefani, I don't think you should keep working for Mr. Marduk."

"What?" Stefani asked. "Why not?"

"I don't know. I'm just afraid he's not a good influence. Besides, what will people think about a young woman who visits the home of an old bachelor every day? With no chaperone—just you walking in there alone. It's not decent."

Stefani felt the blood rise to her face. She hadn't even really thought of this, and because it was a new idea to her, she was able to be casually dismissive, "I don't care what people think."

"Stefani, you should care."

"So, then, I should go back to dancing? You want me back in the club?"

"No, that's not what I meant. I don't think that's a good idea, either."

Stefani kept getting warmer and warmer in her face. She had no idea how red she looked, but if it were anywhere near what she felt, it would probably glow in dim light. "It was good enough for you, but now all of a sudden, I have to give it up." She stood up angrily.

"Stefani, it was never good enough for me. It was just what was available. You have so many more options."

Stefani was mad enough for a moment that she didn't know what to say. She stepped away from the table and walked first into the kitchen, then back over to the table. She pointed at her mother. "You act like things are so different for me, like every door is suddenly open. Well, they're not. There are a few more places. I could be a shop girl, if I wanted. But I don't. Same with a seamstress. But I don't want that job, either.

"Things are different, but they're not that different. Women have the vote, now, but there's no way a woman will ever be elected president. Not in this country."

"Perhaps I am too optimistic, but your father, he always said you could do anything. I believe that, too."

Stefani felt the sting and lashed out. "But what father said doesn't matter much now, does it?"

Her mother flinched. "He also always said you were smart. And that's true. You've outsmarted me, that's for sure." She sighed. Looked in her coffee cup. Stefani guessed that there was probably about a third of a cup in there from the way she tilted it. She set it flat again. "I should get dressed."

Stefani smiled, "Who are you fooling? It's too late to get dressed."

Elizabeth smiled back. "I suppose so. Maybe tomorrow, then. What are you doing tonight?"

"I thought I might go shopping."

"It's too late for that, too, surely. Let's have some dinner."

"Are you cooking?"

Elizabeth smiled, "Pshaw! I may never have been a very good cook, but I know a pogue's way around a potato, to be sure. I think there's some sausage in the icebox, too. That'll about make a meal, don't you think?"

"Put the kettle on for tea and, Bob's your uncle, you've got a fine dinner."

Stefani didn't get to go shopping until Saturday. Then she took the crowded streetcar downtown and began trying to get the items on her list. Some of it was easy: candles and chalk and other basics could be picked up at Woolworth's, but the big item on her list was harder to find. At Neusteter's the woman didn't know where she could find such a thing, but "helpfully" tried to interest her in some rubber reducing garments. Daniels and Fisher didn't have it, either, but there they recommended that she try Lewis & Son's, which turned out to be right.

But then when she found it, she almost wished she hadn't. At more than $30, the black silk robe wiped out all her savings, but she had to have it. Coming home on the streetcar—she was lucky to have saved enough for the fare!—she rubbed the silk between her fingers. It felt so luxuriant, she could easily believe it had special powers.

At home, she began preparations. She drew the appropriate symbols to pin onto the robe, drew the Tetragrammaton on each shoe along with several crosses, and sewed the linen apron—or, more properly, an ephod—she would need. The belt was supposed to have names written on it, and she couldn't figure any way to do that but embroider it. She used large stitches and it looked a little clumsy, but it was readable as the appropriate names.

Preparing the basement space was harder. She could only go down after her mother had gone to bed, and she didn't have the nerve for working down there for very long at a time in the dark. The thing was watching her. It probably knew more than she did about what was coming up, and it made Stefani nervous. But, still, eventually she had the circle prepared.

Then it was time for sanctifying. Not being a churchgoer, she was nervous about acquiring the holy water. But when she went in, she saw an old woman taking some in a small vial, so Stefani just went up and did the same. No one noticed or questioned her.

She sprinkled the holy water and said the words over the belt and the circle, and then everything was ready. All that was left was to wait for a stormy night.

When the first peal of thunder broke into the room, Stefani's heart began pounding. She and her mother were up reading in the main room together, and Stefani worked hard to keep her excitement and impatience concealed. She hoped her mother would go to bed soon, so Stefani could get to her preparations. She didn't want to miss the hour.

When her mother got up and went to bed, Stefani also went up to her room. But instead of changing for bed, she put on the ephod, then the robe, then cinched the consecrated belt around her. She felt safer already. Then she headed down to the basement.

She lit the candles and spaced them around the circle. Then she stepped inside and began reciting the long, chanting poem that was supposed to precede the summons. When she had finished the poem, she could feel the effect it had on her, regulating and deepening her heartbeats, and with them the power of the amulet. Then she called out, "Bound spirit within the sound of my voice, you are hereby compelled to appear. Appear. Appear. Appear!" She continued chanting the command, and with each utterance she felt the force reach out from her into the air. And eventually she felt the spirit. It was now trying to scramble deeper into its cage, trying to avoid the force that sought to bring it out into the light.

When it could not resist any more, the beast appeared before her. It was something like a lion, but with leathery wings and a scorpion's tail. The lion roared, revealing that within its mouth there was a human head. This human head breathed fire. A huge wave of the flame rushed toward the circle. But Stefani stood her ground and the fire broke around her.

Stefani was prepared for this. The demon would begin its appearance by trying a show of strength. This was a bluff, because the demon was powerless to hurt her as long as she was in the circle. The goal was to frighten her to take a step out of the circle. She stayed in the circle and waited for the creature to expend itself.

Eventually, the display was over, and the creature changed into something like a man, but with a sickly pale yellow skin, vicious sharp teeth, and an elongated face. It wore armor like a Roman Legionnaire.

Stefani pointed at the creature, and said, "Damned beast, I compel you to return to Hell. Away! Away!" She chanted, and felt the creature's resistance. It didn't want to move. Although it floated in the air, it had its body tilted and its arms and legs outstretched as though it were pushing on a large obstacle slowly moving toward it.

After a few repetitions, the creature said, "You can sssend me back to Hell if you want, but perhapsss you would rather learn what happened to your father."

Stefani faltered in her chant. Then she said, "What would you know of that? Are you responsible?"

"I am not. Your father and I worked together."

"You lie. My father would never work with a damned, evil beast like you."

"Damned, yess. But evil, no." The creature spread its clawed hands in a gesture of openness. "My ssin was loyalty."

"That makes no sense. All the rebels were banished with the devil. Explain." Stefani made a sharp gesture with a pointed finger, which was supposed to cause the creature pain.

It did flinch, and it cowered slightly, and spoke deferentially. "Of all the 666 prinssipalities, how many demons do you think personally decided to rebel? For most of us, we made no decision to rebel. We ssimply followed orders. When the sseraphim order us, we must ssimply obey."

Stefani thought of this for a moment. It made sense. It certainly made sense that her father wouldn't be working with a wholly malevolent spirit. "Tell me what happened to my father."

"I do not know. I was confined. But I can tell you how to ssumon his spirit. You will see him and be able to ask him yoursself."

Stefani thought about it. She knew it was a bad idea. She knew the beast was deceiving her. Every instinct in her screamed that she must not take the deal the beast was offering. But still she heard herself saying, "Okay. Tell me what to do."

54.   The Nickel of Fate

Stanley, Tarkus, and Fallow agreed that they had successfully thwarted the plan for the fear campaign. There was little talk of the burning crosses the next day, and although some people noticed them and began to worry, most didn't. There was some fear to harness, but not much. That meant the conjurers would have to work harder when it came to creating and harnessing rage. Pretty soon it became clear what shape that would take.

Shortly after Armistice Day, the newspapers started becoming obsessed with a burgeoning crime wave and with their new mayor's reluctance to do anything about it. The police chief had resigned shortly after the election, and the new mayor, Ben Stapleton, hadn't acted on the resignation.

The newspapers claimed that this lame duck chief was powerless to keep his officers under control, which made them ineffective in fighting crime. As crime seemed to be spreading through the city, the newspapers were demanding that Stapleton appoint a new police chief.

The impact of this was felt on the street. People were growing angry, indignant. They were already talking about recalling the new mayor, but they still needed something to push them over the top, a galvanizing event.

And it was at this point that Stanley came in, opened his newspaper, and almost fell into his chair. Fallow and Tarkus were nearby, and they responded to Stanley's wobbly stance. As they rushed into his office, Stanley looked at the story to make sure he hadn't misread it, but he hadn't. Irene Pitcher's body had been found. And now there were renewed calls to bring Otoniel in for the murder.

Fallow said, "Is this the case you were telling us about? The sacrificial victim?"

Stanley nodded. "I have to go out and find some evidence that the kid's innocent. Up until this point, I've been counting on the lack of evidence against him. But now, it's likely the prosecutor will have to move forward with the case. I have to track down some evidence to protect him."

"Why?" Fallow asked.

Stanley looked at Fallow. "He's my client. I was hired to protect him. It's my responsibility."

"That's probably exactly what they want. If he gets caught and put on trial, there's no rage. Justice was served. The mob quiets down. They go back to their homes."

"Except justice wasn't served. An innocent man was killed."

"Not in the eyes of the mob. The system did what they wanted. But if you produce some piece of evidence that gets him off, they will see it as proof that the system doesn't work. They will use it as fuel for their rage. Think of what Saluzar will do with that. I think we need to telegraph Gary Barton—or even call him—to find out what to do next."

Stanley looked at Tarkus, who had been standing back uncomfortably against the wall. "What do you think?"

Tarkus looked bewildered for a moment. Then he glanced at Fallow before saying to Stanley, "I think we need to contact Barton. He'll tell us what to do."

Stanley pounded the desk. "You guys contact him. I don't need to be told what to do. I will protect my client."

Fallow was unfazed by Stanley's sudden action. He said, "Did you get paid?"

"What?"

"Did you get paid? My understanding was you were running a mostly volunteer service."

"No, I didn't get paid, but there are other things . . ."

"If you didn't get paid, you don't have a legal obligation here. The teachings are quite clear on the matter."

"But my heart is quite clear on this matter, too. I know what my obligations are. I know what I have to do as a man and as a sorcerer. You guys contact Barton. I'm going to go find that evidence."

Stanley put the room key on the table, then left. He was sweating. He knew that what he was doing now could potentially result in his expulsion, or, worse, his banishment from the material plane. He would find himself suddenly in the same confinement as so many demons he had put there, himself. And he wouldn't even have the escape of death as an option.

Stanley tossed the case file back on Van Cise's desk. "You can't prosecute this case."

Van Cise said, "And why not?"

"First, it's a tinderbox. It will set this town on fire—there's thousands out there with resentment against the Mexicans, which is already being whipped up by the Klan. This case will turn that resentment into anger, then violence."

"Yes, but, Mr. Fields, that cannot be the concern of the DA's office. If I have a legitimate case with good evidence, I must pursue it. People already know about this case. Not prosecuting it will lead to its own anger. And violence."

"It's not good evidence. Otoniel already admitted to being at the scene, with the people in a vehicle he described. I bet if you gave him a chance he could give a positive ID for the vehicle, and point out the people who were in it, too."

"I know, but none of those things hold water unless you can get someone to corroborate his story that he was picked up by these people. There were witnesses there that claim they saw no such mystery people. Or something, anything, that backs up his version of events.

"You've got to do it fast, too. I can't sit on this case for long, now that the body's been found. The mayor's pretty insistent. He hopes it will stop all the talk about a recall."

"Yeah," said Stanley. He looked around at all the boxes of papers from the Blonger case that still crowded the office. Derrick Biltmore, the defense attorney, nodded. "So," Stanley said, "you say we have to act fast. How long do we have?"

"I can maybe delay this a week before I start to get it in motion. That'll ramp up the publicity, not like there isn't enough of it already. This sort of thing sells papers . . ."

"All right." Stanley and Biltmore stood up, thanked the Colonel, and left.

In the hall, Stanley turned to Biltmore, "So, whaddaya need from me?"

"It's like the DA says—we need some evidence that corroborates Otoniel's story. We need witnesses or physical evidence—something that might make his testimony stand up. That's if we want to get through the trial. If we want to get him to drop the case, it's gotta be something good, something that shows it likely wasn't Otoniel."

Stanley pulled out his tobacco box"This case is moving again because they found the body, right?"

"Yes."

"But no murder weapon, right?"

"No. But they know it's a knife. I think they know the size, too. Let's go to my office."

Biltmore led the way to an office in the corner of the building's basement. The door said, "Public Defender." Inside, there was barely enough room for the three desks and six chairs. Biltmore sat down behind a desk. Stanley sat down in front.

Stanley said, "You got any of the real stuff?"

Biltmore frowned disapprovingly and shook his head. He frowned even deeper when Stanley said, "That's okay," and pulled out his flask."So," Stanley said, "the knife. I'm guessing it's got a curved blade, something like five or six inches long?"

"Where is this coming from? Is there something you're not telling me?"

"So I'll take that to mean I'm right."

Biltmore opened a folder and looked inside. "Yeah. That's right."

"So, how much does it help if I find the weapon?"

"It could help a lot—if you can prove it is the weapon, and that it wasn't in Otoniel's possession at the time of the murder."

"Okay, so there's one thing." Stanley wrote down, *Murder weapon*, and circled it several times. "What about opportunity? What if I show he couldn't have done it?"

"How?"

"The murder took place a couple of days' walk from where Otoniel was arrested. What if I can show he wasn't gone long enough to commit the murder? That seems pretty good evidence he can't be the killer."

"You'll have to get witnesses for practically two weeks—that's how long she was missing before Otoniel was arrested. But if you can show that, we know he hasn't had the opportunity since he was arrested."

"Okay." Stanley wrote down, *Witnesses. Two weeks. Disappearance* → *Arrest*.

"But the main thing you need is to corroborate his story of these mystery people who gave him the money. Nobody else in town remembers them. It's all over his statements. And then, he did get the money, money that might have been in Miss Pitcher's possession when she was kidnapped. Until we prove that these people did exist and gave him the money, he'll hang for sure. Jurors will say, 'Even if he didn't kill her himself, he had accomplices and they did it. Kidnapping and accessory to murder of a white woman is enough to hang a Mexican.'"

"Right. So where's this town? What's it called?"

"It's Californiaville."

Stanley wrote that down. Then he took another long pull on his flask. It was nearly empty, but there was still a good swallow in there. He screwed the lid down, then slipped it into his pocket. Then he folded his notebook and put that it another pocket. "Thanks," he said and stood up. "Any Chance I can talk to the kid before I go?"

"I can give you a pass that'd get you into the jail, but whether he'll see you or not—I dunno. He's been pretty strange since they brought him in. Much different from when I saw him last time." The lawyer wrote on a piece of paper, signed it, and tore it off the pad to give to Stanley.

Stanley took the paper and went down the hall. The jail was pretty near the public defender's office. It was hard to say which was nicer, but the jail was less crowded at any rate. He showed his pass to the guard, who said, "Why you wanna see that spic?"

"What's it matter to you?"

"It don't. He probably won't see you nohow. He's funny in the head."

"Give the kid a break—jail isn't fun for anybody, and I'm sure you guys aren't helping him feel at home."

"Now there's where you're wrong," the guard said, smiling. "We been giving him a real warm welcome." His hand tightened on his baton. "Making him feel real nice and cozy. We want him to feel at home, since this is the last home he'll ever know."

"Now there's where you're wrong."

The guard cocked his head and looked at Stanley. Stanley didn't elaborate, just gestured for the guard to lead him. The guard took Stanley back into the block, and Stanley saw Otoniel. He was off by himself in a corner, looking nervously around the jail. Stanley waved, and made it more than just a physical wave. Something akin to a spiritual tap on the shoulder from a distance. Otoniel started, then looked at Stanley. He stood up and shuffled cautiously toward the bars.

Stanley walked past the cop, who gave a resigned gesture. Otoniel's face was haggard, his eyes sunken, scared, and hungry.

"Get me out!" Otoniel said. He was pretty badly beaten up, with layers of bruising on his face, some starting to turn green, others purple.

"Yeah. Working on it. I can't just snap my fingers and get you out, though."

"They're here!" Otoniel yelled and gestured in a way that made it clear he wasn't talking about his fellow prisoners, who for the most part were as pathetic as he was, except for a jasper in seersucker, who looked like he was just happy to be himself.

"I know," Stanley said. He could feel them. Loathsome harassers sent to torment Otoniel, make him look like a man unhinged by guilt. As Stanley approached the bars, he felt something else. A subtle power that waxed and waned. He located the source. In Otoniel's hand, an amulet swung back and forth. "We can make them go away."

Stanley reached out and grabbed the amulet between his fingers. He could tell it was a saint's charm, but not who the saint was. He put the amulet between Otoniel's hands, pressed between his palms. Then he put his own hands outside Otoniel's.

"Now pray with me."

They were silent for a moment.

"You say the prayer," Stanley said.

"Which prayer?"

"Any one. You pick. Just say it over and over. In rhythm. You'll know when it's right."

Otoniel began, "Dios te salve, Maria. Llena eres de gracia: El Señor es contigo . . . ."

Stanley held his hands together, and listened as Otoniel repeated the prayer once, twice, thrice, as it began to acquire a rhythm.

"Now think that you want them to go away."

Stanley felt the waves of force emanating out from Otoniel now. Not much, just enough to keep the weak, harassing spirits at bay. He let go of Otoniel's hands. "Good. Now repeat as necessary."

Otoniel stopped praying. He opened his eyes and looked around. It was clear what he saw, or, rather, didn't see.

"But how?"

Stanley shook his head. "Maybe they were never really there. Maybe they were just here." He tapped Otoniel's head. "Focus and comfort yourself and you will be surprised at how much you can accomplish. Like getting some sleep. Eating some food. Keep your strength up—we'll get you out of here soon."

Stanley then said goodbye and turned away, wondering if he could deliver on this promise.

Stanley was on his way to Union Station. He knew he was being tailed. The guy tailing him was a mug, none too subtle about the pursuit and that he expected a scuffle at the end of it. He even put his hands in his jacket once to assure himself of something—a pistol, probably.

Because he was such a mug, it was no difficulty for Stanley to get out of sight and jump out behind him. He had seen the man check his pistol, so he quickly reached over the man's shoulder, into his jacket, and pulled the gun out. It was all done so quickly that the man barely knew what was happening. The mug grabbed at Stanley's arm, but missed, and Stanley quickly jumped back out of reach.

"Now," Stanley said, calmly, "why don't you tell me who sent you?"

"I ain't gonna tell you that. But ain't you some kinda private dick? I spose you can figger it out."

"Yeah, I've got a couple guesses. I've also got some guesses about why."

The man put one fist into the other, "To mess you up, but good."

Stanley glanced at the clock. "Maybe, if you had to, but that wasn't really the plan." He wished now he had left himself more time. "Let's get you put away." He gestured with the gun. They went into the alley.

Stanley began trying doors. The third one he came to opened, and he gestured for the big mug to get in among the Chinese cooks in the chop suey place.

The mug looked ready to fight, but he locked eyes with Stanley first. Stanley's jaw set and his finger tightened on the trigger. It was clear what the outcome would be. He went inside.

Stanley closed the door, shutting the protests of the Chinese cooks. Then he grabbed a splinter of wood and shoved it into the door frame. It didn't have to fit tight. It was almost purely symbolic, but it was necessary.

Closing his eyes and concentrating, he reached out for the resonance of the wood. He felt it, the grainy, knotty rhythm that was so faint because the piece was so small. He amplified it slightly, slightly, slightly, until it was wedged tightly into the frame.

He opened his eyes, tossed the gun into the nearby trash can, and rushed to the train station. He was running very late. Stanley ran between the marble columns into the polished granite interior. Fortunately, he had his ticket already because there was a line at the counter.

He rushed across the lobby, glancing up at the board to see what track his train was on. Even from the door he could see that his train was leaving. He ran a few steps but quickly realized that with its increasing speed he would never catch it.

Train gone, Stanley stamped and cursed. It wasn't like it was a regular route. He would have to wait more than a week for the next train. A week he didn't have. If he couldn't get to Californiaville and talk to witnesses, scout the location for the murder weapon, the trial would have to go forward. Van Cise couldn't wait, not with the pressure from the mayor, and with the evidence he had, he couldn't not pursue this case. How was he going to get there? Hire a car? Maybe. Maybe that would do. Or maybe it'd be cheaper to just buy a car. But would Fallow and Tarkus let him get away now? Odds were good that they'd heard back from Barton, and with his explicit order, they'd try to stop him.

Stanley sighed. Without thinking, he had made his way to a streetcar stop. He didn't want to go back to his office or apartment and chance running into Tarkus or Fallow. He needed to think, but, more than that, he needed to drift on the current of Fate. He wasn't meant to catch that train.

The ruse with that pathetic mug had worked, but it shouldn't have. He dispatched of that nuisance quickly, probably losing just a few minutes. It shouldn't have been that close, and it wouldn't have, but for a dozen tiny delays in the morning. Misplaced keys. And wallet. His hat blown off his head and rolling more than a block. A long line at a normally deserted lunch counter. These were clearly the operands of Fate. And now, to find himself unthinkingly at a streetcar stop, fingering a nickel in his pocket.

He pulled the nickel out and said aloud: "Heads I take the next streetcar." He flipped it into the air and he could feel the waters of Fate close in. Not a random flip, but as determined and regular as the ripples from a stone thrown in a pond. Heads.

The streetcar rolled up with a screech and a clang. He whistled as he climbed the stair. He dropped the nickel of Fate into the farebox, smiling at the satisfying rattle and clink.

The streetcar rattled along. The scraping of wheels, screeching of brakes, and, barely audible to the body's ears, the hum of electricity.

Of course, it was this last that was the most palpable to Stanley. The surges when the streetcar accelerated, the slackening when the streetcar slowed, like waves that were not pushed by wind, but drawn by the beach.

After a while, the streetcar stopped turning and winding, and began traveling straight for a long way. Stop. Go. The riders thinned out.

Then, from outside came the loud putter-drone of a large, open engine. A kid on the right side of the streetcar said, "Look, ma, a plane!"

His mother made a dismissive sound. A couple of other kids were looking out the window, but most people barely took notice. Stanley remembered how, before the war, people would take the train across town just for the chance to see the Wright flyer, which might go only a hundred feet or so, if it got up at all.

And he remembered what it felt like when he saw the planes soaring high over the battlefield. His heart leapt out to soar with them.

Of course there was a certain amount of jealousy. You were down in the mud, confined, begrimed, and envirmined, while they were up there free, and at the end of the day able to return to their hangar and sleep in a regular bed, shower, and maybe even enjoy some wine with dinner. But the jealousy vanished the first time you saw one go down. That made your heart sink.

He remembered one that had gone down in no man's land, flaming as it fell, and the pilot, too, who, though burning, tried to make a leap for safety just before impact. His sergeant yelled that they were going to go rescue the pilot. His whole squad volunteered to a man and they ran out to him despite the Jerries' gunfire.

The pilot had cleared his plane, ending up half in a shell hole. Badly burned and broken, he was still alive when they got there, but just barely. His face was screaming, but the only sound that came out was a choking gasp. Then he died. They brought his body back under fire, though luckily they avoided injury, probably thanks in part to the covering smoke from the plane.

But when the planes were up there, keeping the observation planes away, and you could look through your field glasses to see the insignia so high above, it was like Liberty Leading the People, waving her banner over the army of freedom.

Speaking of Liberty, Stanley thought he caught a glimpse of the tricolor insignia on a wing in the field. And is that a Spad? Those were jolly great planes. He rang for the next stop.

He got off the streetcar, waited for opposing traffic to pass, then crossed the street. He headed across the field that was in the process of being converted to an aerodrome. Stanley corrected himself. Airport. They're calling them airports now.

The Spad was on the far side of the field. Its lithe, graceful form stood out against the gangly, awkward rattlebox of a Jenny. The pilot, though, was standing by the Jenny, looking over the shoulder of a man working in the engine compartment.

The Spad pilot wore a flying leather jacket, his gloves tucked under one of the epaulets. He stood up and Stanley saw he wore a bright blue pillbox cap with a small brim. He picked up the cap and ran his hand over his already-slicked hair. He turned his head and Stanley immediately recognized his profile from its aquiline nose, dignified chin, and thin, smart moustache.

Guynemer! Stanley had delighted himself with tales of the French Ace's exploits long before he was old enough to enlist or his country was involved in the war. Then when he had arrived in France, he had heard tales that Guynemer's apotheosis was more than a child's fancy, but since the observers were not

Initiates, he and most of those who could truly sense the supernatural forces had dismissed those tales. But here he was!

Stanley couldn't help crying out the Ace's name, at which the Frenchman looked up with a friendly smile. "Well, hello, sir," he said in good but accented English. "Your voice is friendly, but I'm afraid you have me at a bit of a disadvantage. What is your name?" He offered a hand.

Stanley reached out and took the hand. It had the chill solidity of a powerful spirit. "I'm not sure I want to tell you. I don't know if I'll ever have another chance to have the French Ace at a disadvantage!" Guynemer smiled slightly wider in a good-natured recognition of the joke. "Stanley Fields."

"Good to meet you, Mr. Fields. This is Mr. Mack Spar, a fellow knight of the air."

The man described as Mack stood up from where he was working around, but not in, the engine. He was a little taller than Stanley, slim from a lack of eating rather than an excess of conditioning. He was unshaven for a couple days, but it was still clear he normally wore a moustache similar to Guynemer's. He had wide open, friendly eyes, a dark complexion, and dark curly hair that was unkempt and slightly long. He briefly gave Stanley a puzzled look, then wiped his hands on a rag and reached out. Stanley took his hand.

Stanley asked, "Is this your birdcage, then?"

"Yes. I'm just finishing up changing out the engine."

"What'll that do for you?"

"Everything. It'll increase my speed, range, ceiling, which, to tell you true, wasn't much higher than the ground here."

"Really? How high will you be able to go?"

"Eleven, twelve, thirteen thousand, maybe. I don't know."

Guynemer said, "Truly respectable. At that height, you could challenge an Albatros, something that always frustrated me in my SPAD."

It occurred to Stanley that this meant the plane could take him into the mountains. "How close are you to finishing?"

"Well, I'm about ready to fire it up for a runway test. You want to watch?"

"Can I ride?"

Mack looked at Guynemer, who nodded.

"Sure. The first time we're not going to lift off, but the second time we will."

Mack climbed up into the cockpit and indicated Stanley should climb into the other seat. He reached up to grab the edge, then paused. He pulled out his flask and took a long bolt. Then he handed it to Mack, saying, "For courage." Mack nodded and took a swig himself.

He coughed, "That's terrible."

Stanley nodded. "Where do you think you are, France?" And then he climbed into the cockpit.

The pilot yelled "Contact," and hit the starter. The engine sputtered but didn't catch. He tried it again. This time the engine started and roared to life.

Then Mack tapped Stanley on the shoulder. Stanley looked back, and he could see Mack speaking, but he couldn't understand. Then Mack pointed at his head, and Stanley understood. He took his hat off and put it in his lap.

Then Mack throttled up a few times before beginning to maneuver. They headed over to one end of the field, then turned around.

He throttled up significantly and the plane shot forward.

When they reached what felt to Stanley like it must have been a hundred miles an hour, Stanley gripped the edge of the cockpit, suddenly regretting his decision. He regretted even more when he felt the wheels lift up, though they touched down again quickly. At the end of the field, the pilot throttled down. The plane slowed.

"Sorry, I didn't mean to go so fast. This engine is more powerful and lighter than the one I'm used to. You ready? This time for sure."

Stanley nodded and took out his flask again. He took two swigs as the engine cranked up again. This time the engine revved up higher and it wasn't long before the plane lifted up off the ground and began climbing into the sky.

Stanley began yelling a stream of obscenities as the force of the plane's ascent pushed his stomach down on his bladder and bowels. Then the plane leveled off. For a moment he was weightless, and then he was flying. By God, he was flying! He let out a whoop of delight.

The engine was throttled down, so he could hear the pilot laughing behind him. "Yeah, it's great, ain't it?"

"It's sublime!" Then Stanley looked over and saw Guynemer's ghostly Spad illuminated in the red light of the setting sun. Partly translucent, like frosted crystal, it refracted the light into a thousand starbursts. "It's transcendent!"

Mack laughed again.

Despite Stanley's protests, the flight had to be cut short. Not only because of the failing light, but also because Mack hadn't put much fuel in the tank for this first test.

When they had landed, Stanley didn't exactly leap out and kiss the ground, but he wanted to. Flying was great, but landing was even scarier than taking off, and he was glad to have made it in one piece.

Instead, he extended his hand to Mack, who had already moved back to open the engine compartment.

"Thanks," Stanley said.

"Thank you for helping me test her. With the new engine, I barely felt your weight."

"Perhaps I can help you with a further test?"

"Yeah? What?"

"I need to get into the mountains. I thought you might take me. You can test her ceiling by seeing which mountains or passes you can get over."

Mack hesitated. Then he looked at Guynemer, who nodded. "Okay, let's do it."

55.   Some Men Are Chosen to See

They pushed Otoniel roughly through the doors to the station. The entire trip, he had been trying to decide what to do. That gesture settled his mind. He yelled, "I want to confess!"

That made them pause for a moment. All the police who were watching stopped. Then one of the men holding him slammed him up against a wall. "You don't get to confess, spic. We got all the evidence we need to make you hang. No deals."

"No, no—I want to confess to un otro crimen."

The officer's pale fleshy face was already flushed from the effort of pushing Otoniel around, but it seemed to grow a little redder. "Of course. Every Mexican is his own little brown crime wave. But it don't matter. You're still going to hang."

"Pero, I was not alone. It was a- a- rape."

The officer's jaw worked side to side. Otoniel could hear his teeth grinding. "No deals. You're still dead. Tell us who she was."

"Victoria Guerrero."

There was a moment of silence. Then the cop started laughing. The laughter quickly turned bitter and he punched Otoniel in the gut. "That's for wasting my time, wetback."

The cop rushed him roughly down the corridor. On his right was the heavy brick wall with regular windows—heavily barred and very tall. At least they let in some light, though. On his left were the cells—cages, really.

The cells were made of heavy iron bars with mesh over them. But worse than the cells were the men in them. The word spread quickly about who he was, and pretty soon he was hearing taunts like, "Hey, Spic, you attack white women—come see what a white man can do." And most of the prisoners he was walking past were white men.

Toward the end of the row there was one cell that had a single Latino man. He was chubby and short, with sparse stubble on his cheeks and what looked like it was once a very neat mustache growing out. The door was opened, and the guard bumped Otoniel into it.

The bunks were on the left. They took up nearly half of the floor space in the cell, and they were very narrow beds. Having to share the cell with a portly man immediately made Otoniel angry. But then he realized he would have to calm himself. Being in prison would likely have many worse experiences in store for him. If the threats of the white men were to be believed, it would be much, much worse indeed.

When the taunting men included the fat man in their threats, he said, "I'm not with him—don't lump us together. You all know I'm a good guy. It's him you want!"

Otoniel looked around at the men in the other cells. Through the fine grating, he could see that as crowded as the men themselves would have been in the tiny cells, the cells were packed even more densely with demons, which seemed to dance in delight when they saw Otoniel. They whispered in the ears of the men, who followed the suggestions by shouting ever more vile threats. The demons laughed loudly when the men did as they were told.

The door to the cell closed. The guards shouted another insult, then walked away. Otoniel looked at his chubby cellmate. The man just shook his head and gestured for Otoniel to take the top bunk. He then threw himself down on his own bunk. Otoniel looked at the beds. He put his hand on his own bed. The mattress was an inch or two thick, and underneath there was a hard metal plate. Torturously uncomfortable, Otoniel concluded. He opted to remain standing for a little bit.

All around, the men in other cells were listening to their demons. As they called out the words that the demons put in their minds, the demons, which were at first wispy and incorporeal, grew more solid and threatening. Soon, a demon in the next cell pushed its way through the grate and into Otoniel's cell. It reached out with one of its clawed hands and grasped at Otoniel. Though incorporeal, its hand rasped along Otoniel's skin. Otoniel felt a chill go through his skin, and the hair on his arm turned crumpled, white, and brittle.

Otoniel recoiled from the touch, but so did the demon. The contact seemed to have drained some of its energy. The beast withdrew and began heading back to the source of its power, the man it had been whispering to.

Otoniel realized that with the number of men in the jail shouting their curses, it would likely not be long before a constant stream of demons was coming through the grate at him. In fact, the next one was already beginning to approach him. The physical effects were relatively minor—though the skin where the demon had touched was beginning to turn black—but the draining of his emotional reserve that came along with the touch would soon take everything out of him. Even now, it was all he could do to keep himself from curling up into a ball in panic.

As the second demon approached, Otoniel reached for the only possession he had retained through the search and seizure, the amulet of St. Leonard. When he did, he felt the power of the amulet. And the demon did, too. It hesitated. Then it tried to touch him. It was unable to reach him, despite its efforts. It hissed at him, displaying the snake fangs in its bearlike jaws, then withdrew to its source of energy, another of the prisoners who was very eager to listen to his suggestions.

Otoniel realized that he would need some source of strength to protect himself. The amulet could be part of it, but he had to do what Stanley had taught him to draw out the power. He climbed up onto the top bunk and began praying. And he could only really think of one way to pray, so he began praying the amulet as though it were the rosary. The only ones he could remember were the Glorious Mysteries, but they were good. The Transfiguration gave him courage. It reminded him that some men are chosen to see what others cannot see. It reminded him that this was not madness, it was prophecy.

As he prayed, he let the Hail Marys and the Our Fathers gain a kind of rhythm, and this rhythm stirred up a pulse within the amulet. The power radiated out with his words, and as it washed over the demons, they grew less corporeal again. Not only that, but it seemed they couldn't make themselves heard when they were trying to whisper into the ears of their supports.

The prayers gave Otoniel protection and comfort, but as he prayed, he began to wonder whether he deserved the protection. He had not killed Irene, but there were certainly enough other things on his conscience. The longer he thought about them, the more he felt he really should let the demons come through the bars and drain him dry of all life. So he stopped praying.

The demons immediately felt the difference. Their cackling grew louder and they came up with even more vile insults to hurl. They were soon pushing through the bars and heading toward him.

But then they stopped and looked at him. They began to confer in their rasping, demonic tongue. Then they spat a few incomprehensible words at him and backed off. From the other side of the grate, the demons watched him, but no longer did they goad their hosts, who seemed to lose interest in taunting him. They went back to the various ways they passed their prison time.

Otoniel realized they had figured out what he wanted and they weren't going to give it to him. Instead, they would give him what might be the worst possible pain: guilt without the redemption of punishment.

56.   Times Is Ever So Tough

Early the next morning, Stanley was awakened by Mack. He had slept in a cot at the pilot's bunkhouse for the night. When Mack bumped him, Stanley startled and said, "I'm up. Let's go." He patted his pockets, found his flask wasn't there, then panicked for a moment before he realized he was holding it in his other hand. He smiled and took a quick bolt from it.

Mack said, "That's not a good way to start your morning."

"It's a fine way to start my morning. I'm feeling better already. Besides, what does it matter? You're the one flying the plane, not me. Let's get going."

"You should at least have some breakfast first," Mack said, extending a tin of biscuits to Stanley.

Stanley shook his head. "I don't need anything to eat this early." Stanley began rolling a cigarette.

"Your choice, but it's you who's fetching the fuel." When they emerged from the bunkhouse, Mack gave Stanley two cans and pointed to the fuel hut. Stanley put the unlit cigarette in his mouth and headed over to the hut. He paid for the gasoline and rushed to fill up the cans, but they were taken from him and handed back full.

Stanley walked back a little slower with the full cans. He felt the chill of the morning air and didn't like thinking how cold it would be at altitude. Guynemer was out, too, watching them and waiting. He didn't look like he minded the cold too much, though he was a little hunched over in his flight gear. Stanley handed the cans to Mack, who filled the tanks then climbed into the cockpit.

Stanley stood at the propeller and waited for the call to contact. The little kid in him thrilled.

As a teenager, planes had come to his town, the county seat, and performed at the fairgrounds. Then in France he had seen the mechanics push the props at an aerodrome near his unit's assembly area. He had never thought he would someday be pushing the prop himself.

Mack yelled, "Contact," and Stanley threw the propeller. Mack spent some time testing the controls—Stanley could see the flaps moving around as he climbed in. Stanley was just starting to settle in when then the plane suddenly lurched forward. It roared down the runway and lifted quickly into the air.

Mack shouted over the roar of the engines. "It feels so powerful. It's a completely different plane!"

They rose up quickly and soon they were flying west over Denver, then past the sparse country farms at the town's outskirts and over the small towns at the foot of the mountains.

They were gaining altitude steadily and by the time they reached the Front Range they were able to clear the pass easily. Mack eased off the throttle and let the plane coast. It glided in relative silence over an expanding mountain valley below.

Stanley had told Mack the name of the town, but Mack had explained the name didn't matter that much. The only way to find it from the air was by its location. Stanley told him all he knew: that it was on the railroad, by a creek, and on a paved road as well. So they had to look around. They were following the railroad and looking for a town with all three characteristics. When he saw one, he pointed it out to Mack. They swept around for a second pass. "Now look out for the name," Mack said.

They flew by the railroad stop as Stanley looked out. They were going slow, just over stall speed, and it gave Stanley plenty of time to read the name. Stanley waved to Mack, telling him this was it.

They circled up higher, then turned toward nearby farms. Mack brought them over one for a visual examination. There were some folks from the farmhouse out looking up as the plane swept overhead, but otherwise the pasture was vacant and looked smooth to Stanley. But Mack shook his head and went around for another pass, this time deciding to come down on the road. Guynemer continued to circle overhead. Mack shut the engine off and Stanley climbed down just in time to meet the farmer, his wife, and kids rushing for the plane.

"What you doing here with that machine?" the man asked, very pointedly.

Stanley kept cool. "Kind sir, we're just hoping to park it on your farm for a little while. I'm going to run into town for some business, and when I return we'll be on our way. I'll be happy to pay for the privilege as well as a ride into town." He pulled out a twenty dollar bill.

The man and wife just sort of paused, their mouths slack. The oldest boy said, "Wow. Let's take it!"

The man was eager for a moment, then his eyes got suspicious. "What you need a ride into town for?"

"I have business there. This was the closest landing point."

"What business?"

"A friend of mine has been accused of a crime he did not commit. I am trying to find evidence to defend him."

"You talking about that Pitcher girl what they says was killed up here?"

"Sadly, yes."

"I knew Otto couldna done it. I'd take you in for free, only times is ever so tough around here as of late."

"As of ever," his wife said.

"Shoot," the man said.

Stanley handed over the twenty, saying, "Of course. You're welcome to it. Can you help us push this off the road? And would you be willing to put my friend up for a few days?"

"Of course," the wife said.

"Thank you."

The man, who Stanley had found was named Harry, drove him into town.

It didn't take long for Stanley to find the people that had been charmed to conceal their witness. Stanley was able to disenchant several of them to get good statements and an expressed willingness to testify at trial. Not only that—they told him where the girl had been found.

For a couple extra dollars, Harry agreed to take Stanley out there. The drive was relatively short with clear roads, but Harry said in the winter, when the murder happened, it was nearly impassible to wheeled vehicles. It was easy to get off the road, and then you were stuck for good.

The site was a glacial bowl. At the bottom there was scrub grass and wildflowers. Stanley got out of the car, and as soon as his feet hit the ground, he could feel it—something was stirring here. The presence he had felt from town had its origin here. It was not born here, but it was anchored here, bound by a very old charm. It was partly freed, and reaching its tendrils out. It would still need to be freed, and then get a spirit to guide it across the void. But it was already able to exert some influence in this place.

Stanley walked across the scrub grass, his hands outstretched, feeling the beast below the ground. It did not want to be known by him, it kept moving and hiding itself in its writhing and horrible bulk. In the dead center of the bowl, there was a region where the grass and wildflowers gave way to a darker vegetation. Lower to the ground than the grass, it was the kind of vegetation that should have no place in such a dry climate--hyssop and horsetails, creeping jenny and spearwort—all with dark red-brown leaves that looked just this side of death. This was the site of the sacrifice, and all these plants were feeding off the dark energy spilled here.

But Stanley did feel something else. He wandered away from the central sacrificial area, his hands outstretched, drawn by a presence that was subtle, but morbid. He took a few more steps, then stopped. At his feet was a bone- or ivory-handled dagger, its silver scalloped blade tarnished and stained with a dry brown residue.

"Harry, come over here."

Harry rushed over.

"Look at this."

"What is it?"

"A knife of some sort. I think it might be the murder weapon. I'm going to report it to the local authorities."

They drove back into town, got the sheriff, who was unhappy at being dragged out just when he hoped to be getting home, but when they explained why they wanted him, he became eager and very happy to go.

The sheriff looked at the dagger and exhaled. He didn't know what to make of it. When he tried to lift it up, Stanley pointed out that grass was actually growing around and over it—it had been there for a while. The sheriff agreed and pointed to the yellowed stems below the handle.

Back at the post office, which doubled as the sheriff's office, the sheriff wrote out a sworn statement and the clerk from city hall typed it up in triplicate. One copy was filed there. A second was attached to the knife, now marked and packaged as evidence. The third copy was given to Stanley.

It was very late by the time Stanley and Harry made it back to the farmhouse. That night Stanley and Mack shared a bed that one of the children had been asked to give up for the night. The next morning they were on their way back to Denver.

When they landed, they didn't see the men coming up to the plane. It was Guynemer who said to Mack, "You may want to turn around. I believe you know these men."

Mack turned around. "Yes, I do." Then, to Stanley, "If you'll excuse me."

Stanley watched as Mack walked up to the three men in fancy suits and broad hats pulled low. He stayed where he was, conveniently within earshot of their meeting place.

"Where was you?" said the man in front, short, dark-skinned, with a thin moustache.

"I wasn't here."

"Yeah, we noticed." He looked at the really big guy to his left. "We needed you for a shipment."

Mack scratched his head, looked away. "Hey, I'm not sure I want to be taking shipments for you anymore. I just don't think it's right for me."

"Oh, yeah? Izzat so?"

Guynemer yelled, "Look out!"

Just as he yelled, the big guy started taking a swing at Mack, who was able to dodge back and away because of the warning. He said, "Is that how this is going to be?" He stepped forward and delivered an elbow to the big guy's kidney. The big guy grunted and stumbled. Mack turned on the leader.

The leader had stepped back and drawn a knife, but Stanley had charged forward and knocked it out of his hand before he could use it. The little guy tried to back away, let his other burly companion engage Stanley, but Stanley kept him in the middle as he closed in. A pair of quick punches felled the little guy. Before Stanley could fully turn to respond, the other burly man had closed to fighting distance. Stanley dodged his first punch, but the second hit him on the cheek, sending a jolt through his body. He wavered, but didn't fall, and managed to dance back, dodging the next couple of punches as he got his mind clear.

Then Stanley started working the big guy. He couldn't keep completely away from his punches, but he made sure he gave at least two for every one he got. It was starting to fatigue the tough. Then he put out a lazy punch, which Stanley grabbed and threw the tough to the ground. He was slow to get up, and when he started to, Stanley kicked him in the face. There was a loud crack from his jaw, and the man went down again. This time he didn't get up.

Stanley looked around and saw that Mack was being slowly beaten to a pulp by the other tough. Stanley rushed over and gave the guy a couple of blows in the ribs. He turned partly to face Stanley, and Mack quickly took advantage. It didn't take much of this double treatment before the tough decided to bail.

Mack was panting heavily when he looked over at Stanley. Stanley said, "You're bleeding."

Mack said, "I know. Thanks." He touched his bloody lip.

"Well, if you knew, you didn't have to thank me. You're gonna want to put a steak on that eye."

"No, I meant thanks for bailing me out there."

"Don't mention it. Didn't want to see my pilot get smashed. Never know when you're going to need one."

"Well, if you do need one, you've got one. Just look for me here and I'm yours."

"Look to your eye. And your plane. I have a feeling I'll take you up on that offer sometime soon."

Then Stanley picked up his hat, put it back on his head and waved goodbye. He took the streetcar back downtown. There he looked up Derrick Biltmore. The lawyer was deep in preparations for Otoniel's case.

Stanley said, "Drop everything and look at this!"

Biltmore looked up, "Goodness! What happened to you?"

"Don't look at me! Look at this." Stanley shook the sheaf of papers.

"You've been busy, huh?" The lawyer put down his pencil and grabbed the papers from Stanley's hand.

Stanley sank down heavily in a chair and pulled out his flask.

Biltmore looked up from the papers, "Please. Vice is just down the hall, and those guys can smell hooch a mile away."

Stanley waved dismissively. "Just read."

Biltmore pursed his lips, then went back to reading quietly. It was only a second later that he said, "This is huge. Not only is this evidence going to give us great odds, it can guarantee us some delay. These witnesses have to be depositioned, and they'll have to be subpoenaed to proceed with the case."

"Yeah. And that's not all. Flip to the back." Stanley took another long pull on the flask.

Biltmore thumbed to the last page in the stack. He read for a moment, then exclaimed, "Goodness! Do you think this is it? Could it be?"

"Yeah. I think it's the murder weapon."

"Well, then, that's the case right there. Unless it belonged to the victim and she had it on her when she went out, why would Otoniel buy a silver dagger?"

"And how?"

"Exactly! He supposedly had no money until the day after the murder."

Stanley nodded.

Suddenly, though, Biltmore's face sunk. "But how can we prove it's the weapon? By the time the corpse was found, it was badly decayed. We can't possibly match the weapon to the wounds."

"Blood test. There was blood on the weapon."

"But that only works with fresh blood."

Stanley shook his head. "Used to. Now the Lattes crust test lets us do tests on dry blood."

"The what? I've never heard of that."

"Get in touch with the Federal Secret Service. They'll be able to help you." Rested, Stanley stood up and put his hat back on. "Let me know if you need anything else."

"How could I possibly hope for more?"

Stanley smiled, which hurt on the right side. Definitely going to be bruised there. As he walked down the hall, he began rolling a cigarette. He almost felt like whistling.

57.   Direct Me in the Paths of Victory

Stefani wanted to follow the demon's instructions exactly, but she didn't see how she could possibly do it. It was the silk again.

The demon said that in order to be able to summon her father's spirit she needed a blue silk robe. Blue! There was no way she'd be able to afford another silk robe. And then there was the copper jewelry set with emeralds. The ridiculous expense necessary to even attempt a conjuration made Stefani wonder that anyone would ever attempt to perform more than one in a lifetime.

And yet, her father had never had a job during her lifetime, and he hadn't been born into money. He made money somehow. It must have been through his conjuring, and enough to support his family and to be able to acquire a huge stock of reagents and tools.

That's when it occurred to Stefani that perhaps her father had what she needed. She went into his study and went directly to the closet. There were silk robes inside. Black, blue, gold, silver, and many other colors. She found a small safe in the corner of the closet. One of the keys on her father's ring fit it. Inside were many types of jewels, including copper jewelry set with emeralds.

Stefani could have kicked herself. The only thing was, these robes were too big. She would need to have them cut down to her size. She wasn't sure she even had enough money for that. But maybe if she took them to Caroline at Gold's shop, maybe she could get a good price. An insider price. If not . . . perhaps she could hock some of the jewelry. She didn't like the thought of that, though. Not only because it was father's, but because she was afraid she might need it. She had a nagging suspicion that this wouldn't be her last conjuring.

Stefani put the blue robes into a garment bag and carried them down the street to the dressmaker's shop. She was coming during Caroline's preferred work hours, so hopefully she would be there.

Caroline was there, and she smiled. "Stefani! It's been a long time." Her friend rushed around the counter and hugged Stefani. "Where have you been?"

"I've been working."

"Working? You mean, during the day? What happened? Where are you working now?"

"The club got shut down." Stefani walked to the counter and draped the robes over it. "I'm working for my Uncle Tad."

"That handsome, rich man we met at the café?" She smiled a wide grin and gave Stefani a sidelong look. "I see how you work!"

"Carrie!" Stefani said, feeling a little blush come to her face despite herself. "It's not like that at all. I'm helping him with research."

"Mm-hmm," Caroline said and rolled her eyes a little.

"Anyway, I came here with business."

"Really? Let me see." Caroline came over and unzipped the bag. "Oooh!" she said, reaching out and gently touching the silk. "This is real silk. And it's such high quality. Deeply and uniformly dyed. Dense threads."

"Yes. I need to have it cut down so I can wear it."

"Okay," Caroline said. Her eyes and fingers were still lingering on the cloth. "But silk is expensive to get worked."

"That is not what I wanted to hear." Stefani pulled out all her money and laid it on the counter.

Caroline counted it. "That's not very much."

"I hoped you could get me a deal?"

"Maybe. Maybe if you don't need it right away, and we get to keep any excess. This is really fine silk. Where'd you get it?"

Stefani bit her lip for stability. "What about in three weeks?"

"Three weeks? That should be fine."

"Thank you," Stefani said. She said goodbye and Caroline did, too, though she kept her eyes on the robe until the zipper on the bag was completely closed.

Next, Stefani caught the streetcar out to Thaddeus' house. He was expecting her for work. She wasn't sure yet what she was going to tell him about why she needed the next three weeks off. She walked back to the library with trepidation.

She put her hand on the doorknob, and she could see her hand trembling. Because the information she had used to compel the demon to speak came from Thaddeus' library, she felt that he would know her purpose. But as she headed up the stairs toward his study cell, she calmed herself. All this time, she had been studying right under his nose, and he didn't know a thing. She just had to keep up the act and he would remain just as ignorant.

As she reached the top of the stairs, Thaddeus said, "Oh, there you are. I was wondering what had happened to you."

"I'm sorry I'm late. I had to drop off a dress to be mended." She smiled apologetically.

He smiled back. "Well, that's okay." He rustled through the papers on his desk, then came up with a small slip. He said, "Here's the starting list," then reached out to hand it to her.

"Actually, Uncle Tad, I can't work today. I think I'm going to need three weeks off."

"Three weeks?" Now his eyes narrowed, gaining the intensity that Stefani feared. "Why?"

Stefani smiled shyly and looked away. She turned a little to the side and affected a slight pose. "It's personal. Mom and me . . ."

His hardened glance hit that smile and melted. His own smile returned. "Of course. I should know better than to ask." He turned to his desk and put the paper down. Then he turned back to her. "I got along fine before you were here, and I suppose I shall get along just as well without you." He stood up and stepped toward her. He put his hand on her shoulder. "Only I shall miss your company. Don't hesitate to come by when you are ready to work again."

"Thank you, Uncle Tad!" she said. She stepped back away from his hand. She waved and said, "Maybe I will miss you, too."

As she turned and headed down the stairs, she thought about how easy he was to fool, how even his justified suspicions might be waylaid with a smile and a pose, how her smile and her figure might be all he actually saw of her. The thought made her feel almost as angry as she was relieved.

On the way home, she reminded herself that this was exactly why she needed to take the time off. She needed to be able to isolate herself from people of this world who would distract her emotions. She needed to focus herself exclusively on her father. By the time she got home, she had almost completely forgotten Thaddeus. She had shifted to preparing herself for her next encounter.

Her mother was sitting at the table, staring out the window as usual. Stefani closed the door loudly enough that her mother should have noticed, but she didn't look. Stefani walked up and touched her on the shoulder, and then she did jump. Stefani jumped too.

When they had calmed and laughed a little, Stefani said, "Mother, I'm going to be trying a new diet and wanted to add some things to the grocery order."

Elizabeth looked Stefani up and down, then said, "Stefani, you have a fine figure. You don't need to try any diet."

Stefani was prepared for this, she said, "Not for today's shifts. They don't look smart unless you're slim."

Elizabeth clucked, then said, "You'll never look the way those flappers do, not with our figure. But I suppose you wouldn't be my daughter if you didn't try. Give me the list."

Stefani handed the list to her mother. "And I'll be making my meals myself. It's important for the diet that I prepare my food and eat alone. I'll also be spending most of my time up in my room."

"Oh? And what about your job with Mr. Marduk?"

"I told him I need some time off. I think I'll be looking for a new job when I finish the diet."

"Oh, that'd be wonderful. I do think you have more promise than you've been letting yourself show."

"I hope so," Stefani said, then headed up to her room.

In her room, Stefani washed herself with scented oil according to the instructions of the demon. She scraped the oil away with a copper strigil. Then she dressed and waited for the day to pass. It wasn't long before she became hungry, and it became hard to keep her thoughts focused on her father.

The day passed very slowly, but eventually it was dark and Stefani heard her mother go to bed. Then Stefani rose and headed downstairs to get something to eat. She was starving and a little dizzy feeling. She was reciting the demon's words about the only things she could eat as she headed downstairs. Bread, wine, roots, and fruits. Obviously, the grocery order had not been delivered, as there was little fitting that description. There was a little bit of wine at the bottom of a bottle, so she poured that into a glass. The end of bread was little more than a single slice. There was a potato and an apple.

It wasn't nearly enough, but she knew that was part of the point. She went back up the stairs and waited for midnight.

As midnight approached, she took a candle and her father's hourglass and headed into his study. She went to the small altar she had prepared and removed the veil of white silk from the portrait of her father. Then she turned the hourglass over and went to sit down in the protective circle.

She looked at the picture of her father. It was a small one, just a photo, but it captured his personality perfectly. He had an off-kilter frowning expression, with his bushy moustache tilting high up to his left. His eyes were atwinkle, though, showing that he wasn't really angry. He was just deeply engaged in a thorny problem. The problems were always both vexing and exciting. He loved and hated them. And he always seemed to have one. This expression was the one that Stefani remembered best. She hoped to see it in life again.

When the hourglass had completely run down, Stefani rose and put the veil back over the portrait. Then she backed out of the room with the hourglass and the now much shorter candle in her hands.

As soon as she was out of the room, she became aware again of how hungry she was. That was just the way it was going to be. She went back to her room, blew out the candle, and went to bed. It took her a while to fall asleep with her hunger pangs, but eventually she did.

After nineteen days of this routine, Stefani was barely able to stand, let alone walk over to her wardrobe. She selected a dress and put it on. When she began to put her housecoat on to go do her makeup, she noticed how much the dress hung off her. She looked at herself in the mirror. She was wan and thin. Her eyes, cheeks, arms, breasts—everything—seemed to hang down, as if it were all just as tired as she felt. She sighed, then went back to her wardrobe. In the back she knew she had a dress or two and a brassiere she used to wear when she was smaller but hadn't ever gotten rid of. One of the dresses managed to fit her fairly well, although the skirt was a bit short. That might cause her trouble if she were going downtown, but hopefully it wouldn't do more than raise a few eyebrows for the short distance she was going.

Then she put on her housecoat and sat down to do her makeup. Her face was really pale, and her sunken eyes and cheeks were definitely a challenge, but eventually she made herself presentable. She went downstairs and tried to sneak by her mother.

"Stefani!" Elizabeth called before Stefani had even reached the door.

"Hi, mom," Stefani said as she turned around to face her.

"I've hardly seen you these past few weeks. Come over here."

Stefani came over to the table.

"By gosh, girl, you don't look well. That diet is certainly taking off the pounds, but that can't be good for you!"

"I'm alright, Mother. But I was just on my way out."

"For the first time in three weeks, I bet. Don't you have time to talk to your mom?"

Stefani remembered well how the demon had told her she mustn't get emotionally distracted, how that could interfere with the conjuring. So she said, "Sorry, Mom, but I've got to go."

Elizabeth sighed. "Well, okay. Give us a kiss, and then off with you."

Stefani leaned over dutifully, almost found herself losing her balance, but caught herself on the chair before she actually fell onto her mother. A quick peck and she was back on her way out the door.

Stefani headed out to the dress shop. The sunlight seemed very bright, and the shop seemed so much farther away than it ought to have been. By the time she reached it, Stefani had to sit down. She staggered a little bit coming through the door, then let herself collapse into a chair in the waiting area.

Fortunately, Caroline was talking to another customer, so it didn't seem too weird. Instead of picking up a magazine, as she usually would, Stefani looked at one of the fashion prints on the wall. Or, rather, turned her head in its direction and let her vision unfocus.

She was startled when Caroline practically yelled in her ear, "Stefani!"

"What? Oh, I'm sorry. I didn't hear you."

"Are you sure you're okay?"

"Me? Yes. I'm fine."

"You don't look well."

"I . . . uh—I've been on a diet."

"It looks like it. I think you've lost a lot of weight." Suddenly Caroline put her hand to her mouth. "Oh, no, I hope it fits." She rushed back behind the counter and began looking through the garment bags. "It turns out the measurements we had were really old, and I knew you'd put on weight since then, so I told them to add a few inches here and there. I had no idea you were going to be dieting!" She pulled one of the bags out and hung it on a closer rack. "Come look," she gestured to Stefani.

Stefani put her hands on the edge of the mahogany-finish table and tried to push herself up. The floor tiles suddenly looked so far away that she got dizzy.

She took a deep breath and stood up through the dizziness. She came partway around the corner as Caroline opened the garment bag.

Inside was a blue silk dress. Stefani almost fainted. She barely managed to catch herself on the counter.

"I know," Caroline said, "isn't it gorgeous? I knew exactly which one you wanted—you talked about it so much last time you were here. The seamstress was able to make it right from the picture. Looks just like it. Try it on!"

A dress. Stefani was so mad, her hand curled into a fist and her nails were biting into her palm. She couldn't remember whether she had explicitly said she wanted a robe or not, but how dare Caroline assume anything other than that she wanted it cut to her size. But there was nothing for it now. She would be performing the final incantation tomorrow, and there was no way she could get anything else by then. It would have to do.

"Hey, are you okay? Do you need to sit down again?" She took a step closer. Stefani could see one of her hands out of her peripheral vision.

Stefani took another deep breath and calmed her voice. "No, no, I'm fine. Just surprised and a little dizzy."

"I know how you feel—those diets can be killer. The things we do for beauty, huh?"

"Yeah. Let me try it on."

Caroline handed Stefani the dress and she went to a dressing room. She tried it on.

It was a little tight, but overall she did like it. It was a coat frock with a neat notched collar and long sleeves. It wasn't that unlike a robe. Perhaps it would work.

Stefani came out of the dressing room.

"Oooh . . . I love it!" Caroline said.

Stefani smiled. "I do too."

"Oh, you do?" Caroline wiped her forehead in relief. "When you reacted that way, I was so afraid I'd gotten confused and picked the wrong one. But, really, it couldn't have been any other one—you admired it so much! It looks so toney!"

Stefani said, "It is a high style, isn't it?"

"The latest! And you wear it so well!"

Stefani blushed. She thought so, too, and was embarrassed to have her self-admiration spoken aloud. "Oh, go on, it's not that great."

"Gorgeous, I tell you! Gorgeous! What say you we go out and celebrate with a little lunch?"

Stefani's smile disappeared. "No, no. I can't do that."

"Cause of your diet? If you want, I'll just nibble, too." She feigned dainty eating with her hand. "But I think maybe you should eat a little bit more because you really do look like you're about to fall over right here!"

Stefani managed a little smile. "No, that's not it. It's just that I'm busy this week. Next week?"

"Okay, but since you're putting me off, it has to be dinner. And it has to be someplace fancy."

"Deal. I'll ring you at home."

Stefani changed out of the dress and put it back in its bag. As she closed the bag, she thought, *I hope this works, because I don't want to feel bad about this dress.*

On the way home, Stefani stopped and bought a large bouquet of violets. When she reached home, she slipped past her mother and went upstairs to put the violets in water. That took only a moment, then she began to wait for the time when she could eat her meager supper. Roots, fruits, bread, and wine. She longed for meat, or, really, any decent meal. When her mother went to bed, Stefani snuck downstairs and ate all she was allowed to eat. Then she went upstairs and performed her vigil before her father's picture for one last time before she would attempt the actual conjuring. Then she went to bed, so hungry and tired that despite her anxiety she was unable to stay awake even a moment after her head hit the pillow.

The next day, Stefani locked the door to her room and began her day-long mediation on her father. Her primary emotion was fear. She worried that she might utterly fail, but worse than that, she feared that she might half-succeed, draw her father away from his heavenly paradise and make him unable to return there.

She worried that she might strand his spirit to an interminable and painful exile between worlds. After the pain of his death, she felt he deserved a peaceful afterlife. During the morning, she wove the violets into a crown.

Her worries couldn't keep her awake, though, and as she mediated on her father, she dozed in and out of consciousness all day. Each brief sleep made her feel worse. She had a painful headache that got more intense with each short nap, and by the time evening darkened her room and she had to light a candle—the demon had said electric lights were forbidden during the mediation and the conjuring—she couldn't even stay sitting up. She was exhausted, so she leaned back, thought of the tiny meal she would get to eat, and fell asleep.

When she awoke, the candle was burned down very low. She panicked and grabbed the candle, quickly moved it to see the clock, and noticed, just before the light disappeared—the motion had extinguished the candle—that it was almost time for the conjuring. There was no time to eat.

She put on the blue silk dress with its clasps of copper. One of them had an emerald in it. Then she put on the copper tiara with the twelve emeralds, and the crown of violets. There was an amulet of Venus that had been her father's, which she put over her neck. Finally, she put on the copper ring with the turquoise set into it. She was ready to go into the sanctuary for the conjuring. She had taken care of everything, except, of course, her meal, an omission that she became painfully aware of as she headed into her father's study and almost fainted away. But there was no time. If she was going to do this, it had to be now.

She lifted up the veil on her father's picture, looked at his wry, smirking expression. It made her smile to think that soon she would see it again in life. After a fashion, anyway. She lit the candles on the altar, then headed to the circle.

Stefani took one last deep breath and tried to assemble her reserves. Unfortunately, she found that she didn't have much in the way of energy. She began the conjuration, "Powers of the Kingdom, be ye under my left foot and in my right hand! Glory and Eternity, take me by the two shoulders, and direct me in the paths of victory! Mercy and Justice be ye the equilibrium and splendor of my life! Intelligence and Wisdom, crown me!

"Vouchsafe to be present, O Father of All, and thou Thrice Mighty Hermes, Conductor of the Dead. Asclepius, son of Hephaistus, Patron of the Healing Art, and thou Osiris, Lord of strength and vigor, do thou thyself be present, too. Arnebascenis, Patron of Philosphy, and yet again Asclepius, son of Imuthe, who presideth over poetry.

"Powers carry my words across the vast gulf that separates the land of the living and the land of the dead to the ears of the spirit whom next I name:

"Nikolas Aegis, hear ye these, thine own words, and remember thy way to the plane of matter, 'I dared to do the research, now I must dare to do the work. I have come so far that if cowardice turns me back, it will be worse than nothing I have done, for I will have gained all the dangers of knowledge and none of the benefits of action.'" She chanted the quote again and again. They were some of the last words in her father's notebook, and they struck her as being both potentially relevant to her father's death and her own situation. It was not clear from her father's journal whether he had finally dared to move forward, or whether he had succumbed to fear.

Stefani chanted the quote many times, and with each word, she could feel her power and strength reaching out into the void. The amulet in its velvet pouch throbbed with her words, and she could feel its power bolstering her own, not just in the energy going out, but in her weakened body. She needed it—but for that strength, she might have collapsed while chanting.

The chanting went on and on, until it nearly took everything Stefani had. She thought it must be going on too long, that the conjuration had failed, when suddenly she felt the spirit enter the room. It was like a blue illumined mist, which slowly began to take a more definite shape until it had created a translucent likeness of her father.

It took the ghost a moment, but soon it made a smile. "Stefani," it said, "my girl. I cannot believe it is you. Please, come give me a hug."

Stefani almost did it without thinking, then she paused. "Father, you know I can't do that. You're just a spirit."

"I can still feel. Come to my arms, child."

"I can't. I can't break the circle."

"That's just for protection. You don't need protection from me."

Stefani took a moment to think. Then she said, "I can't. I have questions to ask. You are compelled to answer truthfully." And with that she directed energy down into her arm, extended her flat palm to the image, which cringed slightly. "How did you die?"

The image writhed for a moment, and its color flickered. "Killed by a spirit . . . attempted to cage and control."

"Can you tell me the name of that spirit?"

"No."

"You must know the name of the spirit, if you were trying to control it!" She clenched her fingers slightly.

The image shot through with shards of red, writhed, and blurred. "Please, Stefani, you're hurting me. Release me from this pain and I can tell you."

"Release you?"

"Yes. I am bound in my afterlife to a place of pain. I am prevented from answering your questions. Release me and I will be free to answer—and free from pain!" His face was earnest, his eyes pleading, and his hands outstretched toward her.

Stefani thought for a moment, tried to remember all that she had read in Thaddeus' library. "I don't have that power. I can't have that power. If you are bound in the afterlife, you're bound by greater spirits. I could only release you if you were bound by a human . . ."

She looked at her father's ghostly apparition. It had his eyes, his face, his body, even his expression. But that tear on his cheek was too much. Her father would never let her see him cry.

"You're not my father."

"What are you talking about, Stefani? You brought me here. You called me. And I am glad you did. To get to see you again, one last time, it will comfort me in that place of pain."

"I called you. I followed the exact instructions to bring you here, but those instructions were never intended to bring my father—they brought you!" And with that, she crushed her hand into a fist, putting all her strength into it.

The image writhed and unfocused, becoming completely red and unleashing a horrible scream. When it had finished its suffering, it stood back up, and now it was that beastly figure garbed as a Roman legionnaire. It stood up laughing its horrific laugh. "You have hurt me for the last time, girl."

Stefani said, "Perhaps, but now I will send you back to the torments of Hell."

The creature just laughed. "Try, girl, please!" It gnashed the sharp teeth in its long jaws. A forked tongue lolled out, then snaked along its yellowed and crooked fangs.

Stefani began chanting to force the beast back toward Hell, but she could feel her strength was diminished from the last time she had faced this beast. And where last time the creature had looked like it was struggling against a massive weight or force, this time it merely leaned forward, as if walking in a wind.

Then it lashed out with one of its hands. Stefani felt her power dispersed, and it was as if the hand struck her. She staggered back a step and barely managed to regain her balance before taking a second step back that would have carried her out of the circle.

Now the beast laughed in delight, "Yes, try that again! Then you can come out and play and we can have some real fun!"

Stefani didn't know what to do. She was at the end of her strength. She would have to wait until the spirit wore itself out with the effort of manifesting on the material plane. She slowly lowered herself to the ground, curling up carefully within the circle. She rested and tried not to cry as the demon paced around the protective circle, shouting creative and vile insults at her.

58.   A Terrible Mistake

When Stanley reached his apartment, Fallow and Tarkus were playing cards at the small table. They each had a pile of change in front of them, a sizeable pot in the middle, and from the configuration of the cards, Stanley could tell they were playing five card stud. Fallow was dealing. The room looked and smelled like the men had barely left it over the last few days.

Fallow said, "The Lionheart returns! How was the crusade? I thought you died in France."

Stanley snapped, "I know a lot of good men who died in France."

"Yeah, sorry. That was a bad joke. But you really have put us in a rough spot here." Fallow put the cards down, got up from the table and went over to the stand where the water basin was and pulled something out of the drawer. He gave it to Stanley. "Lookit this."

It was a telegram from Barton. It was short and clear. "PRIMARY MISSION PREVENT CONJURE DO NOT INTERFERE WITH POLICE INVESTIGATION." Stanley looked at Fallow, "Yeah, so? We knew that's what they wanted. No surprise there."

"So what do we do?"

"Just what the telegram says. Prevent the conjure. The evidence I brought will ensure Otoniel's release. And when that happens, we know the Klan and their allies will use the anger that results as the source for their rage spell. Then we interfere with that spell the same we did with the fear one."

"But what do we do now?"

"Now? It will take some time for the evidence to filter through the system, so we'll just have to wait. Deal me in."

They waited and watched over days as the story unfolded in the newspapers. Witnesses were brought in. The murder weapon was revealed. The new blood test was used. The papers explained it in detail. At the end of it all, Van Cise announced that he didn't have enough evidence to prosecute and he would have to release Otoniel. The newspapers blamed it on the lack of an effective police chief. The current chief had resigned on Mayor Stapleton's election, nearly a year before, but hadn't been replaced. In response, the Mayor appointed William Candlish.

They also walked the streets to try to get a sense of the mood in the city. Once it started to come out that Otoniel might not be prosecuted for the murder of Irene Pitcher, the city began to boil with rage. Everywhere white men met they would talk about the Mexicans or spics who were ruining their city and likely would ruin the country if nothing was done to stop them. They would talk about how the spics were sneaking into the country to steal work from true Americans. How they were all criminals if given the chance, and lecherous dandies, too, bent on stealing white women. Someone would have to protect them, because obviously the police couldn't.

Then one day as they were returning home from a scouting mission, Stanley saw that he had a message in his box. It was from Otoniel's attorney, Biltmore. It said, "Our boy is going to be released tomorrow. Good work. The police are offering him no protection when he leaves custody. Perhaps you can help with this?"

"He's gonna be released tomorrow," Stanley said.

"Yeah," Fallow said, "listen." He pointed to the radio behind the counter. The man on the radio was raving angrily. He said that Van Cise was not a true American, because he put the rights of spics and blacks ahead of the safety of American women. Reference was made to the Ward Gash case. The Klan was mentioned and praised for taking a stand in that case. It was hoped that they would also take a stand here, with actions that were proportionate to the more serious nature of the case. He all but said they should kill Otoniel. The hotel proprietor was rapt. His face was clenched in anger.

"Hey," Fallow said to the proprietor, "you believe that?"

"Huh? Yeah," the man said. "Of course. Somebody's got to do something to stop those Mexicans and Negroes or they will turn this country into Mexico or Africa. This is our country here, and we can't let them ruin it!"

Fallow looked at Stanley. He smiled. He always got a kick out of race-baiting with his passing charm. Because people didn't know he was black, he got the chance to hear what they really thought.

Stanley shook his head. He crushed out his cigarette in an ashtray. "C'mon," he said, then gestured for the other guys to follow him.

Up in the room, Stanley took a belt off his flask, then said, "So where are we at? We don't know if they're going to snap the charm tomorrow or not, but they could. If they do, are we prepared to stop them?"

Tarkus shook his head. "We don't know from nothing. If they planning it for tomorrow, they hid it real good."

"So, we'll just have to play it by ear and focus on protecting Otoniel. Chances are they want to kill him. A lynching makes a great focal point for this kind of casting. So if we can protect him, we've got a damn good chance of stopping their conjuring."

Fallow had walked over to the window and he looked down at the street. He shook his head, "It just doesn't feel right. I don't think it's going to be tomorrow."

"Maybe not," Stanley said, "but we have to be prepared."

"I know," Fallow said, "but exposing ourselves like this just doesn't seem right. There's something else going on, and I'm afraid we're going to find ourselves in the middle of something we don't want: a fight. If the crowd turns ugly, we're likely to be the target of their rage as much as Otoniel. And the crowd's numbers will make them deadly."

"Yeah," Tarkus said, "and we can't be deadly in return. We'll have to use restraint, and that means less powerful spells. Which puts us at risk."

Stanley nodded. "Comes with the territory. We'll just have to be extra careful in our preparations. So let's get started."

Stanley thought that in the morning they would have to ask after the door where Otoniel would be released, but they found it easily by the angry mob that was already present, holding signs and shouting. As they neared the crowd, Stanley took out a "Debs for President" button and pinned it on his lapel. The charm worked immediately, as the people nearest them began to look around and shift uncomfortably, even though their backs were turned. As he walked forward, the crowd parted subtly. For about ten feet around Stanley, the chanting was disrupted and people began to shuffle away from him. Without knowing why, people moved out of his way, none of them coming within three feet of him. This made it easy for Stanley, Fallow, and Tarkus to make it to the door through the crowd that the police were having trouble holding back.

Stanley spoke to the officer closest to the door. "I'm a private dick. I've been hired to provide protection to Otoniel Garcia. The kid's lawyer, Biltmore, he knows me."

Even the officer was somewhat intimidated by the charm, and he quickly called someone over to help him. They talked for a little while, then the second officer went inside. When he came out, Stanley, Fallow, and Tarkus were let through the police line.

They waited a few minutes before the door opened and two officers escorted Otoniel out. Biltmore came, too. When they emerged, the crowd's shouting increased in intensity and anger.

Biltmore smiled at Stanley and offered his hand. "I'm glad you came. This crowd looks ugly."

"Yeah," Stanley said, shaking hands, "they do look pretty ugly." He was thinking, *But not as ugly as I expected.*

Stanley went over to Otoniel. The boy looked thin, tired, and pale. His eyes were sunken in and red. Stanley offered him his hand.

They shook and Otoniel said, "Gracias, señor," but in his eyes it was clear he wasn't really grateful for some reason.

Then they had to pose for a few photographs. Biltmore had hired the photographer to take promotional images. He wanted a couple with Stanley and a couple without. Then Biltmore and the officers went back inside. Stanley took the lead with Otoniel behind him. Fallow and Tarkus completed a triangle with Otoniel at its center. Together the four men began to make their way through the narrow channel the police maintained through the crowd.

As they walked, Stanley's charm caused the people in the front ranks of the crowd to quiet down uncertainly, but overall the crowd grew louder as they got closer. There were many angry words, but nothing was thrown, and the crowd seemed to respect the police cordon. As they reached the end of the policed area and found themselves on the open street, everyone tensed, expecting the crowd to rush them, but it didn't. It stayed largely in place, looking on, angry.

They turned around and looked back at the crowd, and Fallow said, "That was a lot easier than I expected."

"Yes," Stanley said. Just then he spotted Saluzar and Dr. Locke in the crowd, looking right at him. They were both smiling, and suddenly Stanley's blood went cold. "Fallow, you were right. We should not have exposed ourselves. This was a terrible mistake."

As they proceeded to take Otoniel to the streetcar, Stanley wondered what Saluzar's real plan was, and whether they really would be able to stop his conjuring

59.   Such a Silly Girl

Riding the public bus could give you a lot of time for personal reflection, unless of course a chatterbox sat down next to you—a constant peril for a young woman traveling alone.

Today, Stefani was unlucky. The chatterbox in question was a young man in a grey suit. The material was cheap, the stitching bad, but the man's constant subject was how well off he was, how he could be driving if he wanted to, and the number of prospects he had for the future, how he was a Stapleton man and would be brought in to the new government, sooner or later.

She couldn't take it. Having barely escaped from the shrieks and insults of the demon when the sun rose and it became weakened, she couldn't listen to this cheap-suited man just blabbering at her. She had to prepare for her discussion with Thaddeus. She got off the bus several stops early and began to walk. The one sure way to guarantee you were free to be alone with your thoughts.

She got so lost in her thoughts that she didn't notice she had been walking with her eyes closed, feeling her way along somehow, but without touching anything. As she walked, she was suddenly bathed in a blinding light. Her reflex was to close her eyes, but they were already closed.

Opening her eyes dimmed the light, but she could still sense it. Now she realized it wasn't light, exactly, it was something else, some other sense that she sometimes thought was light, and sometimes thought was sound—and suddenly she realized that it was the same thing she felt from her amulet as a vibration. And now she was being bathed in it, and it was coming from Thaddeus' house.

It was similar to what she'd felt when working in his library, but different in character, the way a room full of conversations is different from a single orator. She tried, but couldn't pick out the particular voice, but she had a feeling it was there——among so many others. Were there really so many things like that, all vying for attention, all striving to be heard? And all behind the innocuous façade of a colonial house.

And was Thaddeus their master? Was he the master of the thing in her own basement? The thought gave her pause as she was preparing to open his gate. She had felt the terrible potential of the thing in the basement. Would someone really loose such an entity? She opened the gate, closed it behind her and walked up to the door. She took a deep breath before turning the doorbell key.

There was an immediate sound of activity inside, a strange combination of heavy leather-soled footsteps and what Stefani thought was the scrabble of small, clawed feet. It took Thaddeus a long time to answer the door, and Stefani wondered at the noise. It wouldn't be the sound of cats' paws. It sounded more like the feet of small dogs, something without retractable claws. She knew Thaddeus didn't keep pets. Did he have vermin? The sound seemed too large for mice or even rats.

When Thaddeus opened the door, he had his finger in a book without words or symbols on the cover or spine, but his red complexion and rapid breath betrayed some more active occupation than reading.

"Stefani?" His annoyed expression became a too-wide smile, showing not just his smoke-yellowed incisors, but his long, sharp canines. "A welcome surprise. Please, please come in." He held the door open and gestured inward.

Smoke filled the dim interior of the heavy brick house. Sweet pipe tobacco overlaid something sulfurous and earthy.

"Let me get you something to drink. I have lemonade, tea—hot or iced— or, if you'd like, something more bracing."

Part of Stefani longed to get directly to her question, but the part of her that was terrified allied with the part ruled by manners and she replied, "Iced tea, please."

While Thaddeus was getting the drink, Stefani looked around, trying to identify the sound of the scrabbling claws. There were no obvious signs of animals, including no sign of claw damage on the floor or baseboards. But she heard the voices. It was like walking into a room full of gossip-mongers. From everywhere, she felt eyes on her, and dozens of whispers, all too low to make out. She knew that feeling and could not help but fall to a critical examination of her figure. After fortifying herself with a light meal, she had changed from the silk summoning dress into a shift dress from her closet. It was a popular style that had never really suited her, and with her recent weight loss it looked even more like a potato sack. But the item that inspired the most "talk," she felt, was her necklace, the amulet in the velvet bag. It was warm and it throbbed. When she touched it, she felt more than beautiful. She was majestic.

She sat up taller, straighter, and looked around with a natural hauteur. The gossips were silenced. That was a great feeling, like the moment she began her dance and she was suddenly sensual. When all the words and images that told her she was fat and ugly couldn't stop her from knowing she was beautiful—the moment when all the pitiful, disapproving, critical eyes of women were crowded out by the simple, admiring eyes of men.

Thaddeus returned with his eyes on her, admiring and desirous as they fell on her bosom. She took the offered iced tea and sipped. He said, "I have missed your help. Things progress less quickly without you. Hopefully you have come back to work."

"No."

Thaddeus pressed his lips together. He looked her over again, not admiring now, his eyes interrogatory. He leaned back. "Perhaps you have a favor to ask?"

"Yes. I need your help." She explained what had happened.

Thaddeus smiled. "I see." Then he laughed. "Such a silly girl. Oh, you were smart enough to figure out the library better than I thought you would, but what a fool you were to tangle with powers you don't understand and couldn't possibly hope to contend with."

Stefani was ashamed. She lowered her head. She knew what she had done was foolish.

"And why didn't you just ask me for help first?"

"Because I . . . I wasn't sure you hadn't killed father. I wasn't sure I could trust you."

"So you decided to trust a demon? There's the logic of a woman, for you. And now you need my help to get rid of it."

Stefani flushed. She was barely able to squeak out a "Yes."

"You think I killed your father, but I know the truth. He killed himself."

"No!" Stefani slammed her glass on the table.

"Yes, he did. By playing with forces he couldn't control. Just like you."

He pointed an accusing finger.

"That amulet was your father's. It's dangerous. You should give it to me."

"No."

"You could hurt yourself. And others will come looking for it. They could hurt you, too. Give it to me."

"No!"

"Give it to me!" Thaddeus suddenly leapt up from his seat with surprising speed and reached across the table to grab at her bosom.

"I said no!" Stefani yelled, clutching the velvet bag defensively. Suddenly, a wave of energy surged away from her, lifting Thaddeus up and throwing him against the wall. He hit with a thud and a grunt, then sank motionless to the floor. There was a bloody splotch and a small smear that stretched down to Thaddeus' still body.

The gossips resumed speaking. Dozens of angry, accusing voices. Stefani had to get away from their chattering and whatever might be running loose in here. She rose from the seat and rushed out the door, though she didn't know where she was going.

60.   All the Corners Where You Were Afraid to Look

Stanley hated keeping hours in his office. It was just marking time, and he was finding it difficult to focus on the work he had brought to fill that time. He was trying to sort out why Phil Saluzar and his cabal were taking so long to act.

They obviously had enough support to make almost any conjuration easy. And now that Stanley had sprung Otoniel, there must be enough latent anger to bring new people to their cause, so of course they could do it then. Even if it were something dimension-shattering, with the thousands of souls pledged to the cause, they could do it. Unless they lacked some crucial element? It couldn't be that they needed a place of power, like Jerusalem or Ur or Stonehenge, because then it wouldn't make any sense setting up out here.

Perhaps it was timing. Maybe they were waiting on a local ebb of ley lines. Unlikely. There'd been plenty of time for them to get the ley lines at their maximum, and several full moons had passed, too. Of course, he couldn't be sure unless he did the math, but he was terrible at thaumology. Might as well consult a haruspex, it would be about as accurate as his figures. He just remembered the old rule of thumb, "Less than a moon, it may be too soon." Well, it'd been more than a month, so they must be waiting for something else.

He was just about to give up and go home for the day when she walked in. He heard Gail, his secretary, drop her book in surprise, but he felt the woman come in as well. A familiar presence.

He got up and rushed into the front office and, sure enough, though she wasn't wearing stage makeup and she was flushed and sweaty, he recognized the woman who had fled the club. Stefani, Phil Saluzar had said was her name.

She recognized him, too. She looked at him and said, "You?" Then she collapsed—Stanley was barely able to reach her before she hit the floor. And when he caught her, he almost couldn't hold her. It wasn't that she was heavy. She was charged. Charged with power, and with purpose. Stanley suddenly realized she was what the wizards were waiting for.

Stanley looked at Gail, who looked about ready to faint herself, and said, "Please get the door," gesturing with his head.

The girl found her awareness and rushed around the desk to the door separating the outer and inner offices.

Stanley dragged the fainted woman, holding her under her arms. When they got her to the chaise lounge in his office, he scooped her up in his arms. As he had feared, having that close contact with the power almost made him swoon, but he got her up on the lounge. As he put her down, he said to Gail, "Get her some water."

While his secretary was gone, he let himself lean heavily against his desk and took several deep breaths to recover. By the time Gail returned, he was standing up straight, and, he hoped, showing no signs of fatigue. "Thanks," he said as he took the glass, "I'll let you know if I need anything."

Gail nodded and went out quickly, closing the door behind her. When she was gone, Stanley noticed Stefani seemed to be waking up. He knelt at her side and offered her the glass.

"Get back!" she said. Although her gesture was feeble, the wave of energy it released threw Stanley up and over his desk. The glass shattered on the ceiling.

Gail was back in a flash. She looked at Stanley, who was just standing up behind his desk, then at Stefani, then back at Stanley, who said, "She startled and broke the glass. Please get a rag and dustpan."

Gail nodded but barely moved.

"Please," Stanley said forcefully.

This time, Gail left immediately.

Stanley moved to the side of the lounge.

"You," the woman said, meekly.

"Yeah, me. This is my office."

"The sign said private investigator. I came in. I need help."

"Yeah, well, if you want to get it, you need to get that shit under control."

"Sorry. I'm afraid."

"Why?"

"It might kill me."

"It?"

She gestured at the amulet.

"Possible. Especially if you don't get it under control. Where'd you get it?"

"My father left it behind. It might have killed him."

"This sounds like a long story. Hold on." Gail was coming in with the dustpan, rag, and broom. Stanley reached out. "Thanks, doll. I'll take care of this." She looked at Stefani, then handed everything over to Stanley. "Can you get us a couple cups of coffee? One with cream, no sugar." Stanley looked at Stefani.

She answered weakly, "Sugar, but no cream."

"Perfect." He handed the secretary a quarter. "Get yourself something, and don't worry about the change."

"Thanks," Gail said, perking up. She was obviously flagging this late in the day, but now she clutched the quarter tight as she headed to the coat rack.

Stanley took the rag and cleaned up some of the water, then took the broom and dustpan and swept up all the broken glass. He put the pan and broom in the corner, which allowed him to look in the outer office and make sure Gail was gone.

He grabbed his notebook and sat down on a wooden chair beside the lounge. "Now, let's get some basics out of the way. What's your name?"

"Stefani Aegis."

"Now, tell me what you know."

Stefani began telling him about the entire series of events, from her nightmares through her discovery of the amulet. She talked about the conjuration and the demon and her confrontation with Thaddeus.

Stanley listened intently. When she hesitated, he encouraged her with an informed guess at what she was holding back. It wasn't a surprise that she'd hesitate to reveal so many incredible things. The visions, voices, and feelings that were so far outside the normal experience, so readily attributable to a fevered brain.

When the coffee arrived, Stanley poured a little from his flask into his cup. He tilted the flask toward Stefani's cup, but she dismissed it with a shake of her head.

When she was finished speaking, she looked into her half cup of cold coffee.

"It's not too late for a bracing drop," Stanley said.

"No." She took another sip. "It's just, I don't know what to do."

"You came to me. That's what you did. Now I take it from here. Just so happens this might intersect with another case I'm working on, so you're helping me almost as much as I'm helping you.

"First, let's check out your cellar. We'll poke into all the corners where you were afraid to look." He noticed Stefani's expression. "You don't have to come along, but either way I can guarantee your complete safety."

"Okay."

"Now, do you have a place to stay, other than the house?"

Stefani shook her head.

"Hey, doll, come in here."

Gail immediately opened the door and popped her head in. "Yes, boss?"

"Can you help Miss Aegis here find a place to stay?"

Gail nodded.

"Good. And next time you should pause before coming in when I call—makes it harder to guess you've been listening at the door."

Gail's face colored. "Yes, boss."

61.   They Had All the Vocabulary

Otoniel was unhappy that he was being released. The demons had tried to make him suffer by ignoring him, but they could not restrain themselves for long. Restraint is not in their nature. The dark cell with all the jibbering demons around had begun to seem like the place he belonged. It was very much like Hell, and that was where he was bound. He had watched two women be attacked, and he had thought only of himself in both cases.

He could ask forgiveness, but the darkness of the confessional didn't appeal to his soul as someplace he could reveal his sins. He did not care what a priest said. He only cared about Maria, and he did not think that she would forgive him.

Now the door opened and the sun shone on him, and he felt horribly exposed. He felt more than just naked, he felt as if his flayed skin hung about him in shreds and patches, exposing his disgusting viscera. And all around there was a shouting crowd. They hated him, and they were hungry to come up and tear apart his body, eat the succulent, pulsing, bloody organs, but they were held back by something.

Stanley was here, with two companions. Stanley tried to talk to him, but Otoniel didn't really understand him. His own thoughts were too loud. He tried to smile. This seemed to suffice. There were pictures taken. He tried to smile for those, too.

Stanley's two companions arranged themselves around him. One of them was short, stout, bearded, and pale. The other, Otoniel couldn't get a look at. He got the impression that he was medium height, medium build, and white, but if he tried to see his features closely, it was impossible.

They walked through the crowd, which seemed to quiet slightly as they passed. All the faces seemed familiar to Otoniel. They were the ones that chased him away from work sites, the ones that let him know when he had crossed into the wrong neighborhood. They were the ones that told him when he was in the wrong club, and, most of all, they were the ones that warned him he was looking at the wrong girl. A white girl.

Of course he wasn't really interested in those girls. Like the one in the car. Thin, rich, and pale as death. Everyone said that was what men wanted, but it wasn't what he wanted. A woman submissive. Totally passive. A mere lump of flesh. Who could want that?

Otoniel was surprised when he found himself at home. Stanley said, "Go inside. Greet your mother. She will be happy to see you. Keep her away from the door. She may not like what she sees."

Otoniel saw Stanley pull out a small, struggling form. A white rat. He realized he might not like what Stanley was doing, so he rushed inside.

Mama was happy to see him. She greeted him with hugs and kisses. She said, "I always knew you were innocent. I knew you couldn't do something like that. Not my Otoniel." Otoniel went to his bedroom, and she followed. Maria was there, too. She glowered at him.

Mama was the same as ever, though. She touched his hair, talked about how he was her youngest, most sensitive, most precious boy. He wouldn't hurt anyone, couldn't hurt anyone. Far from comforting, her attentions made him feel guilty. He looked to Maria for comfort. But she stood at the door, her eyes red and moist. What happened?

After a while, Mama stopped, pulled back, and looked at him. "Jito, you are so tired. You cannot have gotten any rest. I will let you lie down now. I will go cook something for you to eat—you look like you need that, too." She kissed him on the head one more time, then eased him onto the bed.

He heard Stanley talking to Mama and Maria, telling them that Otoniel was officially cleared and that no one from the police would come looking for him for now. If anybody came demanding Otoniel, they were by no means to let Otoniel out to talk to them, or to let the people in. Even if someone in a police uniform came looking, by no means should Otoniel cross the threshold nor should the people be invited inside.

If they were worried, they should contact Stanley or Otoniel's lawyer. Then Stanley and his friends left.

Otoniel lay in bed listening to the silence, wondering if he could ever enjoy it again. He had lost his right to silence. He deserved to be taunted and beset by demons. He soon would be. The quiet lasted for several days, then the demons came to his home.

The creatures initially came with angry, shouting people. But while the people left, mostly just showing up a few times to throw a rock through the window or otherwise deface the property, the demons stayed, and their cacophonous howls continued all through the night. They had all the vocabulary of Hell and they used every word in their unending stream of fiendishly creative insults and threats.

He felt almost comfortable. Between the demons' hate and Mama's love, he felt like he was right where he should be. But for Maria, he might have survived.

Maria's judgment weighed on him. She continued to avoid him and didn't talk to him if she could avoid it. Otoniel couldn't stand it, so one day he confronted her in the hall. "Maria, why are you so angry at me?"

"You know why!"

"You can't hold a private judgment against me—after all, what was my crime?"

"You raped Victoria!"

"I didn't. But I was there. I was guilty of letting it go on. I took part, and that's my crime. I didn't turn myself in, and that's my crime, too. But your crime here, this private judgment, is almost as bad. You haven't turned me in. You haven't come forward with evidence. You haven't done anything about the terrible crime that you have known about for years. Judging me here in the dark has been your own excuse, your own pretense at innocence that lets these kinds of horrible things keep happening."

He grabbed Maria's hands in his. "Something has to bring these crimes into the light. I tried to get the police to help me, but they wouldn't. God hasn't done anything. I need to seek a different kind of light."

Otoniel rushed to the door. Now the gibbering of the demons was deafening. He threw open the door and ran out. As he ran outside, the demons began laughing, and their sound was like a flock of grackles in the trees. He held out his hands, and yelled, "Come get me!"

But when he was grabbed, it was human hands that held him, not the talons of demons. Shocked, Otoniel looked around and saw the white-sheeted figures behind him. He started to fight, but he was quickly overwhelmed. "Filthy spic," one of them said, "now you'll really pay for what you've done."

62.   All Part of the Plan

The old man and his tall companion had been conspicuously absent since they visited the Mayor's Office. But Bart needed to talk to him. The recall efforts that had begun before they visited Mayor Stapleton hadn't withered away as promised after the appointment of their police chief. Less than three weeks after the appointment, the petitioners had turned in their signatures. They claimed it was well over the 25,000 they desired, and definitely above the 17,000 minimum they needed.

Bart had learned this from the newspaper. So did Stapleton's supporters. They also learned about the court battles that didn't seem to be going so well. Tommy Lowe had come to him grumbling as usual. Things had improved since Coca-Cola Candlish had been appointed. The bootleggers in Bart's coalition had been protected while their competitors were getting raided. But it was a fragile thing, and if the mayor left, so would Candlish, who was pretty obviously incompetent. Lowe was the only one grumbling, but the others were fuming. And Bart himself was afraid. The mayor was his protection. If he went, the whole thing came tumbling down.

So he needed to talk to the old man. After a while, Bart had gotten tired of waiting and decided to send out his agents to track the man down. It hadn't taken long—the man was staying at the Brown Palace, which was almost the first place they looked—so when he got confirmation that the man was in his hotel room, he had Caruso drive him down to the hotel, then headed up to the room, clutching a copy of the recall petition.

He pounded on the door, and it was immediately opened. The old man's raspy voice called from inside the room, "Come in, friend. I was wondering when you would come by."

Bart and Caruso stepped in cautiously. The big man was standing behind the door, the crown of his hat almost touching the ceiling. He stood as if rooted to the floor, and Bart got the impression he stayed there all day. He looked down with too little interest to be deemed contempt at the two men entering. Bart was reminded of the metaphor of the cockroach. He was trying to be a man, but that look reminded him he was not yet immune to squashing.

He hurried into the room. The old man was lounging on a sofa, drinking some clear, viscous liquid. He did not offer a drink or a seat. Bart stumbled over a rug and caught himself on the edge of the other sofa in the sitting area. He tried to speak with as much authority as he could muster, "Well, you coulda come to me, too. Especially since you're the one who owes me an explanation."

"Oh?" the old man said. His face made a smile, but there was no mirth in his eyes. "I'm not sure I owe you anything. After all, what have you given me that wasn't something I already gave you?"

"Well, well, here's the deal: you said that we would have the mayor on our side and he would make the police like we wanted and he would keep 'em off our backs."

"And hasn't he?"

"Well, yeah, but what about this stinking recall business? I thought it was just a ruse to get him to do what we wanted. But now, it's looking serious. It's gone through the courts, and they gotta process the petition. And if they have the signatures, he's out. No way he could survive an election. We barely got him in!"

"Yes, that's what could happen."

"Yeah, but where's all your promises, then? What have you given me, then? When the new mayor comes in and his new chief, the first ones they're going to go after is the people who was connected to the old chief. And that's gonna be us."

"It could certainly happen that way."

Bart was exasperated. He dropped his accusing finger and although he tried to speak with authority, he couldn't help the note of pleading that entered his voice, "I's beginning to think you ain't got my best interests at heart."

The old man chuckled or coughed, it was hard to tell which. Then he said, "My dear Mr. Gallio, if I have anyone's interests at heart, it is yours. You just don't understand the situation. What you fail to appreciate is that in order to keep the mayor as our man, he must continue to need us. The attempt to refuse the recall petition and the court battles were the mayor leaning on his own resources, his cronies in the government and his lawyer friend, Mr. Means. These must fail him so that he will ask us for his help."

"Oh," Bart relaxed. "I sees it now."

"I am glad. Make no mistake, we will win this battle for our Mayor, but it can't be an easy victory. It has to be hard and tenuous. He must feel that he needs every ally he can muster, and that we are the only ones who can deliver what he needs."

The old man's voice was growing faint. He took a drink from his glass and he spoke more strongly. "Your next opportunity to help is coming up. The petitioners do indeed have all the signatures they need to force a recall, but those signatures need to be verified. That will take a lot of work. Volunteers need to copy down the names and addresses and make sure that the people really do live at those addresses. And when mistakes are made, valid signatures might not seem valid. The petition will fail."

"Yeah. I'll make sure he's got all the volunteers he needs."

"Good. I knew I could count on you."

"'Knew you could'? How'd you know I was coming?"

The old man smiled. "You'd better get going. You need time to assemble your volunteers."

"Yeah, right." Bart turned, taking care not to stumble on the carpet on his way out. As he walked past, he gestured to Caruso, who had been standing by the tall man in the alcove. Bart and Caruso headed out the door, down to the lobby, and then back to Morgan's.

He left Caruso in the bar, then went into his office. He made a few brief phone calls, then went out to the bar to wait. It wasn't long before Tommy Lowe, Diego Herrera, Pal Moygnihan, and Fast Frank Wilson assembled.

Tommy Lowe was the last to arrive, but the first to speak, "I was wonderin when you was gonna pull us together and tell us what we're gonna do now that that gasser of a mayor is going down."

"He's not going down," Bart said. "This is all a part of the plan."

"What?" Lowe threw his arms wide and pulled his head back in disbelief. "How long are youse gonna keep listening to this guy? What kind of cockamamie plan could this be? Get the mayor recalled after we worked so hard to get him in office. Makes no sense."

"Just because you don't understand our plan doesn't mean it doesn't make sense. Think of it: before he was elected, he needed us for his votes, but after he was elected, what did he need us for? Nothing, or so he thought. That's why he was so slow in putting our man in charge of the police. He didn't think he had to hold to his promises. But now, with the recall, he needs us again."

Tommy Lowe seemed unconvinced, though the others were nodding their heads.

"He needs someone to confirm the signers. Copy down the addresses and make sure the signatures are valid."

"Sure," Herrera said, "I got people who can do that. Find anyone on the south side you want."

"No, no, no, we'll put those people copying signatures."

"But, boss, some of these people can barely read let alone write good."

"Perfect!"

"Huh?"

"Look. We don't want to find these people. If you find them and they confirm their signature, the petition succeeds. And then we might lose our mayor. But if there's nobody at the address on the card, well, the signature might be a fraud, right? Enough frauds and the petition fails."

Now Herrera, Moygnihan, and Wilson were nodding. Even Lowe seemed somewhat convinced. After some more discussion of the organizational difficulties, Bart dismissed his lieutenants. After they had left, Caruso said, "Pretty smart there, boss. Great plan."

But of course Bart knew it wasn't his plan. And there was something that left him with vague unease.

63.   An Inkling of the Worlds

When they met in front of Stefani's house a couple days later, Carlton was already there. The burly Colorado Ranger was shuffling his feet nervously. Though Stanley might have preferred to have Tarkus or Fallow here, he needed them more for keeping track of Saluzar and company.

Stefani was clearly unnerved by this large stranger, who looked at her with barely-concealed prurient interest. Despite his eyes, his manners were good. He introduced himself, tipped his hat, and didn't presume to offer his hand.

Stefani also introduced herself, then looked to Stanley for a further introduction.

"Carl is here to provide a little muscle."

Carl chimed in, "So I'm told, but I haven't been told what it's needed for."

"It's hard to explain, but your reading should give you some idea of the powers we're contending with."

"Huh?"

Stanley gestured at the half-rolled copy of *Weird Tales* in his hand.

"You mean like the Sphinx?"

"Lovecraft has an inkling of the worlds nestled close to our own."

"But, wait, I thought Houdini wrote that story."

"That's what the byline says, but if you know the master's style . . . That is not the story of an amateur."

Carl thought. "Yeah, I guess you're probably right. What good is muscle against things like that?"

"Muscle is metaphorical in this case. You have always trusted to your brawn, but you have other strengths that lie waiting to be developed. Shall we go in?" Stanley gestured to Stefani.

Stefani climbed up the stairs to the porch. She reached into her handbag and pulled out her keys with trembling hands. She dropped them, but as she bent down, Carlton said, "Allow me."

Stanley shifted uncomfortably and looked at Stefani's grateful smile as Carlton picked up the keys and put them in the lock, which turned heavily. Stefani was reluctant to touch the door, so Stanley reached between her and Carlton to turn the knob and step inside.

An older woman sat at the table. She had evidently been sleeping there. She looked startled, half her face was red, and her hair was disheveled and lopsided around that side. This was probably not the first time she had slept there—the years had not been kind to her, with the marks of many sleepless nights and dozing days etched on her face. Nonetheless, she was still attractive—the resemblance to Stefani was clear.

"What?" she said. "Who are you? Stefani, I was so worried. Who are these men?"

Now Stefani stepped inside. "Mother, these men are here to help me find out what killed father."

"I told you—"

"You told me what you thought. Thaddeus told me what he thought. These men will find out the truth. I hope." She looked at Stanley.

He smiled and raised his hat. "That's my job."

"Who are you?" the woman at the table asked. She was fully alert now, and her eyes were suspicious.

"Stanley Fields, private investigator."

She glanced at her daughter. "A private detective?" Then back at Stanley. "Has she told you this isn't a normal situation?"

"Yes, ma'am, she's told me everything. And I have to say that I think I'm the right man for the job."

The woman looked at Carlton, "And who are you?"

"Carlton Wawkmuller. I'm just here for muscle."

Looking him over, she said, "I can believe that." Then she blushed, evening out the color in her face. She seemed to become aware of her attire and sort of covered herself, pulling her kimono closed with one hand and gesturing toward the table with the other. "Would you boys like some coffee or tea?"

Stanley said, "No, thank you," then paused, looking at the woman.

"Elizabeth Aegis."

"Thank you. Not now. Perhaps later, after we've looked in the cellar." Stanley looked at Stefani.

Her mother said, "No, you can't."

"We have to. Stef, will you come with us?"

Stefani took a deep breath. "Yes."

Stanley gestured. "Open the door."

Stefani reached out and turned the knob. She threw the door open wide. Stanley could smell the odor of stale conjuration, dried reagents, and something else. Something alive, but not corporeal. Something angry and powerful and trapped, perhaps for centuries, mouthing such filthy gibberings that it now sat, practically buried, in a heaping pile of its excremental loathing.

Stanley felt for a light switch.

"It's at the bottom," Stefani said.

Stanley patted his pockets, felt his electric torch, and then started down the stairs.

A few steps down and the smell was stronger. The creature scuttled and scurried around the edges of the space, pulling at whatever binding kept it here.

Stanley turned and gestured for Stefani to follow. She reached out for his hand. The touch was electric.

Carlton followed behind. When he reached the top of the stairs, he wrinkled his nose, "By Jove, what's that smell?"

Mrs. Aegis was mortified—"There's no smell! I keep a clean house."

Stanley turned back to Carlton, "It's not a physical smell. What you're sensing is what killed her father."

"That's a smell I believe could kill!"

"The smell is the least of its offenses."

Carlton's face got grave. "You were serious about that Lovecraft crack?"

Stanley nodded slowly.

"Incredible!"

Stanley led the way slowly down the stairs. At the bottom, he looked around. It was as he expected—one wall covered with alchemical reagents, a couple of tables for preparing potions, another rack full of material components for other conjurations. It was an extensive kit and likely it would prove useful for some types of spells. If he ever needed them. But there was one thing that was immediately useful. On the floor was a large, flat board. It was held under the legs of two tables, perfectly square, at least six feet across.

"Here, help me," Stanley said to Carlton.

Stanley moved to the far end of one of the tables. Carlton grabbed the near end. They lifted it up and off the board.

The demon, which had been trying to remain unsensed, now stirred. Carlton showed a moment of alarm and looked around, but not seeing anything, he was persuaded by the calm expression on Stanley's face. They lifted the other table up and off the board.

Then Stanley bent down and picked up the board itself. There, just as expected, a protective circle inlaid into the floor. Silver, tungsten, and other metals alloyed and beaten into the shape of three crescents in a double circle. Runes ran around the circumference.

Stanley smiled. That was a good sign. It meant that Stefani's father was not deliberately trifling with evil, and was probably not associated with powerful sorcerers.

The creature shifted uncomfortably. Still not speaking. Another good sign.

Stanley moved to pull the board aside and realized that Carlton was frozen, agog at what they had revealed. Stanley pulled a little harder and Carlton noticed the pressure and looked at Stanley.

"Is that . . . a protection circle?"

"Yes."

"Does that mean that what's here is . . . a demon?"

"You could call it that. There are many types of incorporeal creatures. Some of the most powerful are also some of the most malevolent. Power circles are often useful for dealing with them.

"Fortunately, many of the most powerful are also the most craven. It is fear that drives their lust for power. That makes them malleable under the judicious application of force. The circle gives us leverage. Lets us push without being pushed. Now let's get ready. Help me put this aside."

"Of course."

They moved the board over to the wall and propped it up against the alchemical reagents. Stanley then grabbed two white candles from the table and gestured for Carl and Stefani to do the same. He put them down at two points where the crescents met the circle. They were tallow, not wax, and he felt the residue between his fingers and tried to guess at its origin. It could be human. He wasn't sure.

He didn't mention it as Stefani and Carl put the candles down and commented on their softness. Once the candles were in place, Stanley picked up an alder wand sitting upright in a rack at the end of the reagents table. It seemed it had been prepared as a lighter. The tip was burned and it looked like it had once been soaked in essential oils, though those were long since evaporated. The stick was dry enough, though, that there shouldn't be any trouble getting it lit.

Stanley stepped into the circle and gestured for the other two to join him. Once they were inside, Stanley took out his lighter and put it to the alder twig, which burned easily. He touched the wand to the first candle, whispered softly to himself and swept the twig around in a smooth sweep, just touching the candlewicks as he went by, his words and thoughts ensuring that just enough flame leapt to each candle to ensure it would light. Then he extinguished the wand and stood still.

Carl reached for his hand, but Stanley pulled it away, saying, "Not yet. Let me gauge its strength first." Stefani didn't reach for his hand. She looked as white as starched linen and about as stiff. "Don't worry," he told her, "this will all be fine. Better than before. Trust me."

She looked at him and made the effort to smile. She was trying to trust, but the source of her anxiety was deep.

Stanley then began to chant. He chanted first to condition his voice, give it the proper vibrations for addressing the spiritual plane. Then he began to activate the circle. Guttering candles gave the rhythm, as first he brought them all together in successive waves of bright and dim, chattering voices and dancing forms. Then he slowly altered their rhythm until they reached one of the resonance frequencies of the circle. He didn't know the strength of the entity he was facing, so he moved it up the potential well step by step until they were flickering rapidly at the circle's maximum power.

Then he addressed the creature. "Beast, show yourself."

The creature snarled at being disturbed in its hiding place, but did not materialize.

Stanley spoke again, this time more forcefully. "Show yourself!"

At this, the creature hissed, but it came into view. It was a lanky thing, with an oversized head that accommodated even more disproportionate ears and nose. It had a pair of goat horns, but no hair on its head. It was mostly hairless, except for its nether regions, which were shaggy, matted, and foul. It had clawed hands and feet at the ends of its long arms and legs. It squatted on the floor and averted its eyes. Behind, it had leathery wings like a bat's, but with several long, sharp claws atop them.

Stanley could tell this was not a true representation of its form. Although these types of beings didn't really exist on Earth, they all had a form that was a simple diffraction of their otherworldly nature through earthly reality, something that was controlled by natural and psychological laws. As often as not, the form was iconographic. Creatures often concealed their form, though, because seeing their true form was as good as knowing their name, which was Stanley's next question: "What is your name?"

The creature now fixed its eyes on Stanley, but didn't answer.

"Answer!" Stanley said forcefully. The words struck the creature, which cringed briefly, as its assumed form flickered, although not enough for Stanley to get much of an idea about what it truly looked like. The creature responded, "Woodrow Wilson," spitting the syllables through half-shut teeth.

The creature's recovery was fast, faster than Stanley would have liked. It was far too powerful for something bound so long in a cellar, neglected. Stanley tried again. "We know your name isn't Woodrow Wilson."

"No, but he is not unknown to me. He is here with me. Raper of America, destroyer of her youth. Intellectual dilettante and fop, mocked of the nations and despised of his own people."

"Stop! You want us to believe that you are in hell, you exile of the Host?" The creature was stunned and silenced by his words, but not totally cowed.

Stanley reached out and took the hands of his companions. When he took Stefani's hand, he was amazed at the energy flowing through her. She was indeed powerful, but untrained. The rhythm of her power waves were erratic, sometimes surging and other times barely cresting.

Carl's power was latent. It was there, but completely inharmonious and far less than Stefani's.

Stanley resumed his structuring chant, bringing the waves of their power into unison as he had done with the guttering candles. Once he had merged all their power into a single frequency, he looked at the demon again. "Tell us your name!" he commanded.

His hand was almost burned by the surge of power that came from Stefani. The demon shrieked its name in pain, "Gaap!" and it briefly transformed into something like a glowing compass.

Stanley felt a slight tremble in his heart. This was the truth. A demon named as one of Satan's generals. The attribution of rank and structure were of course inaccurate, but they were indicative of the creature's power.

"Was that so hard? Now, Gaap, back in your confinement!"

The demon dissipated into smoke, which drained away under the nearest bench. In his mind's eye, Stanley saw the beast crawl back into its gem-shaped cage. Stanley made the broken "bars" whole again and made the "lock" fast.

Then he opened his eyes and let go of Stefani and Carl's hands. He made a slight blowing gesture with his lips, and all the candles went out with a puff, as if extinguished by a strong wind.

Stefani smiled. "You did it! You did it!" She jumped up and down, then jumped onto Stanley, throwing her arms around his neck.

He was flustered for a moment, then replied, "Actually, you did it as much as I did. Your strength was crucial. And this is only temporary. We have much to do before we can send it away permanently."

"Let's do it, then."

"Now that we have its name, we will, but we need its heartstone. You say you have felt this creature's power. Have you always felt it coming from the cellar, from the creature itself, or have you felt it coming from elsewhere?"

Stefani thought for a moment, then said, "No, I don't think so, except . . . maybe at Uncle Tad's."

Stanley nodded. "We'll make a thorough search, but most likely he has the heartstone."

64.   What Kind of Man

Stefani felt so relieved when the candles were blown out. She could feel the difference. The presence that had haunted the house since shortly after her father died was gone. She couldn't feel it anymore, but remarkably, there were so many other sensations that had been concealed by the overshadowing presence of what had been . . . a demon? Stanley had not been eager to endorse that label.

But she was excited about the difference. She threw her arms around Stanley's neck and thanked him. "Actually, you did it as much as I did," he said, then pointed out that this imprisonment was still only temporary unless they could find the heartstone, which they should begin to search for.

Stefani wandered out of the circle, looking around her in amazement. Suddenly, she felt just how many powerful objects there were in the room. She walked around the room, listening to them. The diversity of their chorus was different from what she had heard at Thad's house. This wasn't like voices. And it wasn't quite hearing, either. It was somewhere between listening and touching, kind of like walking through the orchestra booth as the musicians tuned up. All the instruments were playing, but separately, with everything from out of tune blasts to little snippets recognizable as part of a composition.

She stopped in front of a shelf of stoppered flasks and vials, essential ingredients. She was surprised that she could tell by their "sound" which ones were spoilt, spoiling, or still fresh.

She looked back at Stanley. He was smiling, but it seemed more than an earthly smile—it glowed brilliantly in his mouth and in his eyes. His complexion was luminous, too. He said, "It's a whole new world, isn't it?"

She nodded.

Stanley turned to Carl, "You can probably even tell the difference."

Carl said, "The smell is gone."

"It always begins as smells. Once you begin to hear it, you can influence it. Eventually, you'll be able to see it."

"You're glowing," Stefani said.

"Oh, am I? Sorry. Let me cover up." He passed his hand in front of his face, and the luminosity faded, so that his skin looked normal, except for the growing redness on his cheeks.

"Now that we've got it put away, let's find out what your father wanted it for."

Stefani's heart skipped, "You mean my father brought that . . . demon here?"

"Most likely. Otherwise, why would it be bound here?"

Stefani's mind raced. She thought of Thad's interest in the spirit—and the amulet. "Maybe somebody sent it after him."

"Possible. But once it was bound, why didn't he send it away? Once you have it staked, you can take the time to craft a new heartstone and send it back to its nether origins. He didn't, so whether he brought it or it was sent here, he was keeping it around for some purpose. What that was . . . I'm betting we'll find out in his notebooks."

Stefani felt her lip beginning to tremble. "No." she shook her head. "No. You're not going to . . . to tell me . . ." Her vision began to cloud at the edges. Her eyes grew wet. "Not like the others."

Stanley stood up straight. His eyes grew hard. He chewed up his words and spit them out, "Not going to tell you what? That your daddy was a bad man? Listen, princess, you asked me to protect you and to find out the truth. I'm sorry, but as far as I'm concerned, protecting you doesn't extend to your delicate feelings and daddy worship.

"Every man is half devil himself, and if your father was dealing with a spirit like that, it's possible he was a good deal more than half."

"You're a devil! You're worse than that thing. You should be in there with it!" This time she felt the power leave her.

Stanley grew suddenly luminous again. The light came not from his skin, but from a flat plane in the air that materialized right in front of him. Then she felt the power hit her, like a smack in the face, but it hit her on both sides of her face at once, and stretched from her cheeks to her throat. The force and the sting made her reel.

Carl was quickly at her side, his strong arms supporting her. She was only dimly aware of his words.

"What did you do to her?"

Stanley's voice was loud, angry. "Only gave her back what she sent at me. I warned her once she needed to get that under control."

"What kind of man are you?"

Stefani heard the flick of a lighter. A couple puffs. Then the lighter closed. "The honest kind. The kind that's used to being treated badly because he tells the hard truth. The kind that's tired of being smacked around when he's just trying to be helpful."

Stefani's eyes opened. She saw that Stanley had closed the distance between him and Carl and was gesturing angrily with a lit cigarette in his fingers.

"And if you or she doesn't like that kind of man, I can let that thing back out, and then the two of you can ask it what it's doing here!"

"No," Stefani squeaked. "Please, no. I'm sorry." She looked Stanley in the eye. He put the cigarette in his mouth and took a long draw. It glowed very red. "I think I want to know the truth."

Stanley took the cigarette out of his mouth with two fingers and pointed at her. "You think? That ain't good enough now. You have to tell me you want it. And tell that lug, there, too. I think he cares about your feelings."

Stefani looked at Stanley's hard face and felt the anger well up inside her, but this time she didn't give it vent. She cut it off from the main channel of her thoughts, let it circle like an eddy in her brain. She kept her voice under control as she said, "I want to know the truth. I'm prepared to accept that it might not be pleasant."

She looked at Carl, saw, to her surprise, that there really was compassion there. She said to him, "I need to know." She put her feet under her, pushed out of his arms gently. Once she was standing, though, she gave his shoulder a slight affectionate pressure and said, "Thank you."

He smiled wide and said, "Any time, miss."

"Impeccable manners," Stanley said, his tone bitter, and with, Stefani thought, an undertone of pain. He gestured with his cigarette, "But what you don't understand is that he treats you that way because he thinks you're weak. He's always there with a hand up because he thinks you can't get up on your own."

Carl started, "That's not—"

Stanley waved dismissively. "It's not your fault. It's what you're taught. It's what we're all taught. And maybe there's nothing wrong with it. But lemme ask you, Carl: how would you feel if she knocked you down? What if you were down and she offered you a hand up? Would you take it?"

Carl hesitated. Then he said, "That's different."

"No, it ain't. That's my point." He took a drag on his cigarette. He looked at Stefani. His eyes weren't as hard. They were pleading. "Someday soon, I'm going to need you to pick me up. You have to understand that you're strong enough to do it."

Stefani looked away from Stanley at the shelf of her father's reagents. "My father thought he was strong enough. Look what happened to him."

Stanley shook his head. "You need to step out of your father's shadow. You can be stronger than he ever was."

Carl said to Stanley, "Are you sure you're not expecting too much of her?"

Stanley shrugged and looked at Stefani. "Maybe I'm expecting too much of you. But I'm gonna give you a chance to disappoint me." A little bit of a smile showed on his lips. Then he suppressed it with an impatient shake of his head. "Now show us your father's study."

"This way," Stefani said. She led them back up to the main floor. There Elizabeth was waiting for them.

She was now fully dressed. Stefani recognized the dress as one her mother had worn often about the time of her father's death. It was exquisite, if a decade out of date, and not laced tightly enough to show itself to best advantage.

"Thank you," her mother said to Carl, taking his hand in hers, "I don't know what you did, but I can feel the difference." Carl blushed and tried to explain, "No, no, I didn't do anything," but she didn't pay any attention to his protests. "And you brought my daughter back! I thought you might have sacrificed her!" From her laugh, it was clear to Stefani this was a serious concern, though couched as a joke. And Stefani felt the thing in the basement would have liked nothing better.

Stanley gestured to Stefani that she should lead on, while her mother was distracted with Carl. Stefani led him up the stairs and showed him the door to the study. Stanley looked for a long time at the Baba Yaga and Kali statutes. Then he put his hand to the door for a moment before asking, "Where's your bedroom?"

Stefani didn't gasp, but she straightened up and felt her face get warm. "Pardon me?"

Stanley grunted, "If it's near here, I bet you have nightmares and worse."

"Yes, yes, you're right. It's next door, and I experienced terrors nightly."

"I shouldn't wonder. Shielding is about gone. Totally inadequate."

Then he opened the door, and Stefani felt the power come out and for the first time was able to identify it for what it was. It wasn't awe of her father mixed with pipe tobacco and mothballs, it was arcane power and rare, vital reagents.

Stanley walked in. He looked around the room slowly, hands out, feeling the air, and sniffing. He walked up to the nails on the back wall and said, "This is where the amulet hung, wasn't it?"

"Yes," Stefani said.

He turned and put his hands on the desk. "And this book, it's the one your father was working from when he died?"

"Yes."

"No one came in here to clean who might have put it away?"

"Mother was afraid to come in here. I was, too. I've been in here only once—and I looked at the book, but I couldn't read it. I didn't turn the page, even." Stefani was glad now that she hadn't. With a better sense of the amount and type of power, she was glad she hadn't messed with more of the items in her father's study. She would even regret the amulet she wore, but for the fact that its warm, slow pulse was now perfectly in time with her own heartbeat.

Stanley looked at the book for a while. Then he grunted. "It's clear he didn't know what type of spirit he was dealing with, or what he might do with it. He was testing it, trying to figure out more, trifling with it as gentlemen scientists played with vacuum. Ever see *An Experiment on a Bird in the Air Pump?*"

Stefani shook her head.

"It doesn't end well for the bird. Only in this case, your dad was his own bird. He does tell us about the heartstone. It was a ruby. It should be about this big," he circled his thumb and ring finger, "and have a conspicuous flaw in it."

They searched around for it, but didn't find anything. Then Stefani went down and asked her mother, who said, "I think I know where it is." She told Stefani how Nikolas and Thaddeus had shared the necklace, and when Nikolas had died, Thaddeus had come to collect.

Stanley said, "So that's where I go next." He began to get directions from Elizabeth.

Stefani felt herself begin to tremble at the thought of returning to Thaddeus' house. Although she had put him off once by surprise, she didn't like the thought of facing him when prepared. "I can't go there!"

Stanley shook his head. "I understand. And I don't want you to. I don't know if he's associated with Saluzar and the rest of his unsavory crowd. I'll go alone."

Just then there was a frantic knock on the door.

Stefani looked at everyone. Her mother had lost her short-lived calm and was paralyzed by fear. Stanley gestured dismissively toward the door. Carl said, "I'll go with you."

Stanley said, "Anyone she has to fear wouldn't knock on the door."

Stefani felt irritated at his nonchalance. She turned to Carl and said, "Thank you." She went to the door, put her hand on the doorknob, then took a deep breath and opened the door.

The woman outside the door was just about to turn the doorbell key again. She started. She was young, maybe in her twenties, with dark brown skin and black hair. Her eyes were mahogany and her pupils wide. She smiled and said in thickly accented English, "Oh, I'm sorry." She lowered her eyes. "I am—hm—looking for Señor Fields. His office . . . they tell me he is here."

Stefani looked over at Stanley, who was already rushing to the door, his eyes suddenly all full of concern. He reached out and touched the woman's hand. Just a little touch, but, it seemed to Stefani, meaningful. She felt heat at the base of her neck.

"Maria," Stanley said, "what's happened?"

"Oh, Señor Fields," the woman—girl really, such a young woman— threw herself on Stanley. "Otoniel, he went outside, and they took him!"

Stanley lifted her off him. He stood her on her feet and his strong hands held her shoulders steady. "Maria, that's terrible, but, listen to me: we will get him back." Then he looked around, worried. He briefly caught Stefani's eye, but didn't pause. Then he was looking at Maria again. "But I need you to do something for me. I need these two," he gestured at Carl and Stefani, "to stay at your house for now, just while I'm working on getting your brother back. Can they do that?"

Maria nodded.

Stanley looked at Carl. "I need you to stay with her and keep her safe."

Carl nodded.

Stanley said, "Good." Then he looked at Stefani. He said, "I need you to sleep."

"What?"

"I'm going to your uncle--Marduk's place. Then I will swing by to check on you."

Stefani nodded.

Stanley rushed out the door, running toward the streetcar, which was just pulling up. Stefani watched him go, then followed as Maria led them toward her house. She was trying not to, but she kept thinking angrily that he hadn't put his hands on her shoulders.

65.   Enough Rope

When Stanley reached Marduk's house, the door was smashed. It was closed, and physically intact, but it had been protected by a magic ward, which had been blasted through and just hung like the remnants of cobwebs from the doorway. Stanley almost left immediately to make sure that Saluzar and his people weren't at Maria's house again, looking for Stefani. But, he reminded himself, they might not have gotten the heartstone. It could still be inside. And if it was, he could thwart their plans, no matter what else happened. He might be too late to save Otoniel, but Stefani would definitely be safe.

As expected, the door was unlocked. Stanley opened it and stepped just onto the threshold, not fully entering the dwelling.

Within, the room was a gibbering confusion. There were dozens, maybe hundreds, of spirits trapped in this house. Most of them were minor nuisances, but some were substantial. And all of them had been given free rein of the place. If he were to try to venture into the house, he might be attacked over and over again. They probably wouldn't hurt him, but they would slow him down, and he didn't know how long he had. He needed a better way to search the house.

He rolled a cigarette and put it in the corner of his mouth. He lit it, then closed his eyes. He began to breathe slowly in and out. He wasn't directly drawing on the cigarette, but some of the smoke came into his lungs and left him as an extension of himself, rising, drifting, questing. It floated slowly through the house, long, thin fingers, feeling every surface. The spirits hissed and raged at the smoke, but there was nothing they could do.

There was a suction that drew the smoke onward. The heaviness of power created an ethereal slope, and the smoke drifted down it, under the back door, into a yard where the grass and other plants were blasted and stunted by evil. It was hard to get the smoke across the yard, with the wind, so he took a long, full draw on the cigarette. It irritated even his old smoker's lungs, but he held it for a moment, then released the breath. This smoke was more substantial and made it to the library.

What he felt in the library gave him chills. There was power here, so much of it that he wouldn't know the heartstone until he stumbled directly on it. The power was thirsty, too. Thirsty for anything it could get. The smoke was drawn onward, past the body of Marduk, who had retreated here, counting on his sanctum to protect him, never realizing that the power he trusted would betray him. He lay amid the shelves of books bound in skin and written in blood, twisted, with his blood pouring from his mouth, nose, eyes, ears. He was even bleeding from under his fingernails and his pants were stained dark red. The blood, too, was being drawn down, down into a pit.

Not a pit, a sipapu. But unlike most, this one was not designed to contact the higher planes. This fool had used its power to try and contact a demon, and he had tapped into that ancient spirit that had been so long buried here that otherwise no one might ever have known of its existence.

But now it was known, and it was being fed. It lapped at Marduk's blood as the fluid trickled into the sipapu, and it scented Stanley's blood, too. It sucked the smoke in. Stanley tried to withdraw, but by then it had sunken the chelicerae from its second mouth into the smoke and it began to draw while its other mouths chittered eagerly.

Stanley felt it pulling on the blood vessels in his lungs, drawing, drawing with those sharp mouthparts, and he thought, *Oh God, oh God, the power!* Just this faint touch and it was undoing him from the inside out. His heart was pounding, but it was as if all the blood were going right to his lungs and out of his body, which was becoming anemic and weak.

He sucked the cigarette into his mouth, the ember searing his flesh for a sizzling instant, then he held his breath and swallowed, his teeth clamping down firmly and cutting himself away. He fell to the ground, coughing. Black blood and mucous came out between his lips and dribbled onto the porch, but it was being expelled, not drawn. He lay there for a few moments, regaining his strength. Then he got up and staggered to get a cab.

When Stanley got to Otoniel's house, Tarkus was already there. Stanley looked over the house quickly, made sure their ward was still intact. He hoped it would fare better than the one at Marduk's house. He made sure Stefani saw him. He gave his typical detached smile and hoped she didn't notice how pale he was.

The way she moved quickly to him told him she noticed.

He decided to cut off her concern with some instruction, "I need you to take a nap." He tried not to grimace at the pain of speaking, and was disappointed at the way his voice croaked.

"What?"

"You might need your strength tonight. You've already had a hard day. Getting some rest now could make all the difference."

She said, "I understand, but you look like you need the rest more than me. Will you also be taking a nap?"

"You're right. I do need the rest. And yes, I will also take a nap."

Stefani tilted her head. Her eyes were dubious. "You promise?"

A genuine smile came to Stanley's lips. "Yeah, I promise."

As they left the house, Tarkus said to Stanley, "Fallow was here when it happened. Sounds like what the girl told me. He just came out and got taken. Fallow tailed 'em out of town. He says they're prepping for a ritual."

Stanley swallowed. His saliva was bitter and bloody, and it hurt. "Do you have a drop?"

"Sure," Tarkus said. He passed a flask to Stanley.

The liquor burned badly at first, but it quickly deadened the pain in his throat. "Did he say where they were in the preparations?" Rituals have a certain timing to them, which cannot be violated if they are to succeed. Spiritual energies can only flow at a certain rate, so it takes time to gather them.

"He said it was pretty early, like maybe they didn't know when they'd get Otoniel, and had to start just then."

"Good. That should give us just enough time. I want to set up for some dreaming."

"Dreaming? Why?"

"I want to give that young woman some training."

"She isn't an Initiate is she? The rules are pretty clear that training the uninitiated without approval is prohibited."

"Not prohibited. Just strongly discouraged."

"It's a little more than strongly discouraged. It's dangerous. For her. You'll be putting her at risk. It isn't really allowed, and I'm not sure I can let you do this. This whole thing is spiraling out of control because you wouldn't let that boy be tried for the crime."

"He wasn't going to be tried, he was going to be lynched by the state."

"And now he's going to be lynched by a mob and used in their dark ritual. And now you want to expose this uninitiated woman to the dark powers as well."

"She's already exposed. She's been dabbling in the arts and has made contact with a spirit. She has put herself in danger. She is known to them now."

"So your solution is to give her more rope to hang herself with?"

"Hopefully just enough that her feet can touch the ground when the floor drops out. Look, there's no time to argue about this. If you don't like the way I'm handling this, you don't have to help. You can get on a train back to Chicago. You can even go to Fallow and tell him and take him with you." Stanley fought to keep in the cough these forceful words triggered. He didn't want to reveal how weak he was feeling.

Tarkus grunted. His nostrils flared. Then he said, "No, sir, let's do this."

They went back to Stanley's room. Stanley lay down on the bed. He folded his hands across his chest. He began to chant. After a moment, Tarkus joined in. They were making different sounds, but the rhythm was similar and the sounds blended together until Stanley abruptly fell asleep.

After about half an hour, Stanley woke up. Tarkus was sitting at the table, the deck of dirty cards divided in half as if discarded mid-shuffle. He looked over and said, "Did it go all right?"

"Yeah," Stanley said, smiling broadly. His eyes were very happy. Stanley took a moment and looked around him. His smile vanished, but his eyes still had a little glint. He pulled out his flask, shook it, then took a belt off it. He coughed, then said, "Okay, let's see what Fallow's found."

66.   If It Has a Voice

"Nap," Mr. Fields had said, as if it were that easy. Stefani had never taken sleep for granted, and after what she had seen and knowing that there were other people who were after her, it seemed unlikely to Stefani that she would sleep. But she was in a different place. Maria had given up her room for Stefani to sleep. It was definitely unfamiliar with its combination of Catholic iconography and the little cluster of film magazine cutouts hidden behind the door. Some of the faces she recognized immediately—Fairbanks, Valentino, Novarro—but there were perhaps a dozen men's pictures that had been clipped from magazines and pinned to the wall.

Stefani actually found it surprisingly relaxing to be in this other place. She had felt the ward on the door as they passed through it, and inside the house seemed safe. Maria would sleep with her mother tonight. Maria's mother was also a powerful influence on the home. She was so relaxed and had so much faith in God that it made the entire home feel more secure as well. And this faith was despite her son being taken away from her for a third time. He was in the hands of the Klan, but she seemed sure he would return.

Stefani put her head back and closed her eyes. She began taking deep breaths. Each breath swelled in her chest and joined with a wisp of energy from the amulet. She focused on this energy. It was cool and blue and translucent in her mind. As she breathed, she spread it around her body. First her legs, which suddenly felt very heavy and comfortable. Then she put it on her arms, which sank heavily into the bed. Then she put some in her chest. She found she could no longer take the intentionally deep breaths, but no matter, her next slow breath gave her just enough of the blue wispy energy to spread over her head, and then she was asleep.

Except she wasn't. She was awake. No she was dreaming, she told herself, but it wasn't like any normal dream. Instead, it was like being awake, but where was she? There was a sunny plain that undulated gently and rose up to low, rounded hills in all directions. Atop one distant hill was a large temple, classical in style, but painted all manner of garish colors around the top. The pediment was crowded with figures seemingly jostling for position.

"Hello," Mr. Fields's voice interrupted her examination.

She turned and was surprised to see him sitting nearby on a low stool. He was dressed in a short Greek chiton with pale blue designs along the trim. He held a lyre with seven strings. Otherwise, though, he was himself. Pale skin, gruff face, sunken eyes, even nicotine stains on his fingers. She presumed his legs were this hairy in real life, and his chest—a thick dark carpet came out from under the one-shouldered chiton. He looked so funny she couldn't help but chuckle.

"What?" Mr. Fields said. Then he gestured to the chiton. "The outfit is traditional. It honors our roots in the Mithraic cult."

"Okay, but it just doesn't fit you, Mr. Fields. The Greek gumshoe. It's just funny."

"Oh, yeah. That's my mistake." He closed his eyes and concentrated. As he moved his hand in front of him, his appearance changed. He was no longer the worn, tired detective, but a sun-burnished youth. Smooth of skin with sinewy muscles and a happy, unlined face. The face was still his, just younger and without care. She wondered whether this is what he looked like as a youth. So handsome and open and trusting. Of course, that would have been before the War. "Better?" he asked.

"Yes!" she said, then blushed a little at her eagerness.

He smiled, his bronzed face reddening around the edges. "Well, I'm glad I meet your approval. Now you must choose appropriate attire."

"But I don't know what I should wear."

"Well, let me show you some models." He sat down, concentrated, and gestured. Fading into existence were several women who wore long tunic dresses. The dresses were in many colors, often with a thin line of trim at the edges. Many wore a cloak over their dresses as well. Some had ribbons in their hair, while others had kerchiefs covering all or part of their heads.

"I want that one!" she said, pointing at one that seemed to be made of a lighter material that had a nice line of trim in a geometric pattern around the edge.

"Then put it on."

"Is she going to take it off? She doesn't look like my size, anyway—and how can I dress with you here?"

Mr. Fields smiled. "You don't really dress here. This is not a physical reality. It's all in your mind. Just will it and you will be it. The first step is controlling your mind. If you master that, you will master everything, because everything is mind. That is the first Hermetic principle." He strummed the first string on his lyre. The note was sweet, and she felt she would always remember its tone.

"Okay," she said, "I'll give it a try, Mr. Fields."

"Don't call me Mr. Fields. Stanley, please, though here I am also known as Talus."

"Oh? And how did you get that name?"

"It was given to me at my initiation. You will get one, too, if you choose to be initiated. Now, please, put on your vestment."

Although she knew it was silly, Stefani turned her back to dress. She concentrated and imagined herself in the dress. It took her a while, but eventually she faded away the everyday dress she was wearing and replaced it with the Greek style one. She turned back to Stanley. "Well, does it suit me?"

He blushed a little again, "If one were being honest, he would say that everything suits you. But this definitely looks good on you."

She looked down and she wasn't completely happy. She didn't like the way the folds fell over her large frame, and her arms looked a bit flabby, but she decided not to worry about that. Instead, she adjusted the color of the dress so it became redder, a better contrast against her dark skin, and sharpened the green of the border. "Now it's good."

"If you want, you can take more time—we have all the time we need here."

"No, I'm ready to learn whatever it is you brought me here for—I'm pretty sure it wasn't to learn how to dress myself in my dreams."

"No. I brought you here to learn how to better control your power. You need to understand how it works, and then you will be better able to defend yourself against those who want to use the demon, and to use you."

"Who are these people and what do they want?"

"Well, that is a little hard to explain. First, understand that all religions derive from the Great Mystery. None of us knows from whence we come or where we're going. We believe there is a Creator, but if It exists, It seems unreachable. Its purpose in creating us is obscure. We try to read the signs and interpret Its purpose, which is what creates religions. Christianity is the dominant interpretation here and now, but it derives from two older interpretations, the cults of Mithras and Serapis.

"Mithra was a Persian god that we came to know as Mithras because the cult truly flowered on the island of Atlantis."

"So, Atlantis is real?"

"As real as America or Europe. But it was sunk by the power of the Serapeans. When Atlantis sunk, the Mithraists were reduced in power and it took them centuries to rebuild their numbers and their power. During this time, the cult of Serapis became dominant and even grew to become the state religion under Ptolemy I, who imposed the cult on both Egypt and Greece, driving our cult into hiding."

"So why are these cults fighting?"

"We all serve the Great Mystery, but we have certain theological differences. We all know that suffering is the path to Truth. You, for example, would not have discovered your power but for your father's death and your grief. This pain gave you insight and opened you to the potential of the Mystery.

"Worshippers of Mithras believe that we all must come to our suffering on our own, that the Creator will bring us to suffering as befits Its plan, and bring some of us to truth and allow some of us to remain ignorant. Worshippers of Serapis believe that suffering can and should be imposed on everyone to bring us closer to truth.

"Of course, suffering doesn't bring everyone to truth. For some people, it simply leads to suffering, and, eventually, death. This fits with the Serapean goal. They describe these people as being animalian, coelum defectis."

"See-luh what?"

"Yes. Here's where we get back to our basic teaching." Stanley plucked the first string again.

It immediately resonated in Stefani's mind and brought back the memory of the first principle. "Everything is mental," Stefani said.

"Yes, but there are actually nine classes of mentality. One is called terra and the other eight are called coelum, what you might regard as spirit. The coelum is composed of the five senses, the generative part, the vocal part, and the hegemonic part, which is what we think of as our 'self' or identity. Spirit creatures like the demon in your father's cellar are described as coelum nonterra. They can be composed of different combinations of parts, such as a spirit that is just voice and will, the vocal and the hegemonic parts."

"I understand," Stefani said, "and inanimate matter is terra noncoelum."

"Sometimes, but truly inanimate matter is rare—and dangerous. Magic cannot affect it, so it is often used to make weapons designed to kill Initiates."

"So you're telling me that most matter actually has mind."

"Well, matter is mind, but in addition to its physical existence, it usually contains other parts. Think of the voice of the babbling brook. That's not just a physical sound. It's a spiritual sound as well, which is why it calls to the heart as well as to the ear. And most terra has voice, too. It's essential that you learn to hear it and speak to it, because that is usually how you will influence it."

"So, I'm going to talk to the rocks, and they will listen to me?"

"More or less, yes. You've already done this, but you'll understand more soon. It relies partly on the third principle: vibration."

"Wait, what about the second principle?"

Stanley shook his head. "The second principle is complicated and confusing. Lemme sum up everything you need to know about it this way: there is a whole universe of things like what's in your father's basement and they want to consume our world."

Stefani shivered. "I guess that's clear enough."

Stanley nodded. He plucked the third string. "Everything that exists is but a vibration in the universal fabric. Each thread vibrates differently, and these vibrations determine everything about an object: its composition, its location, its speed. Changing the vibration pattern changes the object. This is what many people describe as 'magic.' It's the essential power you need to learn."

"But I've already started to learn it."

"Yes?"

"Yes. My heartbeat is vibration. The amulet works with that many times. They vibrate together and I can do things."

"Good. The heartbeat is a powerful vibration that can be used to create certain effects. How else can you affect vibrations?"

"Music. Sometimes when I'm dancing I can feel the way music has power. When I dance I sort of make the music mine, somehow, and use its power."

"Good. And what else?"

"Singing."

"Yes. The voice is the most important tool we use for changing the vibratory patterns around us. When you learn the magic words--."

"But you were so against magic words when you told me why I failed to contain that beast? I thought there really wasn't such a thing."

"Not that you can read in books. True magic words cannot be written, and if they were, they would do you no good. The magic words each of us must use are a special language understood only by ourselves and the matter to which we are speaking."

"So, how do I learn it?"

"The way you learn all language. First, you listen. Come with me." He gestured, then turned to head down the hill. His steps were high and light.

As Stefani watched him, she couldn't help but smile. "Are you skipping?" she asked.

"What? Oh, yes." Stanley stopped and began to walk normally. "Sorry. I was very young when I first came to this dream place, and I feel young every time I'm here. I can get carried away."

"That's okay—it's cute." Stefani blushed. Stanley blushed, too.

They were quiet until they reached the banks of a stream. It didn't seem quite congruous with the surroundings. The water and the rocks were more rugged than the rolling, grassy hills, and the water seemed strangely dark despite the sunlight. "It's time to practice your listening. This is a real stream, taken from the mountains and manifested here. What you hear is its true voice. Listen and learn its language. When you feel comfortable, speak, and it will obey."

Stanley sat down on the grass, his legs together and bent similar to a woman riding sidesaddle. It was a surprisingly feminine posture, and Stefani almost smiled, but, she reasoned, he was wearing essentially a very short skirt. It just made sense to sit that way. She sat down in a similar way and began to listen.

At first, all she heard were random burbles and sound. She closed her eyes, took several deep breaths, and relaxed. Slowly a pattern emerged. It began to resolve into something like "Water, water, rocks, rocks, fall, tumble, tumble." Then she became sure that was what it was saying, and told Stanley what it said.

He smiled. "That's what it says to you. I hear something different. Now that you know its language, try to talk to it."

"Talk to it?"

"Speak to it in its language. Ask it a question or give it a command."

Stefani tried to put a question to the water. It took several tries to annunciate properly in the water language, but eventually she asked, "Where are you going?"

"Gravity, gravity, gravity pulls," the river answered.

Stefani excitedly told Stanley what it had said.

"Good. Don't expect sophisticated answers from matter. Remember, most of it doesn't have a full spirit, usually not a hegemonic part that can consider and voice a reply. Now try a command."

Stefani tried many times to voice a command, but the water didn't respond.

Stanley said, "Don't give it a command like you'd command a person. Remember, it doesn't have a hegemonic part—a will that could hear and obey. It's more like pushing with your voice. Command in a way that forces the action."

Stefani tried again. This time she could feel the physical resistance against her words, but she forced them anyway, and when she finished telling the water not to fall, it didn't. There was a place where the water traveled horizontal briefly before crashing back down into the riverbed.

"Good. Now try to tell the water to fly."

This time Stefani tried, and the sounds caught in her throat. There was more resistance to these words. She took a deep breath and tried again. She succeeded, and some of the water shot up out of the riverbed into the air.

"Good. Now tell it to the rocks."

Stefani ordered the rocks to fly, but nothing happened. She tried again and again, but nothing happened. "I can't get the rocks to respond," she said.

"That's because you're talking to them as if they were water. You heard the water talking about rocks, but you haven't heard the voice of the rocks, yet. Listen for it."

Stefani concentrated again. She put the sound of the river out of her mind and listened for deeper, quieter sounds. Then she heard it. The words of the rocks were protracted into long sounds. "Puuuush. Reeeeesiiiiist. Griiiind." She listened, internalized the sounds, then vocalized her command, "Flyyyy!" A small rock flew up out of the water and landed with a thud in the meadow nearby.

Stefani jumped up and yelled, "Wow! Did you see that?"

"I did," Stanley said, also getting to his feet. "Now all you need to do is practice." He plucked a few sad sounds on his lyre. "I have to go now. Keep working on this. The skill may save your life."

Stefani said, "That's it? You're leaving? But there are more principles to learn. You haven't told me much about the Serapeans, either. And how do I learn to create something with magic?"

Stanley smiled. "You're eager, of course, but you can't learn everything at once. If we survive the coming conflict, I will recommend that you become a full Initiate. Hopefully what you have learned will serve you."

"Conflict? What? Wait!" Suddenly Stefani sat up in bed. She heard the squeak of the springs, saying, "Pull!" The house creaked, saying, "Stand! Support!" and, when the wind blew, "Resist!" Stefani realized that nearly everything has a voice, and if it has a voice, it can be commanded.

67.   Punishment for Our Crimes

The two of them went to the place where Fallow said he had seen the ritual being set up. They heard it before they saw it. There were speeches being given, such as might be heard at any political rally of the day, full of talk about the greatness of the country and how it was threatened by forces who would undermine the builders and shapers of this great nation. As Tarkus and Stanley shuffled along through the bushes, looking for Fallow. They couldn't help but overhear what the speakers were saying.

They said that spics were lazy freeloaders who came to this country to take advantage of what Americans had built, that they would never build anything of their own, but only take and exploit what Americans had made. And that included the most precious asset of all: white women. These Latin men would slink around homes while husbands were away, stay out at clubs at night while good, decent American men were sleeping because they had to go to work in the morning, and steal women away, shame and even murder them, then flee to the protection of the laws that were never intended to protect them, the laws that were supposed to protect Americans against spics and their fellow Catholics and communists and Jews.

And that was when they brought out Otoniel. Stanley paused to assess his condition. He had been beaten, but he was standing under his own strength. He seemed surprisingly calm, but not drugged. Stanley had hoped to get a rundown on the Klan's strength from Fallow, but not finding him yet, Stanley assessed the gathering himself. The speaker wasn't Saluzar or Dr. Locke, and he couldn't see them—or the tall bodyguard—among the gathered company.

The speaker then noted that these forces seeking to drag down America could not do it alone, but depended on allies among true Americans. Their allies included soft-headed intellectuals and those who wanted to steal money from the hardworking corporations that helped make America great. And one of those corporations was being challenged even now for the right to its profits. The speaker invited up some representative of the Denver Tramway company to speak.

The Tramway representative wore a blue pinstriped three-piece suit with a red-and-grey striped tie and matching handkerchief. He was a sharp contrast against all the hooded white figures, but he was obviously at ease among them. He was not one of them, but he was known to them and welcome among them.

Stanley had hoped to find Fallow before they had to act. Now he was losing that hope. He would just have to act and trust to Fallow to respond appropriately.

The Tramway man spoke, "I am here to protect the spirit of industry, which in this country is now under attack. A corporation—even one that has been granted a public monopoly—must be allowed the freedom to acquire sufficient profits to pay sufficient revenue to its stockholders and not have those profits stolen by employees who seek to be paid like kings or customers who complain about the price of service and don't appreciate the value of service. These are the voices of socialism that have infiltrated our country. And Denver Tramway is prepared to fight the socialists.

"We fought the employees in the streets, and now we are fighting the customers in the courts. We are grateful that you have followed through on your promises so far. Your mayor and his new city attorney have said they will not pursue the case any further, and their inaction so far makes it clear they intend to follow through on that promise. But first we have to win that case in Federal Court, and we fear that the judge may not see our valuation and our right to profits as we do. We wonder if you can help us with this."

The Tramway man stepped to the side and the Klansman who had been speaking before resumed, "Of course we can. The courts are easy to influence." He gestured to two men who pushed Otoniel forward and forced him to his knees.

They pulled his head back, thrusting his throat forward. The leading Klansman pulled out a blade from its sheath and said, "I hope you won't mind our methods."

The Tramway man smiled, "I think we showed in fighting the strikers that we're not at all squeamish about blood when freedom is on the line."

"I thought so." The Klansman advanced with his knife. Just before reaching Otoniel, he stopped. "Bring out the nigger." Fallow was pushed out of the darkness. He had been badly beaten and was under the influence of some kind of charm. He looked dazed and seemed like he could barely stand. What must have been the tall bodyguard under the robe had to support him as much as direct him.

Stanley signaled to Tarkus to attack. Tarkus led with a charm that was intended to stun the entire company, but there was a ward over the place. Saluzar was ready for them this time, and that would make it a lot harder. Stanley attempted to send a bolt of energy at the Klansman with the knife, but the ward prevented him. He had to stop. Focus. Breathe. Breathing was painful, and he was weak, but eventually the rhythm gave him power, and the bolt penetrated, stunning the Klansman. As he fell, his white robes became spattered with blood. It was too late.

Stanley wanted to give way to disgust, anger, and most of all shame—he had let his friend and subordinate be killed—but he knew that those emotions would disrupt his ability to accomplish what he still had to do. He couldn't save Fallow, but he could save Otoniel. He changed the focus of the energy so that it wouldn't shoot from him, but would stay concentrated around his hands. Then he charged through the bushes into the light, Tarkus at his side.

When they came into the light, they were mobbed by Klansmen. These guys were just poor schlubs who had no idea what they were involved in or who they were up against. They came at Stanley with hands, sticks, and knives. Stanley was a bit of a piker when it came to boxing, but his enchantment more than made up for it. A light touch was all it took to send his assailant flying backward and leave him sprawled on the ground. Even a near miss stunned most men, allowing for a follow-up blow. He might still have been overwhelmed by their sheer numbers if not for the skill of Tarkus. Tarkus' judo moves sent half a dozen men to the ground with ease. And when the inevitable guns came out, Tarkus knocked the wielders down before they could pull the trigger. Stanley was grateful for that, too. With this enchantment, he could deflect bullets, but it was exhausting.

Between the two of them, the hundred or so Klansmen were either knocked down or put to flight. But when this was done, Stanley realized that the leaders had escaped from the brawl. Tarkus had realized this a moment earlier, and he was kneeling beside Fallow's body. Stanley walked over and looked at him. He expected to see the obscuring charm that kept his face from being clearly visible, but instead the features were well-defined and clear. It was easy to identify the man whose blood was all around them.

Tarkus' back was turned to Stanley, but he could tell the big man was weeping. He stood beside him. Suddenly Tarkus leapt up and spun around to face Stanley. Stanley was lucky the big man was too angry to use an enchantment, because the blow that came was strong enough as it was and sent Stanley to the ground.

"He's dead because of your stupidity," Tarkus spat. "Letting that spic out and-and the dreaming. I'm done here, now. I'm going back to report to Barton what's going on here. Hopefully he has a more competent agent to send here and stop this horrible travesty. And put you where you belong—behind bars."

Tarkus stepped off into the darkness. Stanley got up and walked over to Otoniel, who had knelt through the entire fight, his neck stretched out eagerly for the knife. Stanley got out his knife and cut Otoniel's bonds. Otoniel wasn't grateful. "You should've let them kill me," he spat. Stanley felt the emotions behind the words. Deep guilt and intense self-hatred.

Stanley wanted to tell Otoniel that sometimes the worst punishment for our crimes wasn't death, it was often those who made the mistakes that were allowed to live. But the words stuck in his raw and burning throat.

68.   The Supple Creak of Soft Leather

Stefani's nostrils were filled with the exotic smells of spices and chili as she made her way from the bedroom. "That smells delicious, Mrs. Garcia. I can't wait to eat it."

Carl said, "It certainly does smell good. Are you sure you don't need any help?"

The old woman's voice came from the kitchen. "No, no, no. Sit. Relax."

Stefani hit Carl on the knee as she was sitting down at the table. "If she's told you once, she's told you a dozen times."

"Sí," Maria added. "Mama is very stubborn. She doesn't want any help in the kitchen."

Stefani added, "Especially a man like you who knows nothing whatever about cooking."

"Hey, I know a little something."

"Really?"

"Yeah. When the guard's out on the march, somebody has to keep the men fed."

"So you know how to peel potatoes?"

"Pretty much." Carl shrugged. "And I can stir a big pot of beans. Big." He gestured with his hands. They all laughed. It felt good to laugh, and Stefani took part wholeheartedly.

After a while, the laughter faded. Maria said, "Did you enjoy your nap?"

Stefani smiled, "Yes, yes, it was just what I needed. Thank you for letting me borrow your room."

Carl said, "You definitely looked beat earlier today. Mr. Fields was right to recommend that you get some sleep. You look much better now."

Stefani smiled, but she realized suddenly that Stanley had chosen to train her, but not Carl. Even if he couldn't train them both at the same time, surely there was time to train both of them. Stanley said her training would save her life, but what about Carl's? She changed the subject, "Maria, I saw you have a bunch of movie pictures up in your room. Do you go to the movies a lot?"

"Sí—hm—yes. If they let me in, I can sit in the dark and be just like a real American. The theaters are near my work. It's easy to stop on the way home."

Carl was about to say something, but he stopped abruptly, and his expression got suddenly serious.

Stefani asked, "What's wrong?"

"I smell smoke."

They all sniffed the air. Maria got up and went into the kitchen, asking, "Mama?" She and her mother spoke briefly in Spanish. Then Maria returned. "It isn't coming from the kitchen."

Carl asked, "Where, then?"

Maria walked across the room and pushed the curtains aside to look out the window. She gasped.

Stefani rushed over. She pushed the curtain further aside and saw the flaming cross on the lawn. She gasped as well. She felt Carl come up to the window behind her and look out over her head.

"Of all the cowardly!" he exclaimed and rushed to the door.

"No!" Stefani called, but he was already out the door. Stefani looked out the window and saw him rushing headlong at the two white-robed figures at the edge of the lawn. One of them was very short, the other very tall. So tall his robes didn't cover him fully. Even from this distance, Stefani recognized those feet by their enormous size. The small figure must be the wheezy old man.

Carl was running at them, but before he got within ten feet, he was knocked over as if by an invisible blow.

Stefani cried out and ran to her purse. She pulled out her pistol and slipped it in the pocket of her dress. Without training, she knew, he would be killed, but she wasn't fully prepared to trust her minimal training, either. Once out the door, she could hear the roaring of the flames—they sounded like laughter. She ran to Carl's side. He was on his back, conscious but dazed. She tried to lift up his head, but he winced. She let him keep resting on the ground.

She looked up to see the large man coming toward her. Her first instinct was to cry, cower, or run, but then she remembered she didn't have to be afraid of a big man like this. She had the power to stop him.

She grabbed the velvet bag in one hand and got to her feet. Two deep breaths was all it took to summon the power and concentrate it. She spoke to the wind and commanded it to rush over her outstretched hand at the hulking man. It bent the grass, caused the flaming cross to sway, though it didn't affect the flames the way a normal wind would. The hulking man hesitated as the wave washed over him, but he didn't stop.

The old man laughed wheezily. Stefani turned to him angrily. She held the amulet, felt the vibrations there, and worked harder to draw the power out. Then she pushed it out at the old man. The wave hit him and he wasn't just knocked over, he was lifted into the air, then thrown down to the street. Stefani was certain she heard bones cracking.

The big man paused. No, he wasn't just paused, he was frozen, like a statue.

The old man laughed. He sat up. "You do have some fight in you. Very well. That will make this all the more interesting." He gestured to the big man, who had never looked over at him, but began to move again.

Stefani tried to push the old man again, but this time she felt powerful resistance. She turned back to look for the big man, only to find he was right upon her. She tried to dodge, but his arm moved with incredible speed, catching her by the wrist. He lifted her up to the level of his face. Stefani still held the amulet. She swung herself back and forth, and focused the energy in her right foot. Her voice had the supple creak of soft leather, but it commanded great power from her

Oxford. She kicked the big man in the face. He didn't make a grunt or other sound of pain, but to her surprise he released her and began to tumble backward.

Stefani fell to the ground and let out a cry as her breath was knocked out of her. She struggled to get to her feet, but her vision was blurry and before she could manage, the large man had grabbed her again, this time with both hands. Her arms were pinned at her side and she couldn't reach the amulet.

Then she heard the old man talking. No, she wasn't hearing it. It was too quiet and too far away, but the words were somehow penetrating her brain. She was growing dizzier and it was hard to understand what was going on. She could just barely see that Carl was getting up.

Now the old man spoke loudly. "If you interfere further," he said, "You will get more and worse."

Once Carl reached his feet, he ran at the old man, who spoke a brief word and pointed at Carl. Several snakes of flame reared from the burning cross. One of them struck at Carl. He staggered as smoke rose from his charred flesh and now-burning clothes. He took two more steps until another snake struck him and he fell, still.

Stefani couldn't reach her amulet, but she could get the pistol from her pocket. She aimed it right at the old man and emptied both shots into his chest. He laughed, then resumed his quiet words that forced her to drift into an unwilling sleep. The last sound she heard was the pistol clattering to the sidewalk.

69.   Such Little Charms

When Stanley returned with Otoniel, Mrs. Garcia was thankful, but also distraught over what had happened in his absence. She told Stanley everything she saw—the big man who held Stefani limp in his crushing grip, the burning form of Carl, Maria trying to help but being thrown aside. She said she had tried to go out to help, too, but she must have tripped coming down the stairs because she fell at the foot of them and by the time she got up, the red car had driven away.

Otoniel wanted to help. He pulled against the embracing arms of his mother and sister. "No," Stanley said. "You can't help. You're just looking for another opportunity to die."

Stanley knew where they were going. He took the streetcar back into town. He got off the streetcar and walked to the doctor's office. It looked dark and empty. Stanley was convinced, though, that this was where they would be taken. They would be prepared here. For the type of ritual they were planning, they would probably take them elsewhere for the final sacrifice. He hoped they were still here, or, at the very least, that there would be some clue about where the final ceremony would take place.

The traffic from the Denver Athletic Club next door was steady. He couldn't wait for a break. He had to go up to the door, quick and confident, and hope that no one who saw him knew he didn't belong there.

He knew he couldn't take a chance on using his lock picks. He would have to try to knock the lock. He walked across the street confidently and up the short flight of stairs. A quick flick of gold iridium dust into the keyhole. He tried to turn the doorknob twice, just to check its sound. Mechanicals were so complicated, with so many sounds. He listened carefully and spoke to it. To his relief the lock turned. He didn't like to do it that way—little charms could be exhausting and drain him of power he might need later, and he was already so tired—but with the constant crowd he felt he didn't have another choice.

He closed the door behind him. He kept the light off, just waiting for his eyes to adjust to what filtered through the blinds from the electric streetlamp. He looked around the office, but it was clear this was just the doctor's office. The Klan office was elsewhere. He saw the downward staircase, so he went down carefully, holding the handrail and feeling each step gingerly as he passed from some darkness into total darkness.

Once he was down, he turned on his electric torch. This felt better. It was closer to the actual office. He played across the small cellar room with his torch. The entire hallway was lined with swords and knives, and down at the far end stood a suit of armor with a large, bare wall beside it. Walking forward, Stanley could feel that there must be a room beyond the wall that was being used for magical purposes. It took him only a little while to find the concealed trigger that opened the hidden door.

Inside the room was a small antechamber, with a door on the far side. He pushed that door open and was astonished to see that it opened onto a huge, grandiose chamber, almost like a throne room. A large, ornate desk sat on the far side of the room, and the floor was inlaid with the symbol of the Klan.

Stanley walked to the desk and saw that there were several knives on it. Large ones. Stanley picked one up. It was balanced for throwing.

Stanley jumped at the sound of motion. He kept ahold of the knife as he spun around to find the source of the noise. There was Carl, bound and gagged. He was pretty badly burned, but he was struggling. He was alive!

He started to rush toward Carl, but Carl's eyes showed him there was another threat somewhere nearby. Stanley stopped and turned. He saw the big man who accompanied Saluzar everywhere.

Stanley knew the man's strength, and he wasn't sure he could beat him. He threw the knife at the big man. It hit handle first and bounced off. Stanley picked up another one and rushed the big man.

When he got close enough that the big man's arms could reach him, Stanley slashed with the knife. The blade was sharp and cut the man's coat and shirt, but the man seemed unfazed. Dodging the man's hands, Stanley stepped underneath his reach and slashed at the man's chest, again cutting his clothes, but not stopping or even distracting his opponent. Stanley was already beginning to feel himself tire of dodging the man's blows. He would have to end this quickly. He shifted the blade into a stabbing hold and readied for the kill.

He leapt in swiftly and drove the blade deep into the man's chest. It stuck in very solid, as if it had bitten into bone, but it hadn't felt like bone. To Stanley's surprise, the man still didn't react. Now Stanley noticed that there was no blood. Stanley tried to pull the knife out, but it was stuck. And that's when the big man got a blow in, sending Stanley to the ground.

Before Stanley could recover, the big man had grabbed him with both hands. Although Stanley's hands were pinned to his side with crushing force by the big man's hands, his legs were free. He landed a kick to the big man's jaw. It was well aimed and solid, sending the man's head backward.

But there was no satisfying crack of vertebrae or jawbone. Just a dull thud. And his hat fell off.

When the man lowered his head, Stanley saw the mark on his forehead. He was a golem!

Stanley tried to move his foot up to erase the mark, but he was held too tightly now. The crushing force on his chest made it impossible to breathe and it caused so much strain he passed out amid the struggle.

70.   Chain of Life

Stefani woke up and found herself bound in a chair. A big, fat man with a beard was sitting in front of her, working at a table. She could see his hands move, but his body obscured what he was doing. The room was completely white, and, based on the decorations, it was likely a doctor's office.

The old man's raspy voice spoke behind her, "Ah, you're awake. And just in time, too."

"In time for what?"

"To appreciate the miracle of breathing."

At this point, the bearded man turned around and Stefani saw he was working with a powder.

The old man kept speaking, not paying attention to the other man's motions. "We often do not appreciate how magical breathing is. It makes all living things part of their world as they take in the air, incorporate it into their bodies, then expel it along with part of themselves. The act of breathing is the chain of life, each breath a link between the fragile spirit and the material world.

"It can give you power over the world. Like pulling on a chain, your breath can be used to manipulate the world. But the chain can be pulled from either side. Tell us what you've been working on there, doctor."

The bearded man spoke in a surprisingly squeaky voice, "It's mostly opium."

Saluzar resumed, "Opium is a wonderful substance. It gets into your brain and causes pleasure and relaxation. Heart and breath will slow until they reach their harmonic frequencies. And that is when you will feel the effects of the concoction's other ingredients."

"What are you doing to me?"

"Giving you clarity. Helping you see things as we do."

"What do you mean?"

"Help us out, doctor."

The bearded man said, "Sometimes it's hard to think because of all the distractions in our minds. This will help remove all those distractions so you can focus on what we're telling you. Don't worry. This won't harm you. I'm a doctor, sworn to heal, not hurt. Trust me."

"Trust you? I wouldn't trust you any further than I could kick you. Which wouldn't be very far, you fatty!" Stefani struggled against her bonds.

Saluzar tsk-tsked, "Are you trying to hurt the good doctor's feelings? Why, when he is trying to help you?"

"You're not trying to help, you thugs!"

Now Stefani stopped struggling. Instead, she leaned back and tried to find the beat of the amulet, but she felt nothing.

"Don't do that," Saluzar's raspy voice said, "besides, it's no good. We took it away from you." The old man's hand reached out in front of her, with the amulet dangling from its fingers. "Although it seems to want to work only for you. Still, I think you can be made to see the value of cooperating with us. Doctor?"

"It's ready now."

"Good. Light it."

The doctor took a burner and put the flame to the powder. It began to give off a thin, brown smoke. "Enjoy," the doctor said, then went out of her field of view. She heard the door close behind her.

The opium rose in her nostrils. The smell was sweet and she felt the effects slowly penetrating her body. It started in her chest and slowly permeated through all her tissues. She felt warm and light, as if she were lounging on the grass on a sunny day when gravity suddenly began to lose its pull.

She tried fighting it at first, but soon she felt so tired that she wanted nothing more than to drown in the effects of the sweet smell. She felt her breath and heart slow, and she remembered what Saluzar said. She realized she should fight, but she was completely incapable.

Her mind stretched, like pulling glass, and part of her mind, the part that was her self, her will—what Stanley had called the hegemonic part—was drawn so far from the part of her that was breathing that the tie between them felt about to snap. Although it held, it grew so narrow and tenuous that she felt she was not that breathing person there.

Instead, she watched that person there, and her eyes were distant lenses that she could barely see through. All the images were tiny and poorly focused.

And when the door opened, the sound echoed around as if it were happening in a massive, marble room, like when she was in Union Station very early in the morning as a child. The old man came in alone. He looked into her eyes critically. After a thorough examination, he said, "Nod."

That woman over there nodded.

"How are you feeling?"

"I feel ready to serve."

"Good. Take this necklace and put it on."

That woman over there didn't say anything about her arms being bound. She merely struggled against the ropes wordlessly.

"Stop. Wait." Saluzar fumbled a little as he put the necklace over her head. "Break your bonds."

That woman drew on her own strength and that of the amulet. She took a few deep breaths, then spoke a single syllable. The ropes blew apart.

"Good. Come with me."

That woman stood up and followed along behind the old man, who tottered along. He spoke to the tall skinny man, "You stay here, in case our friend Mr. Fields is pursuing us." The tall man bowed.

Saluzar led and that woman followed. They stepped into a red car with the doctor. The car drove, its engine sounding like a poorly organized drum corps in a vast, empty hall.

The car stopped. The old man got out, and Stefani watched as that woman followed him up the steps of a house that looked vaguely familiar, but it was so unfocused and distorted through those distant lenses that she could not be sure whose it was.

When the door opened, though, she recognized it—it was her house, and her mother was inside. She seemed hurt, puzzled, and Stefani could hear her calling, but that woman didn't answer. Instead, she followed Saluzar downstairs. "No!" Stefani tried to scream, but she was so far from her mouth, she could not be sure she made it move, and so far from her ears that she could not hear whether she had made a sound.

That woman stood with Saluzar in the circle. He told her what to do, and she did it, not hearing Stefani's cries. That woman reached out and unlatched the cage that held the beast. It rushed to freedom and ran around the room, breaking glass and knocking over small objects.

But its freedom was short-lived. Using the amulet and that woman's power, Saluzar put it on a leash. He drew it to heel. Then he trapped it in a gem, saying, "We have use for you!"

Then he looked at Stefani, focusing through the distant lenses to actually see her, so far back there. "Thank you. Now that you have served us with your power, you will make an even more fitting sacrifice."

71.   It's a Damn Misprint

It was hot in the cramped car and it reminded Bart he didn't like the thought of going to a Klan rally, but the old man had insisted. Bart had become comfortable working with the Klan from a safe distance, but he didn't like the thought of being among them, even though he was, officially, a member.

Bart had tried every objection he could think of to avoid coming, but all of them were met by the old man's insistence. With each objection, Bart could feel the man's eyes weighing down on him heavier and heavier. Eventually, he had to give up.

And it was definitely an important meeting. Dr. Locke had told everyone that Mayor Stapleton was now going to apologize for his delays and backsliding against the Klan. He was going to ask forgiveness and beg for help in the recall election he was fighting.

Bart's role in the recall efforts were key. The attempt to show how many of the signatures on the petition were false worked brilliantly, for a while. When many of the people couldn't be located, accusations of fraud were raised. They had even arrested some supposed fraudsters who had circulated recall petitions, some of whom had fled the state. They hauled a couple of them before a Klan judge and a Klan jury and got convictions. It seemed like Stapleton was going to beat the recall.

But then it started to come out how badly bungled the efforts were to find people who signed the petition. And then some supposed fraudulent signers came forward to say they were in support of the recall, and it became clear that if there were a problem, it was with the opponents of the recall. Stapleton had to consent to a recall. And that meant he needed every ally he could get.

As they approached the base of South Table Mountain, Bart saw the number of Klansmen heading purposefully toward the center increase. He directed Caruso to take him to a place at a modest distance that didn't have too many Klansmen crowded around. Then he put on his hood and took a deep breath before heading out.

It was almost as hot outside as it had been inside the car. Bart told Caruso to stay near the car and be ready to head out quickly. Then he began to follow the Klansmen toward the base of the road that led up to the top of the mountain.

Bart had been up to the mountain a few times, back when the resort was open. He liked riding up the cog railway. But that had long been disassembled and sold for scrap. And the resort was broken and dusty, the hollow shell of an American dream. And now it belonged to the Klan. And Bart was going up with them.

The dry weather meant that the dirt lot where people were leaving their cars was all dust, and when the wind kicked up, the air was choking and dry. All the white robes were dingy as they all trudged toward the entry point where cars were shuttling people up to the top. A kluxer was checking membership cards at the gate.

Bart shuffled nervously into the disorganized crowd that was getting its cards checked. He moved forward reluctantly, clutching his card tight in his hand. Sweat soaked into the card. He could feel it softening between his fingers. He tried to let other people go ahead of him, hoped he could somehow avoid the meeting, but the crowd pushed him forward because those behind him wanted to get up there.

When Bart was pushed to the front, the kluxer went to checking the cards of other people at the front. While Bart had been wanting to postpone the meeting with this guard, now that he was at the front, every moment of waiting seemed torment. He wanted to get past and be on his way up the mountain.

Then the kluxer turned to Bart and asked for his membership card. Bart had gotten distracted and it took him a moment to respond. His heart was pounding as he handed over the card. As the kluxer took it, Bart could see his greasy, sweaty fingerprints on the paper card.

The kluxer looked up from the card. His eyes were narrowed as he tried to peer into Bart's hood to get a better look at the man inside. "Gallio. That's a dago name, ain't it?"

Bart suppressed the urge to run. He forced himself to say what he had prepared, "It's a damn misprint. Name's Gaulle. French, with a silent 'e' at the end. Every time I try to tell someone that, they think I'm saying 'Gaul-ee' something. 'O' or 'a' or something."

The kluxer was still suspicious.

"Look, I know Stapleton. I was there when we made him choose Candlish for chief. Bring either of them down here. Get Locke or Means or Morley. They all know me."

"I ain't doin that. But I don't think . . ."

"Yeah, you ain't thinkin', that's for sure. You think I'm what, some kinda wop spy? As if they were that intelligent, first, and second—" Bart pointed at the top of the mountain, and his voice almost failed him. "Second, that's the last place any wop is gonna wanna be. Don't you think he knows what would happen to him if he got found out?" Bart snatched his card back. "I'm goin up there, but if you want to have guards waiting for me, go ahead, just tell 'em to have Locke waiting there, too, because he'll vouch for me." He walked over to the crowd of people waiting. He half-expected to get hauled back, but it didn't happen. Then a big Oldsmobile came and people piled in. It was a tight ride, and the road was bumpy, but Bart was grateful to be taking it.

At the top, he piled out and it seemed like the first word he heard was "dago." And as he wandered around, catching snatches of conversations, he heard the same refrains over and over again: "wop," "garlic-eater," "greaseball," and more names he knew were directed at him. Bart found himself trembling. He knew he was going to be found out. He was going to give himself away.

Although the Klan was supposedly very strongly in support of Prohibition, Bart found that there were some guys selling hooch in one of the deserted buildings. The price was exorbitant, and it was swill Bart wouldn't dare serve in his club, but it did have alcohol in it. Bart drank two, and was contemplating a third when it occurred to him it might make him go blind. Besides, it was starting to kick in. Although he was still terrified, he was somewhat detached from his fear. Alongside the fear, he felt a growing desire to prove his American-ness.

Then they were calling everyone to the assembly. Bart made his way over there, found that he was too late to get a chair, and stood with the rest of the overflow crowd. The meeting started normal. Approving meeting minutes and ra-ra-ra for the organization. If he didn't know better, Bart might've mistaken the Klan for any other lodge in town. But he was pretty sure no other lodge could call the mayor up in shame, which is what happened next.

Stapleton was brought forward and made to grovel. After he groveled for a while, Locke promised him assistance and then launched into a speech about America and patriotism and how Stapleton was a good American man who the kikes, kooks, and katholics were trying to bring down. He talked about how the Jews had a stranglehold on the colleges and how they were using that to indoctrinate our teachers, who were then sneaking Jewish ideology into our schools, how mere contact with Jewish teachers could turn your kids Jewish. And then he launched into the blacks, and how nigger music like jazz was corrupting the youth. And somewhere in there the speech became something else, some kind of chant, and Bart found himself chanting along, though he had lost consciousness and was no longer in control of himself.

72. Not the Cries of Free Men and Women

Stanley awoke on the floor. He thanked his mentor again for the false death enchantment. Even a mindless minion like a golem knew how to crush an opponent to death, but only a master sorcerer could tell the difference between true death and false death.

He opened his eyes just a little bit. There was the golem, standing stupidly, his hat back on his head. Stanley's challenge was to get past the golem so he could try to stop the conjuring, which must be happening tonight. Immune to enchantments and physical attacks, the golem has only one weakness, and Stanley would have to be quick to exploit it. He reached into his pocket and pulled out the tear-infused handkerchief. It was long since dry, but it still had the energy from Maria's tears. Using an enchantment to throw his voice, he got the golem to look the other way. Then he got up, ran at the golem's back, and jumped.

He threw his arms over the golem's shoulders and, with the hand holding the kerchief, reached around to knock its hat off. The golem reached back and grabbed Stanley's shoulder, hard. Stanley winced and cried out, but he kept sweeping his hand across the golem's forehead. Finally, he felt the deep-etched letters. He could not have rubbed them out with his hand or washed them away with any normal liquid. But the energy from the tears soaked into the clay, making it malleable, and he rubbed the letters out.

The golem collapsed into a heap of clay, taking Stanley with it. Stanley rolled off the big mound, stood up and brushed clay off his coat and trousers. Then he walked over to help Carl.

Carl was badly burned, and he winced as Stanley untied him. He said, "Carl, I'll get you some help, but first you have to tell me, was Stefani here?"

"Yes."

"Where did they go?"

"I don't know."

"What were they doing here? Any clues will help."

"They did something to her. They took away her amulet, then they did something and gave it back to her."

"If they wanted her to have it, they must have wanted to use her to control Gaap. C'mon, let's get out of here."

Stanley helped Carl to his feet, then up the stairs. They stumbled out the front door and down the front steps. Stanley set Carl down by the side of the road and stepped out to hail a cab.

When he got one, he directed it to Stefani's home. In the car, Stanley chanted softly and applied a healing salve to Carl's wounds. He felt the hot pulse of the burns, and he slowed and cooled them.

When they reached Stefani's home, the front door was open. Stanley told the driver to wait. They got out of the car. Carl was able to support himself, but he hobbled unsteadily, so after a few steps, he went back to the car.

Elizabeth Aegis rushed at them. "Mr. Fields, thank God. They brought my daughter here, but she wasn't herself at all. And they went into the cellar—they undid what you did. It felt so awful. And then they left."

Stanley could feel that the spirit was gone. "Where did they go?"

"I don't know. Please find her."

"I think I might know where they went. I'll get her back, I promise."

Stanley went back to the cab, where Carl was now testing the movement of his legs out of the side of the car. He scooted back inside without much wincing. He was obviously feeling much better.

Stanley sighed. He didn't get in the car because he didn't know where to go. He looked west to the dark shadow of the mountains. He saw something, floating in the distant darkness, a flaming cross. He pointed at it, "What's that?"

"That?" Carl said. "That's a Klan gathering on South Table Mountain."

"That's where we need to go."

"We can't get up there. They guard the paths up."

"Then we'll need to get up a different way."

As Mack promised, the Jenny had no trouble getting off the ground with both men in the front, but that didn't mean it was a comfortable ride. The cockpit was not designed to accommodate two men, especially not when one was as big as Carl.

The plane climbed up over the street lights of Denver into the black sky. They headed straight for the flaming crosses. As they approached, Mack climbed higher over the top of the plateau, then eased back on the throttle so they could glide quietly over the Klan gathering below.

Stanley and Carl looked out of opposite sides of the aircraft. After a moment, Carl grabbed Stanley's arm and said, "There they are! I saw them!"

"Are you sure it's them?"

"I think so. I guess I couldn't see their faces, but it was a fat man, a very little man, and a woman."

"Point to where they were."

Carl pointed and Stanley closed his eyes and felt for Stefani's power. He felt it. It was muffled, but it was there.

"Yeah, it's them." He turned to Mack. "You think you could land?"

"There?"

"Not exactly there—too many people. What about that other part of the plateau where it's dark?"

Carl said, nervously, "Land in the dark."

"No worries about that. I landed in the dark plenty."

"In Europe?"

"No, in Europe we always had good landing fields, but when I was 'storming, you never knew what it was going to be like. Mostly we landed in these farmers' fields, and they almost never had lights. Hold on."

Mack increased the throttle and climbed a while to regain lost altitude, then turned around. He let off the throttle again so they cruised quietly over the darkest part of the plateau.

Mack looked down over the side of the plane and said, "Yeah, I think I can land there. If it's as smooth as it looks." Out into the night air, he throttled up briefly, then turned and cut the engine completely. "The good thing about this Jenny is its very low stall speed. It needed it with the old engine. Now it's just gravy. And great for stunts like this."

Carl said, "Are you sure we're going to make it? Looks like we're very low."

"Hmmm . . . maybe. But if this is going to work, we've got to just hit it. There's not a lot of room, and we don't want to be falling off the other side."

Stanley was beginning to doubt now, too. They did look awfully low.

But Mack knew his angles. They drifted over the plateau almost just as their wheels touched. With flaps and brakes the plane rolled quietly to a stop in the darkness.

Stanley climbed out and said, "Get the plane turned around and ready to go."

"Sure," Mack replied.

"Carl, let's see if we can get in there."

At the top of the cable car, two Klansmen were standing guard. Carl rolled up his sleeves and got ready to walk toward them, but Stanley stopped him. He looked at the men, spoke a few signal words under his breath, then began to focus on his own heartbeat. He could feel it, slightly elevated with excitement and exercise. He worked to slow it, and as he did, he felt it match first one man's rhythm, then the other's. With both hearts under his control, he focused on their breathing. He slowed his heart rate and his breathing, and with it came the Klansmen's. First one yawned, then the other. They both sat down and began talking about how tired they felt. Stanley kept slowing breathing and heart rate until their yawns turned to snores.

"Amazing!" Carl said.

Stanley replied, "Let's get 'em now."

Stanley and Carl took the Klansmen from their posts into the darkness. Though they were handled roughly as they were disrobed, the men did not awaken. Stanley and Carl put on the robes. Then they went out to the gathering of Klansmen, lit by bright bonfires.

The Klansmen at the edges were not paying much attention to what was going on in the center of the gathering. Stanley and Carl easily pushed their way toward the flaming crosses. Then they came to the rows and rows of folding chairs. Thousands of people were here, seated and attentive as if they were listening to Calvin Coolidge. There was nothing for it but to walk up one of the aisles.

In front of the flaming crosses, an imposing man stood in robes, a man that Stanley guessed was Dr. Locke. Behind him was a small robed figure that Stanley guessed was Saluzar. He was surrounded by other men whose robes bore marks of rank in the Klan. Behind them—Stefani!

She was standing, her face vacant, unaware. She wore a plain white robe without a hood.

Stanley looked at Carl, tried to get his attention directed at Stefani, but he was engrossed by something much closer. In front of Dr. Locke, the Klan's dragon, a man was on both knees in a posture of supplication.

"Is that Ben Stapleton?" Carl asked.

"Yeah," said another man. "He's begging us to save him."

"What from?" Carl asked.

"Don't you read the papers? There's a recall. People want to throw him out of office for a bum. The Dragon is making him beg, for sure!"

And he was. The Mayor was groveling in the dirt in a most pathetic way, swearing allegiance before the fiery cross in exchange for support.

After a while, Dr. Locke said, "That's enough." Then he spoke to the gathered people in his loud but squeaky voice, "What do you think? Is he sincere? Is he truly sorry?"

The crowd cheered. A few said, "No," but most said, "Yes."

Dr. Locke said, "You seem to have convinced most of the people." Then he turned to the crowd and said, "Should we help him in exchange for the loyalty he has promised?"

Now the clear majority shouted "Yes!"

"Very well," he said to the man on the ground. "We will help you. Get up!"

Then Dr. Locke launched into a speech about how the Negroes, Catholics (especially Mexican Catholics), and the foreign-born were undermining the greatness of America. He said it was the responsibility of the Invisible Empire to restore the greatness of God's Chosen Nation, the fulfillment of the Protestant dream of her founders who knew that only the great Aryan peoples were suited to the demands of democracy, which required clear minds and uncraven hearts.

The speech, which was never truly coherent, began to devolve into sounds that were not words, or, rather, not English words.

Stanley grabbed Carl's arm. He whispered, "Clench my hand!"

The two men clasped hands.

"Can you feel my pulse?"

Carl nodded.

"Good. Focus on that—don't listen to those words."

The speech changed completely, lost the rhythm of modern rhetoric and assumed a chanting tempo that matched the character of its ancient words, words used since the age of Babylon to draw together worshippers participating in the unholy rites of human sacrifice.

The power seeped out through the crowd, penetrating every body, every mind. As it reached the edge of the crowd, it engulfed the casual hangers-on and opportunists, the men who participated as with any other club to gain personal power, prestige, or professional standing. Soon they were all overcome, all bending their will to that single voice.

They sometimes cheered and applauded, lending their voices to the strength of the chant, but these cries were not the cries of free men and women, they were the sound of physical instruments, like clackers or wind chimes, lending their voice to the force that animated them.

Stanley could feel Carl's hand trembling in his. He clenched it tighter, giving confidence as well as resistance to the unnatural power of the chant.

With everyone bound in service of that single voice, Dr. Locke stopped speaking. The servile ones still thrummed in unison, a choir of spirits bent to sinister purpose.

And that purpose materialized in the air. Gaap appeared, glorious and hideous at once with the power it harnessed from the unholy congregation. It was nearly ready to travel across the void and lead back the malevolent power that could unleash untold destruction on the entire world. All it needed was the sustenance of a blood sacrifice.

Stanley let go of Carl's hand, but he touched the big man on the upper arm to keep him from rushing forward. Stanley then began to build his own strength. With each beat of his heart, he added greater force, but he kept it confined in the tiny space of that single muscle, growing it little by little.

Dr. Locke stepped aside, and Saluzar limped forward. He gestured to the men in robes of rank, and Stefani was brought forward.

She was disrobed and stood completely naked. The old man raised his knife to plunge it into her heart. As he spoke the words to make his knife potent, Stanley unleashed his force, sending the old man tumbling to the ground.

"Carl, grab Stefani and get her to the plane!"

Carl ran to grab Stefani's hand, but he was stopped by the ranking klokards. He set to work showing them his strength and fighting technique.

Stanley ran to the old man on the ground, who was trying to get up. He kicked him back to the ground, then pressed the man flat with his weight. His knees on the old man's chest, he said, "This ends now. I have seen the fruit of these spirits loosed upon the world, and I swore it would never happen again!"

"Fool! We have brought it so close that it may yet slip over to this world. If not today, then we will find another time and place for its advent."

"Then I'll just have to kill you now." Stanley grabbed the man and began throttling him. If there was a faint pang of conscience at brutally strangling an old man to death, it was quickly squelched by his memory of the trenches, artillery, machine-guns, and killing gas, all the fruit of the last time one of these spirits was loosed.

As his fingers tightened around the old man's windpipe, he was startled by the wheezing voice, "You cannot kill me—I am already dead!"

Stanley realized that the voice came with no air through the larynx, and there was no motion of the chest with breathing. It was true! He pulled his hands back in horror, and with them came much of the man's throat, the flesh fragile and fetid.

"These vestments worn to tatters already!" the wheezing voice laughed. "I shall have to talk to my tailor!"

And that's when Stanley was shot in the shoulder. Stanley groaned and reached for the wound as he staggered to his feet. Bullets. He knew their tongue, but did he have the strength to deflect them? He raised his hands and crossed them, palms outward in front of his chest, chanting. Dr. Locke fired both revolvers, emptying them. The bullets seemed to deflect off empty air, but Stanley felt each impact distributed over his lips, tongue, throat, and lungs. His teeth in particular rattled. The effort was taxing, and Stanley could feel his breath waning, but he managed to deflect them all.

Frustrated, Dr. Locke holstered his pistols and drew a knife. Stanley shifted to deflect the knife. As it flew, he suddenly realized it was terra noncoelum, matter without spirit, and it passed through his shield. He realized it just in time to dodge the first knife, but he was not prepared to avoid the second. It struck him in the chest, penetrating deep. He fell over as his body reeled with pain and sudden lack of air. Through his dimming vision, Stanley looked over and saw the doctor, ready with another knife, but the old man waved him off. Dr. Locke came over and helped Saluzar to his feet. Two klokards picked Stanley up. They held him and took him aside to where Carl was being held. His hood was off, and his face, still red with burns, was beginning to bruise.

The old man laughed, the base of his tongue wagging freely before the exposed vertebrae of his neck. "Now, if we can get back to business."

Stefani was brought back to the front. Stanley tried to summon strength again, but he couldn't. He was fading fast. His own breath was not only wheezing, but starting to gurgle as his lung filled with blood. He summoned all his strength and gave it voice, "Stefani, Stefani, that knife is for you. You have the strength to stop it. I know it seems like you are not in control, but you can be."

Stefani turned her head and looked at him quizzically.

73.   One Hundred Percent American

It wasn't as if Stefani awoke—she returned. From down the long, narrow hallway, she came back to her body. She had only the most vague sense of what was going on. She knew she was atop a mountain and that it was night. She was naked, though she didn't know why. But despite the chill in the air, she didn't feel cold. She was too afraid to feel cold, and then there was the heat pouring off the burning crosses.

She heard the old man laughing, the one called Saluzar, and his laugh was curiously otherworldly. It had a hollow rattle like the wind of winter through dry morning glories on the arbor.

And she felt something else, too. The beast from her basement, Gaap, the guide. It was here, and free. The beast looked at her briefly with contempt, but it had no time or energy for her now. It was about to be sent on an errand, the kind of errand that allowed it to curry favor with even more powerful spirits.

Above the three fiery crosses, there was a strange border of irregular shape and purplish-black color that divided the night sky from something else, some other sky, perhaps.

That other sky had a color, but it was an indescribable, unknowable color, one that hurt the eyes, almost burned them with its strangeness.

She turned away and looked at the manifest shape of Gaap, a Roman soldier with a huge, hideously distorted head and batlike wings. It was listening to Saluzar's commands. "I obey, oh master, only I thirst."

And that's when Saluzar turned on her with the knife.

Stefani remembered what Saluzar had done with the fire at Otoniel's house and what Stanley had taught her in that dream which seemed so long ago and yet so vibrant in her mind. She listened to its burn, found that she could understand the words in the chuckling flames.

Saluzar was now directly in front of her. She told herself not to be distracted by the ragged flesh hanging off his dry, exposed windpipe. She focused on speaking to the fire in words it could understand. It harkened to her, but she wasn't able to ask it strongly enough. Saluzar raised his knife, and she noticed the amulet in the velvet bag dangling on its chain from his hand. "That is mine!" she said, and suddenly reached out and grabbed the bag. The pull disturbed Saluzar's knife stroke, and he missed her, the knife sweeping through the air between her arm and her chest.

The amulet came free from Saluzar's hand, and with it the knife, which fell to the dusty ground. As Saluzar picked up the knife, Stefani found the strength to make her request of the flames. She pointed and the fire struck Saluzar as he started to come after her again with the blade. He reeled and fell, smoldering, to the ground.

Gaap said, "I thirst, oh master."

In response, Stefani was surprised to see Bart come forward from the crowd. He picked up the knife and said, "I will show you my blood is American." He plunged the knife deep into his chest. At first, a circle of red appeared around the blade, but it didn't expand. Instead, the blood trickled along the blade to its hilt, then dripped up into the sky and onto the lapping tongue of Gaap. When Bart fell and the stream of blood stopped, Gaap said, "I go, oh master," then turned and dove into that alien sky. It quickly disappeared, as if going around a corner.

Stefani knew what that meant: Gaap was on its way to retrieve a spirit even more powerful than itself. She had to stop it, but how? Then she remembered the heartstone. She saw that as Saluzar was getting up from the flaming strike, he held the ruby Stanley had described. His burnt, mangled body staggered forward a step. He spoke some bitter words at the three burning crosses, and serpents of flame leapt from each of them, but as they swept at her, she cooed at them and raised her hands. The flames held up and perched nervously, like small dogs trying to be uncharacteristically still to earn treats. Then she ordered them back at Saluzar. The flames struck him and sent him back to the ground.

He climbed back to his feet, his limbs hanging by mere ligaments, but the ruby still clenched in his bony fingers. He chuckled, though the sound racked his raggedy body. "Capricious cur! Fire will have its favorites, and it always has been drawn to a sweet voice. But do you speak dust?" His sudden sounds in command of the dust surprised her, and she gasped as the cloud surrounded her. It was the wrong thing to do. The dust swept into her mouth, dry and rasping as it filled her throat. She was choking, and she fell to the ground, looking to Stanley for help.

He lay on the ground, pale and wasting, just out of reach and barely able to move, let alone help her. His tired eyes locked hers, though, and he managed a slow, rhythmic pounding on his chest.

Of course! The magic was vibration, not voice. The voice was the easiest, but the body had other vibrations that could be mustered. Stefani closed her eyes and pulled the amulet to her chest. She concentrated on her heartbeat. The rhythm became something more powerful than just driving blood, it became a pump of energy and it drove out the dust from her throat.

When she opened her mouth to expel the dust she also opened her eyes. Saluzar was standing over her, with the knife in his hand again. She thought she saw surprise on his face, but there was too little flesh to be sure. As she gasped for breath, he lunged at her with the knife.

Stefani kicked him and her strong dancer's leg sent his frail, broken form flying like a castoff rag doll.

Stefani rolled to her hands and knees and had to take several breaths before she could get up. But she was better off than Saluzar, whose movements had degenerated into spasmodic convulsions that lacked any coordination. Except his voice. It still had power as it babbled some tongue she couldn't identify. She didn't want to wait to see what he was conjuring next. She drew out several serpents of fire and set them on Saluzar again and again and again until, suddenly, his voice just went out with a puff.

Carl took advantage of the distraction to break away. This was the first time she was aware that he was here. He kicked one of his captors and punched the other. Both fell. Then he rushed to Stanley's aid, but he was blocked by several klokards. He knocked the first down with just one blow. The second took three blows, but hit the dust just as hard. Dr. Locke threw a blade at Carl, but it narrowly missed. Stefani could not let him throw another.

She coaxed several snakes out of the flame. The doctor had another knife ready, but he would never get to throw it. The fiery snake struck him first. It quickly burned through his Klan robes. His cries were shrill and painful. He ran a short distance, then fell to the ground writhing and screaming.

Stefani wanted to strike him again, but then she remembered the heartstone.

Stefani walked over to the charred and smoking pile of bones. The fingers, though charred and lacking even a single tendon, still clutched the ruby tightly. She pried the fingers away and the hand fell apart, not just into bones, but dissolved utterly into dust.

Stefani held the ruby in her hand. She listened to the throb of its voice. In particular, she found the contentious voice of the flaw inside. She knew she had to destroy it, and fast. Every moment, Gaap was traveling further into the void and closer to that unnamed spirit trapped in the silver. She sang along with the voice of the flaw, harmonized with it, gave it strength until the gem came apart in her hand. There was a sudden cry from some invisible part of that impossible sky.

Stefani sank down, grateful it hadn't taken too long to break the gem, that she had gotten it destroyed before Gaap had returned with its powerful follower. She looked first at Stanley, who seemed barely aware of what was happening. Carl stood in a fighter's stance, turning slowly around to see if any of the klokards wanted to get up and take a few more licks. It didn't seem so.

Beyond, him, a crowd chanted and swayed in unison. The light of fire was in their eyes, but they neither saw nor understood it, they were completely in thrall to something they barely perceived, let alone understood. They had all put on the uniform, but they didn't realize what kind of game they were pawns in.

But then there was a disturbance behind her. Stefani turned and saw that although the region of that incomprehensible sky was shrinking, it wasn't completely gone yet. It rippled like a pond disturbed, and from the disturbance, a tentacle emerged. Slime green, it felt around like a snake nosing its way through grass, then found the shrinking border. The tentacle looped around the edge of the sky as if it were a physical object, like the top of a sack. Another tentacle emerged and looped around the barrier someplace else. Then another and another, until the area was teeming with them, and they grasped and pushed and pulsed until something emerged at the center of the tentacles. You could call it a mouth, but it was really a gaping void with teeth.

But most of all, there was a will. This was the epitome of what Stanley had called coelum non terra, spirit without matter, and the tentacles and the teeth and even the void were just manifestations of its hideous, driving will.

And it had a voice that laughed. It spoke, too, but its words were incomprehensible. Instead, she felt them, like the wave of air when you opened a trash can on a hot day. Smelly and sticky—not just on you, but in you.

Stefani grabbed her amulet and concentrated on the beast, but when she tried to push, the touch of the creature was loathsome and strong. It pushed her aside with a shrug of its quivering tentacles.

Stefani was thrown to the ground. The beast chuckled, its incomprehensible speech slobbering all over her.

Stefani was stunned for a moment, but when she came to awareness, she could see that the beast had enlarged the hole, but it was also pushing up against it so that now it was crowding out the entire strange sky beyond. She could now see the toothed void chomping greedily at their own world, the teeth stained, broken and jagged with obscure bits of flesh stuck around them and embedded in the fetid, bleeding, and suppurating gums. She found herself lost in trembling terror, barely fighting back the urge to scream her life from her lungs before that thing could eat her and take it.

The touch on her hand made her shriek, but only briefly. She looked over. It was Stanley. He had managed to drag himself over to her side, leaving a trail of blood in the dust. As he grasped her hand, she felt he had some strength left, though not much.

"We can do it together."

Stefani shook her head. "I don't want to touch it."

"No . . ." he took a wheezing breath, "don't touch it. Without a circle or a heartstone, we can't push it back."

"What can we do?"

"We can close it off. It won't be imprisoned, but it won't be here, either. Focus on the doorway. Close it."

Stanley let himself collapse, seemingly using no physical strength but what it took to clasp her hand and the increasingly difficult effort of breathing.

Stefani closed her eyes and focused on her own breathing. She consolidated her power, then matched it to the rhythm of her heart. The amulet naturally pulsed in rhythm, but Stanley's heart was struggling rapidly. She slowed it to match her own heartbeat and felt his own power flow into hers.

Then she focused on the portal. The beast was working hard to widen it so it could slip through. So much will and so much power—it was not physical, but it was still bulky.

But the portal naturally wanted to close. It was an abomination to link two places so intrinsically foreign, our world and that. All she had to do was aid it. When she tried to push the portal closed, she felt the force of the beast's tentacles resisting.

The beast gibbered wetly. The tongue of its words made her tremble. Stanley clenched her hand more tightly.

Stefani focused again on shutting that door. The stars didn't want to look on that thing. The earth didn't want to look on that thing. Even the inky black void of space didn't want to look on it. All of creation screamed its outrage against it. She added her voice to theirs and the portal slammed shut, cutting off the ends of the beast's tentacles. These cut ends fell to the ground and writhed there briefly like unearthly worms cast into the light, spewing ichor until their life was spent and they dissolved.

Stefani had done it, but now she was spent. She wanted nothing more than to fall asleep right in the dust, clasping Stanley's hand in her own. But with the disappearance of the beast and the portal, the people around them were starting to return to awareness. They would have to get out of here, and quickly.

Stefani stood up, and was suddenly aware of the chill of the night and her nakedness. Stanley was still on the ground. He raised his hand, his eyes pleading. "I told you I would need your help up."

She grabbed his hand and pulled him up, but he looked very unsteady. Carl enfolded Stefani in the robe that had been dropped on the ground beside her. His strong arms tried to hold her close. She said, "Thanks," but pushed him away. He nodded, his eyes meeting hers briefly. They were full of caring, as she imagined a brother's.

Stanley wheezed, "We've got to go." He pointed to the Klansmen who were struggling to come to awareness.

They started to head away from the flames and into the dark part of the plateau, where she could make out the faint outline of an airplane. It quickly became clear that Stanley could barely walk. Carl supported him.

Their progress was slow, and some of the acolytes were recovering. They raised knives and began to pursue. Stefani knew she had no strength to stop them. Stanley looked completely spent, and Carl barely had strength to support Stanley. The dozen acolytes would make short work of them.

Then Stefani heard an engine. She looked up and saw a ghostly biplane. It swept down and let loose with its gun before rising back into the darkness. As it passed, she saw a crane on its side and the tail painted red white and blue. Several of the acolytes were hit. They didn't bleed, but they were stunned. The rest were thrown into chaos.

They got to the plane, and the pilot said, "Whoa. Who is she, and why did you bring her here?" He was tan—Stefani might have said more than tan, but in the firelight she couldn't be sure—and his black hair was curly.

Stanley said, "We all need to get down."

"I wasn't worried about taking two people up here, but there's no way the plane will carry all of you."

"It has to. She can't just walk out of here."

"No, but I can," Carl said.

"But what if they figure out who you are?"

"Who am I? I'm a white male protestant. One hundred percent American. They won't even ask. Besides, it's the only solution that makes sense." Carl put Stefani in the plane. "I weigh as much as you both put together. And you can't possibly walk out of here. I'm not even sure you can get in the plane."

"Can too." Stanley reached for the edge of the cockpit. His muscles started to tense, but then his face blanched. "I can't."

"I thought not." Carl lifted Stanley into the cockpit. It was crowded, but Stanley said it was a lot roomier than on the way up. Stefani believed it. Carl was a large man.

Carl threw the propeller and the engine roared to life. The plane lifted off easily into the dark night. Carl pointed after the plane and called out. He was quickly lost in the sea of white robes that rushed toward the sound.

74.   The Great Mystery

Gary Barton and his wife Ida came from Chicago for Stefani and Carl's initiation. Stanley met them at Union Station, led them to the taxi. Max's old rattletrap served them for another trip. Gary and Ida spent the trip in silence with their eyes closed. Stanley knew better than to disturb them. They were preparing themselves for their role in the initiation.

St. Leo's had been chosen as the site for the initiation. At first, it had seemed incongruous to Stanley that a Catholic church should be chosen for what would be considered a pagan ceremony, but Stanley knew better than to question the way the spirit chose such things. He left it to Gary to make arrangements with the priest. The two men walked through the church and through the grounds. After a while, they knelt in the pews and prayed together. Then each man administered Communion to the other. They shook hands and Gary gestured to Stanley to stand up from where he sat in the pews.

Stanley said, "So it's all settled, then."

Gary said, "Yes. Men of faith are inherently reasonable, if you talk to them in the language they understand."

Stanley said, "Con them, you mean? I've never seen a Catholic priest take communion from an Initiate."

"Con? I resent the implication. Perhaps you forget that I was ordained by Pope Leo XIII."

They pushed open the door and emerged into the fading light of day. "Yeah, that totally slipped my mind. Was that before or after you married Ida?"

"Before, of course. You sound dubious, but I was truly ordained by the Pope." They turned and walked toward Otoniel's house, where everyone was waiting to hear whether the ceremony would truly be held at St. Leo's.

Stanley rolled a cigarette as they walked. "Excuse my skepticism, but an Initiate of the Mysteries never tells the whole truth."

Gary smiled slightly at Stanley. "Rarely, yes. Before the light of Ceres there are no secrets."

Stanley lit his cigarette. He pulled on it, then blew a puff of smoke. "Ceres. You use the old names with such reverence still. As if there really were gods and goddesses and not just a bunch of people stumbling around in a lightning storm, trying to find their way in the dark by the brief flashes."

"Men and women of the higher planes live in more light than we enjoy. They see better than we see. If sometimes they appear to us and share their wisdom, it is right that we should revere them as gods and maintain their memories."

"Even if they're long dead and gone . . ."

"Denizens of the higher planes may live and die like us, or they may not. We do not know."

"If that's even what they were—we don't know that there ever was anyone who might have been Ceres or Mithras or Serapis."

Barton didn't say anything.

Stanley said, "But what we do know is real is what's in that library. Someone needs to investigate that."

"And you think you're the right person for that assignment?"

"I've encountered it before. I'm prepared to encounter it again."

"Perhaps. Or maybe it's prepared for you. In any case, you still have much to answer for. And this is not your assignment." His tone was final, probably backed by some powerful divination. He knew where Stanley needed to be next.

They walked the rest of the way in silence and climbed the stairs to the porch where Maria, Otoniel, their mother, Stefani, and Carl were all drinking limeade. Stefani was of course laughing at some joke of Carl's. Stanley could not help his bitter reaction.

Everyone was delighted to hear that the ceremony would go on as planned, even Mama. She had an image that the ceremony was something like First Communion, and resisted attempts to have it explained to her. After the news was shared, they all got into cars and rode to Stefani's house, where Ida was helping Elizabeth prepare the place for a celebratory feast.

When they got to Stefani's house, the place was barely recognizable. All the curtains had been thrown open wide and the windows, too. A fresh breeze ran through the house, which was brightly lit not only by the sunlight, but by electric lights and candles. The candlesticks used were of a dizzying variety, originating in all corners of the Earth and made of all manner of materials, from wood and bone to gold and jewels. Nikolas' statues had also been brought out, dusted, and polished. They were placed around as decorative accents by the bar, the buffet, or the band, which played a combination of Greek, Egyptian, Indian, and Chinese music. It all looked so gay and delightful that everyone immediately smiled upon entering.

Ida stood with Elizabeth to welcome each visitor as they entered. Elizabeth seemed happy for the support, and she, too, was barely recognizable. She wore an Edwardian dress of pale green. Cinched tight at the waist with beadwork everywhere and gathered skirts, it gave her a dignity and stature as a hostess that had little in common with the slouched persona Stanley had first seen at the table some weeks before. And she was full of smiles, too. Though her face still bore the marks of her longstanding grief, the smiles and joy she experienced concealed them almost as much as did her makeup.

And Stefani was full of smiles, too. She rushed up to her mother and the two women embraced and chatted. They went around together, talking to people in the crowd, which included both Stefani's friends and people they had met during the course of their recent encounters. She was wearing a green dress similar to the one she had worn during their dream meeting, and it made Stanley think of that time, really the only time they had spent together in private.

Stanley watched her from his corner, where he sat sipping on his second or third glass of wine as a cigarette burned slowly down in his fingers. She seemed so much more vibrant than when she had come to his office: thin, tired, and screaming in terror because of Marduk and Gaap. She even looked more energetic than when he had seen her at Morgan's, where she had been weighed down by grief and by the nature of her work. As she walked around the room, she gave smiles to everyone she looked at, making the bright space even brighter.

Barton surprised him when he suddenly spoke from his blind side, "You should tell her how you feel."

Stanley quickly recovered from his start, "If I knew, maybe I would."

"Don't be so coy. You know how you feel." Gary had a big cigar that was sweet with spices and a trace of cannabis.

"Maybe a little. I barely know her, how can I know what I feel?"

"You can always just tell her what you know. There is magic in language."

"But what's the point? I go back to Chicago day after tomorrow, and from thence, where?"

Barton's eyes were hard and he said nothing.

Stanley went on, "And she'll be an Initiate. She'll have training and then Ida will send her on missions and you'll send me on missions. There's no way we'll be able to be together."

"You'd be surprised what's possible, with Aphrodite's blessings."

Stanley snorted. "If you believe in Aphrodite." He gulped down the last of his glass. "If you'll excuse me, I'm going to secure a little more blessing of Dionysus."

At the bar, Stanley watched the tender pour him a modest glass, then gestured for more. As he was taking the first sip, he turned away. He almost spilled the wine all over himself as he saw Stefani waiting there right behind him. "Woah," he said, "excuse me."

"Hi. I haven't hardly seen you at all these last couple days. Is something wrong?"

"No, nothing. I'm just trying to stay out of the way. Tomorrow is your special day, and you've got all these people here to congratulate you. I just want to stay out of your way. And then Barton's here and I have to help him out . . ."

"My special day? You sound as if I'm getting married."

"It's almost like that. Becoming an Initiate is almost as final and consuming as getting married." He took an unfortunately noisy sip from his wine. "You can't really be involved with other people."

Stefani spun halfway around. It was an elegant move made with a dancer's grace. Her scent reached Stanley's nostrils. Sweet perfume underlaid with just a hint of her sweat. Involuntarily, Stanley breathed deep of it.

Stefani pointed and said, "Gary and Ida seem to make it work."

"Not everyone can do it. They're exceptional."

Stefani whirled back around quickly. Her eyes flashed. "And I'm not?"

"Uh . . ." Stanley couldn't respond. His heart was pounding. His face grew hot. He looked down at his wine. The glass had grown suddenly slippery in his sweaty hand.

"Oh," Stefani said. "I guess maybe I'm the only one who feels it. I feel so good that this is over, and I guess I assumed that the knight who saved me wouldn't just dump the maiden fair, but perhaps I'm not so fair." She started off.

"Listen," Stanley said. He dared to reach out to touch her arm. It was smooth and warm, and the touch sent power coursing through them. Strangely, it made the scar on his hand tingle. She turned around. He let go, put his wine down and began rolling a cigarette. "First. You saved my life. You saved us all. I don't think I thanked you enough for that. Second, it's normal to feel something for someone you meet as we met. In our dreams, I mean. Especially the first time, it's so . . . intimate. It doesn't necessarily mean anything."

"I liked it. I liked who you were there. Without all this," she gestured inclusively at his trench coat, hat, and the cigarette he was now lifting to his lips, "it seemed like you were really you."

"A skinny boy with a lyre?"

"In a short skirt. Yeah, I think that's the real you."

"That's part of the real me. So is this," he gestured to the coat. "And especially this." He loosened his tie and pulled open his shirt collar to reveal the scar on his neck where the demon had been feeding on him after he had been shot in France. "This is what I'm talking about. You don't know me, and I don't know you. How can we talk about making anything work?"

"Maybe that's not what we're talking about. Maybe we're talking about trying. You aren't afraid to try, are you?" Stefani smiled. Her eyes pled.

Stanley damn well knew he was afraid to try. He took a drag on the cigarette, then reached out for her again with his other hand. The touch felt so good, but the enormity of the task before him seemed impossible. He let go. "Listen, after your ceremony tomorrow, I've got to get on the train with Barton and go back to Chicago. I've got work waiting for me there. You will begin your training, and who knows where Ida will send you."

"So that's it, then?"

"Yeah, most likely."

Stanley had been drawing hard on the cigarette. It was burned almost to his fingers. He turned to crush it out in the ashtray. When he turned back, Stefani had been drawn away by some of her girlfriends, and they were all talking and laughing. Stanley watched them as he finished his wine, their laughter resonating in him as if he were a bronze bell, hanging still.

When he finished his wine, he moved toward the door. He was just about to leave when he ran into Mack.

"Mack!" He smiled and shook his hand. Then he put his arm around the pilot's shoulders and steered him toward the bar. "I'm so glad you could make it!"

"Well, thanks for the invitation, but I'm not sure what the celebration is for."

"We're alive and wine is sweet and plentiful. Isn't that enough to celebrate?"

"Surprisingly plentiful. Where did all this come from?"

"It's sacramental, all of it, though how it's sacred we can't tell you." He handed a glass to Mack. "So, what're you going to do now that your employer doesn't have need of you anymore? Find another delivery route?"

"No, no." Mack looked around a little to make sure their conversation was private. "Guynemer wants to keep moving west."

"California?"

"For now. After that . . . he's crossed one ocean. It wouldn't surprise me if he wanted to cross another."

"Where is he going? What is he looking for?"

"I don't know. I'm not sure he knows."

"Do any of us?"

Mack didn't say anything. They had moved over to stand by an open window. Stanley could hear the drone of Guynemer's ghostly engine as the plane flew around in loops and circles.

At the church, they met first in the alcove. Stanley wore a robe with his hood down. As herald, he was to announce the Initiates as they came. A male Initiate attended on Carl. A female attended on Stefani. They both wore robes with the hoods down over their faces. Ida and Barton officiated at the ceremony. They wore robes and masks. Ida's was smiling. Barton's was sad. They stood at the far end of the church.

Carl and Stefani entered in basic robes, but were stripped in the alcove as Stanley talked about birth as descent from the higher planes into our world. Stanley knew that this was canonical and didn't reflect any true knowledge. No one knew where our souls came from or where they went. They climbed down the stairs into the cellar of the church.

It was dimly lit. As they reached it, Carl and Stefani were presented with animal skins to wear. Stanley spoke of the baseness of human nature, which was true enough. They walked through stations designed to represent the seven Hermetic principles: gender, cause and effect, rhythm, polarity, vibration, correspondence, and, finally, mentalism. At each station, Stanley spoke the words.

The seventh station was at the foot of the stairs in the front of the cellar. After Stanley spoke the words, Stefani and Carl threw their animal skins on the ground. Stanley led the way up the stairs.

They emerged near the altar. In contrast to the Jesus hanging on the cross above the Catholic altar, there was a statue of Ceres, representing the opposite poles of death and life. The Jesus was painted wood, his skin dull, his blood dark, the nails grey, the thorns brown with a hint of deep green. Ceres was made of alabaster, painted with a thin sheen of color that allowed light from within the statue to pass outward. She had pale skin, a large smile, and soft green eyes. Her crown was of poppies, bright red petals surrounding a glowing yellow center.

Stanley stepped aside and let Carl and Stefani pass by. Ida and Barton put their Initiate robes on them, but Stanley was thinking about the poppies and Flanders' field. *Take up our quarrel with the foe: To you from falling hands we throw The torch; be yours to hold it high.* That torch that was supposed to represent knowledge, knowledge of who were our friends and who our foes. And even now Ida and Barton were reciting words about how the initiates had entered into knowledge of the Great Mystery, but it was all hollow. The Great Mystery was still mysterious, and none of them, not even Gary Barton, who spoke so confidently, really had a clue about it.

After the recitations were done, Stanley led the recessional out through the church. When they were outside in the light of day, Stanley took his robe off and threw it in the chest where it would be stored until the next initiation. He put on his coat and began to roll himself a cigarette as he walked away.

He had gotten a little distance away when Stefani called out to him. He turned and saw her running toward him, the loose initiate robe of shimmering material dancing around her. She was glowing, flushed from the ceremony, and her eyes were happy. She was smiling broadly. She said, "It's amazing. I feel so different."

"It's always like that after the ceremony. It seems so real then. That will pass."

"But I can feel the power, and surely you must feel it. Don't you believe in the power?"

"I believe in the power. The power is real. But so is a locomotive. It moves, but it's just clanking iron, and all that comes out of it is smoke." Stanley exhaled a puff.

She reached out her hand and touched his cheek. "If that is true, then why do you work so hard?"

Stanley was frozen in the moment, unable to speak. He felt the power come through her hand into him. All his scars tingled.

"The answer is love," she said. "You don't have to deny it to me. I know you love this world, every stone, every blade of grass, and every creature."

They were silent for a moment. Barton and Ida called out to Stanley. Their taxi had arrived. They had to go if they were to make their train.

"I know you have to go, but that doesn't mean we can't meet again. Maybe in dreams."

Stefani took her hand from his cheek. Stanley rushed to the cab. Just before he got in, he threw his cigarette to the ground. He was about to step on it, crush it out, but then he stopped. He got into the cab and let that little ember burn.

Historical Note

This story draws heavily from Denver's rich history in the 1920s. The historical events in the background take place from 1921-25, from the fall of the Blonger Gang through the rise of the Ku Klux Klan, which facilitated Ben Stapleton's rise to power.

The story of the Blonger gang is a fascinating and underappreciated chapter in Denver's history. Philip Van Cise gives a gripping, detailed account of their takedown in *Fighting the Underworld*. Names and a few details are changed to protect individuals who were living in 1936 when he wrote it. You can get a short version of the story (with real names) in *Westword*'s 2008 article, "Philip Van Cise: Scourge of Denver's Underworld."

Stapleton was a member of the KKK. It's unclear how closely his ideals aligned with theirs, but it is true that he leaned heavily on their influence and power to get elected and stay in office. He did kneel before a burning cross on South Table Mountain and pledge his allegiance to the Klan to survive a dangerous recall. However, after the recall had passed, he did work to limit the Klan's influence. If you want to learn more about the role of the Klan in Denver politics, I recommend Phil Goodstein's sensational *In the Shadow of the Klan*.

The occult context for the KKK rituals is fictional, but, like the Freemasons, the organization drew heavily on ancient occult practices for their rituals. In fact, the Klan cribbed many of their rituals from the Masons. Some of the occult history I use is taken from the book *The Secret Teachings of All Ages* by Manley P. Hall, which incorporates much Masonic thought. The seeds of the conflict between the Cult of

Mithras and the Serapeans can be found there, but, as far as I know, my portrayal of these forces is entirely fictional.

Acknowledgements

I have always been a solitary writer, but it takes a lot of help to go from manuscript to book, and I want to recognize those who helped. First, let me thank Tracy. She has always been tolerant of my dedication to writing, and for this book, she not only served as an alpha reader, but editor as well. David has probably been reading my writing longer than anyone on Earth (since my mother passed). He served as an alpha reader and provided vital help and support during the process of publication. I want to thank all my beta readers, too: Bob, James, Kristin, Lisa, Scott, and Sean. The members of my critique circle, LittleSpec, provided vital insight to hammer early chapters into shape, and the Witch Club (Daniel, Kathy, Rick, Scott, and Suzanne) helped me improve the entire novel.

Thank you, one and all, for your support of this project.

Want to read more?

Visit www.writermc.com to find short fiction and other titles by me, both connected and unconnected.

Vote on the sequel to control where the story goes next.